The Loom of Heaven

Franklin Charles Graham

The Loom of Heaven
A Redwood Ridge House Book / June 2016

This is a work of fiction.
Although some places and historical incidents are real, the narrative incidents, names, and characters are solely the product of the author's imagination, or, are used fictitiously. Any resemblance to actual events, locales, or persons, living or dead, is entirely coincidental.

Manufactured in the United States of America

Redwood Ridge House, Navarro, California
redwoodridgehouse@gmail.com

First Edition

ISBN 978-0-9974186-0-6

10 9 8 7 6 5 4 3 2 1

This is a book about family, and
I dedicate it to my own.

Margaret Nell Bond
Franklin C. Graham, IV
Kingman Scott Bond-Graham
Darwin Charles Bond-Graham

With all my love, devotion, and admiration

Prologue

And Coyote said to The People, "If there is no death, the earth will become too small. There will be no room for the cornfields." And, the wise ones spoke: "It is just so. It is best that each should live a limited time on this earth, then make room for those to come." To this day, the *Diné* greet each day's sun, '*Sa'ah naagha éi Bik'eh hózhǫ*, "On the trail of old age, I walk in beauty."

The quest for long life has been a preoccupation of sorcerers, shamans, alchemists, and scientists since humans first asked the question: Is longer life possible? Who can deny that living longer than three score and ten is not desired? And yet, what would a world populated with billions of superannuated humans be like? Would they face a world exhausted of life-sustaining food, resources, and living space? Would war, greed, and pestilence rule? Managing the unintended consequences of extending the human lifespan will demand a great cost. It could imperil the future of all humanity.

Dr. Adam Grant, a molecular biologist, had been consumed with the quest for extending the life span. He resisted every restraint and ignored every cautionary tale. Beside him, Crystal Bayeta, his wife, born Navajo and educated in the ways of both her people and Western thought, watched over him, patient and abiding. Together, with their young ward, Alberto, a victim of progeria, they lived quietly beside the great tear of earth known as *Tseyi,* Canyon de Chelly. Adam relentlessly pursued his research. Crystal Bayeta wove and, at last, became one with her people after so long an absence from her roots.

All was harmony and beauty until, until….

Author's Note: The identification of Navajo Gods within the narrative conforms to the convention applied by Gladys A. Reichard, *Navajo Religion: A Study of Symbolism* (Bollingen Foundation, Princeton University Press, 1950).

Contents

1

Gift Of The Spider Woman

The morning's newspaper for April 4, 1990, headlined a tribute to Sarah Vaughan, The Divine One. For Adam Grant, who stood at the perilous edge of the rim overlooking Spider Rock, the singer's signature song held special meaning. "Send in the Clowns" had been his mother's favorite song, one she said reminded her not to waste time and energy trying to decide what next must be done. Eleanor, his mother, had always been right about the important things, insisting that indecision and delay were often worse than making a bad decision. One could, she would tell him, always alter a bad decision, but never recover the time lost. Staring at the ever-deepening record of the forces of time, pressure, and water that had shaped the landscape of Canyon de Chelly, Adam made up his mind. It was time to return home and tell his wife, Crystal Bayeta, that the time to act had come. To wait would be folly.

The far rim of Canyon De Chelly looked much like it did any other early spring day at the overlook. A crisp turquoise sky pressed down to embrace the streaked, eroding stone walls of the canyon. Ever at odds, change and continuity had shaped the landscape in ways humans can but dimly grasp. A pair of Red-tailed Hawks had circled high above the canyon's rim for two hours, their vigilant stares fixed on his alien presence. In the light of the late sun, the hawks banked and dove down to close the distance. Pale breasts and tawny tail feathers trapped and gathered in the sun's glow. A stubborn chill crept up and over the canyon rim. The hawks had held to their wary vigil in spite of the slipping away of the afternoon thermals. To them, Adam belonged elsewhere, there, far and away down the road. The road—any road—with its dark, striped, monstrous body meant danger. To them, it was an insatiable whipsnake, an alien thing created by malevolent gods.

Adam Grant respected the boundary between man and hawks. Hawks, with their stubborn sense of time and space, possessed no impulse to degrade or alter life's balance. For them, their lives were in perfect balance, complete, integrated, and timeless. *Tseyi*, the canyon below, remained warily guarded by the *Diné*, the Navajo. Its deep labyrinth of jagged, rust-stained rock walls provided sustenance in summer and desperate refuge in hard times. Piñón, juniper, cottonwood, squaw bush, chokecherry, Opuntia cactus, sage, and bee plants fed by undulating streams gave the canyon's floor the look of a lost Eden. *Tseyi* suited Navajo and hawk. Halfway up the vertical rock face rested ancient Anasazi cliff dwellings, crumbling to dust. In shadow and sun, these abandoned refuges manifested the immensity of times past, when the present moment was what mattered.

Adam had stared down at the floor of the canyon for two hours. He wondered that the small stream had created such a huge, magnificent tear in the earth's surface. His reason admitted that it was but a matter of sand, water, and time—erosion. His indecision had clung to him, like the rust-stained patches of snow clinging stubbornly to the canyon's jumbled talus base. He did not want to leave Rimrock, his home. The harsh chill of late winter's wind felt preferable. Its numbing grip had become his intimate, his familiar. It was cold and seductive. Why go? Was it because he, a research microbiologist, had discovered something? Had he dared to believe that it was an absolute good?

<++++++++++>

Earlier that day in Chinle, men sat anxious and expectant in Rose Bia's Café, nursing their third and fourth cups of coffee. Hidden behind their eyes lurked suppressed restlessness. Some of the men had given Adam Grant a sidelong glance as he entered. The younger men shifted slightly on their stools at the counter as he passed by. Making his way to the back booth where Johnny Kabito waited,

Adam heard Joe Silver Tooth, Johnny's cousin, mutter "*adagas*." Adam was indeed suspect. No insult was intended. He took no notice, as it had long since become "just so" that many regarded him as a wizard. Any man who sought to alter the balance of things, as a scientist is wont to do, was *adagas*.

The elders, guarded and silent, filled the booths along the window facing the street. They listened to the young men sitting on stools at the counter, their talk a mixture of Navajo and English. In spite of the unsettled weather, out of respect the young men avoided profanity. The dry, blistering cold of the passing winter had penetrated their senses to the bone, intensifying their heavy anxiety and expectations. In the far corner booth sat four "traditionals", who clutched their cups tightly, warming their hands if not their mood. They stared out the window impassively, with eyes fixed on the eastern edge of sky, where the mouth of Chinle Wash drained out. The runoff from the Chuskas was still running heavy. Before mid-April, movement down onto the canyon floor would be impractical, even dangerous. No horses or sheep would graze on *Tseyi* fresh grass until Auntie Yazzie came down from the Defiance Plateau with her wagon, two horses, and many sheep. It was just so, Johnny Kabito pronounced.

Johnny Kabito, a pleasant man, made his living guiding visitors into the canyon as far as Spider Rock and beyond. *Tseyi* was his intimate ground. "It's the sand, Dr. Grant. Quicksand can eat up man or animal. It don't make no difference."

It pleased Kabito to detail the perils of quicksand and late, sudden rains. Such knowledge invested him with extraordinary insight. He had every right to speak of *Tseyi's* moods. When he opined, other men listened. "This spring is bad. Not been so bad in forty years. Them big four-wheelers not gonna make it past The Rock, not 'til May."

The elders, nursing refills of stale, thick, black coffee, stared out the window in silence. They had heard it all before. They knew that what he said was true enough. The way each man gripped his cup, head tilted down until his face stared back from the swirl of half-cold coffee, confirmed it. For a Navajo, Kabito's voice was too loud. One of the elders had once confided to Adam that Kabito was born talkative. He had learned too many fancy *bilagáana* words. Fifty years of leading pale-faced, talky tourists into Canyon de Chelly's vastness had long ago infected him. "Soon or late", the elder had added, "a Navajo keeping company with all them white folks loses his own tongue." More than once Johnny Kabito had been chanted over. And yet, his talking habit persisted. A certain inner balance was lost. Still, "He knows the canyon," Johnny's friend and cousin said. When it came to matters of sand, water, and time, Johnny Kabito, being Navajo, retained a respectful knowledge and sense of the limits of men and horses.

<++++++++++>

The long winter's hold on the high desert had been tenacious and severe. It had not spared the land or The People. Adam's wife, Crystal Bayeta, had been born within miles of where he stood at the rim. She was not simply of this place, but born to it and for it. As for Adam, her *bilagáana* husband, he slowly had gained acceptance, but still only half-belonged. Rimrock's neighbors were patient with him, even respectful, though they did not understand his ways. To them, his being a scientist implied an alien state of mind, not a small matter.

As a final gust of wind from the north scoured the rim's edge, Adam gripped his coat collar tightly at his neck. It was past time to leave. Indecision, which had clung to his consciousness for weeks, like the dying snow at the bottom of the canyon, had all but melted away. This trip would be the means to his ends. He would go to San Francisco.

He backed away from the canyon rim as a thick, lengthening shadow spread over the near ground at his back. As the sun's glow abandoned the canyon floor, Adam whispered, "When…when will this be behind me?" On the wind-driven frozen air, his question floated unanswered. Where cold reason had failed him, he chose impulse.

Adam was intuitively conditioned to approach every question with a determined sense that the answer to any problem was within reach—given enough time, trial, and error. Boundaries that limited understanding were but edges to press against. It was a frame of mind that showed itself from the time he learned to speak. Jonathan Hardesty, his mentor and friend, had seen this within days of Adam's coming to Berkeley as a student.

<++++++++++>

On July 16, 1945, Adam and Cynthia were born at dawn in a small hospital in Albuquerque, New Mexico. Three months later, Eleanor, their mother, filed for divorce. She was determined that her children would have an untroubled childhood. No child deserved a father's protracted absences and the enforced silences and arguments that characterized the marriage. Strong willed and a capable provider, Eleanor Grant made a good living as artist and gallery owner. Alexander Terman, their father, was a émigré atomic physicist—remote, self-absorbed, and ambitious. After the Trinity test at Alamogordo, he left for Chicago to resume his pre-war academic pursuits. He became a towering, remote, and almost mythic figure in the children's lives. To his credit, however, he never challenged Eleanor's parenting. Nor did he abandon the children's financial welfare. But, in other respects he contributed little.

Eleanor nurtured her children's natural curiosities and emerging interests at every stage of their development. Adam's insatiable fascination with the desert beyond the town's limits helped compensate for the lack of a father figure. From the age of seven, he spent most of his free time out and about the rocky, wind-scoured expanse of sand, seasonal washes, and gullies, tracking and observing all manner of desert life. He would come home holding a snake by its tail, another "friend", to put in his glass terrarium, later returning it to where he had found it. Every desert insect and plant interested him. He collected projectile points, scrapers, potsherds, any artifact left behind by prehistoric Indians. He learned about the hunting and foraging peoples who had lived in the desert. He studied the geology of deserts and canyons. Through the microscope that his father sent, in place of coming for one of the twins' birthdays, Adam observed and classified everything from the silicates in the sands to grasses and cactus fibers. The composition of water collected from springs and seeps did not escape microscopic examination. At thirteen, for his school science fair, he displayed water-born sarcodina, a parasitic protozoan, a cause of amoebic dysentery. Adam had spied sarcodina in a local water supply through his microscope. His biology teacher was disturbed with what Adam had found. Together, teacher and student provoked local health officials by insisting that there existed a health hazard. It was disputed that Adam had indeed identified sarcodina in the water supply. A subsequent search for the source proved unsuccessful. No one, however, could explain the high incidence of infection in residents of the sprawling new subdivision in the desert west of the city limits.

Nothing troubled the young Adam Grant, not even the opprobrium he received for questioning the safety of the water supply. While other neighborhood mothers complained that their teenage children suffered from "the blahs," Eleanor had no such complaint. Nor did it concern Adam that Albuquerque was thought of as a backwater, a "cultural desert." Growing up in Albuquerque had nothing to do with gain or loss of opportunity. For Cynthia, however, it was different. She felt trapped, and her teenage years were an awkward period for her.

<++++++++++>

Adam's talents were recognized early. Before graduating with highest honors from the University of Chicago, two of his senior research projects were published in scientific journals. The one in *Cell*, on a then little understood enzyme, thymosin, came to the attention of Dr. Sheldon Armitage, Dean of Life Sciences, University of California. Armitage pronounced the article intuitive, bold, and methodologically sophisticated. Undergraduate degree in hand, Adam set out for Berkeley with Armitage's letter inviting him into the graduate program. Such a nod meant the fast track.

Eleanor could not have been more proud. She harbored a trenchant distaste for the physical sciences. Her son had chosen molecular biology. No molecular biologist could possibly set the planet on fire. Cynthia, however, posed an anxious challenge for her. Their arguments over physics remained strong and protracted throughout her teenage years. Cynthia insisted that her father's motives were not personal but professional. It was "unfair" to call him a "killer of worlds", or "Teller's apprentice", or one who "tickled the dragon's tail", threatening nuclear disaster for the whole world. Cynthia remained perversely proud of her birth date and its association. It was prophetic, special. Physics, atomic physics, was what she insisted on pursuing, which she did.

Alexander Terman had intensified the conflict with Eleanor by referring to the twins as "Trinity's Children." He fancied their birth date as prophetic, a double triumph for his muscular sense of parenting and physics combined. Eleanor, however, would have none of it. "When the twins were born, you were off in that awful place playing at 'destroyer of worlds.' The children were, and still are, little more than reminders of the day when you said you were never more alive. You speak of July 16 as if it is all about how YOU made the sun rise twice in one day! What hubris!"

As a teenager, Adam had wondered what his father was really like, what mattered to him. His mother's feelings, her vague sense of personal guilt for having married a "bomb maker", influenced Adam's decision to major in biology. In his application essay for admission, he stated a negative motivation for wishing to major in a life science.

On entering Berkeley as a graduate student, Adam Grant immediately caught the eye of Dr. Jonathan Hardesty. Adam sensed that Dr. Hardesty would best stimulate his deepest interests. Hardesty had identified and described more DNA enzymes than any other molecular biologist. Adam abandoned his intent to study under Armitage. Some thought it unwise. Still, Hardesty was affectionately known by graduate students as "the enzyme sleuth." He was also an elder statesman of the North American Biological Society. Personally modest and unassuming, he promoted the talents of promising graduate students and postgraduates. To Adam that sort of attention proved a heady wine. He labored hard and long to prove his worth to Dr. Hardesty.

In the 1960s, molecular biology grew from infancy to adolescence. The iconic letters DNA and RNA were found sprawled across chalkboards on every American campus. The young science bore the marks of a benevolent and creative force. Gradually, research goals shifted from the challenges of definition and description to the complex inner workings of the cell. Federal funding also moved in its direction. The mysteries of the cell became the new testament of science. Adam was determined to be part of its story. For him, the genome was the "prime mover unmoved."

By 1972, Hardesty's estimate of his former student's promise was confirmed. Adam, now colleague and sometime collaborator, was exploring the outermost layers of how replicating mechanisms within the cell trigger and regulate aging processes. His approach focused on how unstable molecules—free radicals—inhibited or interfered with the cell's normal functions. This was an essential key to understanding how and when the cell's functions and maintenance routines degraded and eventually broke down. "The older a cell, the less capable it is to handle its own accumulated garbage," Hardesty insisted. Adam intuitively sensed that it was much more complicated than the accumulation of "refuse and broken parts." He had no ready explanation, but he had his quarry in sight.

There was one matter upon which Hardesty and Adam disagreed, the need for biology to deal with means and ends. Adam did not completely ignore the concern. Yes, there were consequences to manipulating cell functions. Cloning and in vitro fertilization had their critics. Genetically modified plants and organisms drew protests. Stem cell research was restricted. Adam remained aloof. The time and effort it took to fund his research occupied him. He pursued answers as to how, when, and why cells ceased to function efficiently. Was longer life possible? More than epigenetic variability was at work. He had no patience for the public's fascination with quick-fix claims—the litany of vitamin supplements, anti-aging hormones and creams, exercise regimens, stress reduction, diet changes, glandular injections, and more. Experimentation, discovery, and testable results alone satisfied him.

As his ideas matured, Adam linked each piece of new knowledge of the cell to his search for patterns of healthy, long-lived, functions between and within cells. Accepted hypotheses fell away. New hypotheses took shape. The plodding, step-by-step regimen of the laboratory was seductive and irresistible, an opiate for him.

<++++++++++>

He looked toward home to the northeast and thought of the five years of living at Rimrock, its comfortable and self-contained routines. Crystal Bayeta had chosen the site deep within the reservation. Another man might find it difficult, if not impossible, to live in a woman's house. That did not matter to Adam. By right and custom, it was her house. Bea, his pet name for his wife, had supervised construction of the house, except for the north annex, which housed Adam's laboratory. Ben Tsosie's hand was also visible. Ben, a local healer, was firm in his declaration that the laboratory must be placed at the north side, the dark side, and attached only by a covered breezeway. Otherwise, he said, not he or any other Navajo would come near the place. With construction completed, he had come to conduct a Blessing Way rite to make the house habitable, a proper Navajo home. He would have preferred, Bea confided to Adam, to perform an Enemy Way ceremony because of the laboratory. To ease Bea's feelings, Ben relented. She had insisted that *Ana'í Ndáá'* applied only to contact with a dead non-Navajo. Ben agreed. The Blessing Way would suffice to make their new home holy.

For five years, with the first light slipping through the sliding glass doors and onto the bed, if he was the first to wake, Adam would lie in bed, his hand resting on Crystal Bayeta's thigh and watch dawn's approach. When Bayeta stirred, her eyes still closed, she would smile and murmur softly. "It is a good day." One untroubled sun upon another rose and transited over Rimrock to preserve their quiet, peaceful existence.

Whatever the season, the daily routine at Rimrock varied little. Adam and Martin, his assistant, divided their time between experiments and caring for their ward, Alberto. Crystal Bayeta wove and also cared for Alberto. Wednesdays were set aside for Adam's weekly trip into Chinle for mail and supplies. A bi-monthly trip to the Flagstaff clinic with Alberto was equally shared between Adam and Martin. Overnight trips to Albuquerque were rare. Living as they did at "Wizard's Rock," the name traditional Navajos applied to Rimrock, made her kinfolk living nearby watchful. They took to referring to Rimrock as "Crystal Bayeta's outfit." Even so, to them the name, "Wizard's Rock," was also apt. The laboratory made it so.

And, there was the tragic story of which they never spoke. Avoidance of the canyon rim northwest of the house remained strong. "Wizards" had gathered in that place and bad things had happened. No fine distinction was made between supernatural dangers and what was called science.

<+++++++++>

Before Adam set out that morning for Chinle, Crystal Bayeta sensed that it would not be good for him to go off in the mood he was in. He had his brooding look she knew so well. He would certainly drive to the rim after his errands in Chinle. She wanted to ask him not to stand brooding at the rim. But, she could not say it directly to him.

"I awoke thinking about Changing Woman," she said. "From the beginning, The People have known that it is best to die when very old with a quiet wind within. Only Changing Woman has the power to become young again, little by little. When I was a little girl, this was told to me, the story of two children who saw it for themselves, that place where Spider Woman lives."

Adam leaned back in his chair. "Bea, you have told me the story of *Asdzáá Nádleehé* many times."

"Just so—and don't interrupt me." Crystal Bayeta's eyes gathered in the light when she was serious. He smiled and sipped at his coffee, knowing that patience was called for.

"They went into Changing Woman's hogan. There she was, lying down, nearly dead from old age. But, she got herself up. With the help of a walking cane made of white shell, she went into the room to the east. When she returned she was stronger. Then, with a second cane, this one of turquoise, she walked into the south room. When she returned she had no cane, no need of a cane. She went into the room to the west. A little time later she came out. Now she was a young woman again. She went into the north room and returned very beautiful."

Bayeta believed that impeding the course of aging was something only for a god. But that had never been his intention. His work, his research goal, was limited to "adapting" the biological clockwork, not in interfering with it. But she was not arguing over that point. It was her way of touching on the matter foremost in his mind, Alberto. Alberto's condition was accelerating, deteriorating rapidly.

Alberto's fate was at once cruel, impersonal, implacable and immutable. His life was about to be cut off cruelly short, a life marked by pain, debility, and bitter frustration. Most humans could count on the time worn three score and ten. Alberto's journey was coming down to but a score of years. No matter how Adam struggled to explain the nature of progeria, Alberto had clung to a desperate belief that Adam could somehow arrest its progression. Was not Adam working to find the way to extend life? For five years Alberto had wanted to believe that Adam would somehow save him.

"Bea, the boy must accept the fact that my work is not about reversing the aging process. It was never that. All I have found is a way to adapt, and so extend."

"Must you be the one to stake out that claim?"

"Would you have me keep this to myself?" He was conflicted and anxious.

"What if it does not turn out to be such a good thing after all?"

"What do you mean, Bea? I've gone over the research protocol and results too many times to count. This is the breakthrough. I dared not count on it, but it is."

"What will our future be? Others surely will review and confirm your findings. Then, they'll want control, Adam. No, they will demand it. What then?"

"My colleagues are responsible people. They deserve to know."

"That is a foolish thing to say. Do you really think our life will be recognizable once you publish this thing?" Crystal stepped back from the kitchen table to compose herself.

"No, forget that. Let's just focus on the coming next few days. Alberto is dying. He needs you here. This trip only serves your need to prove something."

Crystal Bayeta was plainly disturbed. Adam was not good at working through complicated personal dilemmas. He attacked problems in a linear fashion through trial and error. Solutions to conflicting personal priorities do not lend themselves well to trial and error. His habit of finding an answer by persisting until chance or a serendipitous event led him to it was not infallible. But to her, it was like summer hail, a rare event in the desert, a force of nature. Summer hail was not unlike serendipity or insight. It too could come without warning, a great flash of sheet lightning stretching out across the entire front of an approaching storm. Sudden gusts of cold wind follow, sweeping down from the north. One's nostrils fill with a strange, unmistakable smell—danger. Adam's intent to make public his research filled her with dread, as did summer hail. Summer hail was rare, a force accompanied by lightning. A hailstorm caused headaches, bad temper, and uncontrollable urges. Lightning-charged hail could destroy a cornfield and cause a woman to miscarry. In her mind, Adam's breakthrough was nothing less than a storm's approach. She felt certain of it.

<++++++++++>

Rimrock had become the material framing of their life together. Bayeta wanted it to continue without change. The house blended well into the rock faces surrounding it on three sides. Rimrock was remote, removed from the pressures of modern life. Self-defined routine and purpose governed it. Bayeta's studio opened onto the east patio. The detached laboratory was the north annex. Chiseled into the pine beam over the doorway to Adam's lab were words from her daily dawn prayer.

"With beauty before me, I walk"
"With beauty behind me, I walk"

The hour was late as she worked in the failing light of her studio. For the past hour, Bayeta had listened for the car. Pressing the dye water from a last skein of sheep's wool, a childhood story came to mind, one that helped regulate her firm, purposeful movements working with the wool. Handling wool is best done even paced and steady. Just as she was certain of the means and ends in handling the wool, so was she sure that she wanted Adam not to act in haste or from impulse.

For Bayeta, weaving provided her life with structure and meaning. Her grandmother had told her, "Now you know all that I have named for you. When a baby girl is born to our clan, one must go and find a spider's web, one woven at the mouth of a small hole. Take it and rub it on the fingers and the hands and on the arms of the baby. The baby will grow strong. In time, the child's hands will know the way to make a good web. Her hands will not tire of the task. Beauty will be before her."

Bayeta squeezed the last skein of wet wool hard and tight. It felt good, its thickness and texture even. Hanging it on the drying rack, she thought of the story that clung to her like well-wound warp string. The story came to her often when she sat down to weave. She would flex her fingers and remember. It was the order of things, the sorting of what mattered to a woman, to a weaver. Spider Man and Spider Woman, Grandmother had impressed upon her, gave Navajo women gifts of the first order of things. "Now you will know and act as you should. It is just so." Bayeta set her hands intently to their purpose. She smiled at the thought of the word, loom. Such a *bilagáana* word was inadequate. To her, it was *dah'istl'ǫ́*, the very sound of which held power and meaning beyond words.

In college, Bayeta had learned all the academic terms applied to ethnic lore. Spider Woman, her professors insisted, might be valid as a story, but not literally true. Bayeta privately kept two dictionaries in her head. The *Diné* one she kept private. Her Anthropology 101 instructor showed little patience or tolerance for what he labeled the exotic and quaint. A thing worth knowing must, he insisted, stand-up to objective, rational analysis. Bayeta believed he was abstractly sympathetic to the social and political realities of Indians. But he was inflexible about "things mystical." However imaginative, Navajo myths remained for him but colorful fictions.

"They may enrich our imagination, but do not expect them to be functional in today's world," he said in class. This was a hopeless contradiction to Bayeta. Was he not, after all, a good Jew? He took his Sabbath duties seriously and ate kosher. He read the Talmud in Hebrew. Ritually, devoutly, he observed Seder and Yom Kippur. And yet, of Spider Woman and Spider Man he insisted, "Ah, the stuff of legend, quaint myths." He did not know what it was like to take the wool of sheep into one's hands and weave of it a thing of beauty.

He would never experience the honor of being asked by a woman to erect poles for a loom. What did he know? In his world, machines made such things, not men and women.

<++++++++++>

As the light faded, the air in Bayeta's studio's turned crisp and penetrating. Another sun of the fifth world was plunging into the western ocean, taking with it another of The People. It was just so in The Fifth World. Once, long ago, no one died. On that last day of immortality, the sun stood still, scorching the earth. The earth's waters dried up. Order and harmony failed The People. Coyote came, and he said that death must come into the world. He told of a gift in exchange for a life. Each year would no longer be as a day. The many different beings must learn to live separately. Mountain people must go to the high places and remain there. The people of the plains must now live in that flat place, in their one place. Within the four sacred mountains, The People must remain. Near to the Place of Emergence, from which The People of The Fourth World came up into this, The Fifth World, there the *Diné* must remain. From that time, Death came among The People. Each day ended with a life given. With order and harmony established, the sun would not stand still. The world would remain in balance. For it not to be so, the earth would become too crowded and turn into a burned out cinder.

Such a sense of order and harmony dominated Bayeta's mind as cold air settled against her skin to sharpen her thoughts. She focused her attention on the drying skeins of wool. This new web was to be her best. No commercial dyes, no store bought wools, no manufactured soaps were to be used. This web was to be made the old way. She had set aside the heirloom bolt of deep, red flannel cloth. It, too, was called bayeta, her namesake. Cutting the bayeta cloth into strips and raveling it into thread took time and concentration. The resulting strands had to be of uniform thickness and strength for weaving. For Bayeta, it must be done the old way, and it had to be just so.

The process of cutting, stripping, and twining such flannel anew was a lost skill. No other *Diné* weaver worked with bayeta flannel. It was of another age, from before Bosque Redondo. The old webs made with bayeta were spoken of as special, the highest expression of the beauty way of the *Diné*. Before the century began, however, buyers' tastes had shifted to pictorials, eye dazzlers, the serape style, and weaves identified by provenance within the reservation. The buyer's whim, however, had never mattered to Bayeta. She did not weave to please the buyer, she once explained to her anthropology instructor. He was, she said, using academic terms, to explain the difference between the sacred and the profane. The distinction made little impression on her.

The early afternoon had been sunny with a gentle wind, a perfect time to walk to the well in the company of the Tumecho women. "Ground up Mexican beetles is best," Widow Tumecho inveighed. She insisted that her kin appreciate the one true source of the cochineal color found in the bolt of old red flannel that Bayeta was using. Bayeta had shown them her re-spun "bayeta" yarn with the delicate orange to red hues. For her new web, it suited her design. Seen from a distance, it took on the darkened hues of iron-stained canyon walls. Ground cochineal with a tin mordant was best. The Widow Tumecho cautioned not to add oxalic acid, as some women once did. That would only make it plain and crimson-like. As her kin watched, Widow Tumecho nodded satisfaction as Bayeta worked the wool. The old way was best. Did they not see that it was just so?

The afternoon given over to dyeing wool had pleased Bayeta. Alberto was away at the clinic in Flagstaff, in Martin's care. With her granddaughters in tow, Widow Tumecho had come to help. The well from which they drew water was a good walk south of Rimrock, a safe distance, Widow Tumecho reckoned. There they would dye wool and gossip. The young women had not before used natural dyes. They had not the patience to gather the plants, prepare each dye to the color desired, dye the wool, soak, rinse, and dry each skein. Hearing Juanita complain to Maria drew a silent, chastising look from their grandmother.

"It is best to weave as Spider Woman taught our grandmothers. If not so, time will make the web dull in your eyes," Widow Tumecho insisted. She held up the lustrous wool dyed with cochineal and set it out on the sapling racks to dry in the sun. It had been too long since

Bayeta and women had spent the day together dyeing wool. She had missed their company and gossip.

Juanita, unable to contain her curiosity and not thinking before she spoke, could not help herself. She had seen the row of gas cylinders against the back wall, the roof vents and piping of the building, and had heard the intermittent puffs of venting vapors rising skyward above the roof. To her, the laboratory was a mysterious, living thing. Juanita whispered to Maria that it was a thing that never slept. Juanita, not known for discretion, asked, "*Adagas*?" Does he now work in his ..."

Bayeta gently interrupted her, "Not today. He went to Chinle to do some errands."

The very word, laboratory, was alien in sound and meaning to most on the reservation. Juanita had seen the word in print. But that did not make it any more familiar or meaningful. A laboratory, and especially the one at Rimrock, was a place of unknowable labors that served no practical purpose to those living on the reservation. It was important to Bayeta, however, that mention of the laboratory not break the mood of the afternoon. It was a time for dyeing wool and gathering scraps of family gossip.

When the house construction had first begun, neighbors showed up without notice. Some were kin, reason enough. A "daughter" had been too long away. Men volunteered to help build the house. Two months later, when the foundation work began on the laboratory, the men stopped coming.

A laboratory could be a contaminated place, they believed. They had long experience dealing with uranium ore extraction and the presence of the massive complex at Los Alamos hidden behind high security fences. Assurances that Adam was a different kind of scientist did not impress them. Rumor colored every distinction between physics and biology. And, was not the boxed canyon known as Rimrock "that" place where wizards once brought misfortune? In the end, Adam contracted an Albuquerque firm to finish the laboratory. It was, said one elder kinsman, no small matter. The house could be a sacred place. "That other…it is not sacred," he said.

<++++++++++>

Turning the ignition key, Adam's hand felt stiff and ached from the cold. Barely able to grip the Land Rover's steering wheel, he shifted gears. The grind of metal-to-metal brought him back to the demands of the moment. Crystal was waiting for him. With quiet eyes, patient and caring, she would be watching for his approach from over the rise. The dinner table would be set, had been set for some time.

Adam felt guilty about the timing of the trip. Alberto's condition was grave. His internal organs were collapsing with increasing signs of distress each day. He needed Adam now more than ever. "Can't you postpone? Tell them you can't come. Not until…" But she knew he could not.

Adam saw it in her eyes. He heard it in the pause at mid-sentence. It cost her dearly to ask. She knew that he believed that he could not cancel or delay. The unasked question was most painful to both: How could she cope if Alberto died with only her at his side? What about later? How would Adam bear a sense of abandonment, if? Bayeta had known the sad reality of dying and death. But Alberto's impending death was different. He would never know what it meant to be young, or to live as a mature, independent adult, or to grow old through time, truly old.

As the slope increased, the Land Rover slowed and began to labor in third gear. Adam geared down. He was not paying attention to the road. His mind was occupied with the conviction that he had in fact found a key to life's extension at the molecular level within the cell. Life itself would remain finite, he insisted to himself. But the long-established limit could now be pushed back, recalibrated, redefined. That was victory enough for him. Centenarians would become the new norm of aging.

At the crest of the slope, Adam slipped the clutch into neutral and let go of his uncertainties of what might come. The sky melted into an ashen red glow hard against the horizon. In the failing light, Adam glimpsed home. Rimrock, deep in shadow, lay nested within the red rock walls of the small, boxed canyon. He did not mind that locals called it "Wizard's Rock." Against the dying light, darkened sandstone walls looming on three sides, the house and Bayeta waited.

<++++++++++>

Bayeta heard the car and put aside her concerns about Juanita's chattering on about the laboratory that afternoon. She hurried into the kitchen to finish preparing the salad. Listening for the front door, the stressed lines in her face softened.

"Adam, is that you?"

"Is that lamb stew I smell?"

"Dinner will be ready in five minutes."

"Can I help set the table or something?"

She stood at the door to the study with an apron in her hands. In the time between his offer and her response that nothing more needed doing, Adam had put down the unopened mail and checked the to-do list. Absent from his laboratory since after breakfast, he scanned Martin's lab notes. Unless she acted quickly, it would be too late for dinner or an evening together. Adam stood with a fresh lab coat and Martin's note in hand. For once, they had the house to themselves.

Still examining the notes, Adam turned to see her prim, pleasing shadow reach out across the Crystal pattern rug on the hall floor. It was the rug given to them by Bayeta's mother on their wedding day in Albuquerque. The rug's soft, tempered hues perfectly framed her supple body. Crystal Bayeta was not simply a captivating, pretty woman. In his eyes she was maddeningly soft and appealing. And, in that moment, she was too wise for him. Her apron hung suspended, motionless and poised above the cool slate floor beyond the blanket's edge. It spoke volumes. Could he not smell the sage-seasoned lamb stew and fresh fry bread? Had he not seen the bottle of chilled white wine on the table? Crystal Bayeta, her head tilted coquettishly toward the dinner table, waited. The apron in her hand swayed, a will-o-the-wisp beckoning, whenever she spoke.

"You used wild onion in the stew?" He asked. She nodded.

"Perfect! Only one thing needs doing, feeding the animals at 10. That will only take ten or fifteen minutes."

"I'll give you fifteen minutes at ten o'clock, dear. One minute more and I'll change into a giant spider and eat you up."

"Bea, I promise, ten minutes, fifteen at the outside."

Wrapping his arms firmly about Crystal Bayeta, he plucked her free of the floor. The apron fell to the floor. Their kiss was long, deep, warm, and consuming. She pressed into his frame, sensuous and probing. Whenever he held her like this, and she him, it was as if that first time, that very first time.

That first time had surprised, even embarrassed, Adam. She had moved so deliberately into and upon him. Up to that moment their courting had been restrained, if fast-paced, weeks simmering with the promise of consummation held in check. He had struggled to control his emotions and impulses. Every word, every tentative touch, every look was but half of what he meant. For the first time in his life, he wanted much more than the feel of a woman's hand in his.

On the Saturday of his third week in Albuquerque, she had taken him to a wedding for one of her closest friends. Bayeta was a maid-of-honor. Not knowing the couple, he felt ambivalent about going. He would be out of place. But, he had to be with her. He needed to be with her.

At the afternoon reception, the newlyweds sat and talked with Adam for the longest time, each giving him warm, knowing looks. Others came up to the table to meet Adam, never staying so long that their curiosity, which showed, made him uncomfortable. By five o'clock, the newlywed couple had said their goodbyes and departed. The talk at the tables turned to news of family and friends. The men complained about the dry year and tribal politics. When Adam caught a man's eye, he switched seamlessly into Navajo. Bayeta noticed, sensing Adam's isolation. Before long, she led him by the arm out onto the patio. She had nibbled at the edges of his emotions all afternoon, and this was the moment to be alone with him. Weddings being what they are, she knew her purpose.

It had been an extraordinary, delirious three weeks for both of them. The wedding was the perfect place to let the fragile veil of restraint fall away. Adam had tried for days to find a perfect moment to tell Bayeta how he felt. He had struggled against talking about it, because of how different were their present circumstances. Both had kept any talk of the future vague.

Adam's closest friend, John Sanderson, had hinted to her that Adam, at age thirty-five, was a confirmed bachelor. He had said it as gently as he knew how. Also, Adam was known to be a bit awkward in the presence of an attractive woman. John had squeezed her hand and smiled. "You, my dear, are devastatingly lovely." Being thirty, she was in her prime and wise beyond her years. Dismantling Adam's defenses was what she had set her mind to.

Before she met Adam, she was but a college art history instructor at loose ends. Reluctantly, she had agreed to go to dinner with the man from Berkeley, some molecular biologist. It was to be just a one-time blind date as a favor to John's wife, her best friend at the university. Adam Grant was in town for a three-day seminar on theoretical advances on molecular processes in aging. He was also there, her friend said, to visit his mother's grave. Come Sunday, he would return to Berkeley, end of story.

Three weeks later, however, Adam was still in town. He showed no sign of leaving. He looked forward to attending the wedding, he told her. Being a stranger did not matter to him, he insisted. Could he admit that just being with her was all that had been on his mind since their first date? That she might take advantage of the occasion had not occurred to him, not consciously.

Crystal Bayeta picked her moment well and maneuvered him out onto the patio. Adam had been explaining to a half-drunk cousin of hers something about biological clocks. He kept on about it for minutes without stopping, waving his hands in the air as he tried to explain metabolic, molecular interactions within the cell. She stood listening, waiting for the first sign of his hands coming to rest.

Guiding him out into the cool evening air of the dimly lit patio, she pressed him against the adobe wall. Putting her fingers to his lips, she took control. Adam mumbled a word or two and took a deep breath. His hands shook but his eyes steadied on hers. She pressed hard against him, her right hand cradling his chin and her eyes boring into him. "What is it, Adam? What do you want to say to me, Adam Grant?"

The loud laughs from two young men who came stumbling out onto the patio distracted him. Mildly drunk from champagne, they had spotted Bayeta with Adam. They stood staring for a moment, sizing him up. The taller man said something to the other about having some fun.

As the two approached, Adam realized that he had his arms about Bayeta. He lowered her to the patio's Saltillo tiled floor. Her bare feet settled on to the cool tiles. The shorter man, with a stocky build, was a distant cousin to Bayeta.

"A White man's blanket, just a White man's blanket," he said as he stared at her.

No translation was needed. With one quick, powerful stride, Adam seized the man.

"Don't ever speak that way to my future wife! Not again! Never! Not ever. I'll break you in two where you stand if you do."

The stunned man with one foot off the ground, his throat gripped tightly in Adam's left hand, waved helplessly and went limp. Without another word, Adam set the man back on his feet.

The confrontation was over. Both men retreated, half-running across the ballroom floor and out the double doors into the gathering dusk.

Crystal Bayeta smiled and smoothed her dress. "I accept."

Six days later, Crystal Bayeta married Dr. Adam Grant, a man long overdue back at his campus.

Married ten years, nothing had changed between them. She gave him that look and he melted.

"It was bone cold at the rim today. Warm my insides."

"Come, my husband. Turn out the lights and come."

"What about the stew?"

2

Second First Light

Following Bayeta into the kitchen, Adam sniffed the air approvingly. A pungent, sage-scented stew had been kept warm in the oven. He took olives and red wine from the refrigerator. She prepared fresh fry bread. Since returning from Chinle, he had said nothing of his detour to the rim. His subdued look told her to wait to ask. The turnout on the western rim of *Tseyi*, near the junction with Monument Canyon, was no place for him to be alone. Others would have seen him there, brooding.

With Adam absorbed with stew and fry bread, she thought back to that first time she took him on horseback deep into Canyon del Muerto, the northern spur of the Canyon de Chelly complex. How well he sat in the saddle. How curious he was that day! Everything interested him.

Adam put his spoon down and asked, "Bea, what did you say the locals call that place?" It happened often, their thoughts converging along the same track. She knew what he meant.

"*Tsétah* is the place of crashing rocks."

"There's an immense, raw intensity to it. I like the look of deep, vertical canyon walls, all that red sandstone. From below, it towers so high above, an immensity of time."

"The People try not to go near that overlook."

"Tell it to me again, the story." His mind was trained on that first time they rode together deep into the canyon and how beautiful she looked that day.

"You know Widow Tumecho. Her summer place is there, against the south wall. It takes a time, but eventually each winter ends. The spring thaws everything out. That's when fractured rock walls cleave. Big slabs of it come down. Spring is the most dangerous time. Three of her menfolk had died there when a massive slab came down. They look solid, as if they can never fall down. But they do. That wall near the Widow's hogan was more dangerous than anyone thought."

Bea noticed that Adam was only half listening. "You stopped by Rose Bia's place for coffee today, didn't you?"

"Of course, you know I always do."

"Did you see Johnny Kabito in there?"

"I talked to him."

"He was at Bia's place that day, too, when Manuel stopped in for coffee. They talked. Manuel was impatient that day. Others overheard him, knew how impulsive he could be."

"What was he impatient about?"

"He told Kabito, 'I'm for no more waiting. The grass is growing fat and my horses are thin. They are hungry for it.' " She put her hand on Adam's arm. "Johnny Kabito tried to tell him to wait, a week maybe."

"But Manuel could not be argued out of it."

"It is no man's place to tell another what to do. Anyway, the next day Manuel and his two sons crossed over the Chinle wash with their sheep and horses."

"How long ago was this?"

"I was not ten years old."

"It was that long ago? I had the impression it was more recent."

"A thing like that is never old. Don't you see? To the Widow it was yesterday. Time does not wash away or fade such a memory, or the pain."

"You never said exactly how it happened."

"No one knows, not exactly. Nellie was to follow with the wagon in a few days."

"Why didn't she go with them?"

"It is one thing to herd animals up the stream from the canyon's mouth. But the wagon must wait until enough water gets soaked into the ground for it to firm up to support the wagon's wheels. Six days later, with no rain, Nellie drove the wagon in. When she rounded the last bend, she saw the sheep and horses scattered about. No one was tending them. She could not find the men at or near the hogan. Next morning, she went for help."

"It is a pretty isolated place."

"When the others returned with her, including Johnny Kabito, they could not find any sign of Manuel or her two sons for two days. On the third day, the men found what remained of Manuelito, her first-born. A huge sandstone slab had crushed him. All they saw of him was his two hands and arms up to the elbows. His *ketoh* was on his left wrist. The rest of what was Manuelito rests there still, rests beneath tons of *tsétah*."

"The widow still goes every summer to the hogan with her sheep?"

"Yes, the stone marker is about two hundred yards from of the hogan. She is still afraid to go near it. But that does not stop her from sweeping out her hogan each morning and waiting. But, she never goes near where the men are buried. It is only for the *ch'į́įdii.*"

Adam knew that *ch'į́įdii* meant ghosts, though he pronounced it as chindi. Bayeta used the Navajo pronunciation for emphasis.

"She waits for her men. She waits for the pain to drain away from her heart." The widow could not come to terms with her loss, ever. "Because they are under the rock fall, it is contaminated, dangerous. Each spring she sweeps out the hogan, keeps it for the day her men folk come home."

Finishing his bowl of stew, Adam squeezed her hand resting on his arm.

"Adam, please. When you are seen alone at the rim, people do notice."

"Bea, I'm not superstitious."

"Whenever you stop, someone sees you. Why do you think they call you wizard? It is not because you are a scientist. They have a good idea what a scientist is. It is that you do not show caution for their concerns." She wanted him to avoid going alone to the overlook, alone to brood.

"Adam, they may not know what goes on in your lab. What they do know is that you go to the rim alone. They wonder. They wonder why."

"I watch the clouds pass overhead, the changes in weather, how the light strikes the sandstone, how shadows crawl up from the floor of the canyon. I watch the hawks, this one pair of hawks, and I think."

"I understand. It is your neighbors who do not understand. They mark you as a loner. Loners are either up to no good or something is wrong with them." Bayeta paused, sensing Adam's frustration. She was not questioning his intents. It was the feelings of others that concerned her. "It makes them anxious."

"Bea, if it will make you feel better, I won't stop there. You are right. I should not be seen staring out over the rim."

"Wherever there are crashing rocks, they wonder. Witches or wizards go to such places, alone. If ordinary people act like that, bad things happen to them."

Adam finished the last of his wine and fry bread. What mattered to Bayeta was that her relatives should be at ease in his company. As a white man, he knew the social distance could be difficult to bridge. It was foolish to add to their discomfort.

"Dear, I know you are right. I won't stop looking at all that beauty. But I promise not to stop at that overlook when alone."

What had troubled his mind that day was, for the moment, gone. He set aside the matter of his trip to San Francisco and rumors about his behavior.

"Bea, remember that very first time you brought me here? I had no idea that you wanted to build here, what with that rut of a road and lack of access to power. But I could tell from the way you looked at Rimrock that the remoteness was why you liked it, so raw and perfect."

“It was May 1st. I had quite a time convincing you to come with me. You had received that dean’s letter only that morning. You were in an awful mood.”

“Well, it’s not every day that I get the rug pulled out from under me by a dean, and my wife decides it is time to go hunting for a house site.”

“You were furious about the letter. I almost decided it was not time to show you Rimrock. I did not know if you would even consider us living here.”

Adam smiled. “The Dean did not have the nerve to wait and tell me in person. But, I admit, as things turned out, it no longer stings.”

“I had kept you in Albuquerque. The dean thought you were sort of AWOL. He certainly did not want to tell you in person, did he?”

“I was not very good company that day. The trouble you took making up a picnic basket, negotiating for the horses. And, you painted such a charming picture of Widow Tumecho. You wanted me to meet her because her winter home is close by.”

Until that day, Adam had had little experience with life on the floor of a canyon. He knew canyons by standing at the rim and looking down. Riding a horse into one was new.

“When I was twelve, maybe thirteen, I almost rode down into a canyon. Father had taken Sis and me to the Grand Canyon. Cynthia begged him to let us ride down to the bottom on the donkeys. She used every charm she had. But he said that there was not enough time. He had a plane to catch, something to do with testing another “device.” That’s what he always called them, “devices.” We felt guilty keeping him from his work.”

Alexander Terman had never liked being in New Mexico or any part of the desert Southwest. During the war, he found Los Alamos to be crude, makeshift, and stifling. He was there only because of the project, desperate to be a part of it. Two weeks to the day after the Trinity test, he left for Chicago with two suitcases. Abandoning a wife was a small price to pay for becoming one of Edward Teller’s team that was going to make “the super.” Terman had signed on to be a “gray-eyed, sorcerer’s apprentice,” Eleanor’s parting words to him as he walked out the door.

Adam grew up with a vague apprehension of the emerging nuclear arms race. A childhood marked by a guarded silence between father and son culminated in open hostility the summer of Adam's sixteenth birthday. That day, too, Adam remembered well how his father had felt about their trip to the Grand Canyon. Alexander could be cruel when he wanted. "All that stupid talk of time locked up in stone is useless prattle," he had said. "A nuclear bomb could make it into something useful, a giant water reservoir, perhaps. That's all it is good for." That day, he had insisted that there was no reason whatsoever to go down into it. The day was hot. He was sweating. "All I see is a hole. There is nothing more to it."

Observing her husband's lapse into a brooding silence, Bayeta remained patient. The bright mood of the evening had faded. Thoughts of his father had such an effect on Adam. For her sake, Adam tried to blot out the memory of that trip to the Grand Canyon. His revulsion for his father's work three years later had made reconciliation impossible. At best, a truce was struck when he entered college. By then, Adam had learned to maintain a cool, impersonal politeness in place of argument or recrimination.

Clutching Bayeta's hand, Adam took in a deep breath and smiled. "I enjoyed that day when we sat and talked with Widow Tumecho. Do you remember?"

"Of course I do."

"The sun was so bright, yet in the shade the canyon floor stayed cool all afternoon. I remember the quiet and stillness. Sitting next to the old woman's hogan, I kept thinking of a single phrase, "a pleasant golden hour in the age of mammals, lost before the human coming," something from Loren Eisley. The proof was there in the rocks. But which layers did he have in mind? How high above our heads was that golden hour? What was that golden hour really like? No matter how many times I go to the rim or go down to the streambed at the bottom, I come no closer to recognizing it in the rocks. Is it there, close to the rim or farther down? It has to be above the floor, if he meant the age of mammals. I want to know this, but I don't know why."

"Do you believe that the golden time is in the past?"

"If it is, I am afraid of what the future holds. I am not even sure that I want to know. Life is fragile even in the best of times. Humans have made life tenuous. Nothing is stable or secure. Everyone insists change is good. Whatever happens will end up encased, buried in a wall of stone. Our time will be just one more set of horizontal stains, a speck of time." He looked intently at Bayeta. "I am sorry the neighbors think me odd."

Bayeta rested her elbows on the table, her face nearly touching his. She sipped the last of her wine and put it down. She felt a little silly for going on about how the neighbors react. Adam had never expressed anything but respect for his neighbors. He tried to avoid being seen at the rim, often parking the Land Rover in the shade. He stood next to low trees or rock outcrops to try and not be seen. Still, he was noticed.

Their carefully constructed equilibrium of Rimrock mattered to both of them. When they were living a fast-paced urban life in the Bay Area, she had adapted, even admitting to having "Anglo ways." But, Rimrock was home, was where she practiced her craft, and was where she found her balance between her urbanity and her Navajo self. It was essential to her to nurture her relationships with kinfolk and neighbors. She could not help appearing exotic to Anglos and Navajo alike. Her exceptional beauty made it so: A flawless, bronzed skin, slender waist, and long, black, shining hair combed straight and down her back. Her presence disturbed most men and intimidated their women. This pleased Adam immensely.

With the house bathed in the quiet coolness of a full moon streaming through the windows, Bayeta handed Adam the fruit bowl to take it into the living room. "I'll make the coffee." Embracing him, she pressed the bowl suggestively into his ribs.

Adam settled comfortably into the deep, soft leather chair near the fireplace. His concerns over the trip could wait. To eat a ripe peach, sip hot coffee, and watch the fire with Crystal Bayeta beside him was all that mattered in the moment.

"Adam, you did confirm the plane reservation, right?"

"My brother was not at the Institute when I called."

"What if the flight is full?"

"Herman's secretary insisted on making the reservation. I tried to tell her to wait."

"You need to tell John that you can't give the talk tomorrow in Albuquerque."

"Damn! I completely forgot."

"Adam, you need to call John now and cancel. He'll understand."

"No. I won't leave John hanging like that, not on such short notice."

The difference between can't and won't was calculated on his part. Adam often hedged between alternatives. He could put a thing off, as if he had no choice. Or, just as likely, keep to his plan in spite of obstacles. He liked to think he could have it both ways. John, she knew, would understand, if he put off the talk. As Adam's best friend, he would know that Adam had a very good reason. In the past five years, he had had to reschedule his annual guest lecture to John's students twice because bad weather made the trip too difficult.

"Bea, John is going on to San Francisco, too." He hesitated for a moment, distracted by an incomplete thought. "I will keep my promise and not let down his students, especially the graduate students. They need more exposure to how similar mammals are to our own physiology and evolutionary adaptations."

"Adam, you can't always have it both ways."

He said nothing. But, his sinking lower into the leather chair showed that he had his mind made up. It was no use discussing the effect it was sure to have on Herman. His half-brother, as Director of The Evergreen Institute, expected him to arrive tomorrow. For five years, he had provided funding for Adam's enzyme researches. That alone allowed Adam to pursue his real passion, longevity research. Adam insisted the two lines of research were unrelated. Bayeta doubted that Herman saw it in the same way.

"Adam, you told them you would fly out Thursday morning. You know how Herman is when kept on tender hooks. He's touchy, egotistical. Don't antagonize him."

Her words made him remember how Herman behaved when he refused to install a secured computer link between the Institute and Rimrock.

"Yes, remember how he went on and on about the computer link. He insisted it was needed. He's still miffed over it. He had no right to insist, knowing that I would reject it out of hand."

"I know that, dear. But isn't it time that you let it rest?"

For five years the incident had rankled Adam. Bayeta tried for months to convince Adam to forge a truce, even if a cold one. Adam reluctantly agreed to a computer link through the university at Albuquerque. Adam made certain to segregate his longevity work and stored his data on a personal PC with a removable disk drive. The institute's funded research alone flowed through the computer link at the university via BIOCOMNET. Doubly careful, he corresponded with colleagues by way of the regular mails. At first, Bayeta thought he was just being obstinate. In time, however, she became aware how close Adam was to proving his lifespan experiment. Intuitively, she saw the danger. Such knowledge could be dangerous to possess, even unholy. To her, a natural life's span was a sacred boundary, not one to breach. And, to what end? Adam's trip only heightened her fears.

"Dear, Herman is expecting you to arrive before noon tomorrow."

"Herman is not my concern. At the conference my work will get attention. Some inkling of what I have been after is already known. What I have to say can only be said once. I must decide how much to make public." He paused to focus his concern over Herman. "Most importantly, I have no intention to let his institute near this work. It has nothing to do with his precious institute. That's why I'm keeping away until the last possible moment."

She saw Adam glance a third time at his watch. Her hope for an evening alone together had lost its momentum. It was nearly 10 o'clock, time to feed the animals. Time was against her. The feeding schedule was invariable, inviolate.

He rose from his chair. She pretended not to notice. Her eyes were on the fire. Once he crossed the laboratory threshold, he was beyond reach. The lab, unlike her studio, was a world apart with secrets and an alien language. In five years she had not interfered with the demands of his laboratory routine, not once. In the moment, what concerned her was his insistence that John Sanderson took precedence. Adam enjoyed his annual talks to students and the interactions with them. He looked forward to it, though he never spoke of missing the atmosphere of the classroom.

"I want to talk about *Sorex vagrans*, Bea."

"So, Herman waits his turn behind a quarter ounce furry thing." The irony in her voice did not penetrate his consciousness.

"Bea, Herman can wait. I need more time. I don't know how he or his people might react to the news at the meeting. They have no stake, but that may not matter to them."

"Even so, he expects you before noon."

"I'll phone from Albuquerque and tell him I was unavoidably delayed."

"Now you are being unfair."

"He knows how remote Rimrock is, how hard it is to get away. I'll call him from the university. An unexpected family matter came up. I'll mention Alberto."

"Have you told Herman how serious Alberto's condition is?"

"No, I haven't. He does not care about Alberto. Why should he?"

She thought, what would Herman think if he knew? She said, "He doesn't need to know."

On his way to the lab, Adam knew that Bea's concern over Herman had not been resolved. She would be listening to his steps in retreat on the Saltillo tiles. He felt guilty leaving the matter unresolved. Bayeta called out, "I'll put a fresh pot on the stove." Any other woman would have complained at his retreat. But Crystal Bayeta stoked the pine logs in the fireplace and quieted her mind. Pitch-laden and smelling of the forest, the logs spit spirals of embers up the chimney. She sat in her chair watching the fire and amended her list of to-dos for the coming day. Adam would be absorbed in detailing and crosschecking his latest results into the early hours. He was compulsive about leaving no variable or observation unaccounted for. He had a list to prepare for Martin in his absence. Martin was capable, but he did not take initiative. However tedious it was, Adam would take time to detail instructions.

The fire died down. Bayeta thought of their first years together. She half dozed. Those first five years, before Rimrock, were crammed with frenetic over-doing and travel. That first summer, they blanketed Europe. The second summer it was South America and Australia. More trips to Europe and the east coast followed, with a foray to Canada. Adam talked of going to Russia, Israel, Romania, and China. In one three-week period, in the fourth year, Adam squeezed in Delhi, and three days each in Sri Lanka, Melbourne, Tokyo, and Seattle. Stepping off a midnight flight to San Francisco, Bayeta was completely exhausted. She had lost five pounds, in spite of the rich food at every stop. Adam, to her astonishment, was completely unaffected. He could not wait to get back into his lab to digest the results of his meetings with colleagues, visits to their labs, the conferences and lectures. Throughout it all, he was oblivious to scheduling conflicts, flight delays, and late-night invites. He saw only opportunities to buttonhole one more colleague, even if only in a hotel lobby, no matter the hour. How like children Adam and his colleagues could be at such times. An idle parting comment could easily turn into an impromptu symposium in the corner of the hotel lobby or even an airport lounge, adding yet one more complication to their schedule. Bayeta did not really mind. She understood enough about his work to feel the excitement he and his colleagues shared. He was in his element. Language, place, customs posed no barrier to their intense conversations.

How odd it was, then, when the travel and interactions with colleagues came to a sudden and complete halt. For the last five years, Adam had secluded himself in his laboratory and traveled no farther than 300 miles to Flagstaff or Albuquerque, and one brief trip to California. Bayeta immersed herself in her weaving, family, and caring for Alberto. Her family was close by in Window Rock, Chinle, or the slopes of the Chuska Range to the east. Adam's closest friend, John, was in Albuquerque. Occasionally, a former colleague or current correspondent made it an occasion to meet up in Albuquerque.

Of late, however, Bayeta had become apprehensive that things were bound to change. Adam's impending brush with fame, or perhaps notoriety, would complicate things. The thought, her fear, of Rimrock becoming the past and not future, was disturbing. Rimrock meant peace, quiet, contentment. It was fifteen miles beyond the last strip of decaying, paved road, self-contained. How easily life beyond Rimrock could become unrecognizable and unpredictable, unwanted change. She feared most for Adam, that he had no real grasp of what was about to happen. He was absorbed with work in the lab and with Alberto's accelerating decline. His habit was to narrow his focus to one or two things and ignore everything else.

Bayeta's father had seen it the first time he met Adam. "Daughter, I do not say he is simple-minded. But when he talks science, can he keep anything else in his head?" He had listened carefully to everything Adam said that evening, how he said it, what he said. It mattered to George Slim that a man speaks well, that his speech has certain knowledge.

"Daughter, you look at him with warm, soft eyes."

"What else do you see, father?"

"His wind blows strong. You say he is good. I believe you. He is a good man. One thing only: He is *bilagáana.* Can good come from mixing your blood with his?"

"Father, I am 30 years old. I know my heart. I have not met a man of my own people who can make me happy. This man makes me happy. Eat with him, just the two of you. Ask him anything. Tell him your mind."

At noon the next day, George Slim met Adam for lunch. He liked Adam and put aside his long-standing feelings about mixed marriages. It was in Adam's favor that he was not Ute or Cheyenne. Ute and Cheyenne men had married into his clan. Two marriages ended badly. Adam also had a direct nature, no affectation. Adam gave George Slim an outline of his science, a brief one. But, he could not keep from talking about Crystal Bayeta, how much he wanted to make her happy. That evening, George Slim took his daughter aside. "It is good."

"Then, I have your blessing?"

"He is a good man for you. He wants to make you happy. Only one thing: He does not think like our people. He does not understand that he cannot ***make*** you happy. That, you must do for yourself. Happiness is not a thing one gives to another."

"Father, be happy for me."

"I am content." He squeezed her hands. "Daughter, I am old. I have lived with old ways. I tell you now that others will talk. They will speak of disharmony. They will say that you were not born for him. Your mother will talk about family, their feelings. I will speak for his wind, a strong spirit. It is good to have such a spirit, a strong wind. One thing only, sometimes he will not see how his wind blows in another's face."

"What are you saying, Father?"

"All living things have a wind, daughter. It is the breath of life, and it is more. One cannot live without having it. Some possess a black wind. Your mother does not think about such things. She only wants things to be calm and peaceful. We must wait and see."

Bayeta had little time to reflect on her father's nuanced meaning. It was enough for her that her father saw in Adam a strong wind. She had his blessing.

That evening, at her apartment, George Slim watched Adam from across the room. When it was time to go, he said good night to his daughter. "A strong and steady wind stirs up life in the desert. How quickly it comes."

Of course, he wanted to see his daughter settled and happy. George Slim and Ninaba saw her unmarried state not unlike the desert in winter—waiting for the thaw of a spring to come. He had never expressed such feelings to her, but all the same it was so. For her part, Bayeta sensed her parents' concern and was grateful it remained unspoken. Now, they could see for themselves that their daughter had chosen well. Ninaba took her daughter aside that evening. "It is good", she whispered. Bayeta answered: "My heart has spoken."

<++++++++++>

Between midnight and 1:00 a.m., a pipette slipped from his hand, shattering to pieces on the cement floor. Then, a simple equation failed to compute. It was imbalanced. Adam surrendered to his fatigue and scribbled a final note in the log.

Before going to bed, he felt his pants pockets one last time for something to write with. Since 10:00 p.m. he had mislaid one pen after another on the lab counters or his desk. With sleep pouring over him, he wondered how many pens and pencils one could lose in one evening. If Alberto knew, he would scold him for being so absent-minded. Stooped with age, Alberto often stood holding five or six recovered pens and pencils in his gnarled, stiffened hands. Each morning, until a month ago, Alberto had performed his task of retrieving and reminding, picking up the pencils and pens and lining them up in two neat rows. They were, he was fond a saying, soldiers in formation ready for action. It pleased Alberto to collect every mislaid pen and pencil and return them to service.

Adam felt the chilled air penetrate his half-unbuttoned shirt. A stray detail on cellular repair mechanisms kept turning over in his mind. The calculation error was about those repair processes. Across the ceiling above the bed, he could almost make out the solution. He reached for a pencil to write it down, but sleep overtook him.

Driven to its limit, a mind falters. In his deep but restless slumber, Adam shivered. A dream lured him ever farther into the recesses of the canyon, its towering, vertical walls cold and dark, loomed over him. He heard himself asking: "Where was that golden hour, where?" But the walls did not answer.

<++++++++++>

At 3:30 a.m. Bayeta rose from bed as gently as she could manage. She dressed and washed her face. Adam lay crumbled in a heap on top of the covers. As she breathed in deep, the cold air forced an involuntary shudder down her back. She picked up the clipboard on the nightstand. The last entry on the log sheet read:

Day 1441 Alpha Group 11 PM
Blood Analysis Pending Check Glomeruli Filtration Rates

Bayeta squinted and focused intently on the entry above it, written in pencil by a shaky hand.

Alpha 11 expired No sign of lividity :043 AM
Tray # 112A4-11 Frozen for Analysis :058 AM

With dawn still hours away, she shook her head. Another Alpha was dead. Alphas were dying off rapidly now, one after another.

This latest event would further delay his paying attention to the details for his trip to San Francisco. Bayeta spread a wool blanket over Adam and picked up his log sheet. It told her what she needed to know. He had fed the animals at 1:00 a.m. With Alpha 11 logged and frozen, he could sleep a little longer. The automatic food dispensers were set for 4:00 a.m. Bayeta set the clock radio for 4:30 a.m.

Warming her hands as she walked into the kitchen, she decided to finish spinning the warp yarn. Her hands were stiff from the cold air. Spinning was a slow-going task. She did not mind. A good foundation took time. The warp yarn was almost long enough to string, almost long enough. The churro wool was strong and springy. It would make a fine foundation. With fresh coffee poured, she quickened her steps to the studio.

<++++++++++>

George Slim had said that Adam had a big wind. He believed that every living thing possessed a wind, the breath of life itself. In the ten years since George Slim first sized up Adam, his judgment had not altered. It pleased his daughter that he believed that. To a woman in love, a father's blessing is like gentle summer rain that falls on one's parched skin. It washes away anxiety and apprehension. He approved her choice. To George Slim, however, his assurance implied much more. The wind within any man must carry a song. Bayeta trusted her father's sensibility in such matters. Her father had sensed a deep, constant, and strong force. It affected everything about him. At thirty, Bayeta wanted to have children and begin a family. She had had enough of city living, of Albuquerque, and of her fast-paced life in an academic community. Adam was irresistible. Her life, she believed, could correct its course with him. This, too, was what George Slim hoped for.

The years advanced, however, and her hopes to begin a family remained unfulfilled. Adam was not aware of her growing anxiety. How many times had she wanted to sit him down and tell him? But of late, as never before, he was too deeply preoccupied. When her parents visited weeks earlier, George Slim told her to remain patient.

"You must wait for the season to ripen, my daughter. He must first finish this thing you call his obsession. Until it lets go of him, he is like tumble-weed in a storm. This thing in him is master. It will pass."

George Slim did not understand the intricacies of Adam's obsession. He knew nothing of what Adam called the coding of life. But, he knew enough to wonder if it could interfere with the limits nature imposed. "You want to bring longer life to people."

"I think it is possible, yes."

"Do you believe that it is a good thing?"

"Isn't that what you believe?"

Direct questions made George Slim uncomfortable. He had no reluctance asking them, only to have to respond. His habit was to ignore questions. If one needed answers, in time they would come out of their own accord, in their own way.

"So, you want this for all people, do you?"

"I do. Life is precious. Whatever can be done to extend life is important."

He studied Adam for a long moment, and then he said, "Yes, life is good. Death is a good thing, too. Maybe the path one travels is not always long. But every path is a gift."

"I'm not sure that I know what you mean."

"Such knowledge will come to you when you need it. When death came to the First People, they did not understand. They did not know that without death the world would become very crowded and there would not be enough food for everyone. They, too, when death first came to the hogans, believed it was a dark wind."

Bayeta had entered the living room just then. She sensed the substance of their conversation. But, she did not pursue it. Her father's vision encompassed both the fair wind that made a man good and that wind which could come out of nowhere to rage against the light. The thought that Adam could be capable of rage or unpredictable behavior simply was not something she wanted to hear. John Sanderson had told her how uncompromising he was about the potential of his science. He was against any attempt to confine, constrain, or regulate. God help the skeptic who would put limits on it. And yet, oddly, he did not see physics in the same light. Why the exception?

She put aside her memory of her father and Adam talking of man's nature. Finishing her coffee, she focused on the last pile of natural, un-dyed wool to spin for the warp yarn. Widow Tumecho's flock of churros gave such good wool. The Widow took pride in her sheep. Their wool was not crimped or too oily, not like that of merinos. It was ideal for carding and spinning by hand. It did not require dyeing or washing. Its natural oils allowed the wool to come off the spindle as one smooth, even strand. She tested each skein with her hands for strength and tension before adding it to the spindle batch.

Half an hour later, with the warp yarn ready for stringing, Bayeta turned to sorting each ball of yarn, examining them for uniform thickness and texture. How clean and natural were the lanolin rich fibers. She sorted the yarn into four baskets. Working right to left, she placed the first basket to the east. Two unsatisfactory balls she put aside. She gave thanks to the widow's sheep for such wool, feeling how firm and uniform it had spun. Bayeta found her rhythm in the sorting and emptied her mind of all other concerns.

For the hour, Bayeta sorted and estimated the length of the warp yarn. Satisfied with the amount, she was ready to string the warping frame. That would take time. She turned to gathering up the tools she needed. George Slim had brought her a new cloth beam and yarn beam. She set her favorite batten and heddle beside them. Two shed sticks rested by the door. As she handled her two weaving forks, she saw that one was worn down, too much so to be suitable. Another would be needed. But she did not want to use just any comb, not like those she had seen at the trading post. There was no time to have George Slim fashion a new one, however. Perhaps Widow Tumecho's brother could make it. He was a good man. She could trust him to make a good one, with smooth rounded edges to each tine. She wrote a note to herself to stop by the Widow's camp on her return from Albuquerque.

<++++++++++>

Adam had stretched out under the blanket. In his half-waking dream a phantom midday sun penetrated down to the canyon floor. His bride reined in the dappled gray at the last fork of the trail. One branch led in a northerly direction. The other drifted eastward along the talus slope. It led to the summer camp of "those born to the Jemez clan." Reluctant to disturb the enfolding silence, Bayeta leaned over in the saddle and whispered to Adam. "They are a wise band, the Jemez. They knew Carson, or someone like him, was going to come."

"Did the soldiers find them?"

"Some were marched off to Bosque Redondo. Others hid. They all suffered from hunger and starvation. Carson and his bunch were not soldiers. They were New Mexico volunteers, outlaws and drifters. Real soldiers would have behaved better."

"I am not so sure, Bea. It was a pretty rough time. The Civil War was raging in the east. Men fit for regular military duty were in short supply."

"Adam, Carson's men burned all the hogans. They burned the cornfields. They slaughtered all the sheep and horses. My great grandmother could read and write. She wrote down the date, March 6th. That's when the long walk to Bosque Redondo began for her.

Adam pictured a woman standing by the stream, a proud and defiant look in her eyes. It could have been Bayeta's mother's grandmother, the one who had learned to write *bilagáana* words. She had written how it felt to be forced to go on the long walk and later to be placed in the school at Fort Defiance. She recorded how Colonel Carson's men acted when they came into *Tseyi* for Barboncito, his men, and for their women and children. The schoolteacher at Fort Defiance harshly scolded her for speaking of it. It was not so, the man said. "The teacher was an ignorant man. I wrote down the truth on a piece of paper and hid it."

"They came, promising food and shelter. Many walked to Fort Defiance. The soldiers burned the hogans. When the corn came up out of the ground, they burned it. The streams flowed red from the blood of sheep and horses."

Bayeta had amended the tale before with harsh exactitude. "Our people were the first to experience the scorched earth policy." She never referred to Carson by rank or by his first name. He was simply Carson, "fearless slayer of peach trees." Reducing the hogans to ashes and slaughtering the animals was not enough for the irregulars. Even the peach trees, scrawny at their best, were hacked down. Nothing, absolutely nothing, was to remain that could sustain life in *Tseyi*.

"Our mothers all cried and suffered. We were prisoners, no better than slaves. Our lives were like a poor, old weaving coming apart in the wind. In 1865, at Bosque Redondo, one outbreak of smallpox took 2300. To bear the pain, women wove blankets. They wove and grew silent. The men also were silent. They could not make a crop. The soil at Bosque Redondo was poor. Little rain fell for the corn. When the crops failed, the government did not honor its promise of food. The men who did not die lost the will to live."

It gnawed at reason that the hogans were reduced to ashes, and the sheep rotted in the arroyos. Carson returned one more time to make sure no peach tree was left standing. He went to his grave in 1868, as the *Dine'* walked away from captivity. Nothing short of filling in *Tseyi* would have satisfied Carson.

Adam's image of Carson drained away, replaced by the image of Crystal Bayeta. Tall, slim, and beautiful, she sat proudly in the saddle. The stained face of the rock-wall canyon framed her perfectly. On that day, their fifth anniversary was days old. A mystery dwelled within her, behind her dark, all-seeing eyes, heightening his sense of joyful confusion. It was time to see that her dream came first, Rimrock.

It took time for concern over intermarriage to fade for some. In the first year of marriage, for Bayeta and Adam, two worldviews of custom and tradition melded into one. Love narrowed the differences to insignificance, but not his sense of wonder of her. Within her, behind those dark, vigorous eyes, a subtle repository of custom and belief remained untouched. How could he penetrate such a deep knowledge of being and place? He had found the one woman capable of sustaining his soul. On that ride, eight hundred feet down from the canyon rim, they were riding into a great mystery. No other woman had affected him so deeply. Eleanor had indeed opened doors to many mysteries. But, she was not, in herself, possessed of mystery. Crystal Bayeta, however, possessed a centeredness and sense of mystery beyond his knowing. And yet, it was she who guided and completed his sense of being. Even her most casual look as she walked into a room was enough to refresh him. Her dark, deep, quiet eyes ignited fires within him that he had not known were possible. When she spoke to her family or to a friend in Navajo, he felt an emotion beyond expression or translation. He could but listen. On that ride into the canyon, he had watched her smooth, bronzed skin absorb the sun's rays. As she leaned to one side in her saddle, the fresh, pungent scent of horse sweat and aging leather filled his nostrils, and she touched his hand. Half-blinded by the intense morning sun, his hand tingling at her touch, he felt wholly enmeshed within the orbit of her being. He was embedded in the moment, as if he was a thread that her fingers were working onto her loom. They returned each other's gaze, wanting nothing but for that moment to last, and last, and last.

Beyond the last bend of the stream, they rode at a slow pace, rock walls above them, standing in wait. The long, cool shadows of morning slipped away with a suddenness that startled him. His eyes tried to focus on the shapes ahead, disordered chimeras dancing in a sudden, pulsing glare. Only the languid swish of a horse's tail brushing back flies broke the silence that engulfed them. The horses' hooves stirred the dwindling waters of the dying stream. Molten mirrors, the water trapped and held fast the crisp, bright hues of cloudless sky and rust-red cliffs above. A ribbon of fresh smoothed sand, an abandoned carpet of a late winter's torrent, eased their progress. The western talus slope, a jumble of fractured sandstone blocks, glowing pink and streaked rust-red, hemmed them in. The north wall, cloaked in ashen purple and muddied brown shadow, lured the eye toward its somber repose. Cottonwood roots stretched out into the damp sands along the stream's edge defining the limit between water and sand. Massive slab-shaped boulders, fractured chapters of time, lay in confusion, estranged—an ancient text from a golden age lost before the human coming.

The trail wound its way deep into the canyon etched by water, time, and pressure. Bayeta led the way, her long, blue, velveteen dress weaving its undulating hues through wind-born cottonwoods and stream-side shadows. On solid ground, the horses' hooves invaded the silence. Round the last bend in the streambed, a soft whisper of wind, dreamy and primal, invaded Adam's senses. At the foot of the far talus slope, sheep gnawed on fresh spring grass, content. Bayeta smiled. She cocked her head listening, happy, knowing the grass was green.

Reining in his horse, Adam adjusted his eyes to the shadows of the near ground. His saddle's leather crunched, and the bridle fastenings jangled in synchrony with the steady gnawing of sheep. *Tseyi* was indeed a world apart. The canyon nurtured the spirit and offered refuge. The world of getting and taking, of comings and leavings, where life's balance could come undone, had been left far behind in place and time.

Adam was unprepared for the effect of the canyon on that warm spring day. He saw at once that *Tseyi* was at the heart of what it meant to be *Diné*. It was much more than two hundred million years of sedimentary rock, compacted sandstone. Along the talus slopes grew piñón and juniper, abiding survivors of the Miocene Age, sharing the present with the tireless gnashing of sheep's teeth on sweet grass and sage bush. Such tenacious grass and bush had endured every drought, every seasonal flood of the ages. Yearly cycles, eons long, delineated the advance and retreat of frost, snow, thaw, rains, heat, and wind. Fast within the depths of the canyon, Widow Tumecho's churros kept to their nature and purpose, growing fat.

Something moved in the nearby shadows. Bayeta stiffened in her stirrups and leaned over her saddle's pummel and whispered, "Ninaba and George Slim's daughter comes."

From the phalanx of cottonwood at the stream's edge came the muffled hint of giggling and the rustle of sateen dresses. "We see you. We are over here!"

Bayeta answered, "*Yá'át'ééh*, daughters of Manuel Tumecho's daughter."

Widow Tumecho's granddaughters stepped beyond the shadows into sunlight. Waving to Bayeta, they smoothed down their dresses, giggled, and waited. They stood before the slender, greening cottonwoods, budding leaves shimmering in a light breeze, roots clinging at the edge of the stream's seasonal meander. Bayeta dismounted and joined them. Adam dismounted and stood a little apart. He waited for formalities of greetings laced with family history to be exchanged. For his benefit, they began to speak in English of the summer to come. With pleasantries exchanged, the girls slipped back into Navajo. Adam understood. They did not know him, had only just met him. The gossip of family could embarrass him.

Juanita was a child of eleven. She smiled shyly at him. She pointed for Adam to follow her to where the flock was grazing. He tried to make small talk. She grinned and hurried on. As they reached the flock, she stood looking down at her bare feet, wiggling each toe, as if counting them out. She was missing school today, Bayeta said before he followed her down the trail. Tomorrow would be different. Her mother would insist that she return to school. She must not miss two days in a row.

Adam was charmed to be led by a child about the canyon. She smiled brightly and pointed at things as she ran ahead of him. But she did not speak. Children, all children, had power over Adam. He was defenseless against their curious, sidelong glances and ready smiles. Juanita disarmed him and held captive his undivided attention.

<++++++++++>

Adam's dream of that day five years ago slipped back into memory with Maria's daughters watching him. They stood half in shadow, a blinding sun flooding the expanse between them. A black lamb on unsteady legs trotted by, making for its mother.

At the Tumecho summer outfit in the canyon, the widow proudly pointed to her granddaughters' looms, both small but sturdy, set to each side of her own. Juanita raised her arms, stretching all her fingers, each one strong and straight. He watched the girls draw and tamp down weft strings, their battens spanning between the evens and the odds. Bayeta stood talking in Navajo to the child. What was it that they said? Later, she told Adam, "That child is so like the daughter I wish for. I will not always be young."

Adam wanted to tell her what he had felt watching the girls at the edge of the light. But for a reason he had not fathomed, he did not. At their looms, he saw the intense expression on their faces, how each finger, strong and straight, worked at the loom. That day, he had glimpsed the floor of time. The walls whispered to him, just as did the girl's working at their small looms. "Now is the time, here, now."

Often, Adam, at odd moments, would remember that day. It was a jumble, rather like the slabs of crumbling, fallen sandstone strewn along the talus slopes. Three women sat in the shade of Cottonwood trees talking in a tongue only they understood. Bayeta laughed, brushed back her hair, and blushed. Was it family gossip? Did he suspect why the Tumecho girls looked at him so? Their eyes never quite met his. Did their fingers sketch his outline, those repositories of centuries of endurance and hard won skills? Their soft, smooth gestures migrated from velveteen laps to lips and back again. Their knowing smiles, all but hidden, carried meaning not meant for him to decipher.

Bayeta had teased Adam about that ride into Canyon de Chelly. "They thought you a good catch, Adam. You sit a good saddle. Maria says you have strong loins."

"Bea, what they saw was my pale skin and pale eyes."

"No, you did have a good tan. As a pale-eyed white man, you passed."

"They acted very shy with me."

"Adam, they were much taken with you."

"Did it matter to them that I was a white man?"

She gave him a long look. "It is what the men think that bothers you, not them."

"Yes, I admit it. They see me at Rose Bia's almost every week. Some nod. A few nod hello. But after five years, we still don't really know one another."

<++++++++++>

When Adam had finally lay down on the bed, sleep overtook him and the image of his dead Alpha 11 retreated. The dark dream of his father, which had haunted him for twenty-five years, forced a sudden gasp of breath into his lungs. His forehead broke out in sweat. He smelled the acrid, steamy odor of a Devonian swamp. An ancient inland sea lapped at his feet. Having tossed the covers off, a dry, salt-free draft forced a shudder to run up his spine. A chill wind of an arid, dimmed world enveloped him. Nearing consciousness, sweat trickled down his nose as the dream disintegrated. What had his father said of deserts and canyons? He did not believe they held answers, only lies. But then, he had never met Juanita and Maria.

"Adam, it is time to get up."

Bayeta stood at the edge of the bed holding out a cup of hot coffee.

"Drink this while it is hot. Come."

He shook his head and rubbed his eyes. The smell of fresh coffee reached his brain.

"What time is it?"

Beyond the glass door to the patio, the moon's pale reflected glow outlined ragged-edged rows of thin clouds slipping eastward. He dried the sweat on his forehead with the bed sheet. Warming his hands on the coffee cup, he looked up at Bayeta. "Bea, what do you think our future will be like?"

"Why are you asking such a question? Why now?"

"I'm not sure." He took a sip of coffee and sat up in bed. "Does anyone really think about what their future will be like, what it should be like?"

"I don't think about abstractions. One can't really prepare for it, not really."

"It was wrong to bring nuclear weapons into being."

"Adam, you've had that dream again, the one about your father."

"Sort of did. It got mixed in with something else."

"It is enough to face each sun as it comes. How we make use of it is what counts."

"The Day of Trinity changed everything, you know. It was not about making a better world or securing the future. Some say they brought Mega-death into life."

"Your father was a part of that. He could not help himself, Adam. The world was at war. Men go to war to win, to use whatever means."

"Maybe I should not go to San Francisco."

Bayeta stood at the door, hall light filtering through her form. She was deep in prayer. "Wherever I go *hózhǫ́* radiates before me," she whispered in Navajo. "As far as I gaze around me, earth extends its beauty."

What was to come, be it a warm golden hour or a cold dawn, had nothing to do with her life at the rim of *Tseyi.* A once shallow sea, *Tseyi* held its secrets well. In time, it would come to hold even her life's record. Not Carson, not the bomb, not all the science of the age could make it otherwise.

Adam, at last fully awake, followed Bayeta into the kitchen. His purpose was set. He had to go to San Francisco. Now, it was for others to measure the weight of his discovery.

The search for longer life had consumed so many searchers and their patrons—kings, emperors, and visionaries, even madmen. The dream of longevity was as old as alchemy itself. It was alchemy. It was as old as Homer's world. Plato's Timaeus spoke of "that sort of death which comes of old age and fulfills the debt of nature." It was said to be the least painful of deaths, and accomplished with pleasure rather than the pain. Adam knew well the story of Orpheus' descent into Hades to carry back to the living world his beloved Eurydice. As a biologist, he accepted that death must be, but only with old age. He believed that the lifespan did not of necessity have a fixed, tethered limit. He had labored to reset the standard measure, to extend life in time and blunt the sting of inevitable death.

Pouring his second cup of coffee, Adam listened to Bayeta's prayer.

> "Give me the strength of *'sa' ą na' yái*
> Give me the body of Long Life
> Give me the mind of *Bike xójó'*

Give me the mind of Happiness
Wherever I go beauty radiates around me.
Give me the body of Long Life.
Give me the mind of *Bike xójó'*
Give me the mind of Happiness.
Wherever I go beauty radiates around me."

3

Flower of Kent

On the road drifting south and east from Rimrock, the desert showed no sign of life. Predawn travel in the desert is to be avoided. A car engine's noise and headlights unsettle the dark time that defines night in the desert. A lacework frost resembling a spider's dewy web framed the car windows. Bayeta gripped the car blanket more tightly about her legs as frigid air stole up her back. A fogged over windshield or the heater not turned on, those were the options.

A dense unbroken shroud of cloud obliterated the stars and the moon. The universe beyond, its boiling fusions piercing the great void, for the moment, did not exist. What did trillions of nuclear furnaces have to do with life on the predawn desert floor? The dark time was best to avoid, best left to the forces of chaos.

Adam struggled to keep the Land Rover on the eastward track, more rut than road. He counted the infrequent dirt side-roads that hinted of habitation to sharpen his attention. He did not look for lights down the turnoffs, knowing that the generators would be idle before dawn. The power grid did not extend this far into the reservation. It was built to serve Las Vegas, Phoenix, and Los Angeles. For those who lived here, coal-fed power meant smoke stacks, acid rain, and lung disease. Rubbing her sore eyes, Bayeta remembered the first time Adam complained of his eyes stinging.

"The Four Corners plants," she had said. She and Adam were both well acquainted with the black haze in the air to the north. "It's worse than Los Angeles smog," he added. Bayeta's father called it "invisible poison." The bulk of Black Mesa was being transformed into smoke. Desert water was being diverted for a slurry pipeline to carry Black Mesa coal to the plants.

"Progress is for white men in white suits," George Slim said. He knew of such men only from a movie he had seen about a madhouse. "Only the inmates were sane. Only the custodians wore white in the Cuckoo's Nest." Adam respected the subtlety of how Navajos described things. He had noticed from the beginning that Bayeta shared her father's penetrating wit. On this predawn drive, with Sawmill in sight, his mind focused on her concern about the San Francisco trip. Might his discovery upset the balance of things? What consequences had he not considered? Had it all been a mad venture after all?

For a few more miles night ruled with impenetrable stillness. He imagined the time when The People first wandered into the canyon country from the north. Wedged in among the settled Pueblo Peoples, the *Diné* occupied land defined by four sacred mountains. There, they stayed safe behind the door at night. George Slim had told him so: "No sane person goes out into the desert at night. It is unlucky."

Bayeta's hands ached from the chill. Her habit was to rise with the dawn, prepare coffee, and weave for an hour or two before others stirred. She wished she were back at home, in her studio sheltered from the cold. At her loom, she could await the promise of a new sun's warmth penetrating the glass doors. It was the sun that gave form and substance to life in the desert, not the cold dead of night.

"Adam, I am making a new weave."

"I saw you preparing wool. You've been with Widow Tumecho."

"Would you like a poncho, one in a traditional pattern?"

"What a question!" She smiled. "I also noticed the stains on your hands."

"Vegetal dyes, that's all."

"When?"

"When what?"

"Will I see it when I return?"

"Sometimes you do surprise me, Adam. You know better."

"You weave so fast."

"And, how long has your all-important experiment taken you?"

"You mean since I left Berkeley?" His hand made an expansive wave at the road ahead. "Oh, it took no time at all, a mere five years."

She gave him a wry smile. "Just that long, is it?"

"Well, I've had ideas since graduate school. Five years ago, that dust up with the review committee settled it. I decided to go all out for it."

"And you dare talk as if I can make a weave in a matter of days. Well!"

There was a definite edge in Bayeta's tone.

"Bea, I didn't mean…"

"Do you know that it takes days just to select which sheep to shear? I had to wait for Widow Tumecho's churros to be brought in for shearing. They are best for making long warp string, hundreds of yards of it. Maria and Juanita helped to wash the wool and beat the sand and grit out. You remember them, don't you?"

"You clean the wool by beating it?" Adam was glad the subject had turned to sheep's wool and not what was uppermost in both of their minds.

"Don't interrupt." Bayeta ignored the bumps and hard, sidewise slipping as Adam maneuvered over the ruts, trying to avoid the soft shoulders on each side of what some called "The Sawmill Road."

"It took a week to card and to spin the wool. Tomorrow, if I have time, I will string the warp to the loom and sort wool." Adam reached over and squeezed her hand. She squeezed back. "We experimented with dyes for two days. Widow Tumecho shared her special way of preparing the indigo. She uses blue corn and blue clay that she digs from near Massacre Cave. It is a deep indigo. It is not like the trading post dye from the Caribbean. It will not fade."

"The color matters that much?" He gave her a mock quizzical look.

"You know it does. Don't tease."

"When might I see this new weave?"

"Be patient. I have Alberto to think about, too, you know."

At first light the day began to show color. The road became less bumpy and the turns evened out. She closed her eyes. The day ahead would be a long one. "I will work fast," she said softly. "But, I don't want Spider Woman to scold me for weaving too much in a day." She meant more than she said.

Bayeta's reticence was tied to her inner sense of balance, her capacity in finding harmony and avoiding misfortune. Within days of their first meeting, Adam had noticed how intuitively she calculated her need for balance in all things. George Slim once said as much. "My daughter follows the beauty way. Nothing can make her go fast or slow. My daughter makes her own time. Sickness is a stranger." Adam had asked George Slim what he meant, how sickness was a stranger to her. "Ah," he said, "sickness is not always physical. In time, you will learn that from her."

Adam half perceived that he meant that she possessed a body-centered wisdom. George Slim admitted that such insight came to him only of late in life. But for his daughter, he said with conviction, "It came early. She was born with it."

At age ten, Bayeta had made her first large web. Her father was on the mend, and her maternal grandmother, Ruby Yazzie, announced that the family would make summer camp at the old hogan close by Massacre Cave. Deep within Canon del Muerto, comings and goings would be impractical. Life in Window Rock, she insisted, had made them all hungry for quiet and beauty. "It is a good place to stay put." She had a garden layout in mind for George Slim to plant and tend. The stream's water was sweet, good for drinking and bathing. Sheep would grow fat on fresh grasses. There would be fresh lamb to eat. All that was needed was hauled in by wagon.

As that summer wore on, George Slim redeemed his health. It was not his fault. Men drank. A man forced into idleness sat with other men and drank, drank to forget. The late spring rains had been heavy that year. George Slim kept busy hoeing weeds and inspecting the corn by hand for insects. The hogan required repairs. Ninaba insisted on a wood floor. At first light each day, George Slim got up to feed the fire and put water on the stove for making coffee. Before the garden work, he gathered firewood, checked the corral, inspected and filled the oil lamps. He took upon himself many tasks, except tending the sheep.

Grandmother never once spoke of George Slim's troubles. Even so, young Bayeta understood the need to keep to the canyon that summer. As son-in-law, it was an awkward relationship for both of them. By custom he spoke little to the women. He kept busy with the garden and away from idle talk of hard times. By summer's end, George Slim again lived in his own skin. He talked of finding wage work and returning to the homestead in the Chuskas' foothills. Grandmother knew it was to be just so.

The women organized each day to prepare wool for spinning, dying, and weaving. For the women and Bayeta, it was the best of times. Her mother was an expert weaver and quick to pick up on market trends. Each new web commanded top price in Gallup or Flagstaff. One Sedona dealer regularly inquired about her rugs. She specialized in storm patterns. Against the soft grays and off-whites of natural, un-dyed background wools, her rug's black lightning with serrated edges could be explosive, disorienting. When dealers told Grandmother they needed Eye Dazzlers, Ninaba and Grandmother made Eye Dazzlers. When demand shifted to chief blankets or pictorials, she adapted. But, Eye Dazzlers were best left to Tec Nos Pos weavers. Ninaba made sure that her daughter heard and understood: "You cannot keep to a pattern if its price goes down. Chief's blankets will always bring a good price. Make good webs and you will not go hungry." It was advice that she repeated often as she wove.

Grandmother Yazzie schooled her granddaughter in technique and pattern. But, for a ten year-old, stories of Spider Woman and Spider Man held a special fascination. The tales were of the origin of weaving, the gift of Spider Woman and Spider Man. Bayeta longed to be worthy of the gift, to be recognized as a good weaver, and not just a girl.

Grandmother Yazzie taught Bayeta names of ancestors, places, and events. A name, she said with firmness, is like a web's design. Each name possesses a spirit. If a name is not right, nothing good comes from it. There was also a proper way of things and that was that. If one did each thing in the proper way, and called each thing by its proper name, all would be good. When Grandmother spoke of weaving, it was all about what came from within. "You see it inside first. If it is good inside here," she pointed to her head and heart, "the web will fill your loom with beauty. It comes out of you. Only then can you make a good web. The web's spirit will be good, if it is good inside you. Do not hurry, Crystal."

She chose to call her granddaughter Crystal, a name with its own special meaning. "Practice with every sun. With the sun in the east, sit down before your loom. Until the sun is behind your shoulder, weave each day. Your hands and fingers will become true and strong."

George Slim made her loom with straight and smoothed juniper wood. He built it with care, lashing the sky and earth beams tightly to the upright beams planted firmly in the ground. He wanted his daughter to have the best loom upon which to make her first big web. He placed the loom between mother and grandmother. Before long, however, such impartiality satisfied neither one. But for Bayeta it was hard to choose one over the other. That was to be avoided. Bayeta asked him to move her loom to a new place, one sure not to offend.

By mid-summer, Crystal, as Ruby Yazzie preferred to call her, had developed the habit of watching her grandmother weave. The elder's constant little attentions proved irresistible. Grandmother was very old, knew things only a woman of great age could know. How to cut and ravel flannel to make it into yarn was a thing to learn. Flannel raveled and re-spun made the finest yarn. Border selvages were best black or deep blue. An escape line was best near a corner. Every convention prompted a question. Grandmother was very wise. Mother also possessed answers, and her instructions were good. But she could not match a grandmother's inexhaustible inventory, one rich with stories. Grandmother remembered best the very old stories about old enemies. Each story possessed an answer a young girl should know.

Grandmother said before the *Diné* came, *Tseyi* was home to the Anasazi. In that time, there were many people living in the canyon.

Antelope House, Ledge Ruin, White Ruin, and Mummy Cave were their homes. Grandmother took Crystal to see for herself that the stories were just so.

In spite of George Slim's efforts, breakdowns and delays were to be expected when a trip to a ruin was called for. The aged pickup's motor was unreliable. The rutted meanders in deep sands were barely passable at their driest. Even so, each excursion that summer kindled Bayeta's imagination. They visited Massacre Cave three times. A forbidding place, it was contaminated by the spirits whose bones were scattered about the cave floor. The entrance, near the top of a sheered rock face, was reached only by sliding down into the cave's mouth, a brave thing to do. Talk of *ch'įįdii,* what white men knew as chindi, was enough to discourage most. But for Crystal, the adventure of it was more powerful than a young girl's fear of long-dead spirits. A kind of history of the cave was written in books, telling of Lt. Antonio Narbona's Spanish troops invading *Tseyi* on a cold January day in 1805. They had come to subdue a party of troublesome, elusive Navajos who always managed to slip away without detection after raiding nearby Spanish settlements. The secret location of "Two Who Fell Off" had been safe. But then a terrible thing happened. The hiding place was given away by a woman's cry for vengeance. The Spanish troops below heard, and the result was certain. The soldiers opened fire indiscriminately and without clear targets. Bullets bounced off the walls of the cave, killing many. The cave became a tomb for all who hid there. From that day, it had become contaminated. The un-avenged spirits of the dead remained there.

"But what about the men who dig in the ground for bones," asked Crystal?

"They find things that maybe are not bad, pieces of old weavings. I have seen the pictures. Scraps, but my eyes see them whole." Ruby pointed to her favorite blanket, indicating that it was of a very old design. It was a simple weave, three feet by six feet, of un-dyed brown and white wools. Ninaba seemed almost envious of the blanket. She seldom looked at it hanging over her mother's bed at

Tseyi. "It whispers to her of the old times. It is a simple thing, but it warms her heart."

Crystal learned many things that summer: How to card and spin wool, to identify plants for making natural dyes, the best use of different wools and fibers, and how to avoid missteps in stringing warp and making straight weft lines. The women used few words. Instruction was best given by a guiding hand alone. Reluctantly, Grandmother made some use of commercial, aniline dyes. Ninaba said nothing until alone with her daughter. Commercial dyes, made of coal tars, she said, made for less ideal dyes. But Grandmother was now too old to make her dyes from vegetal matter. The gathering, boiling, and preparing took much time and effort. Grandmother still walked with Crystal and pointed out each plant to pick. Sagebrush, snakeweed, globe mallow, sumac berry, and rabbit bush grew close to camp. George Slim took Crystal up to the rim for juniper berries and the gambel oak bark. Only *ch'il gohwéhi*, Navajo tea, could not be found. Grandmother, however, knew well this would be so and had brought a large bundle of it with her. When needed, George Slim made a small fire down by the wash, near two large cottonwood trees that served as shade. There, Crystal practiced making dyes as grandmother watched. Grandmother had thought of everything. George Slim was on the mend. Her apprentice was quick to learn and willing.

Ruby Yazzie also made an effort to teach Crystal how to pattern. In this matter, no compromise was allowed. One did not come to know how to pattern by being taught techniques. One had to use the mind's eye and know their origins. She drew patterns in the sand or on paper. Some were as old as Bosque Redondo, even before that time. Every blanket or rug she had ever woven came quickly to mind as she drew outlines of them in the sand. Ninaba kept silent. It was best not to confuse her daughter with competing patterns. To Ruby a web with horizontal stripes was best. Such a web was simple and clean. She did not speak of *Serape* or Saltillo designs. They, too, were old. A poncho's design, both women agreed, was best kept simple and clean.

Ninaba wore her patience well that summer. Her husband was on the mend. The days were sunny, and the food from the garden nourished them. The morning light was given over to weaving. Each web brought a good price. That summer, the buyer in Sedona wanted complex designs. The rich women tourists from the East Coast snatched up Eye Dazzlers and Pictorials. Ruby kept silent about the market for such patterns. Ninaba spoke of how money bent one's mind to please rug merchants. "Waste of a good loom," she said. Crystal grimaced, knowing how much the money was needed. A good chief's blanket would always fetch a decent price, in time.

Ninaba completed four weaves that summer, each showing great skill. She had a good eye for what would endure the craze of the moment. Crystal studied each weave with appreciation. The weft lines were perfectly straight and tight. Grudgingly, Grandmother Ruby acknowledged that their value would hold. When the summer ended, they would climb out of *Tseyi,* and Ninaba's daughter would be hers again. Grandmother Ruby was pleased that Crystal had been instructed in the old patterns.

<++++++++++>

In the dawn light, Albuquerque still two hours on, Bayeta's thoughts kept returning to that long ago summer. The memory came and went without conscious context or closure, a jumble of images. Watching the road ahead, she put the pattern of that summer back in her mind's storage. What was ahead was what mattered. Even as a young girl, Bayeta viewed travel as something to endure out of need. Her childhood had been traced out by annual relocations from Window Rock to the summer home in Canyon del Muerto. At boarding school, however, the pattern changed. It was then that she learned that travel from home could be unsettling. Now, in the present, she was reminded of its dangers, the uncertainties it implied.

Bayeta's apprehension of travel was not a matter of distance or inconvenience. Automobiles and trucks broke down. Desert roads disappeared in sandstorms or downpours. The social and physical landscapes beyond the four mountains of her homeland, *dinétah*, could be disorienting and alienating. But then to grow up and to fly from San Francisco to Rome, then Rabat, on to Hong Kong and Sydney, and have to cope, that was to live with an acute disorientation.

Watching the desert begin to take on light beyond the headlights, she tried to focus on Adam's list of skeptic conjectures. Might his findings be rejected out of hand at the conference? Would Herman claim that The Evergreen Institute funded Adam's aging research? Did his hermetic life at Rimrock engender skepticism? How could such progress be made in an isolated laboratory? Who would believe that real scientific research was still possible under such conditions?

For five years, he had designed, conducted, monitored, analyzed, and reviewed—on his own. Now, with success at hand, Adam wanted to trust that fair evaluations would confirm his results, his achievement. His data fit neatly into a coherent result, a compelling pattern of experimental confirmation. Bayeta admitted that he had to go to the conference. But it did not make her apprehensions less acute.

"Bea, I have to do this. The life span is not a fixed thing. Life expectancy of most people has increased because of advances in medicine, food production, progress in controlling infectious diseases, better health habits. How is what I have accomplished any different? No, such a discovery cannot be withheld. You once told me that scientific facts are like layers of stone exposed by the elements. Once exposed, they are visible and have a story to tell. Well, all I have done is exposed a new layer."

"Adam, I sometimes feel that your work, however beautiful and fine grained it is, can be washed away in a flash flood. Ignorance and greed can sweep away every good thing that comes their way. What good is there in not using more caution? You know, you have not really prepared for this day. You have ignored the possible consequences, only looking at what you think are the good sides."

"I don't believe that, Bea."

"I remember being trapped in *Tseyi* in a late spring storm. A gentle rain can nourish the corn and grass. But a sudden downpour washes away animals, trees, a newly planted garden…and men. If a storm erupts over this, it can sweep you away before you can find high ground. Are you prepared for that?"

"Yes, when I spent a year in Cambridge, I came to understand that. I realized then how even an accident, like an apple falling from a tree, changes everything."

"Adam, be serious. To discover an existing force of nature is not the same."

"You know that I planted that apple tree in the patio to remind me of the possibilities."

"You mean that scrawny thing that you ordered from...from where?"

"Woolsthorpe, it comes from Woolsthorpe. Newton lived there during the plague. It's an heirloom varietal, The Flower of Kent."

"Well, it has not produced so much as a handful of apples. And don't change the subject."

"My discovery will change how we measure the lifespan. But for that to happen I must reconnect, get back into the stream of things, as you so ably put it."

"Adam, I don't want to see you carried off by this thing. As for Newton, yes, he hid out in the country until the plague ended. I do remember that much. I, too, can learn from history. Don't you think it a good idea to wait?"

"Bea, nothing is going to carry me off."

"Make sure your colleagues back you up. Let them shoulder some of this load, Adam. You don't want to find yourself alone in this."

"Jonathan will go over my findings. Others, those working on enzyme and molecular processes at the cell level, will be able to independently confirm the results."

"All that will take time, won't it?"

"Well, as you say, maybe that won't be a bad thing. Up to now I've kept it all under wraps. No one even knows that I've been working on this problem."

Adam stared out at the soft, gray gloom of desert taking shape and definition in the early dawn light. His mind was focused on something he had only dimly noticed when it happened a few weeks ago. "Someone at Berkeley, I forget his name, asked Jonathan, 'What is Adam Grant up to out there in the wilds of Arizona?' He told me it was not the first time someone had asked him."

"What does that suggest to you?"

"Why would the question come up at all? Yesterday, when I talked to John, telling him I was coming to his class, he said that someone had phoned him, someone he'd met at a conference. He asked for a copy of one of his papers. John sensed it was odd, as it is posted on the internet. Then, out of the blue, he asked the same thing."

"And now, Adam, you realize it might not have been an innocent question."

"Now I wonder. At the time I did not."

"People do wonder how you can continue to work and publish and at the same time keep yourself aloof. You were established at Berkeley. Then, you drop out of sight. Now, well, some are bound to wonder why you are resurfacing, why now."

Bayeta dimly perceived a pattern. She believed nothing happened without some sort of pattern behind it. For five years, she had listened to Adam talk of method, experiment, replication, analysis, review, and confirmation. It was all not so different, not in her mind, from how she approached her loom. Her approach to a new weave was no less exacting. It, too, required precise intent, controlled method, purpose. Both, she knew, exist to produce something of value, something meant to be good of itself.

The car labored up one ridgeline and then sped down the other side, one ridge after another, into and out of an endless ribbon of ruts. Dawn was slowly advancing to vanquish another night's cold grip.

Bayeta dismissed the impulse to dwell on what might have been. The last ten years had been good years, and she did not regret leaving teaching. She did enjoy teaching. Campus life was a comfortable state of being. But when she married Adam, that all changed. The suddenness of it none of her friends or family had anticipated. Her colleagues were happy for her. Still, they thought it so unlike her to so drastically alter her life. She was not the type of woman to be so carried away by any man, so some said. She told them that it was inevitable, even if they did not believe it. Truth was, she was done with Albuquerque. Course preparations had lost their freshness. Too many students were unmotivated. She questioned why some came to class at all. She found herself talking technique, composition, expression, but not doing. She became wary of having to apply labels and use multicultural babble. Before she met Adam, Bayeta knew something had to give. She did not want to be "one who can't, but teaches."

Nor did she believe in coincidence. Things happened because they were meant to happen. Had her fatigue of Albuquerque influenced her immediate attraction to Adam? Perhaps. That first evening together, at dinner, he had asked her, "Do you like teaching?" It was not an idle question on his part, but rather inspired insight. Her reply was automatic, "Of course, I do." Her answer, however, did not satisfy him.

"But do you see yourself as a teacher? If I can put it another way, is it enough?"

She went flush and fiddled with her napkin. "Please, call me Crystal."

"Then, you must call me Adam. I think we are past formalities, don't you?"

"Yes, well, I suppose we are." Her napkin fell to the floor, ignored.

"I have a friend who insists that friends call him 'Hardy.' Jonathan Hardesty, Doctor Jonathan Hardesty. Acquaintances address him formally. He's a Nobel Laureate. His most admired scientist was Doctor J. Robert Oppenheimer. 'Oppie' was what he preferred to be called by friends. Most people I know, those I like, try to avoid formalities. With you, I would like to dispense with formalities. Wouldn't you?"

"I shall call you Adam."

"Some call you Crystal. But, I like the sound of Bea. It is, well, more intimate."

She blushed. "You may call me by that name, if you like."

Before she realized, he had leaned over the table and kissed her cheek. "Beatrice, Bellissima mia." It would be weeks before Adam admitted to her that his impulse was to gather her up in his arms and kiss her lips then and there. Being in public, however, he resisted.

But what had begun as playful probing within the first hour had progressed to an intense, but suppressed, urge to abandon pretense. Her lips burned. She began to fuss with her hair.

"What was that question you asked?"

He smiled and chewed on a piece of bread. "Do you like teaching?"

"What about you, do you like teaching?"

"It stimulates me. But I am most at home in the lab. I have ideas I want to test. I also have a good bunch of graduate students. They take up a lot of my time." He paused for a moment. When he resumed, he was more pensive than before. "The hardest part of teaching is the necessity to focus on what is already known. Before I lose my edge, I must focus on what we don't know, what we can come to know."

Abruptly, he changed the subject. "You really are beautiful, Miss Crystal Bayeta."

"You promised to call me Bea." He looked at her for a long moment. "Please do so only if...."

"I can't believe that no man has..."

"What? Carried me off? How do you know it has not been tried, many times?"

"They have all failed. You are too wise, and much too beautiful, I think." Her naturally bronzed skin tones could not hide her blushing. "When I look at you, I think of Beatrice." He said it with a strong Italian inflection. "But, Da Vinci's Beatrice was not as beautiful as you."

She steadied her gaze and met his with equal intensity. A minute passed in silence. With difficulty Bayeta broke free of his gaze and regained her composure.

"Perhaps it is too soon. Please, for the present just call me Bayeta."

"Are you afraid that others will take us to be lovers?"

"You can be very direct when it suits you. But, yes, I am a bit shy."

He reached across the table. "I will do as you ask, though it is against my will."

She did not withdraw from his touch. Words failed her. She felt his touch and her cheeks become feverish. It was not sexual, not in an ordinary sense. It was more like sharing a private confidence.

Adam steadied himself. "Tell me what it feels like to weave. I want to know."

"I can try, if you are really interested." Adam sat back with an attentive look. She searched for the right words. "A feeling—a sensation of a sort—comes when I sit down before my loom. I don't know how to describe it, wholeness, perhaps. Before I begin, I close my eyes to concentrate—to see the pattern come to mind. It, the pattern, speaks to me. Then, taking time, I sort the yarn and my tools. My mind sort of, well, empties out everything but them. If I cannot free myself of distractions, from what else the day brings, I stop. Even when I am not weaving, when I have other things I must do, the pattern of the weave stays with me. Only when I cut the strings and take it from my loom, am I free of its hold on me. Then, it is a thing of its own. I might put a single thread into the weave near the end, an escape line. In that way, my spirit is released. Yes, it is like being possessed."

"So, you plan it all out, from the beginning?"

"I can't say that I have it all worked out in detail, not in a way I can describe in words. It is more as if my fingers weave what my mind already sees. In that way, the pattern works through me, not from me. I'm sorry, but this is very personal. It catches me, sort of. I don't catch it. A weaving, a truly good one, comes to life for and by itself. When others see it, comment on it, and compare it to other weavings, I don't listen. Once it is done, it exists on its own, exists for itself."

"I always thought that an escape line is an intentional flaw."

"Adam, you do surprise me."

"I grew up with Navajo weavings and silver work. Mother knew a good number of Navajo weavers and silversmiths. In her gallery, she made room for their work."

Bayeta smiled. This man, this man who had taken hold of her hand, made her feel special. She did not resist the impulse to run her fingers across his open palm, looking for his escape line. When at last he slowly, almost intangibly, withdrew his hand, she blushed. Her eyes searched the room to avoid his gaze.

In ten years, her memory of that first evening together seldom escaped a day's notice. Beyond the car's lights, uprooted sagebrush scraped and bounced across the road and into oblivion. A confused jackrabbit almost collided with the front fender. Daylight was breaking over the eastern ridgeline. Adam complained of the beating the car tires were taking on "The Yellow Brick Road." A visiting friend of Adam's had named it so. Adam gripped the steering wheel tightly and shifted into second gear.

It was a struggle to keep to the road. "We are not in Kansas anymore, Dear."

"Only fifteen more minutes, Bea." Beyond Sawmill the road was graded and graveled. "We'll be on the state highway soon."

"Do you remember the date?"

"What date is that?"

"When we first met."

"Of course I do, March 20th. Isaac Newton died on March 20, 1727, one day short of spring."

"Oh, come now. It is not flattering to hear that you remember because of that."

"It should please you. He is a hero of mine."

Bayeta smiled. It was enough to hear him say that he loved her.

"He, too, did his best work hidden away in the country. When The Great Plague of 1665 reached Cambridge, the university shut down. Newton fled to his farm in Lincolnshire and remained there for two years. After that, he lived sixty-two years. But, those years in the country were the most productive one in his whole life."

"I can take a turn at driving when we get to Window Rock."

He reached over and squeezed her hand. "You are my Flower of Kent. You fell from the tree of singlehood and made all the difference to my life."

Patting his hand, she said, reprovingly, "Don't get poesy on me."

"We'll stop for coffee in Gallup and stretch our legs."

"I need a warm place to sit while you call Herman." Her tone was matter of fact but gentle. "Please, do it?"

"You will have hot coffee and a warm place to sit."

"Please, Adam." Her tone now took on a definite, insistent edge.

"Bea, it won't be dawn yet on the coast. He doesn't even know that time exists at that hour. Before nine or ten in the morning it is impossible for him to stitch two words together. If I call him before ten, he'll only growl and whine."

Adam was right. The timing was not good. Contact with his family was never easy. He avoided his father. He liked his sister, Cynthia, but mention of their father often brought on an argument, she being on good terms with him. Adam could deal with Herman, their half-brother, though not without strain. He harbored a visceral distrust and personal dislike of Herman. It pained him how much he depended on Herman for funding. Adam usually kept his emotions in control, but not without it taking a toll. Herman was always quick to complain of sarcasm in Adam's tone and not let it pass. Verbal skirmishes could last for weeks, ending only when Adam, to please Bayeta, made the call to smooth things over.

What Bayeta could not fathom was how neither Adam nor Herman allowed personal animosity to interfere with the flow of funding. Perhaps it was Herman's stubborn family loyalty that made the difference. Adam insisted that results of the research funded by the Institute was the reason. Bayeta was skeptical that was all there was to it. Herman had made Adam an exception, but family ties could have little to do with it. Like a gallery owner she once did business with, Herman, she sensed, had his own purposes. The gallery owner took her work and sold it quickly, at high prices. She could tolerate his sexual innuendoes and ignorance of art, only so long as the end result was satisfactory.

Adam never talked about what it cost to maintain his laboratory. It had to be a substantial sum. Some expensive equipment, such as the electron microscope, was on loan. Many expenses had to be accounted for. It worried her that at some point he might find that what was expected from him in return would be too high a price. She had no faith in things freely given, any more than in coincidence. What compounded her concerns was that Adam was an anachronism. Even the out-of-the-way annex or basement facility on a university campus was becoming an anachronism. Basement labs, improvised equipment, and solitary experimentation were part of the past. World War II's "big science" approach saw to that. Massive pools of government and corporate money now powered research. The once revered entities of invention—Edison, Westinghouse, DuPont, General Electric and Sarnov—lived on. But they had given up basic science, in favor of applied. Funding had become a managerial function, a matter of top-down decisions, secrecy, market focus, and military priorities. The public had little interest in to what ends science was applied. Science was refashioned to be entrepreneurial, controlled, accountable, applied. Brookhaven, Battelle, Aberdeen, Los Alamos, Sandia, Livermore, Woods Hole, and Cold Spring Harbor seldom now made headlines with breakthroughs in basic, fundamental research. Elite committees, boardrooms, and political priorities captured attention, defined merit.

Bayeta marveled at how quick-footed Adam was at keeping his laboratory going. A molecular biologist, he took pains to focus some of his work on a few fashionable and popular lines of research. Such work paid the bills and provided Herman's institute with added visibility. He also admitted that the cumbersome bureaucracy of university-based funding requirements gave him an edge. He framed his research in simple, bold terms and promised results. He got results and remained visible on the pages of Cell Biology, Science, Molecular Biology, and The Cell. That impressed Herman and the directors at The Evergreen Institute.

Adam ignored debates over the ends of research and what corporate-managed science implied. Privately, he knew what went on. Others carried on the debate over the Petrie Palaces, Bio-Bins, Gene Factories, and Chromo-Holes. The concerns over patenting of the human blueprint for profit raged on. Profit ruled priorities for the new age of healthcare and medicine. Gene implants, embryo and fetal therapies, cloning, stem cell implantation, and drugs for everything from obesity to cholesterol levels, diabetes, and psychiatric dysfunctions absorbed so much science.

Something more personal and troubling, however, had taken root in Adam's mind shortly before he made his decision to leave Berkeley.

He had not sorted out his disquiet, but it was there just the same. His concern focused on how some of his colleagues became preoccupied only with applied research for pharmaceuticals. Many of them had a reputation as serious scientists. But large salaries, corporate grants, and the opportunity to remain on campus with little or no teaching bothered his sense of proportion. A colleague who shared laboratory facilities with him became embroiled in the patenting and marketing scandal over a new drug called "Pleasure Plus." It was prescribed as an SSRI class drug for depression. The marketing campaign, in which his colleague participated, focused on women and children diagnosed with a wide range of symptomatic criteria. Double blind clinical trials had been conducted on campus, with pharmaceutical funding. His colleague took an undisclosed payment, an "honorarium." Only when the research was discredited and the drug was found to be no more effective than a placebo, did scandal ensue. But, it was not withdrawn from the market.

The last time Adam spoke with his disgraced colleague, who had moved on to a high-paid position at the pharmaceutical in question, the man told him not to be naïve. "There are two-dozen drugs out there, just like ours," he insisted. "Why should it matter to you? People use them every day, with prescription. Politicians have their silly little war on drugs—Columbia, Mexico, Afghanistan. They don't give a shit what we do. The FDA? It's in the pocket of the big pharmas. No one is complaining about the harm done by Prozac, Valium, Vicodin ..." His words fell away as he waved goodbye and walked out of Adam's office for the last time.

For five years, Adam had ignored the debates over the harm caused by so many pharmaceutical drugs. He had no special insight. Therefore, it did not concern him. At Rimrock, Adam insulated himself from such "external" issues. Bayeta, however, now sensed that Adam's trip to San Francisco, in some ill-defined way, could threaten Adam's comfortable illusions of invincibility and self-efficacy. He had been uniquely fortunate for five years. Why did he believe it could last?

"Adam, could you pull over for a minute?"

Adam slowed to a stop at the next pull out. Crystal Bayeta got out of the car and walked a few steps toward the first light of dawn. Her soft voice reached out to the coming of light, to the new day. The first rays of a new sun were breaking free of the eastern horizon. Adam listened as she prayed.

> "In the house of long life, there I wander.
> In the house of happiness, there I wander.
> Beauty before me, with it I wander.
> Beauty behind me, with it I wander.
> In old age traveling, with it I wander.
> I am on the beautiful trail, with it I wander"

4

Talk At Table

Herman Cockroft, Adam's half brother, was self-absorbed, petty, and self-indulgent. He detested physical labor and the smell of his own sweat. A creature of habit, he never rose before eight-thirty, arrived at his office punctually at ten, and left at six sharp. Adam grudgingly admitted that Herman Cockroft possessed a talent for administration, or so he gave the impression.

Adam never understood how a director of a science research institute could live as Herman did. He looked ten years older than he was. The opaque band in the cornea of his right eye indicated the onset of *arcus sinilis*. At odd moments, involuntarily, he clenched his jaw and wrinkled his forehead, adding to his prematurely aging appearance. He had a thin, receding hairline and globular, piggish ears. A tic at the left corner of his mouth, which accompanied the clenching of his jaw, hinted at a small, but deep, neurological deficit. He had a forced, taut expression when he smiled. He often used an expression that betrayed a sentiment that he would rather be somewhere else. On the rare occasions Adam met with Herman, Herman appeared easily bored, if the focus was not about him, his importance.

Setting aside Herman's physical characteristics and habits, what heightened Adam's wariness of his half-brother was the company he kept. He surrounded himself with older men, men with stern, hard demeanors, men who knew power and privilege. They exacted a price from others at every opportunity, even if it was but token subservience or to be held in awe. Their demeanor was unmistakable—that inured, steeled determination to gain advantage at every turn. Such men are born old. Although Herman mimicked such a disposition, his attempts were pitiful. His drinking and poor health habits crippled his every attempt to display such characteristics. Herman's ego, however, deceived him into believing that he could master his ambitions. A daily dosage of palliatives provided the deceptive mental gloss he needed to keep up appearances. Carol Longstreath Cockroft, his wife, finally gave up her attempts to make him more human, if not loved. After a few years of the marriage, she no longer cared. Theirs, Carol stubbornly persisted, was a "conventional marriage," a "convenient arrangement."

Herman's early morning caller knew all there was to know about Herman's health and habits. They mattered little to him, so long as Herman played his part and was compliant. Herman, the administrator, was well suited to play his role. That he took orders from another, no one, except for a select few insiders, was the wiser. For all appearances, The Evergreen Institute was an independent science foundation. Herman's caller, however, deftly, secretly, pulled the strings.

The phone rang again. On the fifth ring, Herman's hand scoured the floor near his shoes. Like a toy top winding down on its axis, his head gyrated and tipped over the edge of the bed. Raising the receiver to his ear, he heard a loud, insistent snarl. Still shaking off the dim, humid remains of a bad dream, Herman snapped to attention.

"Herman! Goddamn it, Herman, wake up! Where in the hell is that ass-hole, that misfit brother of yours? Well? You told me you had everything under control!"

Desperate to placate William Henry Schwann, Herman tried to calm him. But words and courage failed him. The long and typical harangue began. Herman shook uncontrollably. The flow of debasement continued uninterrupted for two full minutes. When, at last, Schwann paused to catch his breath, Herman tried to defend his efforts, but his violent shaking made his words slurred, indistinct.

"Everything is in hand. Trust me, it's barely..." His sweaty palm lost grip of the phone. It fell on the bed like a thing alive, some black, growling thing that might well bite if touched.

"You listen to me, Herman, listen goddamn good! It is now six. Six, that's what time it is, goddamn it! What in the hell do you think we do in La Jolla, sit on our asses pickling our brains 'til the sun comes up? You, I know it, drank yourself into a stupor last night! It's getting to be a nightly ritual with you, Herman. Well, if you touch another drop, so much as one goddamn drop, until I have what I want, I'll have your balls for breakfast on a platter!"

Herman had not heard the words, but he guessed the substance. The man was a beast, a beast and his master. Desperate to gather his wits, Herman picked up the phone.

"You have exactly one hour, no, goddamn it, fifty nine minutes to locate that brother of yours. He did not get on that plane last night. Get your ass in gear. Now! Phone my office the minute you know where he is. Find him. Find out why."

"I'm sure it is just an unforeseen delay. He's likely… Well, I don't know, but…"

"Shut up. You find him. Find him in the next fifty-eight minutes. Do you hear me?"

"He's probably in…" Herman's voice trailed off. Pointless to argue, he sat mute.

"Fifty-eight minutes, Herman. One of my newspapers has a reporter in Los Alamos. He's already being sent to Albuquerque. He's to find that brother of yours and keep track of him. From now on I want to know exactly where he is. Do you hear me? Keep Anton informed. He will be in constant touch with me. Do you understand?"

"I'm sure that is not necessary, I mean…" Again, words failed. To involve Anton Mueller made him nauseous. He wiped the sweat on his face with the bed sheet. The acidic taste of his own sour, malt-laden sweat invaded his nostrils and revolted him. Again, the phone slipped from his hand. He stood up and stared at the phone. He did not listen, did not need to. He knew what was expected.

"This is no time to be stupid, Herman." Schwann's tone was threatening. "This is too big a matter for you to handle on your own. Do you understand, Herman? I must have it, must have it."

The phone went dead. Herman knew but one thing: Find Adam before Schwann's man, Anton, did. Herman did not like Adam, never had, but he did not want to think of what Anton Mueller might do. Anton was a thug, a silent, brooding thug, Schwann's muscle man.

Who was William Henry Schwann to hold such power over Herman? To the world at large, he was just another wealthy businessman, albeit a very wealthy one. Billionaires were becoming common enough not to attract undue notice. For over forty years, he had been building his holdings in pharmaceutical and health provider companies. Averse to publicity, he also controlled a number of newspaper and media outlets to better shape his image as a successful businessman. Out of the public's view, he was in a position to place directors on company boards and affect their policies and investment strategies. Over time, such maneuvers as mergers, leveraged takeovers, and interlocking directorships gave William Henry Schwann effective control of twenty corporations. His holding company, Schwann and Company, was more than simply a large conglomeration. Schwann saw the value of patent holdings. By 1985, Schwann and Company, a 40 billion dollar enterprise, had become a major player equal in clout to the Hunts, the Koch Brothers, the Getty's, and George Sterling of health maintenance provider fame. By 1990, Genetrix, the patent arm of Schwann and Company, posted revenues of ten billion dollars, with projections trending toward doubling over eight years.

Herman had few illusions as to how he fit into Schwann's plans. He would be tolerated as long as, and only as long as, he provided Genetrix access to new drug research. Such access had to remain obscure to outsiders and FDA regulators, however. Herman's administrative abilities, his mania for detail and organization, kept the connection between Schwann and Company and the institute out of reach of public scrutiny. Still, Herman understood how tenuous was his position. He drank to forget.

"I may be a terrible shit," he told himself as he dressed and sprinkled his suit with Old Spice, "but I'm no fool." His headache was becoming almost unbearable as he rushed to find his car keys. Two hours of sleep would not hold him up long, not for what he must do before noon. Fear and adrenaline would have to suffice, if he was to make it through the day.

<++++++++++>

The early morning traffic was headed mostly in one direction, west. Truckers hauling over-weighted loads bore down on slower moving passenger cars, nearly sweeping them off the road. The railroad tracks, shadowing Interstate 40 for one hundred and fifty miles, carried freight to and from Pacific ports. Adam pointed to the Gallup city limit sign. Gallup was their usual stop before Albuquerque. For one hundred years, it had served as a buffer zone between Zuni and Navajo.

Bayeta roused herself from half-sleep. "What is today?"

"It's Thursday."

"Thank God it's not Friday."

Adam nodded. Every other Friday was government checks day. On such days, for too many years, the sidewalks and alleys in the run-down parts of town would be crowded by late afternoon with Navajo, Ute, and Pueblo men in search of oblivion. The men stood, sat, or lay down at street corners, curbs, or grassy strips. A few made for home by midnight, the money gone. Some drifted about the streets and alleys for days. The Indian Health Service did what it could. Bayeta knew the bi-monthly ritual had much abated, but that did not erase her memory of it.

When she was five, her father was a regular to Gallup's streets every other Friday. George Slim was not a weak man. He had been a hard worker and good provider. But in the space of two years, cancer took his brother and two uncles. He was especially close to his older brother and to his uncle, Red Point. His brother, Hastin, was in his early forties. He, too, was said to have been a good provider for his family. Both of his uncles, veterans of the War in the Pacific, had lived through hard times. Surviving Japanese suicide attacks and snipers, they did not lack courage or a sense of responsibility. Both code talkers, they had served as forward spotters for artillery and air strikes. They faced every danger at the leading edge of war. Returning home, however, they found most of the marriageable girls already chosen. They lived as bachelors. It was just so, men without wives. They worked hard, lived with their sisters' families, drank to forget, and died before their time.

Red Point was the first to contract a persistent cough that progressed to a "wasting away." The Indian Health Service could do little to help him. He died. Brother Hastin went next, a victim of the same cough and "wasting away," but not before going mad. Five months later, Uncle Joe died. Before he went, however, George Slim came down with the same symptoms, cancer.

Bayeta's childhood was cut short by the daily presence of her father's dull stare and listless brooding. She saw that same dull stare in other men's eyes, too. She saw such men drifting down Gallup's streets when her mother took her in search of her father. Each time, when at last they found him, she saw how he fixed his eyes on the pavement at his feet. He could not face daughter or wife. His big hands trembled when he raised them to cover his mouth, as the coughing rose up from his lungs. Those big, strong hands, idled and weakened, trembled as he fought for control.

The Indian Health Clinic at Window Rock did what they could. Ninaba found ways to keep him home on alternate Fridays, monitored his medicines and saw to it that he was warm and fed. His sickness wore on into a second year, then a third.

In January of the third year, mother-in-law Ruby organized a healing ceremony. At the end of the year, George Slim was declared in remission. Kerr-McGee's unventilated uranium mine, the one near Shiprock, had not claimed him. He had endured two operations and a heavy regimen of medications before Ninaba could accept that her husband was spared. Ruby Yazzie, however, could not accept the prognosis until an Enemy Way Chant was sung over him.

George Slim, at forty-two, was through with the mines, and of regular employment. His earning capacity was not promising. "I am like them millions of tons of tailings," he told his family, "used up. I go to decay in the sun." For ten years he had sought oblivion with Thunderbird and Gallo.

In 1960, early spring, George Slim was picked up from the floor of a main street saloon for the last time. His little girl, Crystal Bayeta, stood at the open door, the torn Raggedy Ann doll in her hand illuminated by the glare of the hot sun. The look she gave him was not one of disappointment or disgust. It was one of confusion and need. Ninaba had used her last, desperate ploy to make him see what he had become. Within the week, Ninaba and her mother had decided. It was time to move down to the summer hogan in *Tseyi*. For Crystal Bayeta, it was to be the most magical summer of her childhood. Life would never again be so hard or uncertain.

Adam slowed to a stop at the light. Gallup was not much changed. It was the place between—between Flagstaff and Albuquerque, between Navajos and Zunis, Ute and *bilagáana*. In the surging, emergent global economy, Gallup was a marginalized outland. It supplied a commoditized world with coal, uranium, cattle, corn, and cotton. Extraction and exploitation were the way of things for Gallup. A chill raced up Bayeta's spine. She leaned over to grip Adam's arm. "You said we were going to stop."

"The Fruitland Cafe is just ahead."

"I hope Melanie's coffee is better than the last time. You can't cut it with a sharp knife."

Adam laughed. "She does make it thick, doesn't she?"

"Does she have any idea how bad it is?"

"Her morning trade is mostly truckers. Once, she installed a new Brew Master. She was so proud because it made coffee without grounds in the bottom of the cup."

"That's not the coffee I remember."

"Well, within a week of getting that machine her business dropped off. Melanie said that most of the truckers began parking over in front of Joe's Place, across the highway. She tore that fancy machine out and put the old West Bend back in place. 'You think I'm gonna let that old fart poison all my old customers?' That's what she told me."

"It sounds like something she'd say."

"She's half Navajo, you know."

"Adam, she looks Mexican."

"Her father was. He was shot and killed by a policeman, a case of mistaken identity."

"Sometimes you do surprise me with what you know."

"I know a lot of things like that, that's all."

"You been drinking her coffee behind my back, is that it?" Tilting her head in feigned jealousy, Crystal gave Adam a sly look.

Adam saw the Fruitland Cafe ahead and slowed down. "Her family lived in Albuquerque. My mother used to buy weavings from Helena Quintana, her mother. They were very good, mostly blankets and rugs with stripes. Hers always sold quickly. You know the one I wanted to put in the new house?"

"You mean the one I put away?"

"Well, that's a Quintana weaving. Her family comes from the Burnt Water area."

Bayeta knew and respected the style. But she was not comfortable with it. It clashed with her mother's weavings in the house. She had hoped that Adam had not noticed its absence.

Entering the cafe, Bayeta motioned toward the counter. All the booths were occupied. "The counter's fine. All I need is coffee."

The waitress was pouring coffee before they were settled onto their stools. The steam rising from the cups was inviting. Warming her hands on the cup, Bayeta reached over with her right hand and gently stroked Adam's forearm. "Adam, call him."

He gave her a tense look. "I will." Bayeta waited for a different answer.

"Bea, I'll call. Trust me. He won't like hearing that I did not take the plane last night."

"By now he knows."

Melanie Quintana, the owner of the cafe, came over to greet them. With both hands held out to Adam, she looked very pleased. "Well, I'll be! How long has it been?"

"Melanie, it's good to see you, too. How have you been?"

"Oh, you know me; I'm good, real good!" Melanie was by nature outgoing, even flirtatious. Men found her attentions flattering. Women found them irritating. She had a way of ignoring the woman beside any man. Melanie was not consciously rude. She was an attractive woman who liked men, but had little success with them or with marriage. Still, she bathed in the attention men paid her.

"You do quite a business this time of the morning." Bayeta looked straight into Melanie's eyes, steady and sure, without a hint of annoyance.

"It used to be just the truckers. They're a rough lot. Now, we get the Church Rock crews and some from that new strip mine west of here. See those fellows taking up my booths? They come off shift covered in mine dust." Melanie leaned over the counter, her tone at once confidential. "Makes more work for me and my staff. We have to clean the booths twice a day now."

"That's the price you pay, Melanie, for all the extra business."

"It isn't what some folks think." Her tone shifted. She was serious now. "All that coal gets made into electricity for L.A. and Vegas. I'm told that some of that coal even gets shipped off to China. What do we get out of it?" She motioned toward the men and lowered her voice almost to a whisper, looking to make certain her words did not carry. "We get what's left behind: Holes in the ground and sick people. We get miners from the uranium digs, too. A week ago, the yellow hats shut me down for more than half the day. That's the Nukes for you. It's 'cause of those miners. They had one of them incidents. They never call them accidents or let it get in the newspapers." She had a look of disgust on her face. "Those men up at United Mine got radiated. Before they knew what had happened, a bunch of them were in here after their shift. Well, later, in come the Nukes. One minute I'm in business, the next thing I know they close me down and post a damned radiation sign on my door."

Adam was interested, but it was Bayeta who pressed. "What exactly happened?"

"Ripped two of the booths clean out. The boys always sit back there near the side entrance. One of the men got a really big dose. He's a good guy, always orders pie or cake with his coffee. He leaves a decent tip, too. Anyway, they found this hot spot. Tore both booths right out and brought in a crew of cleaners wearing masks. I had to find two new booths. You should see the forms they want me to fill out just to get reimbursed. Them bastards!"

"You will come out all right, Melanie. What about the men?" As she spoke, Bayeta reached out to grip Melanie's arm. "What about those miners?"

"Most of them will check out OK. But one guy told me that they can't work in the mine for a while, something about the doses they got. One old guy, an old-time Indian, he got it bad. His family is up by the Colorado line, living on the Res. They fired him right off. The other men aren't happy about it. No fault of his own. He was just in the wrong place. The mine manager said he was careless and fired him. All he gets is two week's severance."

"You said he lives on the Res.?"

"He's Ute. He has family at Ute Mountain."

"You say they fired him?"

"That's always the way of it. Nothing shows up right away. But in six months or two years, the miner gets cancer. The mine goes on as always. No one makes a stink. The company says it has a great safety record. That's 'cause the men die at home, can't prove it was the mine's fault."

Talk of things nuclear had troubled Adam since he was a teenager. It also troubled Bayeta, but in different way. The atomic test sites, the laboratories, and the mines were part of the histories of people who grew up in Arizona and New Mexico. Bayeta knew men whose insides were burned out by inhaling radioactive dust from mining yellow cake. Many of the men she saw as a child on the streets of Gallup had been miners. George Slim was one. He was a lucky one, however, having survived two operations, losing forty pounds, and unable to ever again work underground.

As they got up to leave, Melanie called out, "Come back soon, Adam."

Back on the road, Adam said they could make Albuquerque by nine to meet Cynthia at La Posada for breakfast. Bayeta wondered aloud, "Do you think your sister will ever marry?"

"I doubt that, Bea. Menopause is catching up with her."

"She's still a beautiful woman, Adam."

"Beautiful but with a difference; she doesn't much like men."

"Adam, that has nothing to do with it."

“I did not mean to imply *that*. It’s just that she hates men her age. She calls them used goods.”

Few acquaintances recognized that Cynthia and Adam were twins. They did not look alike. Cynthia was shorter, delicately framed, her skin nearly as pale as the moon. She resembled their mother in many ways. Eleanor has also been diminutive and had thick, dark hair. Whatever mother and daughter lacked in height, they more than made up for by having a strong, elegant bone structure. In any crowd they stood out, remarkable women with long, swan-like necks. Standing side-by-side, their heads stiffly poised on long necks, they attracted notice, even from the most unobservant of men. They moved through a room in stately fashion, each step deliberate, but not for effect. Neither acted as if she was aware of the effect they had on friends or strangers, men or women.

Puberty for Cynthia marked the beginning of a long retreat into one’s self. Her room became an inviolate space, reserved for herself alone and her books. She never acknowledged the need for friends or company. Her state of self-absorption lasted for years. Cynthia refused music lessons and showed no interest in anything resembling artistic creativity. She never wanted a pet. Indeed, the first serious sign of strain between Eleanor and her daughter surfaced over a stray cat that took up residence under the porch steps. It was a beautiful angora, and not feral. Mother suggested that it would be company for Cynthia. She could keep it in her room. But Cynthia ignored the cat. Weeks later, Eleanor discovered the cat wrapped in plastic in the refrigerator. Opening the plastic, she saw that the animal was half-dissected. The smell of formalin overwhelmed Eleanor as she dropped the specimen tray on the kitchen floor. Later, Cynthia was resolute that she had found the cat dead on the porch two days before. Since she needed a science project for biology class, why not the cat? She would not admit that the cat caused the scratches on her arm. An uneasy silence grew between mother and daughter for a long time after.

Although the physical resemblance was remarkable, mother and daughter were poles apart in temperament and attitude. Cynthia was like her father in such respects. Alexander’s influence in her late teenage years was manifest. He regretted only her sex. In spite of infrequent visits, he nurtured her budding interest in physics. She developed an almost perverse enthusiasm in all things "atomic."

Adam, on the other hand, by the age of ten was out exploring the open desert west of town sunup to sundown in his weekend forays. He almost never let a weekend go by without hiking into the foothills near to Petroglyph Monument and the desert to the west. He grew into a somewhat dreamy teenager. Everything in nature excited his imagination. He was constantly capturing animals and releasing them back into the wild, after, that is, "studying them."

Eleanor was the model of a loving and devoted mother. She treated both children equally in the things that mattered. But Eleanor could not hide her disappointment in Cynthia's growing passion for physics, and by extension for her father. Upon graduating from Berkeley, fourth in her class, Cynthia announced that she had no intention of wasting her life on a man, any man. Her mind was set on physics, albeit a man's world. Alexander saw to it that opportunity came her way. His near celebrity status as a physicist exerted a strong influence on her. He reciprocated in kind.

In spite of their differences, brother and sister did keep in touch after college. The one thing that stood between was mother and father. Since his sixteenth year, Adam's feelings about his father had turned rigid and uncompromising, deeply distrustful. Cynthia and their mother reconciled, though slowly. Over time, the twins learned to avoid arguments over parents. They struck a truce and kept to it.

<++++++++++>

Ashes from her half-smoked cigarette snowed down on the notepad on which she was making her to-do list. Cynthia cursed and brushed them away. Then she spilled coffee on the note pad. The phone rang. Cynthia tried wiping the list dry, gave up, and answered the phone.

"Yes? This is Dr. Grant speaking."

"Cynthia, it's me!" Herman's voice sounded shaky and anxious, barely recognizable.

"Is that you, Herman? What on earth are you calling me for at this hour? What's the matter with you? Don't tell me that you haven't been to bed yet."

"Now Cyn, let's not start off on a bad note." Herman was never one for banter. "I'm trying to find Adam. Have you heard from him? Do you know where he is? There's no answer at his home or the laboratory. I've, well... I must, absolutely must get in touch with him immediately."

"At this hour, you called me for that?"

"You know that I would not call unless it was extremely important."

"Cool your jets, Herman. It just so happens I am having breakfast with Adam at nine. In fact, I should already be on the road, if I am to make Albuquerque by nine."

"Thank God! You see, he did not make the flight as promised. I was concerned."

"Herman, now I know something is wrong. When was the last time you cared a shit about Adam? All you want from him is the research he does. It helps polish your image at that "chromo hole" institute of yours. Even Father knows it."

"Goddamn it, Cynthia, I am concerned. Please don't start in on me this morning."

"What's the big deal? So what if he shows up later than you planned?"

"Well, you see, it's just that we expect him. I've gone through hoops to get everything lined up for him. He's going to foul up everything by being late."

"Herman, if he agreed to be there, he'll be there."

The silence that followed was not like Herman. She expected more whining from him. With the silence becoming awkward, Cynthia took a more insistent tone. "What does it matter to you, anyway? He's only half a brother to you to begin with. Besides, Adam doesn't like being handled."

"Please, Cynthia, don't be flip with me, not this morning. This thing of his, this research he has done, well it is really, really, well..." Herman cut short what he began to say. He had said too much, implied too much. "Forgive me for not asking, how are you these days?"

Cynthia instantly picked up on his course correction. The last time they had spoken was a year ago in San Francisco, when she was with Father. She inevitably encountered Herman at their father's house. For a minute or two, they exchanged inane pleasantries. That was it.

"I'll tell him to call you, Herman. When I see him, that is. Satisfied?"

"Yes, thank you. I must hear from him. It is vitally important."

"I'll tell him, Herman. What more do you want? I will tell him that it is vital, critical, and immediate. Call Herman! OK?"

Cynthia was on the road to Albuquerque ten minutes later. The drive gave her time to think. Had Adam produced something important enough to warrant Herman's nervous state when he did not show up as planned? Why did Adam commit to attending the conference? It surprised her that Herman implied that he had something to do with that. One thought kept returning: Herman had cut himself short. His near hysteric tone struck a nerve with her. If only he had finished his sentence. Then she might have some idea what to tell Adam, tell him what bothered her about Herman's call.

The two disagreed about many things, but Herman was not one of them. Cynthia called him a "smarmy toad." Adam agreed that he could hardly stand Herman's fawning and self-absorption. Father, however, insisted Herman had a talent for administration and organization. Running an institute, Alexander said, demanded a specific skill set. "Herman values symmetry, habit, and order. Leave the round pegs and square holes to him. He'll get them right." Did it matter that Herman had no talent for abstract thinking? Setting policy and priorities at The Evergreen Institute was in the board's hands.

Herman related to others only with effort. His home life was dysfunctional and chaotic. He secretly hated his father. Cynthia and Adam knew, but never spoke of it. Alexander knew, but was content to allow Herman to play the dutiful son. He was good at fetching and carrying. Herman served his purposes. He also co-managed a family trust, an acknowledgement of his near mania for order and concrete results. Herman's financial acumen seldom failed him. What Herman did with his personal investments did not concern Alexander. That Herman was known to venture into speculative investment instruments with his own money, a kind of perverse reaction to his conservative management of the trust's portfolio, was his private affair. At age fifty-five, Herman was desperate to free himself of his father's dominance. Such over reaching for quick profit failed to serve its purpose, which kept Herman tightly bound to Alexander. Of late, he had been playing too close to his margin calls to increase his investment in Genetrix. Adam's latest research, of which Herman knew nothing, or was supposed to know nothing, was at the center of Schwann's plans for Genetrix. Herman believed that his Genetrix stock would at last free him of Schwann. Until it did, however, Herman had to insure that Schwann did not know of his stock manipulations.

<++++++++++>

On entering the dining room, Cynthia's mood brightened. She had put aside Herman's frantic, early morning call. Seeing Bayeta and Adam, she smiled and quickened her steps.

"It's so good to see you, sis. Life is treating you well?" Adam stood to pull out a chair for her.

Cynthia leaned over to kiss Bayeta's cheek. "Crystal, you look radiant this morning."

"Thank you, Cynthia." She gave her sister-in-law a wry, knowing look.

"I mean it. In spite of your having that long drive, you look fresh, radiant actually." For once, Cynthia's words had the ring of truth. For today, the two could set aside their wariness of each other. Neither had reason for being cool toward the other, it was just so. As the waiter poured coffee, Cynthia busied herself laying out her daily pills.

"Cyn, are you still taking those awful things?"

"Yes, and I am getting better. One is for hypertension. This one is for anemia. I did take your advice, though. Those pills Father insisted that I take, well, I chucked them. They made me feel grungy, off key. Goddamn drug companies, they're out to hook us all on useless nostrums and poisons." Adam leaned back and looked intently at his sister. "I should slow down a bit, too, for my own good. Fusion research has become a weightlifter's game. Every experiment requires apparatus that weighs tons. The mechanics and pipe fitters, damned tinkers, they've all but taken over."

"Sis, you have always known that today's physics is more about engineering than theorizing."

"It makes me feel old. Anyway, we've been getting some really good energy returns, nearly as much as we put in. Give it five years, no ten, and we'll really show progress.

Bayeta smiled and asked, "Enough fusion to close down Black Mesa?"

Cynthia smiled. "You will live to see Peabody gone. They're giving up on that slurry pipeline. One day, people will realize that nuclear power is clean and not all that expensive."

"If that proves true, I'll be delighted for you, sis. We still have days with pollution so thick that visibility at Rimrock is affected. The one benefit is intense sunsets, all those reds and deep purples. If physics can make nuclear power safe, we will gladly give up the view."

"Adam, that's just about the nicest thing I've heard you ever say about anything to do with nuclear power and physics. One day, you might even stop quoting Mom."

"She had reasons, sis. She knew only its 'terrible queerness,' as she often put it."

"What made you think of that old saw?"

"Do you remember Melanie Quintana?"

"Sure." Cynthia turned to Bayeta. "She had her eye on Adam, you know." Adam grinned. "She once caught you with Daphne Reims, in the girl's locker room." Cynthia leaned back and laughed. "Melanie said that seeing that was almost enough to turn her Dutch."

"Oh, come on. Daphne was in no way like that."

"Oh? Anyway, Daphne did come out senior year." Adam blushed.

Bayeta pinched his arm. "You never told me about Daphne, Dear."

Cynthia was not ready to let Adam off the hook. "All through high school, the girls laid traps for him. He played hard-to-get. But, that only encouraged them."

"Daphne was a nice enough girl. We were just friends."

"Brother, how you lie! That's not what Melanie Quintana said. The two of you were half-stripped, quite guilty." Cynthia seemed determined to make Adam blush. "She was not the first."

Bayeta had not heard any of this before.

"It did not go any further than petting. Besides, my first real crush was Cassie. I really liked her. I wondered for years after high school what happened to her."

Cynthia's mood changed abruptly. She lowered her voice and leaned across the table. "I see her in town occasionally. She married right out of high school. She's divorced, raising a son on her own."

Adam remembered now. "That's right, sis. You and her brother, the hippie..."

"Henry. His name was Henry, Adam. Yes, I liked him. I really liked him."

"Would you have married him?" Bayeta's question was innocent enough.

"Henry was a great guy. He was sensitive, moody at times. We dated for over a year, whenever I came home from college for holidays. In my sophomore year, he proposed. But, I could not just drop my studies. I was not ready to marry anyone." Bayeta nodded that she understood. "What made it even worse was that he did not want college. He flunked out. His parents separated and were going through a nasty divorce. When he showed the ring, I just couldn't accept." Bayeta leaned forward and gently touched her arm. Cynthia took in a deep breath. "His mother found him in the garage on Christmas Eve. It was too late to do anything. She blamed me. Cassie, however, did not blame me. We keep in touch. She had hopes that Adam would rekindle his interest in her."

"You loved Henry."

"I did like him. But if I had married Henry I would not be a senior scientist at Los Alamos, or a professor, or live at Woodmere. None of that would have come true. Life is about choices, isn't it?"

"How on earth do you keep up that white elephant, Cynthia? It is so huge and drafty." He meant the Woodmere house, Cynthia's house in Santa Fe.

"It's not all that big. Besides, Tina and Vesta tend to the housework and upkeep."

Adam leaned back and motioned to the waiter for more coffee. He decided not to pursue the subject of Woodmere's "venal vestal virgins." With the plates cleared and fresh coffee poured, Cynthia reached into her pocket for her cigarettes. A note fell out with the pack. It had completely slipped her mind. "Herman called me."

Bayeta's eye caught Adam's look. "Herman called, you mean this morning?"

"Yes, you do remember him, Adam, our esteemed half-brother? From the sound of his voice, I'd say he is in quite a state, hung over and in panic mode. Of course, that is nothing new."

"I take it he did not call for a friendly chin wag."

"Now, don't be snide. He is trying to locate you."

"I will see him in California, tomorrow morning at the latest."

Cynthia steadied her look. "He sounded pretty rocky, Adam. Actually, I'd call it jaded. I gather that you've upset some plan of his." Cynthia shook her head. "No, that's not quite it. He sounded scared. His voice shook." Adam feigned indifference. "The question is, why?"

"Come on, sis. So I decided to take a later plane. One day more or less can't make any real difference to Herman." Cynthia gave Adam a skeptical look. "When I do see him, let me tell you, I'll give him good reason to worry. But that is a matter for another day."

"He said something about planning a luncheon in your honor with the Institute's directors."

"I don't remember him saying anything along those lines. I would not have agreed to it."

"Well, I've delivered the message. He wants you to call him, ASAP."

Bayeta softly reminded Adam, "You promised to call. Don't put it off."

"All right you two, I'll call him right now."

Adam walked out of the dining room to find a phone, while Cynthia studied Bayeta's expression. For a long minute, neither one spoke. The waiter poured more coffee and collected the check. It was ten o'clock and the dining room had emptied out, except for them. The sounds of post-breakfast cleaning mingled with the rasping of the un-oiled hinge on the service door to the kitchen. It was rare for them to be alone together. "Adam still doesn't like using phones, does he?"

"Disembodied is how he puts it. He complains that it is can distract him when he is working in the lab. He never answers it. Actually, I think he disconnects it."

"When you and Adam built your home, I wondered if Adam would or could adapt to the isolation. However much it resembles a peaceful, secret garden, I had my doubts. But, clearly both of you are content with it and the way things are. I was wrong to worry."

"We both are occupied with what we believe is important. And, with Adam I feel free and respected. Adam does not see Rimrock as isolated, not with his work. Whenever the walls close in, and they do, we come here or to Flagstaff. Of course, we also have our ward to care for."

"I thought once…"

Bayeta finished Cynthia's sentence for her, "…that our marriage was a mistake?"

Embarrassed, Cynthia looked down at her coffee cup and shrugged her shoulders.

"As his sister, knowing him as you do, you believed him too restless to settle down."

Cynthia nodded. "I did." She gave a sigh, as if relieved. "But, you've settled him."

"For the first five years, what with Berkeley and the travels, he often was restless, with a kind of insatiable energy. He needed to stop and take stock, but his research and duties at Berkeley made that impossible. Travel only made things worse. Yes, leaving Berkeley made all the difference."

"What will happen now?"

Bayeta looked surprised. Surely, Cynthia could have no inkling of the sea change she and Adam were about to face. "Cynthia, you are very perceptive."

"I don't know anything, not really. But, Herman, and also something Father said, has me wondering. What has Adam been up to? The tea leaves tell me he has done something big."

"He has. When he makes public his breakthrough, I want him to take a break. Maybe we'll travel. We both like Europe, Rome maybe, Seville, anywhere where we can be ourselves."

"Is that what Adam wants?"

"For the moment, Alberto is his constant concern. The boy—God, I hate thinking of that young man as a boy—has not much time left. Adam's sense of failure makes it all the harder on him."

Cynthia could see that it was a painful subject and spoke of the prospect of travel. Bayeta understood. "Well, I'm not sure about Europe, too many contacts there to keep him away from. He has mentioned Mombasa, the Seychelles, a place to sit on the beach. More than once, I've found a scribbled note about hotel and flight packages. There's no talk about a next big thing, the next experiment. This research took five years, and he has to see it into print. I don't know if he has the energy to start another big one. After this, he doubts that he can garner big enough grants, or institutional backing, or graduate students to work with. How he accomplished what he has in five years still surprises him."

"Crystal, I want to know why Herman..." She took in a deep breath. "No, let's change the subject. I really should wait for Adam to tell me. May I ask you something personal?"

"I have no secrets."

Cynthia smiled and softened her tone. "Why does Adam call you Bea? John Sanderson says it is not a shortening of your maiden name, Bayeta. I know it is clumsy of me to ask."

"Ah, you know that we Navajo have secret names. Bea is not one. Adam should tell you."

"It was a queer thing, Herman's call this morning." Cynthia could not quite let it go. "He sounded scared of something. I had a funny feeling that he has finally lost his grip."

"It would not be the first time Adam has unsettled him."

"This is different. It's more what he did not say. He began to, but then abruptly changed the subject. I could swear he said something like 'Adam's new thing.' Whatever did he mean by that?"

Bayeta hesitated. Adam should be the one to tell her what he had done. He could tell her in scientific terms that she would understand.

Cynthia abandoned restraint. "What has my brother done? What has he been up to?"

"I'm not the one to tell you. As for Herman, he should not know a thing. Adam is adamant that he has no obligation to Herman's institute. Maybe Herman was referring to an enzyme study he's just completed. But that is in press, and Herman should have a copy of the unpublished draft."

"So, there is something that Herman is not supposed to know anything about, right?"

"Adam refers to it as his Greene Lyon project."

"That's a funny name."

"Moving to Rimrock made it possible for him to devote his attention to it."

Cynthia had a sudden insight. "I see. It all fits." Bayeta tried not to react. "I remember how he talked when he left Berkeley. He did say he was at last free to work on what makes us age the way we do. He's always believed that people should have the benefit of a longer life. He argued violently with Father about it, about how no research ethics committee should try to control his work product. Adam was against partnering with corporations, the commoditization of the commons. Adam hates that."

"Yes, he does hate it. It was a big factor in the decision. Rimrock is isolated, as you say, but it is also free of external demands and controls."

Cynthia thought for a moment about what Bayeta said. "Yes, I see. His interest in progeria has more to it than just Alberto's condition, doesn't it?"

Bayeta nodded. She was near to tears. "You know how much he loves the boy. Until a few months ago, well, before that, Adam actually thought he could do something for him."

“Is there nothing that can be done?”

“We make him as comfortable as one can. We try to fill each day with good things, little joys that do not tax him too much. We read to him. Adam takes him on short drives to the canyon rim. Alberto putters about the lab when Adam is working.”

Bayeta looked down at her hands, gathering in her thoughts. “Sometimes, he still thinks like a child. He believes in magic, anything that might miraculously arrest the decline, even restore him. He wants the youth he never had. Adam has done all he could for the boy.”

Cynthia could not repress her anxiety. “You’re not suggesting…”

Bayeta interrupted, “Of course not. Alberto is our ward, under our care and protection, not a test subject. For five years we have comforted and loved him. Maybe it crossed Adam’s mind once or twice, but no, he knows better than to do anything like that.”

Bayeta wiped her tears as Cynthia made an effort to brighten the mood. “And, John…?”

“Adam insisted on giving his annual talk to the biology forum. He loves to do it. It gives him a break from the routine of Rimrock. He won’t admit it, but he misses teaching.”

“Five years is a long time to be out of the classroom.”

“Once Adam decided he’d had enough, he resigned. He looks forward not behind. The day he resigned, he asked me if I minded living in Albuquerque again. The Berkeley house went on the market the next day. But, I said no to Albuquerque. I wanted to be done with urban living.”

“It was all decided in little more than a day?”

“Almost: He called Alberto’s parents the next day to ask if Alberto could come live with us.” Cynthia knew the broad outline of events, but not how precipitous they were. “Ironic, isn’t it? He wanted a laboratory all to himself with no interference. He wanted no more chasing after grants and kowtowing to bureaucracy. He wanted to help Alberto and learn by watching how he coped with his disease. The parents were only too happy. They were by then worn out with caring for him.”

"And, what did you want?" She did not believe that the decision was all Adam's to make.

"I wanted to come home. Rimrock was just a bare patch of ground, but I knew exactly what I wanted to make of it. So, it is five years later and both of us have had exactly what we dreamed of."

Adam returned from his phone call. He looked relaxed and satisfied with himself.

"Did the two of you come to terms?" He'd caught Cynthia's look.

"We talked about Rimrock. I was about to tell her how you handed me the sketch for your lab and told me to call the contractor the day after I showed you where I wanted the house at Rimrock."

Cynthia could not resist bringing Herman back into the conversation. "As I remember it, you had a verbal commitment from Herman within a month of leaving Berkeley. He even gave you on loan some valuable lab equipment. Father thought the whole idea impractical, absurd even. Odd, isn't it, Herman, of all people, going to bat for you. For once, he ignored Father's counsel."

"Poor Herman, I have been a burden to him."

"Don't be smug, Adam. You do owe him something."

"Something, yes, I admit it. I have repaid his largess with a stream of productive research that helped to put a shine on his precious institute."

"Now, tell me about this latest flap with him." Cynthia was not to be put off.

"It is over a lunch he set up. In spite of my objections, he went ahead and planned it."

"It has to be more than that, Adam. You've been a no show more than once."

"Yes, I have indeed. But this time he wanted to make a big show of it. Only God know why."

Cynthia pressed, "You have something up your sleeve, Adam. That's why you have decided to attend the San Francisco conference. You've not been to an academic meeting in five years."

"Maybe so, but that has nothing to do with Herman or his institute."

"What on earth are you up to? More of that old Greene Lyon stuff?"

"I don't want to talk about it." Adam squirmed in his seat. "Well, I have made something of a breakthrough, yes. If I am right about it, we have the means to extend the human lifespan. My work with *Sorex vagrans* shows that the protocol can, in fact does, work. The conference is the best opportunity to bring my colleagues, those working along similar lines, into the picture. That is why I am going. Giving a paper on enzyme studies, the abstract I sent in, is just the excuse."

"Jesus, Brother, how important is this, this thing you've done?"

"It is big enough, big enough." Adam was now desperate to change the subject. "Oh, did I tell you, Herman tells me, but I don't believe it, that I am on the short list for The Morgan Prize. It is flattering. But, I'm sure someone else will receive the award."

Bayeta looked surprised. Adam had mentioned the possibility, but until that moment had not thought of it being a realistic possibility. Being nominated was enough.

"It is eight hundred thousand. Herman told me the board of The Evergreen Institute doubled the amount of the award. God knows why. Maybe they do need to polish their image."

Cynthia looked confused. "That does not sound like Herman."

"Lately, nothing surprises me when it comes to Herman. He's become overly solicitous. He asked me if I needed additional funds for the lab. He's such a tight wad that his offer makes me wonder. Last month, when I sent him my quarterly expenses for the grant administrator, he not so much as objected to a single item."

"See, there has to be a catch. Herman is many things, but generous he is not."

"Well, whatever the case, it is nothing I need to be concerned with."

"You don't really believe that." Cynthia took a deep breath and stared. "He calls me in an absolute panic. You've gone missing, he says. He has to know where you are. He expected you to be at this La-de-da luncheon with the board of directors. Herman expects something from you."

"Herman can be devious. Well, no matter, he knows nothing of my *Sorex vagrans* work."

"Sometimes, Brother, you can be dense beyond belief. What do you think he meant when he asked me this morning about your 'new thing'? He clearly insinuated that I knew something."

"He said that—he said 'new thing'?"

"He did. More to the point, he caught himself and clammed up."

Cynthia leaned back and gave Adam her most skeptical look. The mood at the table became subdued. Adam struggled to absorb Cynthia's insight. Reaching for his coffee, he began to say something, but his words trailed off. Like the stale coffee in his cup, the conversation had gone cold.

"Sis, do you remember how we used to argue over physics? You would get so mad when Mother or I said that physicists were trying to write the last chapter of life on this planet. At the time, I believed that. The arms race was turning physicists into cold warriors."

"Adam, what does this have to do with Herman?"

Adam was folding and unfolding his napkin as he thought, as if turning the pages of a text. "I'm not sure. After years of probing, I have succeeded. But I don't feel pleasure in the fact. We have come to understand how dangerous the nuclear age is. We've stepped back a bit. But in its place, biology might be the new threat, a different kind of threat. I've been writing up my results and giving some thought to how they might be applied. I'm not that good at thinking about possibilities." Adam wiped his brow. "Am I sounding as if I'm making an apology?"

"For Christ's sake, Adam, just what have you been up to?"

"It was progeria that first gave me the key. The trigger for the disease is in the genetic expression of the cell. Locate the faulty gene, alter or turn it off, or just re-program it."

"It sounds to me as if it does have something to do with Alberto."

"Well, it did, but only in an indirect way. I knew that I could not help him. The point is: By watching him, I thought about how to reset the biologic clock. The cell's replication mechanisms turn on and turn off. That is the key to it all. Biological mechanisms involved at the cell level in aging, in normal human beings, can be reprogrammed."

"You mean you can change the length of the life span?"

"The hard part was identifying which genes are involved and how they function or fail to function properly. Then, modify their processes through selective inhibition and stimulation. Of course, others will need to replicate my experiments and procedures. I used *Sorex vagrans*, my shrews, instead of white mice. That will be criticized, but that is a minor concern."

"Adam, are you sure about this?"

For the next ten minutes, Adam outlined his research and findings. His procedures were complex, but Cynthia followed much of his reasoning. When he finished, she had more questions.

"Adam, we've got seven billion people on earth who need to be fed and sheltered. How is the world going cope if all of them live longer?"

"Modern medicine and health systems have already extended the average lifespan by twenty-nine years in this century. My work is just a logical extension of that trend." He knew he was beginning to sound defensive. "We're getting ahead of ourselves. It will take time to approve trials. Can a double-blind trial even be done? With shrews answers came quickly."

"Who else uses shrews in research? What line of shrews did you work with, anyway?"

"Cyn, a shrew's lifespan is two years. Their body temperature is at 99 degrees. A human's heart rate is one-thirteenth that of a shrew. Their intestinal system processes an amount of food equal to their entire weight each day. It is easy to induce chronic conditions of stress, a variable with immense implications. Shrews make a perfect experimental vector, more so than white mice."

"What if you have manipulated a shrew to live a month or two longer? What does that prove? Experiments on white mice show that they live longer simply by controlling diet."

"Cynthia, with my Alpha group, I am within days of the four year mark. Thirty percent of them are still alive. I have shrews that have lived to be twice as old as nature allows."

"Adam, if you are half-right about this, promise me that you'll not rush into anything."

Bayeta touched Adam's arm to interrupt. "Cynthia, what a difference it would make for someone like Alberto."

"My God, Adam, tell me again that you haven't experimented on that boy."

Adam looked taken aback. "I have not. I admit that his doctors are at a loss to explain how he has survived this long. But it is more to Bea's care than anything else."

Cynthia was not totally mollified. She knew how much deteriorated Alberto's condition was when he first came to Rimrock. To survive so long and to mark it down to love sounded fanciful to her. "Please, just tell me once more that you have not…"

"…done something unethical or illegal? Is that what you think?" She could not look Adam in the eyes. "Before this goes any further, let me tell you. The fact that he has survived four years beyond what the doctors originally gave him is due solely to his will to live, that and Bea's care."

"Maybe you should not tell me more about this, Adam."

"When Alberto came to us four and a half years ago, in biological terms he had the body of an eighty-year-old man. He was aging six times faster than normal. Worse than that, the deterioration was accelerating. Christ, the boy was only eighteen-years-old. Do you know what that means? He had already outlived most other victims. How many specialists did we take him to, six? They examined and evaluated Alberto for months. Two flew in from Europe. Each one reached the same conclusion, giving him less than six months."

Bayeta shuddered. "You never told me that."

"Yes, I know, Bea."

"You did not need to carry that burden alone, dear."

Cynthia was determined to carry her concern to the limit. "Adam, you are so naïve. Do you think that others will not suspect that you made use of Alberto?"

"I did not use or abuse him."

"All the same, there will be those who will say that you must have done something. What else explains Alberto's miraculous beating of the odds? You may want to limit explanation of your success to shrews. But there are those who will suspect that your experiment was not limited to test animals."

"What do I care what others think?"

"Adam, I'm only pointing out the obvious. I won't believe it, not for an instant. But..."

"Look, Alberto was born poor. His parents, did you know, died three years ago in a car accident? What then would have happened to him? No one would have stepped in to care for him. Except for us, he was a lost cause. Alberto's malady strikes one in eight million. The heart and internal organs begin to deteriorate by the age of one. At age three, the signs of the disease are unmistakable. From that point on, childhood is a thing of the past. Growth retardation sets in. At ten, a progeria child is bald. Arrhythmia is a daily concern. Skin turns leathery and wrinkled before a child is old enough to say its name. Bones become weak and brittle. Most progeria victims die between the age of twelve and eighteen. Alberto is twenty-two years old. He has had four plus good years with us. We helped him to feel and experience some of what life has to offer. At Rimrock, he was free from ridicule and prying eyes. He developed appetites and interests. Plants and flowers give him the most pleasure."

Bayeta looked to Cynthia. "He is so desperate to live. Death terrifies him. No matter how much we do for him, deep down he is a very sad young-old man. It's not because he is old but because he was never young. He's never been in love. He will never be a father." Tears filled Bayeta's eyes. "The garden is his favorite place. There he sees living things grow and thrive, live a full cycle of life."

By now, Cynthia, too, was in tears. "Does he know how little time he has left?"

"I think so. Martin took him to the clinic early yesterday morning. His kidneys are failing and he needs dialysis. A health service nurse is scheduled to come with a portable machine."

"I'm so sorry. I know how much you love him."

Adam sighed. "Well, that is how it is. He will die and we will bury him. I try to ignore his bouts of depression. I'm used to his coming into the lab, his puttering about. He helps Martin care for and feed the animals. Martin checks the cages before he comes in, not wanting him to see a dead animal. He is quite bright, you know. He keeps score. He wants to know everything about their charts—hormone levels, thyroid, even the endorphins levels.

"He keeps up a pretty good front, but his body is telling him. The last time Martin and Bea took him to Flagstaff to have Dr. Himes examine Alberto he came back and asked me to tell him how much time he has left. I didn't know what to say. He just looked at me and said that he needed to know how many books to select. He did not want to start one and not finish it."

Bayeta said, "He does not sit with me anymore for afternoon snacks. We used to sit and listen to music together. Now, I bring his snack to his room. It's too cold for him to sit outdoors. But, he insists that he wants to sit under the apple trees, the two Adam planted between the house and his lab. He wants to live long enough to see them flower. They are late this year."

<++++++++++>

As they drove to campus, Bayeta asked Adam to drop her off on San Mateo Boulevard.

"I'll catch a cab back to the faculty club when I'm done. John is meeting us at one o'clock?"

Adam agreed. At any rate, he wanted a few minutes alone with Cynthia.

Halfway down the campus drive, Adam pointed to cacti and flowers in bloom. This did not fool Cynthia. He was trying to find a distraction.

"Adam, I have something to ask you. I always assumed that you call her Bea because it is short for Bayeta. She says no, that it is something else."

He pretended not to hear, but his smile betrayed him. "Cynthia, I have a problem. As long as my hunt for answers was elusive, I didn't think about what a result could mean. I didn't ask myself why I was doing it. Now I have submitted a summary in a paper for *Science*. But, well…"

Cynthia waited, but Adam hesitated to go on. With the silence weighing on both of them, she replied, "If I were you, I would not tell

Herman. That is what you are asking yourself. If he could understand it, he would press you for control. You don't have to tell me that you have no intention."

"You do see my problem. Others are working along similar lines. Cell modification studies are going on all over the place. Cancer research is unraveling the matter of how to get a cell to stop replicating. Stem cell research is heading in that direction. I just got to my goal line faster, that's all. I have found a key to editing the cell's metabolism, mediating its functions."

"Tell me again about the animals, the shrews. How many did you use?"

"I started with two hundred. It was a huge undertaking to get that many healthy animals to work with. I began with ten breeding pairs and had their history going back five generations. I randomly assigned them to either the experimental or control group. I used one hundred as the control group. As expected, they all died within the first two years. I introduced variables at intervals. Shrews reach adulthood at four weeks. Remarkable, isn't it?"

Cynthia squirmed in her seat, impatient with Adam's beating about the bush. "You said that the controls all died pretty much as expected, within two years?"

"The mortality curve was absolutely to form. Everything, from cage size to temperature control, lighting—everything—matched a shrew's daily and seasonal cycles. When the last of the Beta group died off two summers ago, I knew for sure that I was on to something. On day 730, out of one hundred Betas, four were still alive. One lasted two years and nineteen days. All of the Alphas were still alive. I then split up the Alphas into two groups. One group was continued on the baseline hormonal therapy. The second group had their dosages increased by 50%. Of the fifty Alphas on the increased regimen, thirty-four are still alive. Over the coming month, the surviving ones will likely die. Not one of my experimental animals died short of two years and four months. The last group of Alphas, had they been human, I estimate that on average, had nineteen years in human terms added. Imagine that!"

"Adam, did they breed?"

"Breed? Yes, sex and bearing were variables that had to be included. That helped to maintain as normal a hormonal and emotional state as possible. Nor did I neuter them. That could have complicated the hormonal data. Females survive a little longer, actually."

"Does Father know what you've been working on? Maybe you should talk to him."

"I already know what he would say."

"You are too harsh with him. He understands the role of science in society, grant him that."

"He understands all right." Adam checked himself. "I'm sorry, Cynthia. I don't mean to be argumentative. I do value your opinion."

"He might give you a fresh perspective. That is my only point. After all, you do say that he knows sin. Unanticipated ends, he's an expert on them. You've accused him of it often enough."

Adam nodded. Alexander had often, at least of late, seemed focused on arguments over means and ends, even invoking Newton. The twentieth century had less to do with the invention of the atom bomb, he insisted, than did Newton and his notes on the apple falling from his tree at Woolsthorpe. The bomb, he believed, was little more than the ripened fruit of the 17th Century.

"You still haven't told me."

"You are referring to Bea?" She smiled. "It is my short form for Bayeta. But there is more. She is my fair Beatrice, my beauty, Beatrice d'Este. She is Leonardo da Vinci's fair maiden. She is Boccaccio's Beatrice. At our wedding, I saw her in prayer, with her mother beside her. It was such a beautiful sight. I heard 'I walk in beauty before me…' That phrase was repeated four times. What I felt that day was what Byron alone could express so well: 'She walks in Beauty, like the night. Of doubtless climes and starry skies…'"

Cynthia completed his line, "And all that's best of dark and light…"

"So, you do see. She means more to me than life itself."

"She's worried for you, you know that. You need to be careful."

Adam parked the car in front of the physics building as she finished her thought.

"I have to go."

Walking up the building's steps, Cynthia took a long look back over her shoulder. There he was, she thought, adrift in a sea of students. They were all so young, so full of life. But they were not all young people hurrying between classes. Her eyes fixed on a man. The man, a dark hulk of a man, was standing stiffly beside a car parked fifty feet down the street. He was watching Adam and alternately glancing in her direction. He was fifty, a little older. He looked out of place. And, he looked vaguely familiar, the sort of face one does not forget, even if one has never met him. Who wears a suit like his in this weather? He must not be from here, she thought. She stepped inside the building, and her thoughts turned to the reason for her visit with a colleague.

It felt good to Adam to drift into the flow of young people on their way to class. They all looked so young and fresh, buoyant with promise and potential. Seeing them rush by in the bright sunlight reminded Adam of what Hardesty, his teacher and now friend, once called him, his "little apple, an immature but ripening fruit, his Flower of Kent." Adam did not fancy himself fitting such a grand description, but it flattered him, nonetheless. The safety and remoteness of the fields of Woolsthorpe in Newton's time did mark a beginning of great things. But Adam did not equate his discovery as so momentous, nor was it anything like The Day of Trinity. Had Newton sensed the ultimate ends to which his *Principia* would be applied? Would his Unitarian frame of mind allowed it if he had?

Adam set aside his quandary over means and ends. Alberto was his more immediate concern. He had once promised Alberto that he'd live to see Newton apples ripen and to taste them. Alberto wanted to sit in the sunshine of a late afternoon and have *The Open Door* read aloud to him. But first, he had to get through the next four or five days.

5

Tickling The Dragon's Tail

Miss Morgan hesitated at the door, nervous and reluctant. Her employer's rule was absolute. He was not to be disturbed between noon and one. No exceptions. Nevertheless, she felt compelled to knock and enter his office. Contravening his standing rule was certain to unleash a barrage of abuse from Mr. William Henry Schwann. She could stand what was to come. She would have the weekend to recover.

"Sir, you have a call on line one. The caller insists that it is urgent."

"No interruptions! Must you always ignore my orders? Get out!"

"Sir..."

"Get out! I will deal with you later. Now, get out!"

She was frozen in place, knowing that it was best to take his abuse now, rather than later. "Mr. Ryder insists that you will want to talk to him." She was caught in a double bind. Putting Ryder off meant more trouble for her later.

"Morgan, get out! Terman is due at one, no interruptions until he arrives."

Still, she stood her ground.

"Goddamn it, woman, what is it?"

William Henry Schwann had not so much as glanced in her direction since she entered his office. She was used to his moods and, of late, was considering walking out without a hope for a good reference. She could take only so much from "that man." With her knees shaking, she spoke. "Sir, this is the third time he has called. He's that reporter, the one from the San Diego Times. You did say..."

"Morgan...!" He cut himself short. "Yes, I'll take the bastard's call. Now, get out!"

She retreated, closing the door silently behind her. Anne Morgan knew that Schwann had never before spoken to the man, Ryder. So, why would he take the call from this bothersome reporter? It was not at all like him. Schwann never dealt with employees of a subsidiary company. He paid others to do that. Late the previous afternoon, she had been ordered to track down Donald Ryder. One of the secretaries down the hall volunteered that she knew him slightly. She had once dated him when he came into the office on an assignment. They both had laughed as she looked up his number. "What," she asked, "can THE great man want with Don?"

What did connect Donald Ryder to William Henry Schwann? A graduate of the UCLA School of Journalism, Ryder was, by all accounts, a competent reporter. Schwann's paper would not have employed him otherwise. As it turned out, his assignments were not the sort upon which to build a more promising future. He longed to fit the role of investigative reporter, but for him the big story, the one to make his mark, never materialized. He had had his moments when he thought, "This could be the big one." More than once a promising lead had come his way, only to be scooped up by a syndicated "headline hog." Or, if the story turned out not to have "legs," he chalked it up to bad luck.

On this Thursday, it rankled him that his editor insisted he contact Mr. Schwann directly and without delay. He did as he was told, trying three times without success. Knowing that his editor would be angry if he failed to reach the man, it was a relief to hear a voice on the other end of the phone, if it was indeed Schwann.

Just that morning, as he lay in bed, he thought of getting his fishing gear ready for opening day of trout season. He also thought of some of the stories he had chased over the last ten years, the ones that got away. He remembered the time when he was in Washington D.C. to cover the National Nuclear Security Agency meeting on plans to upgrade Los Alamos. A next generation of nuclear weapons, multi-purpose in design, called the "inter-operable system" was on the agenda. Since science and technology were his beat, he understood what a one-size-fits-all weapons system implied—bigger bombs, better bombs, and more bombs. In Arizona and New Mexico nuclear weapons were news to his paper's readers, jobs for Los Alamos. There was to be no mention, however, of the corporation controlled by William Henry Schwann and Company, one of the major contractors. His editor also was quite definite that mention of plutonium pit manufacture was to be kept to a minimum.

On that November morning as he had walked out of the Mayflower Hotel, he ran into an old classmate who worked for Congressman Boland. His classmate, Ryder remembered, was a puffed up sod who talked too much. Ryder found himself sitting with the man in a coffee shop on Wisconsin Avenue, listening to a disjointed tale of a secret arms deal that involved a Latin American group called Nicaragua Contras. Laws, his old classmate said, were being broken, heads would roll, even as high as inside the White House. It was heady stuff, but not for attribution. Ryder had sensed that he was being given a leak, something that could stir the pot for the committee for which his classmate worked. Ryder later called a friend at The Washington Post to pursue what his flannel-mouthed former classmate, now informer, had told him. The Post contact had quickly changed the subject, claiming he knew nothing of arms to Iran. But Ryder had not mentioned Iran. Ryder smelled the big one, a byline, and even TV interviews. This was THE big one, and he had the inside track.

On the second day of digging and running down leads, he had a call from his editor. Where was the story on appropriations for the Los Alamos upgrade? Ryder told his editor to forget that, he was on to something bigger, much bigger. An hour later, his editor called again.

"Look, Don, we provide local and regional news, period. The lab and the jobs that come with it are what our readers want. Leave the national stuff to the big boys. We'll take their stuff off the wire if it comes to anything and be done with it. You stay focused, hear me?"

No amount of protest made a difference. To end the discussion, his editor drove home his point.

"You do remember World War II, don't you? By '45 our readers did not give a damn about the war news. The day they tested the first A-bomb, and believe me it made one hell of a big bang out in the desert—lit the whole sky up—well, all they wanted was the football scores. Who won, Chicago or St. Louis? You get the point? Now, get your ass over to the hearings and cover what I sent you there to cover."

<++++++++++>

As he walked across campus, Adam focused on what tack to take for his talk. Student reactions often surprised him; they asked great questions, if he caught their interest. Hard against the western flank of Sandia Peak, he could see hot air balloons coming down after a morning aloft. He imagined John Sanderson being in one of those baskets. A retrieval van would have to make quick work of packing up the balloon for John to make it to lunch on time.

Even on gusty mornings, John, a master pilot, fearlessly took on the thermals. He understood probability as well as anyone and took to the air only when he felt it safe. Mary, his wife, saw little humor in his hanging the print of Brueghel's *Landscape with the Fall of Icarus* over their fireplace mantle. She had wanted to hang one of Bayeta's weavings there. John had insisted that a rug would only become sooty in that spot. "But," Mary countered, "what if it is Icarus who gets his wings singed?" Icarus had indeed soared too close to the sun, while peasants in the field ignored his fate. On a day like this John probably needed no reminder of fate, if one overreached. Adam's thoughts returned to the life of *Sorex vagrans*. The shared kinship of humans and shrews was a good starting point. John would appreciate that.

John's favorite print had always reminded Adam of J. Robert Oppenheimer's fate. Like Adam, John believed Oppenheimer was an inspired scientist. A native of New York, he was at home in the high desert of western New Mexico. Yet, it was there that he chose to "tickle the dragon's tail." The race to first-use was motivated by fear that overcame all objections. Day of Trinity, however, stunned

Oppenheimer. "I am become death, the shatterer of worlds." The fire ball rising up from the desert floor of Jornada del Muerto had told him that in an instant the world was changed forever, as had science itself. Was there no limit to be placed on knowledge? For some, physics had come to know sin. Oppenheimer had fled the desert, never to return.

Afterward, Oppenheimer had tried to promote a debate of means and ends. The temper of the time, however, was that science, all science, must focus on brave new frontiers, and the cold warriors dismissed any suggestions that caution be applied. John Sanderson was no cynic, but he had already expressed his concerns that Adam was not paying attention to unintended consequences.

In front of the Faculty Club, Adam waited for John to appear out of the turbulent flow of students rushing between classes. John spotted Adam first and waved. "You look great!"

"Unhealthy habits and strong drink, that's what keeps men fit. As for you, you look awful."

"Lowly slave to paperwork, that's me."

"John, you could have said no to the chairmanship. For someone with a lab to run, it is insane to take it on. What does Mary think of you being department chair?"

John pointed down the walkway. "Ask her yourself, once she's had a couple glasses of wine."

In her early forties, Mary looked fit and content. John never tired of telling friends how beautiful she was. It was as if he could not believe his own good fortune. Mary did have fine, strong features. An anthropologist, her face weathered and lined from years of fieldwork, she gave the appearance of one used to the feel of wind in her hair and dust on her clothes. Her tinted glasses disguised the intensity with which she surveyed the world about her. Her eyes, when she put aside her glasses, were like amber coals at the heart of a campfire and could catch and hold any man's gaze, even Adam's.

"Hello Mary. I am glad you are joining us."

"John almost didn't tell me it was today. He wanted you and Crystal all to himself."

"Nonsense!" John looked a bit embarrassed, "Actually, I was hoping Crystal would show up first. I would have spirited her off, leaving you two to fend for yourselves."

Mary hugged Adam and smiled mischievously. "Marrying Crystal saved many a marriage, you know. Even my John was under her spell."

Mary's jest was tongue-in-cheek, but it was not an idle one. John had once found himself captivated by Bayeta, though at a distance. As colleagues, Bayeta and Mary often sat on the same committees and became friends. As such, Mary sensed John's interest in Bayeta, not that she reciprocated. But when Mary introduced Bayeta to Adam, nature took its course.

"By the way, I ran into Crystal a little while ago. She was walking up Lomas Boulevard looking for a present for Alberto. She said to start without her. She'll be along."

The hostess led them to a table by the windows. Familiar faces called out greetings to John and Mary. Some, a surprising number, recognized Adam and greeted him as well. The show of attention was unexpected, even a little embarrassing to Adam.

It was Harold Masterson, a cell biologist, who came over to the table with a copy of the San Francisco Chronicle in hand. "Front page stuff this, Dr. Grant. Congratulations!" Adam asked to see the paper. Quickly scanning the headline, he admitted that he was surprised.

"It says that you're still on the Berkeley faculty," Masterson said with a knowing smile.

Adam shifted uncomfortably in his chair. "I've not stepped foot on that campus in five years." He finished scanning the paper and handed it back to Masterson. "Now I understand what Herman hinted at on the phone. How on earth did he know?"

Adam pushed his chair back and stood. Gripping the table, he steadied his balance. "I have a surprise in store for Herman." John looked puzzled, as did Masterson. "I'll tell you later, John." With that, Adam went looking for a phone.

<++++++++++>

An agitated wind gnawed at the deck railing beyond the dining room's windows of the Torrey Pines Golf Club. By noon the La Jolla cove had darkened as the wind whipped up an ominous froth, a rare event and one certain to spoil the day for hundreds of beachgoers. Looking grim, a cluster of golfers, having abandoned their carts at the edge of the green, stood idly in the hallway. On entering the dining room, Alexander Terman tried to shake off his mood brought on by the weather. The drive in from Palm Springs, never pleasant because of stop and go traffic on the interstates, was especially bad on this day, compounded by a massive pile-up at the interchange of I-10 and I-5. It was no time to be late. No time for the terrible sinus headache coming on. He braced himself, determined to keep to the business at hand, no matter the provocation to come.

"It looks like we are in for a blow." Without rising to greet him, William Henry Schwann put his papers down and stared at the grey, unsettled day beyond the windows. "That daughter of yours..."

"I talked to my daughter this morning," Alexander said, ignoring the slur. He would never have let it go unchallenged from another man. Schwann, however, was the exception. "She's very pleased with her fusion experiment. It is showing results." Schwann paid no notice. Alexander pressed the point. "I would not be surprised to see her making a headline or two before long."

"Fission or fusion, it makes no difference."

"Henry, there's a fortune to be made from..."

Schwann cut him off. "Do not address me in that manner," he snarled.

Alexander took a seat and waved to the waiter to pour coffee. For once, he had got under Schwann's skin. And, Schwann had not rattled him. It was a small victory, but a victory nonetheless.

"How much profit is in turbines, fuel assembly rods, shields, control room installations, and transmission systems that your companies produce? You should pay me more for the advice I give."

Their relationship had become strained of late, each apprehensive of the other's motives. Since Three Mile Island, no new plants had been licensed. Schwann had become burdened with his holdings in aging operating plants. Alexander's technical advice on reactor designs was of little use recently in an industry hampered by regulation, rising costs, safety problems, and maintenance and storage issues.

Schwann spilled his cup of coffee as he raised his hand to speak, "Well?"

"She had breakfast with Adam this morning. He is definitely in Albuquerque."

Staring out at the agitated pine branches scraping at the window, Schwann grimaced.

"She said he plans to take a late flight to San Francisco." The muscles in Schwann's face relaxed, but only slightly. Still, he said nothing. "Leave her out of it," Alexander grumbled. She knows nothing."

Schwann clenched his jaw, his mouth twisting into a bitter grimace. "What exactly did she say? I can't believe he has told her nothing. They are close"

"She knows nothing. Leave her out of this." Alexander had no intention of telling Schwann what Cynthia knew. Nor did he want to raise the matter of Schwann's involvement in the awarding of The Morgan Prize, one more manipulation, one more ploy to achieve his ends.

"The sooner he turns over his research to Herman the better. I want this settled before the end of the week. He'll take that damn prize and with it our thanks. That will be the end of it." Of course Schwann was behind Adam's selection as the recipient of The Morgan Prize, had been all along. But before that moment, Alexander had only guessed at it.

"Mind what I say, Alex, not one word about Genetrix, not one. I blame Herman for that mistake. I could have had the rights to all of his work, if only Herman had done what I told him to do. Your precious son would have come along willingly. Five years ago his ego was hurt. That's when to buy and sell the likes of him."

"Henry, we've been over this before. Yes, Adam's ego was bruised, but not so much as he would agree to any kind of exclusive contract. He would never do that, never. Herman could not have gotten far with him on that score. Besides, who knew?"

Schwann had already determined, before Alexander arrived, that Adam had to be dealt with once and for all. He had dismissed Adam as a talented but "screwed up idealist." The fact that he had run off to "hole up in the desert, married to that savage," was too much for Schwann to comprehend. But now Adam had something he wanted, something he had to have. He could not stand not possessing it, whatever the cost.

"What was it that half-breed assistant said? Dr. Grant is like an alchemist, a wizard. He can turn lead into gold if he puts his mind to it. Yes, that's how he put it. Well, he's conjured up something that I paid for. I will have it."

"I don't believe Mr. Atsidi used the word alchemist."

"Alchemist, fool, mad scientist, what's the difference?"

Schwann's temper was veering dangerously toward its extreme limit.

Alexander tried to deflect Schwann's spleen. "You should give Herman some credit for knowing that Adam has the touch. After all, he may well have succeeded where that institute full of assholes and puffers have not."

"Well, if that's so, that's a hundred million down the goddamn drain. Maybe, for once, Herman has picked a winner. So, Adam, your son, has put that whole complex full of half-cocked puffers to shame. For once, I believe Herman. My own people, not Herman's, confirm it."

"All right, Henry, I did not come all this way from Palm Springs to be raked over the coals." Alexander spoke as if, for once, he had the initiative. He was not his usual guarded self. "I'm due at the airport. Tell me what it is you want, so I can go."

"I've had some stupid reporter sent to Albuquerque. He's to get a read on your son's work. Damn fool! He had the nerve to call me to complain about being pulled off a puny story. When this is done, I will see that he's good and taken care of."

"Adam cares nothing for the press, Henry. Since he left Berkeley, what with that mess the papers made of his resignation, well, he just is not one to speak to press people."

"Alex, this reporter's specialty is science reporting." Schwann's eyes had not strayed from the weather's turmoil brewing out in the cove's waters. "He'll keep tabs. Then, if necessary, Anton will do for me."

"Anton?" Alexander stiffened in his chair. "What's Anton got to do with any of this?"

"Anton will see that he shows up at Evergreen. I want this, and I will have it…"

"You don't need to belabor the point, Henry."

"If you know what is good for you, and for both of your sons, do not fail me, Alex."

<++++++++++>

Anton Mueller existed to do William Henry Schwann's bidding. To say that he had a life of his own would be a gross overstatement. He had no ambition but the serve his master. Since his posting at The Evergreen Institute, he scrutinized every aspect of its security. As such, he knew the backgrounds and habits of the staff and associates, every last one. Every secret, the smallest venal weakness or one-time indiscretion, was exploitable. Mueller had handpicked the security guards, old-line toughs. Though told to be discreet, by nature he preferred direct, muscular methods. Although nominally an institute employee, everyone knew or suspected otherwise. It was dangerous to speculate about Mueller.

Soon after Anton Mueller took charge of security, Herman's deputy director, a brilliant neuro-physiologist, was the first to leave. Dr. Pearl had had no character flaw or dark past that Mueller could exploit. Even his thoughts about Herman Cockroft and his way of running things, he kept to himself. Anton Mueller, however, found a weakness. A stunningly beautiful laboratory assistant was put to intern in his lab. Dr. Pearl, a man with a frigid wife, did indeed have a need. It took the intern five weeks to lure him to her Berkeley apartment. He was desperate for affection and amazed that such a woman would find him attractive. Pearl succumbed. The next morning a messenger appeared at his office door with a plain manila envelope. The photos could not have been more devastating. A note was attached: "If you resign, these will not be posted. The choice is yours, Doctor."

Two security men found Dr. Pearl in the bathroom throwing up and hysterical. He left the building before noon, never to return. By 2:00 p.m. notice of his resignation was circulated. He was rumored to have flown to Europe with his Austrian-born wife and their two children. No one spoke openly of Dr. Pearl's resignation, or of Mueller's role, although the sudden departure of his attractive intern, last seen shaking hands with Anton Mueller the next day, fed the rumors for a while.

As unexplained as Dr. Pearl's leaving was, a more disturbing example of Mueller's methods occurred weeks later, and involved a security guard suspected by some of being a small time pusher. Over a period of months, the guard provided small quantities of cocaine to a number of staff members. Stationed at a side security gate, he could make an easy hand-off as an employee drove home at night. Occasionally, he could also deliver while making his rounds. Some transactions were videotaped, implicating a dozen people, including a promising endocrinologist. Schwann had little interest in exposing users. Why waste the leverage? A well-timed threat of exposure from Mueller would suffice when need arose.

Dr. Lloyd Simpson's cocaine use began simply enough. He often worked late in the lab, hoping to attract notice. The pressure to get results, however, led Simpson to use cocaine to fight off fatigue. His use became a daily thing. The guard, Guenther, kept him supplied and the price low.

Things began to unravel for the unfortunate endocrinologist when he violated institute policy. He had submitted a research paper for publication without first having it reviewed by the patent and publications officer. In frustration, he announced that he would shake free of the institute. What followed that evening was never adequately explained.

In the police report a janitor recalled Dr. Simpson entering the lab late at night, and as he cleaned the hall outside Simpson's office, he heard loud voices coming from the lab. The janitor thought a guard had entered a short time earlier. The guard, however, insisted that he was on rounds and did not see Dr. Simpson. He swore that he was at his desk in the lobby when the "event" happened. Had he heard anything? No, the guard insisted. In any case, he volunteered, he would not have heard anything hitting the ground beneath the window of Dr. Simpson's lab, as it was out of sight on the north side of the building. The window posed a problem for the police. A key was needed to open any window above the first floor. It was kept in a locked drawer at the security desk in the lobby.

Dr. Simpson's body was not discovered until 7:00 a.m. the next morning. A quarter ounce of cocaine was found in his lab coat pocket. The coroner's report listed Simpson's death accidental or suicide, by falling out of the fourth floor window. A month after the inquest, Guenther took a security job at Schwann and Company, San Diego. In the months that followed, many of those on Mueller's list, provided by guard Guenther, found reasons to resign. Rumors of each resignation took a toll on morale.

<++++++++++>

The more Adam Grant thought about the award, the more his mood changed. The cash award alone should have buoyed him. He told John that the amount was, as he put it, "a bit over the top." As for the selection committee's reasons, "Well, someone's hand has been jiggering, hasn't it?"

Just then, Bayeta entered the room and smiled as she joined the table.

"Adam, you look very…" Just then, she saw the newspaper on the table. "Herman was not exaggerating, then, was he? Well, my darling, you have earned it." Turning to John, "What do you think of our boy wonder, John?"

John was well qualified to gauge the merits of Adam's research. He had already agreed with Adam that two on the award short list had produced solid advances in cell biology at twice his rate.

With a puckish smile, John said, "Chock it all up to his impeccable taste in women,"

One of John's colleagues came by the table to pay respects. At a discrete distance, Anton Mueller watched with special interest. He trusted that he'd have a free hand to act, if need arose, when it arose.

Mueller, an immigrant from East Germany, was Teuton to the core, known by some as the "Little Prussian." Rumor had it that he had once worked for the STASI. Whatever the facts were, Mueller knew his craft well, like his father before him. Having grown up in a communist system, he learned what one must do to be a model servant to the state. Now, as Schwann's man, he had proved the perfect instrument. For the moment, constrained as he was, he gnawed at his pastry and watched.

"Yes, of course, it floors me," Adam admitted. "It also bothers me, being so out of proportion."

Mary was the first to react. "Alright, I'll bite. What have you done? Can you tell us about it?"

Adam wanted to let the matter rest.

Mary, however, had the scent. "What have you been up to?"

John tried to deflect the direction in which his wife was headed.

"Adam, my dear, has a charmed life. If I didn't know better, I'd say that he uses conjuring and spells to uncover what he's after."

Adam had been momentarily distracted by the staring look of a stranger at the back of the room. Had he seen the man earlier, seen him on the path? "I am sorry, Mary. What were you asking?"

John gave his wife a stern look.

But Mary would not be put off. "If you don't mind, John, I want Adam to tell us. No more beating around the bush." She turned back to Adam. "You are our dear friend, Adam. But, people do talk, you know. Every time you and Crystal come to Albuquerque, rumors start up again."

"Mary, what on earth do you mean?"

"Oh, you know how petty and envious academics can be. They possess curious natures, so they gossip. You live a hermetic life out there at Rimrock, yet, as a scientist you produce. It makes people wonder. Yes, it's a charmed life. Some say it is even unnatural. Others have to earn a living teaching and begging for grants, or go off to work for a corporation. They can't do what they really want. They are in a rat race just to keep their vitae fresh. But there you are. You answer to no one. You answer to no one and do as you please. It unsettles them."

"What do I care that others talk?"

John was uncomfortable with his wife's probing. "We should not pry, Mary."

"Look, at Rimrock we are not all that isolated. There is more to do than we can handle. If Bea felt otherwise, she would tell you. Just this morning, Bea got up at three wanting to string warp yarn before we left. I had to check on the animals and leave instructions for Martin. Even if we had another hundred years with no interruptions, there would not be enough time to finish what we have started."

"Crystal, do you feel as Adam does?" Mary had never accepted Crystal's claim that Rimrock was all her idea from the beginning. Crystal was once so involved with Albuquerque, with Mary, with teaching, and with students and friends. Mary still felt the loss of her friend's regular company.

"Mary, when I was here at the university, I painted. It was not possible for me to weave, not really. My Navajo self was starving. I painted. I worked in clay. But those things are only art. I used up all my time talking art and doing art. But I wanted to weave. Weaving is part of who I am. It is necessary in order to live. When at my loom, I am whole. In Albuquerque I felt less than whole. Yes, I miss my friends, especially you, but I saw no other way."

"You could not live here and weave? Adam could join the faculty and do his research."

"Can you imagine what it is like to sit at a loom and constantly hear traffic outside? The phone rings, and you stop what you are doing. At Rimrock everything I need is there. Our neighbor, Widow Tumecho, has a fine herd of churros. The yucca root to make soap with is outside my door. Every plant I need to dye with grows on the hills or down in the canyon. I am at peace there."

Adam reached across the table and kissed Bayeta's hand. "She's making a blanket for me. I am a willing captive for her loom."

"Crystal, I want to understand how much weaving matters to you. But is it enough?"

"Rimrock itself is a loom, heaven. It stands straight and free from the turmoil of modern life. There, we own our time. We do what is important, free of distractions."

Mary still had a perplexed look.

"Before Adam, before we met, I wasted so much time. As an art professor, classes and students took all my time. That's not the point. I had some time on my hands. I wasted it. I dated men who were not for me. I went shopping twice a week looking for things I did not need. I was at loose ends and lonely. If I had not met Adam, I would still have returned to the Res." John asked if she ever felt lonely at Rimrock. "Being alone is different than being lonely. Adam and I are together. We have Alberto. Martin is at the lab six days a week. People do come and visit, even you two."

"Adam, I hate concede the point. Obviously, the desert suits you two."

"It does. Nor are we out of touch with what is going on in the wider world. As for academia, I have had my fill of it. To be honest, I had no idea that things would turn out so well."

"I do wish you had stayed involved. I know you've never been political. You insist that a scientist must be judged only on the quality of the work product. The funding criteria at NSF and NIH are too restrictive. Too much depends on applied ends and corporate interests."

"John, sooner or later, I would have left. The pharmaceuticals and genetic engineering labs had been siphoning off my best graduate students. Christ, every time I turned around, I saw them becoming little more than paid apprentices to those damned puffers."

"Adam, we face the same thing here. We can't keep the recruiters off campus. Our best young faculty members are being lured away. They can't live on fifty or sixty thousand. They see their former students making twice that. Adam, I'd give anything to get you to come here. What do you say?"

For five years John had asked. Adam never said no outright. He did not want to hurt his friend's feelings. Both knew, however, that fifty percent of any grant went for administration. He lacked the tact and patience to put up with that, to say nothing of the oversight.

"Take a half-time appointment, one semester a year. We've got more than enough laboratory space and a stockroom full of unused equipment. Hell, with senior staff leaving, I'll have two empty labs by June. See Albert Merkl over there by the door?" Adam turned to look. "He's talking to NIH. He'll be gone. Jane Harmon, his wife, she's retiring early, says they want to travel."

Mary nodded. "Jane's actually in Bethesda this week looking at houses. She insists that Al is undecided. If so, why did she cancel her classes for the week and go to D.C.?"

John had a stressed look just talking about it. "Both Henderson and Burns are up for tenure. I'm not even trying to argue Merkl out of his decision because we need his tenure slot. With the freeze on hiring, I have to threaten to slit my wrists just to get one of them tenured."

"If you have a hiring freeze, why try to add me to the mix?"

"For you, I can handle the dean, even the vice president. Besides, with the publicity that goes with The Morgan Prize, you can come through the door writing your own ticket."

"John, let's just say that I will think about it."

"Please. You can't hide away in the desert forever. No one knows what you are cooking up in your lab. You stay cooped up out there like a hermit. Sure, you do good research and you publish. But you are not making friends by keeping yourself aloof. They envy your freedom."

"I must be free of constraints. The institute has been generous and has not imposed restraints. They seem well satisfied." John stiffened. Adam patted his arm. "I know you are a critic of The Evergreen Institute, John. But, they have been good to me."

"If you thought about it, really thought about it, you'd have concerns, Adam."

Bayeta gripped John's arm. "What are you implying, John?"

Adam was beginning to look defensive. "I've had no trouble in five years."

John then softened his tone. "Adam, nothing is free, not any more. There are strings. You just don't see them. It is all too neat."

John had met Herman Cockroft but once, prowling the halls of a conference in San Francisco. He did not like him. Why Adam dismissed him as harmless was beyond him. Adam made no secret of his dislike for Herman. He detested him. So, why did he have this blind spot?

Bayeta had her own reasons for agreeing with John. She tried to change the subject. Finally, Adam regained his balance. "John, I'll be careful. I don't intend to scorch my wings. The sun is close enough as it is, thank you."

"Please think about my offer, just one semester a year, four or five months, no more."

With lunch served, conversation turned to catching up on friends.

As they all got up to leave the dining room, Mary went on ahead with Crystal. "I know Adam will listen to you. John is worried, thinks Adam is, as he puts it, 'tickling the dragon's tail.' John knows things. He distrusts The Evergreen Institute." Bayeta nodded but said nothing.

<++++++++++>

Alexander Terman could not recall Adam agreeing with a thing he did or said. He tried, in his own way, to avoid argument. The gulf between father and son had remained unbridgeable for thirty years. By his sixteenth birthday, Adam had grasped his father's role in the "defense of the nation." He would not listen to any reasons for needing an arms race.

Alexander's character and disposition were Lutheran to the core, tempered by a personal ambition to take part in shaping the terrifying power of a nuclear-armed military. Within the theoretical section at Los Alamos, he made no secret of his distrust of a lasting peace or stable relations with the Soviets. For her part, Eleanor did not hide her abhorrence of Alexander's role. The very place she called home had been turned into a "frightful, queer playground." Jornada del Muerto, the Apaches ancient hunting ground for pronghorn, had become a death's tract. In defense, Alexander quoted a New York Times reporter who witnessed the first test: "How was such a creative force born in such a place, fit alone for Apache, a few miners, and ranchers?" Alexander was proud of the phrase, "creative force." "Let there be light," the reporter proclaimed. "On that moment hung eternity. Time stood still. Space contracted to a pinpoint." Trinity was the most important event in Alexander's life. He would never again feel so god-like.

Clinging to the thought of his great moment, so long dead, Alexander stared out at the angry weather beyond the Torrey Pines Golf Club windows. The heat of the air in the room reminded him of that long ago day with malignant precision. He now harbored a secret admission: He should have listened to Oppenheimer. If he had, he would never have met Schwann.

Alexander regretted his alienation from his son, Adam. It was his fault. He knew that. Things could have been different. He had once wanted to work on proximity fuses or microwave radar. With a sense of irony, he compared Adam to William Henry Schwann, Jr. Had the boy lived, he would have become a perfect adjunct to William senior. Schwann had labored toward that day when his son would take the helm. But, with the boy's diagnosis of Huntington's disease at age 17, Schwann was denied his wish. Schwann divorced his wife, blaming her faulty genes. The "flaw" could not have come from him, not him.

It never crossed Schwann's mind that his son might not have turned out to be as ruthless, as malignant, and as dangerous as he was. He had had such plans for the boy. When the first signs of the illness appeared, as slight, involuntary movements in his facial muscles and fingers, Schwann denied it was anything more than growing pains. The tremors progressed to his hands, toes, and shoulders. His face became twisted and grotesque, a fixed, macabre expression that signaled that the boy was going mad. Near the end, each attack began in an arm or a leg, intensified, and spread to the whole body. He was consumed by an unending, torturous unwinding. The "dance macabre" proved too much for the father. Schwann fled at the first sign of each onset, unwilling to watch. He was helpless, embarrassed, embittered. After six years of home care, Schwann had the boy put in a nursing home. Within months he was dead, the cause of death listed as pneumonia.

In light of his son's death, William Henry Schwann resented Adam, resented that he lived "a charmed life." Adam had good health and an exceptional mind. The alienation between Alexander and his son mattered not in the least to Schwann, except as a means to demean Alexander when it suited.

Schwann believed history was governed by blood, a commanding force that pitted men against each other. Born the son of an undistinguished provincial branch of the Schwann family, he claimed nobility. His grandfather insisted that his lineage stretched back to the German knights who ruled an Estonian duchy. Schwann, like Alexander, grew up anti-Russian and Lutheran. This was the tie that bound both men. It was a bond Schwann could trust, could put to use.

Alexander Terman, son of Ernst and Friida Jogeva, unlike Schwann, was heir to seven centuries of subject status, a trait that ran deep. Estonian children were taught the rigid division between master and servant. Alexander grew up fearing Prussians and Russians. In the Jogeva family, survival was the highest good. They felt inferior to Prussians. William Henry Schwann was Prussian to the core, a true Junker, one destined, ironically, to dominate Alexander.

Fingering the rim of his coffee cup, a sullen mood overtook Alexander. He stared out at the Torrey pines recoiling from the strong gusts of wind beating against the windows. He wished that he had never seen the Pacific Ocean. It was nothing like the shores of his homeland, nothing.

"Americans have no sense of history, Alex. Leave the masses to their TVs and shopping malls. That is all they want or need. Keep them content in their ignorance. Destiny is in our hands, not theirs. We give it meaning. We shape it. We control it." Schwann's tone was oddly confidential and inclusive. Alexander but half-listened. It would be dangerous to argue. Let Schwann spout his tired, stale, Nietzsche sermonizing, whatever his purpose.

But he could take no more of it. "Henry, I am tired of hearing it. I know it by heart." Schwann gave him a hard look. Alexander took a deep breath and regained his sense of caution. "Yes, of course. We are all sinners in the hands of an angry God. Man is born of and for sin."

"Alex, you need to take better care of yourself. You look tired. Lately, you have become argumentative. I find that tiresome. Perhaps, you do need a rest, a good, long rest."

"Your concern is touching, Henry. There will be time enough for the worms."

"Don't be sarcastic! It does not suit you. We're cut from the same cloth, you and me."

Alex raised his hand as if to object. "All I ask is that you leave my son out of it."

"Herman? You lost him long ago. He's vain and weak. He serves me well enough. So long as he does, he need have no worries."

"You bought and paid for him just as you did me."

"He was easily seduced."

"I don't want to hear it."

"Schwann took in a deep breath. "As for Adam, I don't give a damn about him. He can go his own way. But this discovery, well, that is a different matter entirely. I paid for it. I will have it. He will turn this over to Herman, and that will be the end of it, a fair exchange."

"Henry, he is not about to turn it over, not to you."

"That would be a pity. Don't you agree?"

In a dull, flat tone, Alexander responded, "Do not count on me to influence him. He is not one to listen to me. He never has done so."

Demands and veiled threats continued. Alexander pretended to listen. But it was the weather beyond the windows that absorbed him. The La Jolla cove stretched seaward, its arms gathering in the approaching storm. He wished that his life had turned out differently. What if he had never left Estonia, never heard of physics? He would have chosen a quiet life, if only. But he knew better. Fear had compelled him to flee his homeland. Ambition drove him toward science, physics, and ultimately to Los Alamos. And, why into Schwann's orbit, a natural born predator, why did he get involved with the man, why?

Schwann continued to hammer away. Alexander pretended to listen. What else could he have done? He remembered the day when Adam irrevocably turned against him. Eleanor had had the advantage, had mixed reason with emotional content. She had raised Adam to think that way. Then, that day came when his girlfriend's father appeared at the house. His son's attack was withering. How was Alexander to know that the girl's father, Dr. Urikami, was that Urikami?

Adam knew that Nancy's parents had been interned at Manzanar until the end of the war in 1945. Born at Manzanar in 1945, Nancy was born a prisoner. It was but cold comfort to the Urakami family that an atomic weapon helped free Japanese-Americans from imprisonment. Her father insisted that he would have chosen continued captivity, if it meant no first use of the atomic bomb.

The Grant family lived a few blocks down the street from the Urikami home. Nancy's father often came by to pick her up before dinner. That day her family had planned to observe Day of Trinity after dinner to reflect on the first use of the atomic bomb. Dr. Norman Urakami, a committed pacifist, wanted his children to share his commitment to the abolition of atomic weapons. Yes, he knew who the twins' father was. That did not cause him worry over Nancy's feelings for Adam Grant. Indeed, Mrs. Urakami had developed a friendship with Eleanor Grant. Her weavings, displayed at Eleanor's gallery, sold well. White Cranes flying over snow-topped Mt. Fuji was a favorite image. The two did not speak of the internment at Manzanar. The Urakamis needed the income, and Eleanor took pains to promote her artwork. She considered Fumiko a friend.

On that day, at six, Norman Urakami stopped by the Grant house to pick up his daughter. She and Adam had become inseparable. He harbored a private qualm, but believed that young love seldom survives the test of time. Let nature take its course, he told his wife. On that hot, late afternoon, however, everything changed. Walking up the path, Dr. Urakami saw Alexander Terman standing at the bottom of the porch. Staring in disbelief, he recognized him immediately. Until that moment, he had repressed his feelings towards Terman. With steeled determination, he ignored Alexander Terman and called out to Nancy.

Nancy and Adam had been alone in the ramshackle shed at the back of the house, the "museum" for his desert fossils, plant specimens, and science projects. She loved everything that interested him. Nancy was the loveliest creature Adam had ever seen. It took all his will to keep from kissing her until his lips were bruised and blistered. They held hands, kissed, and talked.

"Why does my dad call you and Cynthia the 'Trinity Twins', Adam?"

"People talk too much. Besides, it really has nothing to do with us."

"Can't you tell me?"

"I suppose I can. Only, please don't talk about it to others."

Nancy agreed.

"It reminds Mother of the war. Father was supposed to be with her when we were born. The night before, she had to call Father Thomas to take her to the hospital. Father was away, at the big test. Only, she didn't know that. It was a secret. When Dr. Michaels delivered us, he told mother that just as we were being born the bomb went off. He did not know it then, only that there was this big flash of white light that flooded the delivery room. He said that he almost dropped one of us on the floor when it happened. Later, he claimed that we were the first children born in the atomic age. He was proud of being the doctor who delivered us. He's the one who first called us "The Trinity Twins."

"Do you see your father often?"

"Father was supposed to come for our birthday. When he does, mother will get one of her headaches. It lasts until he leaves. It's always the same."

Nancy gripped his hand tightly. "I have a secret, too. I don't know if I should tell you."

"We should not have secrets. Kiss me." He held her and kissed her.

At length, she drew away. "My father was at Berkeley. He knows some of the scientists who went to Los Alamos. We're not supposed to talk about that, either. We, too, have secrets."

Adam let her drop the subject. She wanted only to imagine what it would be like to be his. But before she could say what was in her heart, she heard her father calling for her from the front of the house. She squeezed his hand and smiled. "Will I see you later?"

At the beginning of the war, Dr. Urakami was an up-and-coming radiologist. Radiological science was in its infancy. Potential medical uses had only begun to be recognized. Importantly for Norman Urakami, radiology was one of the few specialties open to a scientist with an Asian-American background. At the Lawrence laboratory his future looked bright indeed.

Within weeks of Pearl Harbor, however, FBI agents came for him. He had already been denied access to the Cyclotron Lab, over the objections of Seaborg and Perlman. None of the many letters vouching for his loyalty and talents made a difference. War hysteria had swept the west coast.

By late 1944, unknown to the interned Dr. Urakami, the scientists at Los Alamos concluded that a test was necessary in the coming months. Germany was near military collapse. Attention was shifting to the war in the Pacific. Little was known of the effects of radiation on animals or humans. Norman Urakami was one of the few who had any knowledge of its effects. But, as an intern at Manzanar he would not have the chance to take part in or even discuss the potential dangers of radiation.

When the camps emptied at the end of the war, the Urakami family made their way to Albuquerque. He stood no chance of reinstatement at Berkeley. A position with the radiation section at Los Alamos was offered him. But he did not accept. The bomb dropped on Nagasaki contained plutonium. His ancestral family roots were there, in Nagasaki. Generations of Urakamis had worked in the iron factories. They were Catholic. They had opposed the militarist faction in pre-war Japan. He abandoned any thought of working at Los Alamos. Father Thomas secured a position for him to teach science at the Catholic high school.

Fumiko Urakami was born into the Hiroshige clan, the daughter of a renowned weaver. Her mother's tapestry depicting Mt. Fuji had been displayed at the World's Fair on Treasure Island, San Francisco, before the war. Fumiko's mother was a casualty of Nagasaki.

At the end of the conflict, Dr. Urakami still harbored hopes of contributing to research on the peaceful uses for radioactive elements. But, he had not reckoned on men like Vannevar Bush, who promoted what they called "best science." Bush and the atomic establishment accepted, even promoted, a regime infused with secrecy and security. Physicists had become the elite of modern science. The military's priorities dominated research agendas as the Cold War set in. Talk of peaceful uses for the atom were abandoned. Those who objected, like Dr. Urakami, ended up teaching high school science.

Then, in 1960, after so many years, he saw Dr. Terman on Eleanor Grant's front stoop. An involuntary shudder ran through his body. Rage rose up in Dr. Urakami's mouth. He stammered, "You! You and that Teller! You two have dragged the world down with you, your madness!"

Terman had recognized Dr. Urakami. He had direct knowledge of his case, of his being listed as a security risk. Terman had harbored an unspoken aversion to working with foreign scientists, even though that was what he, himself, was. He never liked Fermi or almost any of the "foreigners" on the Manhattan Project. Such men had qualms about using atomic weapons. As for Nagasaki, Terman knew perfectly well that military considerations had never entered the picture, not seriously. To him, the bomb was an object lesson for the Soviets, not Japan, which was on the verge of total collapse, even before Hiroshima. No technical demonstration was required. Stalin needed an object lesson. Terman believed that the Soviets would invade the whole of Europe, including Estonia, his homeland.

The afternoon when Norman Urakami returned for the last time to the Grant house, two days after his encounter with Terman, it was 109 degrees. His nerves were raw and agitated from lack of sleep. As he wiped sweat from his hatband, he apologized for coming unannounced. Eleanor asked him to come in and have a glass of cold lemonade. He thanked her, but declined. She would understand, he said softly, his eyes riveted on the porch's wood steps. Race had no part in it, he said. Their children could not continue their friendship. He bowed and took his leave.

Eleanor was speechless. She refused to believe that the sins of the father could devolve to her son. The war was over and done with. But the damage had been done. No explanations, no apologies could mend the breach.

When Nancy asked her father why she was not to see the Grant boy, he told her about the burn wards. He had read the technical reports of the effects of radiation on the victims of Hiroshima and Nagasaki. No proper treatment protocols existed. Many died because of ignorance, not intent. More troubling to Dr. Urakami was the implication in the reports that physicists viewed the victims as objects of study. They were preoccupied with charting the severity of radiation exposure and survival rates. The reports gave matter-of-fact details of how men, women, and children slowly and painfully died as they burned up from the inside out. No one knew how to help them. Radiation poisoning was a new phenomenon. It was believed that once exposed there was little that could be done. The pain could be masked with opiates. Worst of all, the law forbade members of the Atomic Bomb Casualty Commission to treat victims. They were to observe, record, and remain uninvolved.

Nancy Urakami stopped seeing Adam immediately. Adam, hurt and confused, lonely for his lost Nancy, demanded to know why. Eleanor tried to explain. "You know that your father made bombs, Adam. He tested bombs. He made bigger bombs, better bombs. He tested ever bigger bombs."

"But what does Nagasaki have to do with any of that," he asked her.

"It was unnecessary to bomb Nagasaki," she told him. "Yes, some objected. They were against first use. I knew some of them. Oppenheimer and Szilard argued for a technical demonstration in the Sea of Japan. Most of those at the Metallurgical Lab in Chicago, Franck, Bohr, Hans Bethe, even Wilson opposed using the bomb to end the war. Japan was within days of collapse, we now know. The nuclear arms race is terrifying. Teller, your father's boss, had to have his "super" bomb. Anyone who objected was labeled a communist."

Before his sixteenth birthday, a relationship with his father might have been possible. Adam had harbored a need to feel good about what his father did. He needed a father figure. But Alexander Toomas Jogeva, Lutheran to the core, believed in election and predestination. All men sinned. When he left Albuquerque in 1945, he accepted that his children would grow up knowing little of his role in making bombs. Eleanor would see to that. He willingly chose destiny over marriage and family.

<++++++++++>

On their way to the lecture hall in the biology building, John challenged Adam to abandon his usual lecture. "Why not wing it, see what happens?"

Adam had the same idea. He had brought along a PowerPoint program, excerpts of what he planned for San Francisco. "Great idea, John, let's do it."

John called the room to order and began his introduction. "I am pleased to welcome all of you to this, the sixth colloquium in our spring series. The subject for today…"

Absorbed with re-organizing his PowerPoint slides, Adam smiled mischievously. John continued: "Our subject for today is *Sorex vagrans*: Our Least Known Relative." A brief chuckle rose from the audience. "You may well ask what is *Sorex vagrans*? What has such a tiny mammal to do with today's frontier in experimental biology? In a word, *Sorex* vagrans has provided Dr. Grant the key to his research on aging at the cell level. By no means is Dr. Grant an alchemist, yet, in Sorex vagrans, has found his familiar, his guide into the spirit world of the cell."

John could not contain how pleased he was with his own impromptu turn of phrase. But, enough of gilding the lily, he thought. "Dr. Adam Grant is this year's recipient of The Morgan Prize. His impressive body of research is too long to list. His work on unraveling the role enzymes play in cell regulation is unparalleled. To fathom the depths of cell function and viability over time is essential to understanding how humans age." John turned to Adam and whispered, "I wanted to make sure they knew how important you are."

Adam blushed as he took his place and adjusted the podium's microphone. He took time to frame his opening remarks. As the lights dimmed, he saw that the students had note pads at the ready.

"Today, you won't need to take notes." They chuckled again. Most put down their pens and pencils. Adam pressed the button and the first image appeared. It was a view of Canyon de Chelly, at its confluence with Canyon del Muerto. Rising from the canyon's floor, a magnificent layered stone spire loomed before them. Adam winked at Bayeta, who sat to the side in the front row. She understood. He called it nature's walled cathedral. Widow Tumecho's hogan was the next image he selected, her cherished Churros in view. "I give you a golden hour..."

6

Future Tense Dreams

The great beast's nostrils flared. His steamy breath fouled the air. His glinting, leaden gray, ironclad hooves struck the unyielding pavement stones. The great beast lunged into its traces, straining against rigid, forge-tempered bonds. The whip cracked over his bulging, riveted hindquarters. This five-ton hulk, a tinker's fevered work, eyed the gathering crowd. The coachman's inflamed lashing yet unbidden; no man dared to stand ground before it. "A beast from Hell," a voice whispered. "Aye, Hell's Horse," a second affirmed. The coachman cocked his lame ear and declared, "Nay, tis' The Future!"

A placard was riveted to the carriage door with bold black letters proclaiming: "No feed. No cost. No will. No rest." All swore there was a fearful captive energy surging and sparking through those wrapped and bound steel sinews. This was a construct to marvel. Of bellowed lungs, steeled ribs, well-tempered joints, and cold-rolled skin, such a marvel was for the ages, ageless. The coachman, how well and true he held the reins. His eyes had the glint of grim resolve in them.

The coachman stood and grandly waved. "Come closer. Observe this wonder, this great and magnificent electrified steed. Observe how finely wrought this steel-framed slave. The future awaits YOU! Step up! The price is but a pittance. Cash only. No credit. No half-fares. No free ride. Who will be the first to step aboard? You will be carried into the bright future, in full comfort, mind you!"

The beast, stayed only by the coachman's firm restraint, stood inert. Like-minded men of means pressed forward and mounted the carriage. "The road ahead is straight and level," barked the coachman. With willing charges seated, the coachman gripped the reins, cracked his whip. "Imagine! What wonders await you!" The giddied passengers begged haste. "On to the future!"

On command, this great beast's welded, plated shoulders tensed. Discordant scraping, metal-against-metal, cleaved the expectant air. With two cold, dead eyes fixed to the distant horizon, the beast wrenched free of its station. Passengers howled as one: "On to the future!"

From the curb, a lone boy waved farewell and turned his back. He had but a pebble to pay his fare, no coin. He gripped his pebble, a beautiful, but worthless thing, and tossed it over his shoulder.

A desperate cry of disbelief rose up from the expectant crowd. Mouths fell slack-jawed in confusion. Who among them had hurled that stray pebble that nicked the flank of that great, armor-plated beast. There was no cause. Lurching unbalanced to one side, the great lumbering beast, The Future, did stumble, did strike the pavement, instantly devolving into chaos and flying sparks. This wonder spilled out its anguished charges and settled on the cobbled path—dissembled, disemboweled, a heap of plated steel, wires, failed rivets. The confused coachman struggled to his feet, his whip still in hand. "Who dares such a deed?" The exposed clockwork innards whirred, wheezed, and wound down, drowning out the coachman's protests. The pedestrian mob curbside laughed and shuffled near to comprehend. "How quickly its balance is thrown," said an old man. At the edge of the crowd, another man patted the boy's head. "That creature will not again stand. Thank God." He smiled down at the boy. "Spun of unnatural ambition, such a thing was bound to end that way."

Someone was shaking Adam's shoulder. "We're here, Doctor. It's time to get off." With the dregs of his dream melting away, Adam tried to stand, only to slip back down into his seat. The other passengers continued up the aisle. As he gathered his senses, he inventoried the outline of his dream. This time, for the first time, he thought he had sensed the whole of it. Before, each time he woke from the dream, he recalled only fragments, seldom the same ones. But now, had he the whole of it?

The man who had sat next to him again shook his shoulder.

"Oh, it's you, Mr. Ryder? Forgive me. I'm still a bit uncoordinated in my legs. You go on ahead. I'll catch up with you in the baggage area. We can talk there."

At carousel 4, Adam spotted Ryder. The last bags were coming off the conveyer belt. "Forgive me for ignoring you. I was tired and just could not stay awake."

"You did look dog-tired. If you can, I'd still appreciate a story." It was the fourth time the reporter had asked. "Dr. Grant, I can, if you prefer, keep it under my hat for a day or two. I promise."

"It's not that I don't want to give you something, Mr. Ryder, it's just that..."

"Look, it's obvious that there's a story here. Tomorrow, or the next day, you will be surrounded by the press. I could use a good story. Why not give me something now?"

"All right, but promise me you won't print it until the award ceremony. I need time."

"Agreed, if, that is, it is an exclusive."

Adam lowered his voice. "I've been working on something for five years, a work not published or talked about before now. Is it significant? I dare to say that it is."

From the public address system, Adam heard his name. He was being paged. He excused himself and walked to the phone on the wall to take the page. Ryder, meanwhile, found his bag and also retrieved Adam's. Returning to where Ryder waited, Adam apologized. "I am sorry. It seems that the Institute has sent a driver to pick me up and deliver me to their guesthouse. I have other plans, but..."

"You don't have family here to meet you?"

"No. Well, I do have family here, sort of. My father is in his eighties. He's not the sort to come and fetch me at an airport. Then there's Herman, my half-brother. He sent the limo."

Ryder saw the sardonic twist of Adam's mouth. "You and your brother are not close."

"For someone I've just met, you do pick up on things, don't you?"

"It's in my nature, Doctor. I am a reporter. Remember?"

"Well, Herman is Herman. We don't agree on things, that's all."

"Okay, so you are not close. No story in that. Your father, however, is THE Dr. Alexander Terman, the physicist? Why not tell me about him? What influence did he have on you?"

Adam was having second thoughts about talking about his research. The diversion would give him time to reconsider.

"He once wanted to be a biologist. Science was the only way for an ordinary man to rise above his class. He grew up in Estonia, but Germany was where one had to go if he wanted to become a scientist. Schleiden and Schwann, two men who helped establish modern cell biology, were German. But then, one of his schoolteachers in Tartu saw him on the street one day and gave him a copy of Einstein's 1905 paper. He thought Alexander would want to read it. It was so compelling, how energy, mass, and motion came together. Having read H.G. Wells, he immediately saw a connection. He determined to become a physicist, to be a part of that new world. Einstein's science made H.G. Wells' world real. The atom could be harnessed. Then the Great War intervened. Depression followed. Reluctantly, he gave up on the idea of a German university."

Why Alexander Jogeva had left Eastern Europe was plain enough. The Germans, Russians, Poles, and Swedes had all occupied Estonia. Too few people and undefended borders made his homeland a backwater. Walking the streets of Tartu, listening to "My Fatherland Is My Love," he found the fear of Russians sweeping back into the country was unbearable. Seven hundred years of vassalage had stripped Estonia of hope. At age seventeen before the first frost, Alexander Jogeva emigrated. His father gave him a small sum, enough to get him to London. He never saw his homeland again.

Alexander never spoke of the early years after emigrating, except in the vaguest terms. He had enrolled in London University and took a degree in early 1926. He moved on to Cambridge as an associate at the Cavendish Laboratory. He changed his name to Terman. His English by then was so fluid that few could tell that he had not grown up in England. It was there, in Ernest Rutherford's lab, that Alexander Terman, the once street urchin of Tartu, saw his future.

At Cavendish, Lord Rutherford served as midwife to the new science, nuclear physics. On an experimental "bench" little more than an assemblage of three tables, a low filing cabinet, a row of shelving, and an odd assortment of hand-made apparatuses attached to wires, dials, gauges, and glass, the atom was first split in 1917, revealing for the first time the proton. The chaotic mass of wires strewn overhead and attached to electrical posts seemed fanciful. But to Alexander that research "bench" was the future, straight out of a Wells novel. Rutherford had described the atom much as the solar system with satellite particles circling a nucleated center. At last, physics had a model to work with, a means to explore radioactive elements, and, ultimately, to make an atomic bomb.

Another physicist said of the atom that it "lay like a jewel unbroken and unworn." Rich in theories, physics needed the means to probe further through experimentation. There had to be a way to pry it open. Alexander's talent for constructing experimental equipment soon attracted notice. A born tinker, Alexander helped to translate abstract concepts into material proofs with the devices he constructed. By June of 1936, he had come to the notice of Compton in Chicago. A position was created for the young "Cavendish Mechanic." Alexander left Europe, never to return.

Donald Ryder had listened patiently to the sketch of the life of Alexander Terman. But, Adam Grant was being evasive about his own work.

Before Ryder could redirect their talk, Adam heard his name called. The opportunity, for the moment, was lost.

"Adam, there you are! How are you, my boy?" Through the crowd strode Jonathan Hardesty, his mentor and friend. Adam, surprised, turned on his heels. "Has it been five years?"

"Jonathan, what a wonderful surprise!"

"Adam, you look exactly the same. Life, I can see, agrees with you." Adam returned the compliment.

Objectively, Jonathan Hardesty looked fit and vigorous. "I feel tip-top since my by-pass, ten years younger, in fact. God! How I hated feeling old."

"I planned to call you first thing in the morning. Bea sends her love."

Motioning to Donald Ryder, the three men retreated to a quiet corner. Adam introduced Ryder to Hardesty as a science reporter.

"So, Adam travels with his own press these days?"

"He rates it, Dr. Hardesty. I have been trying to get a story out of Dr. Grant. He's been spinning stories about his father instead. He is an elusive quarry, an artful dodger."

"Ah, yes. But, Alexander Terman is a most interesting subject." Hardesty sounded slightly agitated at the mention of Adam's father. He turned back to Adam.

"The news of the Morgan has the department buzzing. Congratulations." Ryder nodded appreciatively. "He was the best student I ever had. He's done more good science than any five of my former students."

The expression on Ryder's face was electric. He had suddenly made the connection. "Of course, you are **The** Dr. Hardesty, a Nobel Laureate!" He reached out again to shake his hand. "I did a piece on you five years ago. There was a huge stink about research oversight at Berkeley. You made quite a speech defending academic freedom. You said that university based research was in danger of becoming a slave to business and corporate interests."

"Yes, something of the sort." Hardesty's expression was strained. "It was a difficult time."

"Wasn't Dr. Terman also interviewed on TV, an opposing opinion?"

Adam interrupted, "Yes, my father interfered. We were defeated, in part because of him."

"I'll be damned if it isn't a small world. Wheels inside wheels in academia, isn't it?"

Before Ryder could pursue his new line of interest, a young man in a chauffer's uniform approached. He identified himself and reached for Adam's bag. "My instructions are to take you directly to the guesthouse at the institute."

"I appreciate it very much. However, my friend and I have different plans."

"I am sorry, Dr. Grant. But my orders are quite explicit. The Director instructed me to see to it that you arrive safely. The Director will be very upset if I do not deliver you, sir."

"Young man: How old are you?" Adam was not inclined to obey. The driver was twenty-one. "And, how old do you think Dr. Hardesty is? Or better still, myself, if you prefer?" The driver hesitated. "Never mind; the point is that we are all of the age of consent. Your service is not needed."

Jonathan seconded Adam's decision. "Dr. Grant and I have some catching up to do. I'll see to it that he arrives safely at his destination."

The young man persisted. He had his orders.

"Look," Adam insisted, "I am not coming with you. However, this is Mr. Ryder. He's booked in at the Claremont. I'd like you to drop him off on your return to the institute. As for me, I'll find my own way. Is that clear?" With no other option open to him, the driver nodded compliance.

Adam shook Ryder's hand. "Buy me breakfast. I'll give you a real story then."

Ryder followed the driver out the door. Adam admitted to Jonathan that he was relieved. He had no intention of giving an account of his work on the fly. "You and I do need to talk."

"Adam, you've just had a taste of Institute subtlety."

"Jonathan, I see that murky dismal coming on. Don't go fey on me before we reach town."

"I'll buy you a drink and bring you up to date on the goings on here."

"Good. First, the Buena Vista, then we'll walk over to Scoma's for black cod and oysters."

On the drive into the city, Jonathan talked about problems facing the university. Although retired, he remained involved in political and economic issues that affected research. It was his passion. Adam nodded off before Jonathan turned onto the Embarcadero. A hard rain was thinning out the Thursday night crowd in and around Fisherman's Wharf. A parking space miraculously appeared two doors down from the Buena Vista on Beach Street.

"Adam, you didn't hear a word that I said."

"I'm sorry. I know how important it is to you, Jonathan. You and John are just alike."

"Sanderson is a good man. You do know he really needs you in Albuquerque. He's only talking one term out of the year, a few months. He needs someone like you on his side. Things there are not yet too far gone in his department. He can also use some help with the Coalition."

"So it was John who phoned and told you I was coming."

"He phoned. He told me that you need looking after."

"John worries too much."

"If he says you need looking after, you do. I do know a thing or two about your quest."

Entering the Buena Vista, Adam spotted a window table that was free. Hardesty ordered wine. It had been five years since Adam had been in San Francisco. As they settled in, Adam broached Jonathan's concern.

"You know my passion for cell regulation and aging. The key is at the cell level. You thought it was not a promising direction for me to go in. The Methuselah Strain you called it. Well, progeria provided a connection, quite by accident. Progeria is classic Mendel, an autosomal recessive. It took a lot to decode a healthy cell's aging cycle.

"Jonathan, what really got me going was the case of a woman named Megan Casey. Today, she is 29 years old, near death, but she has lived 29 years with progeria. Talk about an anomaly! Figure the median age at thirteen point four. You always said to look for the outlier and not ignore it. I saw how devastating a single gene mutation can be. Progeria is not just the deficiency of growth hormone or increases in heat-labile enzymes or altered proteins. The protein defect leads back to cells in the anterior lobe of the pituitary. I found an inverted insertion in the gene sequence. An idea came to me. What if I could mediate gene regulation in healthy cells?"

"Adam, have you found a cure for progeria?"

Adam sat back to finish his wine. His look was one of defeat. "How I wish." Hardesty had steered toward a sensitive personal matter. "No, but I have found the means for retarding the aging process in the average, healthy human being."

Hardesty's head jerked involuntarily. He tried to shake off the vertigo flooding his consciousness. For almost a minute neither spoke. Both stared out the window towards Alcatraz Island with the rain bouncing up from the street. Finally, Hardesty raised his head and stiffened his back.

"Adam, after all we went through years ago? You went ahead anyway?"

Staring at the tourists braving the rain along Beach Street, Adam nodded. "Jonathan, what happened five years ago is history. Thinking back, it is, and was then, irrelevant."

"I don't agree. Yes, the committee was narrow-minded in its rejection of your position. Still, there is need for responsible oversight. One can't just go off and do science these days without it. I gather you did, anyway, in that hermetically sealed laboratory you put together. I told you then and I tell you now, science cannot be done in secret. You have to allow others to have a voice."

Adam cleared his throat to object, but Hardesty waved him off. "What has always concerned me is that science can bring on unanticipated ends, unwanted consequences."

"Jonathan, I put my lab together with trust monies Alexander set up for me. Some foundation money also came to me. I do not have to have a damn committee to answer to."

"That's not the point. Without oversight and review, one could open Pandora's box."

No one else could speak so bluntly to Adam about his work. Jonathan, however, had trained and directed Adam's graduate experience. He had molded, disciplined, and sharpened Adam's native acumen. He had also tried to teach Adam to avoid shortcuts and to clearly define his goals. Adam, however, had little patience for restraint and caution. His passion for research carried with it a kind of blindness to limits. So promising was Adam as a graduate student that Hardesty looked on him as the son he never had. The old enzyme sleuth had found in Adam a kindred spirit, his intellectual heir. His one daughter wanted nothing but a quiet, ordered life. Marriage and children were everything to her.

The rain had stopped: a chance to walk over to Scoma's. "Five years is too long to go without good seafood. The usual fare in Albuquerque or Flagstaff is frozen salmon or frozen halibut steak. On occasion crab or lobster can be had, but Bayeta does not like either one."

On entering Scoma's, they saw that it was crowded. The line of waiting diners looked daunting. Auguste, the Maitre d', recognized Jonathan. Oddly enough, August also immediately recognized Adam.

"What a pleasure to have you gentlemen for dinner." He made a sweeping gesture toward the dining room and led them, without paying heed to the line of hopefuls.

"The Chronicle did a fine article on The Morgan Prize, Dr. Grant. Congratulations. Tonight, champagne is on the house." With that, Auguste seated them and instructed the waiter to bring a bottle of Korbel Brut. How many times had they celebrated a success at Scoma's? It was Jonathan's favorite fish restaurant.

Jonathan sipped his glass and chuckled. "Here you are, with a million-dollar award, and Auguste won't even let us pay for the bubbly." Adam smiled impishly. "Now, tell me everything."

"How's Mary?" Adam was not quite ready to talk of serious matters.

"Mary is happy. She and Ira, and the five children, are all fine. I am enjoying being a grandfather. I may even be a great grandfather before you know it."

"Everything turned out the way it should, then."

"Yes, although ..." Hardesty's candor was always one of his signature traits. "The one thing I regret is how dense Ira Borden is. Every time we are together all he talks about is building codes and sports. To him, the world's fate is tied to football standings or baseball playoffs. He knows I watch only basketball. He never goes to the games with Mary and me. Oh well, I do have delightful grandchildren, and they keep me on my toes."

With dinner ordered, the two continued to talk of family and friends. Jonathan, however, kept inching back towards the essential topic of the evening.

"When you first came to California, Sheldon Armitage tried to co-opt you to work under him. He was not happy when you signed up for my seminars. Since his visit to Cavendish in '36, he had been your father's close friend, even though Alexander chose Compton's lab in Chicago and not Berkeley. When Armitage became Academic Dean, Teller was invited to Berkeley to become the Director of the Lawrence Livermore National Laboratory. Alexander once told me that he decided to come to Berkeley after you entered graduate school in the hopes of mending fences with you. Of course, he was still one of Teller's termites.

"You probably never knew the full extent of Alexander's involvement with the heavy-handed security and internal controls that confronted scientists. Armitage and your father even tried to squash the Bulletin of Atomic Scientists. They wanted Gene Rabinowitch listed as a security risk. Teller and Strauss saw to it that Oppenheimer's security clearance was never restored. They hated Oppie's stand against the Enewetak Atoll test. In the face of public indifference, the last straw for Oppenheimer was seeing Teller picked to head the Livermore lab. Teller had come with one purpose, to perfect HIS 'Super'. Armitage gave up being Dean to work on biological agents for the military."

"Jonathan," Adam did not want to talk of bombs, physics, or Berkeley, "Alexander's work was a mystery to me. He visited us only when there was a test in the desert. In 1959, it had to do with some test at Los Alamos. Mother said he only came to New Mexico to 'tickle the dragon's tail.' "

"How did that affect you, I mean, as a child, a teenager?"

"Whenever there was a test, even as far away as Nevada, Mother made us stay inside for days. Fallout terrified her. I was 9 when they blew up Bikini with a 15 megatons bomb. The fallout from that was incredible. We had bomb drills at school. Teachers would march us down into the basement where huge boxes marked civil defense were stored. We practiced diving under our desks at the sound of the air raid siren. We laid flat on our stomachs, with one hand over the back of our necks as protection against flying glass. I told no one that it was all because of what my father did. I was sure that he, personally, was going to blow up the world. But most of the time I simply did not think about it."

"Anyway, to return to Armitage, he was furious with me when I assigned you to my lab."

"I have never asked you why you did that."

"After I met you in the hall that first day, I looked you up, the two publications you had co-authored while still an undergraduate. The methodology was quite sound, even innovative. I thought: What can Armitage do for you? He was long past doing good work and was living off the work of his graduate students, putting his name first to their papers submitted for publication. His real interest was defense contracts. Anyway, I saw that you signed up for my seminar on genetics. For the rest, nature took its course. Sheldon died two years ago from bone cancer. I believe he was too fast and loose with the radioactive tracers he used. He boasted how harmless they were."

Adam remembered. "He always talked about transuranic elements, especially americium."

"Near the end, they gave him massive doses of morphine. The pain had to be excruciating. He lost his mind. My Martha was a friend of Lois Armitage. She told Martha her husband once admitted to her that he had been careless in the lab. He admitted it only once, shortly before his mind went." Emptying the champagne bottle, Jonathan finished his tale, and waved to the waiter.

"Jonathan, maybe we should forego another bottle. I've got to call Herman. He'll be in a foul mood, but I do need to call."

"Nonsense, you have not had nearly enough bubbly to make that call. Herman, on the other hand, is no doubt well lubricated. I'm told that he practically lives at that goddamn Kosmoi these days. That club is for degenerates. Some say that he even stays at The Manse on the grounds of the institute, when he's too drunk to drive."

Adam could see that Jonathan was enjoying the wine. "What are you talking about?"

"You mean about the Kosmoi? You don't know? He's been put on the board of the Kosmoi Club."

"I don't know anything about it, Jonathan."

"I forgot; you've been in the desert communing with snakes and lizards. Well, let me tell you about reptiles!" In spite of the alcohol, or perhaps because of it, Jonathan was suddenly quite animated. "The place smells of old, mutant creatures! All the clans gather there: The Chestertons, Armitages, Cockrofts, Talmidges, Hammonds, and let us not leave out Schwann. They're a cancerous lot. They have set themselves up as some sort of grand council, the self-appointed Ephors and Archons of capitalism. The self-anointed protectors of corporate power and greed."

"Jonathan, what are you talking about?"

"I forgot to mention Alexander. Your father is a member. When he first arrived in Berkeley, Alexander once told me that reading Einstein's 1905 paper as a teenager instantly changed his life. He wanted to be a physicist because he recognized the immense power hidden inside the atom, something he saw as a veiled exotic. It was his temptress. What kept Alexander in Berkeley was the likes of Teller, Armitage, and of men like Schwann."

Was the liquor talking? Whatever Jonathan was driving at unsettled Adam. "I know that Herman's mother, Alexander's first wife, is a Cockroft. There was some talk of the Cockrofts helping to found a private club. What is sinister in that?"

The waiter interrupted to clear the table and pour more coffee. It gave Adam time to look squarely into Jonathan's eyes. He saw for the first time how old Hardesty looked. Retirement had clearly affected him physically. He still kept an office in the department and made an effort at research to benefit a handful of graduate students. But knowing Jonathan as he did, Adam knew it was not enough. He would insist on being involved in Adam's plan. Sanderson's call had ignited that fuse."

"Now, my boy, let's get down to cases. What about this Methuselah work? What have you conjured up for the wide world out there, the world beyond Rimrock?"

Jonathan knew that it could not have come about easily, even for Adam. Nor was it of necessity by design. The controversy at the university five years ago had pushed Adam into isolation. One year before, quite by chance, he had been asked to consult on a progeria case. Adam had worked with one of the physicians to test autoimmune responses. Nothing like it had ever so frustrated or saddened him. He tried to imagine how the boy felt, how he suffered. The boy of almost eleven was aged long before his time. Adam could not help staring at his chin and mouth. He could not look him in the eyes. The boy had milk teeth and a receding chin. He kept reaching out to one of the physicians, asking to be fixed. He didn't care if he had to stay "crinkled and breaky." He just wanted to live. His sister, sitting in the outer office was a normal eight-year-old, already half again his size. The doctor wanted to try a new treatment of intensive vitamin-E in combination with a growth hormone. Another wanted to try synthesized hormones. What about injections of vasopressin? What role might thyroxin play?

It was already too late for the boy, and they knew it. Talk of the build-up of free radicals was pointless. The boy's kidneys were failing. Adam reviewed Harmon's work with mice using BHT and MEA. But Harmon had used healthy mice. Within the month the boy died while watching TV. Dr. Swift called to say that it was a massive coronary. He made a point of saying he died while watching *The Captain from Castile*. The doctor asked Adam, why that movie?

Months later, Adam got another call. The doctor was treating a seventeen-year-old. Would he consult? He would, knowing beforehand that the same questions about hormonal therapies would come up. This time, he was asked to examine tissue samples and blood sera. The patient was not so far gone, and Adam wanted to know more about this disease. He had often used the immortal cell line, Henrietta Lacks 1951, in his lab. But this was a chance to look at cells that were radically different, prematurely senescent. Progeria cells were non-cancerous cells programmed to die after only a few doublings, ten or twelve. What if…?

Between questions and observations from Jonathan, Adam explained how he got from testing cells of a progeria victim to deciding to use a common shrew as his experimental vector. He was looking for mutations affecting metabolic and cell division processes. Adam reasoned that his insight into progeria had opened up new ground before him. The challenge became irresistible. He had questions to explore about antibodies, restriction enzymes, protein synthesis regulation, mitosis, and more questions.

At five minutes to midnight, Adam finished his account. Hardesty agreed: The research approach he had taken was sound. It went well beyond Adam's previous work. But, how did Alberto fit into all this? Jonathan knew about Alberto, though he had never actually seen the boy.

"Alberto knows it is too late for him." Adam paused for a moment to wipe a tear. "He's not taking it too well. Nothing I have done is a cure for progeria. My protocol works only on basically healthy, relatively young individuals. Ones willing to undertake a long-term intervention."

"How is Crystal taking the latest prognosis of Alberto's condition?"

Adam had departed Rimrock before the latest results were communicated. He hated himself for leaving her at the airport and subjecting her to the long drive home alone, and of what awaited her. She was, he knew, also worried about his future.

<++++++++++>

Bayeta arrived home at 11:00 p.m. and looked in on Alberto. Martin told her the drive back from Flagstaff had drained him. She felt guilty. He had wanted to be awake when she returned, but his body did not allow it. Martin had made a fire and let him sleep on the living room couch. The two roasted marshmallows. What did it matter, Martin said, what Alberto could and could not eat? So much had been denied him. Martin had not the heart to withhold marshmallows, only two marshmallows.

Seeing Alberto withdrawn into a long-delayed sleep, she could not hold back tears. How many times had she carried Alberto, this man of twenty-two, to his bed in her arms? It was a thing no mother should have to endure. Not being his biological mother made no difference. He was a son in all other ways. The burden of his frail body she could bear. It was the certain knowledge that she would bury him that was unbearable. As she gently drew the covers over his body, she tried not to see, not to calculate or compare how much his skin had shrunken and tightened its grip on his brittle bones in just the last month. His body was transforming itself by the day, desiccating before her eyes into a living, mummified man. Her hands trembled as she smoothed the covers.

For her sleep would not come easily, if at all. "I'll work at my loom," she said aloud.

In the hallway, Martin appeared. He'd been in the kitchen.

"Are you all right, Martin?" He stood fidgeting with the door handle. He did not look up, his eyes averted. "You must be exhausted," she said. "Go to sleep. We all need some sleep."

Martin gave Bayeta a quick, furtive look. "Don't worry about me."

"Martin, are you sure you are all right?"

"I've got a lot on my mind, that's all." He retreated to his room and closed the door.

Martin was by nature reserved, not one to show his feelings. Something was eating at Martin. For the moment, however, she was too tired to press him. He would have to be the one to speak first. Questions only drove him into stony silence.

Drinking coffee so late had set her nerves on edge. With sleep out of the question until the caffeine wore off, she would work in her studio. The warping frame was laid out on a large worktable with large balls of warp yarn beside it, yarn from Widow Tumecho's sheep. Stringing the warp was physically demanding and required great precision. She flexed her fingers wide and estimated the time it would take to complete the stringing. The task needed to be completed without stopping to insure equal tension on each wound strand of the warp. She had at the ready two dowels notched at 1/4" spacing to mark placement of each strand. A small ball of bayeta yarn was also set aside as twining cord for the bottom and top of the warp loops. Having settled on the time involved, she stood before the frame and reached for the yarn. With one end tied to the bottom yarn beam, she closed her eyes and prayed.

As the stringing progressed, she forgot her cares. With precise repetitions, at once automatic and hypnotic, stressful and mechanical, the warp yarn was stretched between bottom and top beams in a continuous, unbroken series of elongated figure eights. She lost track of time, of time and worry.

The weft's pattern would grow horizontally, to a width of 79 inches. It had taken 316 windings of the warp yarn. She sighed relief, the foundation all but complete.

At last, with the final length of warp yarn played out at the right side of the warping frame, she tied it off. This was to be a tight weave. The spacing between each warp strand must be as small as possible. She picked up the ball of twining cord and twined it between each strand of the warp. This selvage strand, top and bottom, was to be of the same yarn as her weft. She inserted the cord at the top of each warp strand with one twist. "The spacing must be so", she whispered. "It must be just so." Time passed. At last, with the twisted cord between each warp strand, top and bottom, the task was complete. Three hours it took without rest.

The warp was ready to remove from the warping frame and install on her weaving loom. Holding the bottom warp strands gathered in her hands, she inserted the binding cord. Fatigue was taking its toll, but Bayeta kept working until she was ready to hang the top yarn beam in place and secure it to the tension bar. With the bottom attached, she stood back and examined the effort for evenness and spacing. Then, she knelt, and with five short lengths of cord, secured the cloth beam to the lower loom beam. Her joints ached. Bathed in the soft light of the lamp on the worktable near her emptied warping frame, she walked back and forth, her hands gripping her waist. She stretched her back and examined the warp. Tightening the tension bar at the top of the loom beam would complete the task.

It took time to tighten and adjust the tension bar. With the lamp in hand, she studied the evenness of spacing. Eventually, she was satisfied. It had not been without suppressed apprehension when she began. She was tired. Such exacting work should not be done in the dark of night with only lamplight as guide. Pent up tension in her hands had flowed into the final tensing of the warp. Content with the result, she experienced an upwelling of fatigue. The skeins of yarn set aside for the first panels rested in the basket at the right side of the loom.

In the hour before dawn, the house folded in upon itself as if bound up within a tight ball of thick, indigo yarn. With a moonless sky above, a chill seeped into the studio where the glass door had been left ajar. Bayeta listened for the first rustle of dawn's creatures. How often she had worked in her studio until dawn. She listened for the first sounds of their ward, Alberto, when he stirred from a restless sleep. He often awoke disoriented, tangled up in sweat-stained blankets, uncertain where he was or how long he had been feeling pain. At such times, he needed her most.

It was best to weave in the light of day. Yet, her pent-up tension demanded that she weave toward dawn. It unsettled her. It compelled her. The vision of it held within, spurred her on. The only sound in the house was that of her batten being drawn across warp strings, a soft imperceptible scrape of weft drawn across warp, the tamp of the comb settling each weft line into place. Her hands were numb from the cold that had crept into the studio. A pot of Navajo tea would do nicely.

With the pot on the stove, Bayeta took out the bag of Cota stems and small leaves. To make it strong, she put ten stems and as many leaves into the boiling water. Good Navajo tea takes fifteen minutes to steep. Bayeta made use of the time by setting firmly in her mind the new web's pattern. Viewing the brilliant pink hue of well-steeped Navajo tea, her mind's eye focused on the foundation. The hidden figure eight warp winding mirrored Adam's consuming passion for the cell's double helix, that which made all life possible. As with weaving, Spider Woman's gift bound purpose to design. She prayed for Adam to resolve the how and to what ends his work was destined.

Her grandmother had set aside four bolts of baize, purchased from the Hubbell Trading Post in 1910. When Crystal Bayeta was born in 1950, the precious heirloom stock grandmother called Manchester cloth was given to Ninaba for the child. From that gift, those four bolts of flannel cloth, Bayeta was given her name. Its vibrant red, the color of a summer's setting sun and the red rock walls of Canyon del Muerto, had shown in the infant's eyes. Bayeta cloth was a part of the *Diné* story, the time when her people had died at the hands of Spanish soldiers in Massacre Cave, 1804. Then, bayeta cloth was called Spanish wool. She would never admit to it. No, bayeta was older than even Massacre Cave. The English had made such cloth since the 16th Century, the time when the *Diné* moved south into the canyon lands. It was suitable for the finest weavings of which any Navajo woman was capable. Of such ancestry, it was free of the taint of Spanish treachery and of the captivity of Bosque Redondo.

Crystal Bayeta had her purpose firmly set in mind. Her pattern called for a large, broad weave. She had cut and stripped and unraveled the bolts, twisting the threads into fourply yarn. At last, this heirloom bayeta would find its place on her loom. Yet, it was not to be a simple textile, no *yistłł'ó'nígíí'*. It was to be her finest, a *diyogí*, a true Navajo blanket. Her grandmother and her grandmother's mother would have been proud of it.

Settling down before her loom, Bayeta reached out for the old ironwood comb, a gift from Grandmother. Grandmother's batten, too, was there, long smoothed and polished from use. She adjusted her shed rod, separating the alternating warps. The heddle was attached by loose loops to the shed rod. Moving back and forth across the loom, each panel would build up one section upon another in lazy lines, the traditional way for such a large web.

Balls of deep indigo yarn were in the basket to the left of the loom. Her re-spun bayeta yarn was to her right. Widow Tumecho's natural white wool she distributed to her right and to her left. Bayeta closed her eyes to imagine a classic second phase chief's blanket of an unknown *Tseyi* weaver who had evaded Carson's troops in 1864. She, too, had used bayeta yarn for red, a deep indigo, and a natural white—the colors Bayeta must use. She imagined how it would hang about Adam's shoulders, not as a poncho, but as a "chief's blanket" wrapped about his shoulders. It mattered most that the pattern be straight and clean of line. How well the pattern would settle about his shoulders was important, its end-folds like the moth's wings at rest. This is how it must be. She prayed.

> In the house of long life, there I wander.
> In the house of happiness, there I wander.
> Beauty before me, with it I wander.
> Beauty behind me, with it I wander.
> Beauty below me, with it I wander.
> Beauty above me, with it I wander.
> Beauty all around me, with it I wander.
> In old age traveling, with it I wander.
> I am on the beautiful trail; with it I wander.

The sound of weft yarn threading through warp strings, the batten sliding into place, the firm tamping thuds of the comb was all that stirred the air. Time was lost, ensnared within the reach of her hands. The yarn felt strong, good to the touch, evenly spun, rich and yet subtle of hue.

With dawn's approach, Bayeta stopped, the first of 19 bands, three inches, in place. She imagined the interplay of red and indigo that would dominate the head, the foot, and the middle ground of her weave. It would be just so.

In the distance, an owl's last hoot marked the end of night. First light was at hand. Life stirred on the desert floor. As she walked to her bed, she thought to set the alarm clock for seven-thirty. A long day was ahead. Alberto had been gone four days. It felt like four years. How very old he looked last night, tangled in his blanket, his hands shaking as if trying to fix a last marshmallow to his roasting stick. Martin told her how much he complained of the bedpan, embarrassed beyond words. His kidneys were almost gone, collapsing within. The doctors in Flagstaff were of one opinion—a week, maybe two at the outside. If he could be hospitalized, perhaps a little more time was possible. There, they could intervene if he had a coronary—a grim prognosis. One function after another would continue its decline, then fail utterly. He would lapse into a coma, if not seized by a massive coronary. Bayeta needed Martin to be on hand so long as Adam was away. He was very fond of Alberto and felt that he, too, had somehow failed. Any death deeply affected Martin. He was not so modern a Navajo as to keep his fear of death in check. He half-believed in a time when there was no death.

Alberto had struggled bravely against the inevitable. Even now, with his body telling him, he could not bring himself to accept it, not completely. For four years had not Adam told him that doctors do not have all the answers? His latest visit was no different. He wanted to believe, in spite of everything to the contrary, that a miracle, something, anything, would save him. But when Martin slowed the car to turn off of Interstate 40 and on to Highway 63 North, Alberto had asked how soon. He had always taken such great pleasure in the trips to Flagstaff. They were a change in routine, a genuine outing. And each time, the doctors, seeing how well he was managing, expressed cautious optimism. He would ask, could a cure be not far off? The matter of time had lately consumed Alberto's thoughts. Martin, watching the road ahead, did not smile. Then, only then, did Alberto know, truly know.

At seven-thirty, Martin's knock at the bedroom door awakened her. Coffee was made, he said. He would be busy in the lab until after 10. "It is really good news for Adam, isn't it?" Under his arm, he had the Thursday edition the Albuquerque paper she had left for him on the hall table. "There was no mention of his big project, though. Why?"

"He has yet to tell anyone. Oh, John Sanderson knows. He'll make some statement at the meeting. Adam wanted to wait, but what with this award, it forces things."

"Would you want him to keep this a secret?"

"Part of me does. No one can say what changes it will bring."

"Will he go back to the university?"

"Our home is here, Martin. Things will stay the same as much as possible." Martin turned to go. The set of his shoulders betrayed his inner distress.

Fifteen minutes later, a second cup of coffee in hand, Bayeta went down the hall. At Alberto's door, Bayeta stood for a long time, the coffee in her hands going cold. She listened to his shallow, uncertain breathing. He must have been cold in the night. In his fretful sleep, he had twisted the covers about his legs and exposed his shoulders. On the floor near the nightstand lay the half-open copy of Boccaccio's *Decameron.* Why had he chosen ribald tales from the 14th Century? Once, when asked, Alberto grinned slyly and insisted that he liked stories of gay young men and women who fled to the countryside. She did not care for the too-close analogy to Alberto's plight and Rimrock, a refuge from the world. Martin told her that Alberto had another reason. Boccaccio's young people had fled Florence for the countryside, desperate to avoid the plague. Was he not like them in spirit? He wanted to escape his own terrible, personal plague. Rimrock was a refuge from contamination. Alberto clung to a desperate wish for death to pass by and not settle upon him.

Before Martin had taken Alberto to Flagstaff, Bayeta had read to him, for the third time in as many weeks, Don Federigo's story, *Falcon.* The boy in the story died for the want of possessing an old man's incredible falcon. It was not, Alberto insisted, for lack of the man's generosity. Half-hidden among the cushions on the floor near the living room fireplace, he smiled and told her of his wish. "When I go, you must live and be happy." Deep within his sunken, half-closed eyes, she glimpsed such sadness. The quivering of his frail chin, as he smiled, carried a mild rebuke that he could not suppress. It was true, she knew; his life's thread was so short, all but worn through.

After breakfast, Bayeta looked in again on Alberto. He was still asleep, stretched out beneath the added blanket she had used to cover him. His buzzer was within reach at the headboard. When he woke, he would buzz. Until then, she would weave. Being idle, she found the waiting now frightened her.

<++++++++++>

Adam and Jonathan sat and talked for hours. It was, of course, all about biology and family. A few minutes past 1:00 a.m., they drove into the Claremont parking lot. As Adam held the entrance door open, Jonathan gave him a playful belt on the shoulder. Adam had outlined in some detail his research on the drive from the city. "You are a sly bastard, Adam."

"How you can say such a thing?"

"Yes, you are. Herman is probably in an alcoholic trance worrying what's become of you."

"Oh, that. Well, I wanted to call him from Scoma's Restaurant. But you kept on so about your enzyme studies." Adam gave him a knowing wag of his finger. "Anyway, he knows that I've landed. That driver reported back. As for me, I prefer staying here at the Claremont. I don't like the idea of staying at the institute's guesthouse. It makes me feel obligated and of being watched."

"Confusion to the enemy," Jonathan boomed. He was feeling his wine. At the desk, Adam signed in and asked the bellman to take his bag. Adam pointed toward the bar.

"Martha will wait up for me. Do you know, we have not spent an evening apart since I retired?"

Jonathan asked if it was the same for him and Bayeta. It was. Alberto's condition was in part the reason. She was at home now caring for and watching over him.

Once settled in the lounge, a nightcap of brandy in hand, they sat staring at the lights across the bay. At the north end of the city, a low, thick fog was rolling in through the Golden Gate. The lights of the Presidio blinked and dimmed as the fog rolled eastward, spreading its veil across the far shore.

"I was born there, you know. We lived in one of those spotless, three story row houses on Laguna Street. The Palace of Fine Arts is three blocks north. Every Sunday, rain or shine, Pop and I walked over to the reflecting pool on the Palace grounds. Of course, in those days it was more like a lagoon. Pop took me to see the Panama-Pacific Expo when it opened in 1919. Quite a show it was. There were palaces dedicated to Education, Liberal Arts, Agriculture, and every sector of society. Yes, it was quite the thing. Later, during the depression, they put up lighted tennis courts inside. I played tennis there, and Pop came to see me play every Saturday."

"We often sat and talked on a bench by the lagoon, about life mostly. I'd carry the bag of stale Wonder Bread to feed the ducks. Life was good." Jonathan paused to sip his brandy. "I got pretty good at identifying the ducks. Some were greedier than the others, gutsy beggars. There were the skittish ones and the noisy ones. One duck in particular, Snoopy, was the comic of the bunch. He would hold back at first, waiting. Then, at just the right moment, he'd start up quacking, more like a laugh than a duck quack. The other ducks would suddenly look at him and waddle aside. In he'd come, to stick his bill right into the bag for bread. I liked him best. Pop had names for most of them: Hitler, Stalin, Roosevelt, Myrna Loy, and Laurel and Hardy. We matched every duck to the right celebrity personality. He'd light his pipe and wonder out loud about which duck, I mean, which personality, was in the news that week and how they had behaved."

Adam shifted uncomfortably. "I never called him Dad or Pop, or anything other than Father. Mom had some choice names. He was 'The Shatterer of World's,' 'the Dragon's Tail Tickler,' and a 'H-Bomb Boomer.' For a long time, I didn't care so much what it all meant."

Jonathan interrupted. The brandy had gone to his head. He was feeling nostalgic. "My father died in 1935. A snapped cable assembly got him."

"You never spoke of it. How did that happen?"

"He was quite a man, my dad. He was a crew chief on the Gold Gate Bridge project. It was the depression, and he had to feed his family. He kept telling me that he made sure his insurance premiums were paid up, else they'd cancel on him. He put in a lot of overtime to pay for those premiums. I forget how many other men died, maybe ten or so. The builders were so proud of their safety record. But dad seemed to sense that he might not live to see the bridge complete. The insurance paid off the house mortgage and bills. A little money was left, enough for me to go to college. What parents do for their children. If only my father had lived to see me finish."

“Yes, what parents do for their children,” Adam echoed.

“He had so much to do with my goals, you know. He was always bringing up the future. Be a teacher, he kept telling me. I still wanted to be a pilot. All my heroes seemed to be aviators—Lindbergh, General Mitchell, and Wiley Post. They led exciting and gallant lives. Still, Pop kept at me: Be a teacher. I was certain that teachers were the sort that others didn’t care if they lived or died. Luckily, I had great professors in graduate school. They kept after me to do basic research. I had a talent for detail. Eventually, I developed a good nose for enzymes.”

Jonathan finished off the last of his brandy and stared out at the city clothed in fog, his eyes trained the Golden Gate Bridge. “Pop was right. I gained some notice. Winning the Nobel, however, caught me dumbfounded. After Stockholm, I could not settle back into work or the classroom for almost two years. The notoriety almost ruined me. No one would believe I was just lucky in picking a line of research. They expected more of me, and later, well, I had no new big idea to satisfy them.”

“You got over it.”

“It got over me, Adam. With that damned prize, I almost lost it.”

“Jonathan, you are drunk. I don’t think you really mean…”

“Oh, yes I do! You, on the other hand were born for science. I saw that the first class you took from me. You were obsessively curious about everything. And, you were so stubborn.”

“I’ve been lucky, too, Jonathan.”

Jonathan raised his hand to silence Adam. “Yes, you have been lucky. So many would give their right arm for what you have done. But they do not have your luck. You always had a nose to smell out elusive quarry and pursue it to the end.”

“You were the one, Jonathan, who taught me to pay attention to outliers, the anomalies, and the loose-ends that others ignored or dismissed. Besides, who is to say that I have it made? I gave up my university appointment. I’ve become an outlier myself, an isolate. I live quietly…”

“Did, that is the operative word, Adam. You did live quietly. Now, that is over for you. That is what you need to see before it is too late. It could already be too late. The Morgan Prize will fade from people's memory. Grant money will dry up. How far can a million go these days? But, forget all that. My point is that if you publish this Greene Lyon of yours, you'll have no peace."

"Jonathan, why do you think that? My research has always stood up to scrutiny."

"My boy, my dear boy, a storm is about to break over your head. This thing will fly out of your hands. If it turns out not to be the blessing you think, who will they blame? You have no idea what it could mean to the world at large, do you? It is not all roses to live a hundred years, you know! Oh, I suppose that never occurred to you. Who is going to support all those superannuated codgers? You could upset the balance, the population pyramid. Have you thought of that?"

"Jonathan, we've both had too much to drink. New discoveries change things every day. I can't just bottle it up and keep it secret."

"The hell you can't! You have every right. No, you have an obligation to do so." Jonathan lowered his voice, deadly serious in his tone. "You must be careful, Adam. This thing can blow up in your face. Such a thing has huge economic and social implications. Christ, man, don't you see that?"

Before Adam could respond, if he had a response, the waitress interrupted. The bar was about to close. It was almost two in the morning.

They walked out onto the balcony across from the reception desk to take in the cool night air. In the garden below, the old palms cast long, tenuous shadows across the pathways. A couple could be seen embracing. Two cats prowled the flowerbeds.

"I've had a bit too much to drink. And, Martha is waiting up for you. You better go."

Jonathan had exhausted his concerns on the matter for the night. Adam promised to come by the house in the morning, a short six blocks down the hill. With that, Jonathan Hardesty said goodnight and walked through the lobby and out the doors. Adam felt chilled. It was time to try and get some sleep. He had promised to meet Ryder for breakfast.

7

Smells from the Swamp

Staring at her calendar, Marcy Adams flipped to Friday, April 6. The digital clock on her desk clicked to 9:59 AM. She counted to 20 and said, “The Director will see you in a moment, Dr. Terman.”

Alexander Terman, seated near the inner office door, ignored Miss Adams. It was easy to ignore her. She was plain, middle-aged, and gave no sign that she was anything but an impersonal and efficient secretary. Herman Cockroft cared only that she be efficient, precise, and discrete. Unless asked a direct question related to her duties, she almost never spoke. With stiff, well-practiced precise motions, a habit of a lifetime, she adjusted her pocket mirror to arrange a single misplaced strand of hair. Alexander watched without interest. He smelled her heavy perfume, a languid musk. His stomach tightened involuntarily. Nothing about Miss Adams stirred the faintest interest in him as a man.

The intercom buzzed. “Dr. Terman, the Director will see you now.”

Alexander stood and turned to the door. Miss Adams tracked his movements with one eye, judging him matter-of-factly. To her, he seemed a spent vessel—old, wheezy, ground down. No sign of personal recognition penetrated her defensive, emotional desert. She did not care for him, or the likes of him.

As he reached for the door, it opened from the inside. Herman stood with his hand extended in an awkward gesture. His first words betrayed a mixture of relief and discomfort. He could not control his diffidence toward his father without a trace of confusion. "You are looking fit and trim, Father."

Alexander did not take Herman's hand, for he saw that he had someone with him. Herman turned his head toward the man, "Well done. You know what to do."

Alexander recognized the man, every inch a Junker, whom he called "The Little Prussian." Only William Henry Schwann, however, ever openly referred to him so. Without so much as a nod to Alexander, Anton Mueller brushed by and marched out of the office at a quick, stiff-legged pace. Alexander grimaced. He had no impulse to recognize the man, only his departure. Neither man cared for the other.

"I am sorry that you had to wait, Father. Did Miss Adams keep you company?"

As the door closed, Alexander turned to give Herman a hard look. "Don't be an ass, Herman."

Herman feigned surprise at the outburst. "Whatever do you mean?"

"That damned Medusa guarding your lair, why do you keep her?"

"If you say so, Father. Well..." Herman motioned for his father to sit. "Shall we get down to business?"

Once seated behind his desk, an orderly expanse free of papers, Herman keyed his intercom. "Miss Adams?" He did not wait for her response. "Hold my calls. Hold my calls, except for Mueller. Yes, except for Mueller. And, if you please, we'll have coffee and Danish."

Settling into the couch, the kind of soft, overstuffed affair that made the person in it appear diminished by its sheer size and how low one sank toward the floor, Alexander waved his left hand toward the door. "I don't like that man, that cold bastard. You should get rid of him. Get rid of him, if you can."

"Father, we've been over all that."

"He's Schwann's man. You cannot trust him. He struts about like a Nazi bully boy."

"Yes, well," Herman hesitated, his hands trembling. "He is good at what he does. One can't do without security these days."

"Herman, it's your show. I'm just a retired old fart, as you like to tell that wife of yours. But mark my words: He answers only to Schwann. Who should know better than I? Get rid of him."

Herman shrugged. What was the point of arguing?

"As you wish, I say nothing more about him." His expression tensed. "Have you located Adam?"

"Yes. He was on the plane. Only, my man lost him in traffic coming in from the airport."

"Christ, Herman, what's this double-speak? You mean Mueller tracked him!" Alexander stared at Herman. "One day, you will go too far. Whose idea was it to send that cretin?"

"Yes, Mueller was on the same plane. Anyway, Adam is here. Well, he checked into The Claremont at 1:00 a.m. He prefers that drafty old barn to our guesthouse, I assume. He was there with an older gentleman. They were making a night of it, drinking."

"You're not serious? Adam doesn't drink anything stronger than a glass of wine. He does not have an appetite for the stuff, not like you do, Herman!"

"Last night he did. He dismissed the driver sent to pick him up. Then, he went on the town."

"Am I to suppose that Mueller was shadowing him just to make sure he behaved?"

Herman ignored the question. "Mueller tells me the bar tab was paid for by credit card, by Hardesty."

"You have been a busy toady, haven't you? All this nonsense having Adam followed. This business with Mueller is too much. You are going to spook Adam. Where will that get you?"

"I'm doing what has to be done, what I have to do. And don't you preach to me! You know why. We're both in the same soup, you know. For both our sakes, Adam has to come round."

Alexander ignored Herman's defense. "Hardesty, you said? He can cause trouble. Adam will tell him everything. Worse, Adam will listen to him. All this scheming will go up in smoke."

"Don't you think I know that? Before it is too late, Adam has to come around." For a long moment, Herman fell silent. Regaining his balance, he pleaded, "Look, Father, Adam's work will end up in someone's hands. He's not equipped to develop it into a full-blown result. Here, we can see to it…see to…"

"You mean Schwann will see to it. I hate every second of this dirty business. But, that is why I am here. And let me tell you this, even if your office is bugged, I don't know if I care anymore. What if Schwann gets his way? What if just this once he does not?"

"Father, I'll pretend that you didn't say that. What we need, what we need to do is…"

"For now, just leave Adam alone. Let Mueller come near him, and it will end badly. Schwann is in a particularly nasty mood. Anything can set him off. Best you not say a thing about Hardesty."

Herman got up to pace back and forth between his desk and the window. "I must keep Schwann informed. He is sure to ask. What I don't tell him, Mueller will. You must see that." Herman continued to pace, wringing his hands, sweating. Alexander waited, used to Herman's moments of near panic. Herman had a look of defeat on his face.

"There is more to it than just Adam. We are losing too many scientists here at the institute. I am not getting results. Yes, you are right about Mueller. He is heavy-handed. But there is only so much I can do. Don't you see that?"

The door to the outer office opened. Alexander rose to his feet as Miss Adams rolled the coffee cart in. "Will that be all, Sir?" Without waiting for Herman's reply, she continued to check the tray. Nothing was missing. Alexander took coffee only with heavy cream, no substitute. The small pitcher was full. The brown sugar lumps were for Herman. Two spoons, two napkins, two pastry dishes, and two forks were laid out in precise order. With a stiff about-face, she left, closing the door briskly behind her.

Herman poured himself coffee and nibbled on a bear claw without pleasure. He did not like the pastry. He ate it out of habit, nothing more. "Adam needs convincing."

"He will insist on publishing. He is not a fool. I suspect he's also filed a patent application."

"But..." Herman's hands shook so much that he spilled coffee on his tie.

"Why did you think The Morgan Prize would make the difference? That's the hook Schwann cooked up as bait. In any case, Adam made up his mind to come weeks ago. At the meeting, he may give the institute some small credit, though God alone knows why. But turning over his data and treatment protocols, do you think for one second that he will? He may be ignorant of Schwann's intentions, but he believes that a scientist must control the fruits of his labor."

Herman was shaking so hard that he had to put his cup down. "We've paid his bills for five years. He has to know that we have every right, every right and expectation."

"You won't get far with that. He believes science should have no secrets or prior constraints. Well, maybe he knows better than that. But, he chooses to believe otherwise."

"Jesus Christ! I have to make..." Herman lost his train of thought, was reduced to wringing his hands.

Alexander stood up, as if to go. "Herman, get a hold of yourself. And, keep that God damned Prussian away from Adam." Herman had not heard. "Herman! I mean it. Get a hold of yourself. Unless Adam on his own comes around, you are sunk. Have Mueller handle things, and you won't have a chance in hell."

"You're not suggesting it's my fault?"

"It doesn't matter whose fault it is! You could have avoided all of this if you had not compromised that Martin fellow to spy on Adam. That's a mistake. That's what got Schwann all excited. Adam will find out, you know. When he does, you'll have hell to pay. Why did you corrupt that little bastard, anyway?"

"Schwann made me. He insisted that Martin Atsidi could be made to tell us how far Adam had got. Well, don't you see...I mean...Schwann would have done something even more drastic."

Alexander stared at Herman in disbelief. "You still don't have a clue, do you? If you had not been such a snoop, Adam could have published his results before Schwann had any inkling how far he'd come. No one would have been the wiser. All that nosing around, where has it gotten you? Now, Schwann must get his hands on it. Schwann's put Mueller to it. This is spinning out of control."

Herman jerked his head, an involuntary spasm rippling through his body. He was not a healthy man, not in any sense. He lacked physical strength. His hands were putty-like, limp. Herman was a weak creature fated to waste away ever so slowly. He was not a stupid man, though he often acted stupidly. When it came to his own mortal coil, his habits constrained him from doing anything about his general physical being. If he paid it any mind, it was to freshen up his drink and shake away momentary insight as an unwanted distraction.

"I don't want to even think about that."

"You should never have told Schwann you had any idea what Adam was up to."

"That was impossible. With Mueller here any secret is dangerous, impossible."

Herman gave Alexander a defeated look. Both knew that it was so. One way or the other, Schwann was determined to have his way with them. Father and son, each in his own way, had become his captive.

Herman steadied himself. "What am I going to do?"

"I've been sent to tell you one thing. Adam has to come around before midnight Monday. If not, more than one boat will be swamped. Billions are at stake." Alexander walked to the window and looked out. "More than money is involved, Herman, much more."

"How can Adam be made to come around? Has the great man considered that?"

"Adam is to receive full recognition, full recognition and a royalty. It will make him richer than he could ever imagine. You will promise that the institute will continue his funding. Do not so much as mention Schwann's name. The institute will ink the agreement, not Schwann, as far as Adam is to know. Offer no more than four percent, not without talking to Schwann first. He is to turn over all materials—raw data, test results, and the detailed treatment protocols. Schwann is very, very determined. Bring Adam around by Monday."

"What if I need more time? We can't rush him. He's not going to want to be pushed."

"Monday afternoon, Schwann is flying up then. He'll be at the Kosmoi Club by five. He expects this settled by then. Get it over and done with by Monday without fail." Alexander took a step toward the door.

The phone rang. Herman cupped the receiver with his hand. "Wait, it is Adam." Alexander stood waiting.

"Hello, Adam. Good to hear that you've arrived safely. You know, the guesthouse would be more comfortable. Why not stay here?" Herman tried to pretend that Adam's checking into The Claremont was not a snub. "Father is here in my office. We were just having coffee and chatting about the boys."

Gesturing to Alexander, Herman nodded with relief. "I'll see you at eleven, then. I'll have a driver pick you up." Herman listened for another moment, his body movements betraying the anxiety rising within him. "Wouldn't you be more comfortable at the guest house?" Sweat trickled down his face. He licked his lips to collect the drips on the tip of his nose. "Oh, well, of course, if you prefer it to..."

With a bored look, Alexander watched Herman perspire and twitch. He had given up being concerned.

"Well ...you see, I thought we'd show you around the institute, have lunch after, you really should see some of the facilities we have. Perhaps you could meet some of our current research fellows."

Another long pause followed, with Herman nervously twisting in his chair. The chair's casters squeaked angrily. Without another word, he hung the phone up and reached for his handkerchief.

Alexander turned to leave. The substance of Adam's response, Alexander could guess. "For your own sake, Herman, do bring Adam around. You are pitiful when you sweat."

Herman sputtered a half intelligible defense, something about unreasonable demands being forced upon him. How many times had Alexander heard it, especially of late?

"I'll show myself out. Is the reservation for twelve-thirty? Go home and change into a clean shirt. You are perspiring like a pig."

"Maybe we should not use the club. I could try to shift things around."

"Don't be stupid. The Kosmoi is more private. Never air your dirty linen in public."

Alexander walked out of the office and hurried out of the building. The Claremont was only blocks away, and he did not want to see Adam until lunch. He needed the time to think. He still felt some measure of affection for Herman, mixed as it was with disappointment. His son was weak, unable to control his drinking, his nerves, or his timidity. There was self blame in this, Alexander knew well enough. As for Adam, he was equally conflicted. Adam had long ago rejected every claim Alexander made on him as a father. Alexander could not conjure up a time when the two of them did not circle each other warily. Adam had turned from confusion to distrust, from distrust to rejection. The fault he did not disown. Now, however, did any of it matter?

There had to be some means to escape the web Schwann had spun. Herman needed bolstering. Adam needed to accept the reality that his work was best left in other hands. It was inevitable, so far as Alexander could reason. The means to delay the advance of age was too valuable to thrust upon the world as it is. Men of power must always find the means to control such a weapon. A weapon it was. He could not but think of Adam's discovery as anything but a weapon. The irony of it, to a man whose life was occupied with thermonuclear devices, was not lost to him. His son had indeed tickled the dragon's tail. He had vastly different motives, but it, too, was a matter of unintended consequences. As Alexander walked to his car, he imagined that he saw a mushroom cloud rising overhead. He momentarily had lost all sense of place. He was standing on a ship's deck, waiting. In the distance, Bikini waited in an empty ocean for the countdown to end, for Castle Bravo to rise. The cloud's mass hovering over the parking lot did resemble a mushroom.

<++++++++++>

Donald Ryder flagged the bartender for another Bloody Mary, a double. The day was still young but he had not slept well. What if Grant did not show? But, he waited. He needed a story

A minute later, Adam appeared.

"Good morning, Mr. Ryder. How did you sleep?"

"Pretty well, thank you. Please, call me Don. It will make me feel less like a hungry reporter."

"Fair enough," Adam said, attempting to put Ryder at ease. He knew, however, that Ryder had a job to do. Adam looked about the room, examining every table. He had promised a story and so he would. "I'm hungry. Let's order first."

"Sounds like a plan. They have an omelet cook at the ready over there. It is a perfect day for breaking some eggs. I assume that he can make a decent omelet."

"The last time I stayed here, they were good." Adam understood the double meaning.

Choosing to ignore the subtlety of Adam's response, Ryder said, "Have you stayed here often?"

"I used to live down the hill not far from here. When friends came to town, we often brought them up here for Sunday brunch. This is the first time I've been back to Berkeley in five years. Some things can be counted on not to change, at least not overnight."

"It must have been difficult to give up your teaching and the laboratory facilities here. I understand that you had to set one up on your own. It's not the sort of thing one expects a scientist to attempt these days."

"It was hard. But, I had help. The Evergreen Institute provided, or should I say, loaned me a good deal of equipment, an electron microscope, one of the EM301 series. A liquid chromatography machine, even an amino acid analyzer was found. Things worked out."

The waiter poured coffee. Ryder listened to Adam's summary. For years now, Adam had not thought about the delays and the time it took. Building the laboratory wing took time, what with so much detail in configuring counter space, shelf space, refrigeration, gas tank connections, venting, safety bracketing, where to station the centrifuge, how much generator power was needed. Attention to such details is not expected of a research scientist. Planners, designers, and facility administrators are available for such things on campus. The scientist is expected only to identify the needs. Yes, Adam admitted, only once the lab was up and running did he realize how complicated the logistics. Gone was the Cavendish era when physicists tinkered away in basements and constructed experimental apparatuses on second-hand tables. Adam saw that Ryder's interest was flagging.

"You can't imagine how intimate the relationship is between the experimenter and his work space. When he or she had to personally create it, work the kinks out, make it fully functional, that was when it was intensely personal, an act of love, really."

"Excuse me, what were you just saying?" Ryder had listened, but was impatient to get down to cases.

"Oh, I was just thinking back to how much work went into putting my lab together. The hardest part was getting things to run smoothly. Only when I found a good assistant was I satisfied."

"Does he live out there, too, at Rimrock?"

"Yes. We're quite a little community. There's Bayeta, our ward, Alberto, my laboratory assistant, Martin Atsidi, and myself. A handyman and his wife, who sometimes does light housekeeping, live just over the rise to the west. When we need extra help, other neighbors can be relied upon. Some are still, well, a bit shy of me. Bea takes care of most of the details."

"So, for five years you have concentrated on experiments?"

"Half of my time goes to research that I had started at the U. The other half, my aging research, is what matters most to me. If you like, I'll tell you a bit about it."

For the next half hour, while he picked at his breakfast, Adam outlined his research. With twenty years of science reporting, Donald Ryder had a basic understanding of how a biology lab is run and the fundamentals of DNA genome research. As Adam spoke of DNA, genes, chromosomes and the like, he kept up. But, as Adam's monologue steered to issues concerning autophagy, autophagosome markers, lysosomes and other technical sidebars, Ryder's understanding lagged behind. He did not interrupt, however, not until the matter of shrews as experimental subjects came up. That was a surprise. Adam acknowledged that using shrews as a baseline for measuring and factoring in mammalian metabolism was complex. But it was precisely the shrew's accelerated metabolism and similar structure and bodily functions to larger, longer-lived mammals that made them a perfect analogue. Adam, Ryder intuited, seemed to view shrews as almost little people, only more direct in their struggle to fulfill their needs. Shrews had become his familiars.

"Doctor, might your discoveries lead to extending human life? I don't mean to suggest immortality or anything like that, but let's say by a decade, maybe even two?"

"In broad terms that is the result. I have proven that much. There's still a lot of testing to do. A refinement of schedules and treatment regimens need more attention. Those are but details, not the means."

"Are you sure? Will your findings hold up to scrutiny, to being replicated?"

"My methods and experimental results will be replicated, tested. Granted, the procedures are exacting and complicated. Accurate assays of test subjects are required. I can see a full-scale clinical program up-and-running within a year. That is, if approved for testing in humans."

"And then what? Do we stock the pharmacy shelves with 'bio-chronic" something or others?"

Ryder's tone had turned hesitant, confused. The idea was too radical to absorb over coffee in the Claremont's breakfast room. Could the autophagy system, Adam's term, be regulated? Basically, Ryder wanted to accept what Adam said. Many scientists had picked away at the edges of life extension for a hundred years, longer if one chose to include the alchemical tradition. But, arriving beyond speculation into application, well, that was a leap.

"Doctor, what if not everyone is to be allowed to take advantage, I mean given…"

"Some people will choose not to. It is a demanding regimen, decades long. But if one wants to live well beyond three score and ten, what's the alternative? Some people smoke, ruin their livers with alcohol and toxins, become obese, and refuse regular checkups. Life is full of choices."

"Is it that simple to you? Life is not a matter of choices for most people."

"There are a hundred ways people behave that are not good for them. A successful, sustained regimen on the part of the individual requires commitment over the life span. It is not easy to coax human cells to work faster, better, and longer than what evolution has programmed. Older people, especially, must accept that the efficacy of any such regimen declines with age. You can't expect someone whose body is already compromised to receive much advantage. Damage and decline, atrophy if you will, cannot be reversed. I don't care what today's miracle products you see on TV claim. At best, they only mask the underlying decay."

"Remember what the poet once said." Ryder's expression became strained, as he groped for the quote. "'Do not go gentle into that good night, Old age should burn and rave at close-of-day.'" He repeated the last phrase, "at close-of-day," and became silent.

For a moment, both sat watching the young people gathered below at the edge of the hotel's garden. They all were slim and tanned—immortal.

"None of them have definite plans for how to occupy themselves in their second century of life," Ryder finally said. Adam gave no sign of having heard. "You do see those bodies down there. What might they think of your discovery?"

Adam nodded. "Life is still on the upside for them. Life is good. They will want more of it. Yes, they will want what is made available to them."

Ryder was not ready to let it go. "Perhaps some can pay. You do understand that there will be a price, a dear one. But believe me on one point: Most will not have the means. Some believe in the cycle of life, one in which they grow old, retire, even to die to make room for others. And yet, our world is now obsessed with the youth culture. Being young, or just looking young, is the new standard. If they think of it at all, the average person hates the idea of aging. Anyone over forty is not to be trusted. The world is undergoing a huge change, age segregation. You could be putting into hyper-drive the age-old war between the young and the old. The difference will be that the old, perhaps the very old, could become a new majority, a new standard.

Are we ready for life in a world in which most people are retired and old?"

"You mean to suggest that young people will be burdened with caring for the old, the super old?"

"Yes, that is precisely what I mean. It would be nothing short of a social and economic revolution."

"We've always been divided by race, gender, and class. The rich take advantage of the poor. Women don't trust men. Men don't understand women. There are a hundred ways to pit one against another."

"And you, Doctor, may have just invented the one hundred and one way."

Adam defended his work as a logical, inevitable advance. If not him, some other scientist would find the way. Why shouldn't a person's birthright be a long and fulfilled life?

Ryder believed such a view was naïve, but did not press the point. Adam was proposing to change the rules. One more domain of life was to be manipulated, altered without a clear understanding of consequences. It was only fair to ask, benefit for whom? For twenty years, he had reported on issues surrounding cloning, genetic engineering, artificial insemination, overuse of antibiotics, the cost of medicines and medical procedures, and the marketing of body parts. One thread ran through all of them, the cost. To him, life extension at a price had potential to unleash unanticipated and incalculable costs. But, he did not raise the issue with Adam. He liked Adam and did not want to antagonize him.

For his part, Adam did not want to leave Ryder with a wrong impression. "Look, ten or twelve percent of our population lives beyond the age of retirement as it is. That is better, but not by much. I believe that all people ought to have a life beyond seventy, eighty, and ninety. Why not expect to do so?"

"Dr. Grant does your friend, Sanderson, or Dr. Hardesty for that matter, agree with you?"

"I cannot say they do, not entirely. They insist no one can know what the future is going to be like."

"Thank you! While this could be the greatest boon to the drug companies since aspirin, it may not be what this overpopulated world needs just now, not if it is to survive to a ripe old age."

"Why do you focus on the drug companies?" Adam's demeanor was at once intensely focused.

"I think you see the world as straight, a clean place. You don't question motives or look for the fly in the ointment. But I tell you this: Something smells. I can't put my finger on it, not quite, but in the last twenty-four hours I have felt it." As he talked, he continued to look out at the Claremont's grounds and toward the San Francisco skyline.

"Look, I am a good reporter, if allowed. I have not lost my sense of smell. I know when I smell swamp gas. I know when I feel the ground shaking. I know when things go bump in the night."

"Don, don't be cryptic. Tell me straight what it is that you think you smell."

With a tense smile, Ryder leaned closer. "It's just that...." He hesitated.

"All right, Don. You have a point to make. Now, tell me."

"Yes, I smell something. I can't quite identify it, not quite yet. I'm a fisherman, you know, and the smell of dead fish is in the air." Ryder flagged the waiter and ordered another Bloody Mary. Perhaps drink in the morning was an occupational hazard, Adam thought. "A fish rots from the head first."

With a fresh drink in hand, Ryder took a healthy swallow. "You see, for me this all started yesterday morning. I was on assignment at Los Alamos. Fusion research is worth a story. At least I thought it was. But you know about that. Your sister is on the project. I like that kind of story. It's not the usual stuff Los Alamos is known for. Lately, stories on thermonuclear weapons design, pre-programmed decision making models, and a new plutonium pit production facility get big yawns. The cold war is over, so why bother? I figured a new source of energy, a clean one, is worth reporting on, a byline in it for me."

Ryder took another big swallow of Bloody Mary, downing what was left of it. "Anyway, I get this call at the crack of dawn. I haven't even opened my eyes yet. It's my editor. He asks, am I sober? I can hear him swearing as he hands the phone over to the publisher. The publisher has never as much as said word one to me for as long as I can remember. Why should he? All of a sudden he's talking, all nice and smarmy. I get the point. Whatever he wants, just go with it. I'm to get my butt down to Albuquerque. He means immediately. I'm to find you, get a story. What story? Forgive me, Doctor, but listening to your talk about shrews, well!"

"You do see the point—about the shrews, I mean?"

"Now I do. But at the time I was pissed. Why pull me off a perfectly good story? I got my pants on and asked myself: Who is behind this? I do some of my best thinking when putting my pants on. My editor is not too bright. As for the publisher, why talk directly to me? He never has before, never. I know this secretary in his office pretty well. I call her after I get to Albuquerque. We've dated a couple times. Anyway, she tells me that there was this call that made the publisher jump. He made her track me down. I was out drinking with a buddy. They gave up trying to contact me by ten. She was sent home, end of story. Except, she tells me the publisher, her boss, was in a sweat. Schwann, himself had called him."

"Wait a minute, what's this Schwann got to do with any of this?"

"Connect the dots, Doctor. Connect the dots. Schwann owns my paper, or controls it." Ryder looked pleased with himself. "Now why would this Schwann go to all this trouble? Why send me to Albuquerque? My friend, the secretary, had written down Schwann's phone number. She gave it to me. God bless secretaries who think of such things. I decided why not phone him direct.

"You did that?"

"You bet. He was pretty peeved; I mean real pissed. He swore, and he gave me some crock about you being news for getting The Morgan Prize. The locals in Berkeley or San Francisco could cover it, I said. He told me to just shut up. Shut up and do what I'm told, he says."

"Is that it?"

"Before I could get another word in, he hung up. So, it was on to Albuquerque and the shrews."

"Schwann already knew about the Morgan. Now, how did he know that?"

"There's more. I drive down in time to sit in on your lecture. That's when I saw him."

"Him, who is it you saw?"

"Him! You have no idea, do you? He's been dogging your tracks since yesterday. You had no idea, did you?"

"There was just that once, just once, in the faculty dining room. A man eating alone...every time I glanced his way, he seemed to be staring. I wondered if he knew me. I think he was behind us when we left."

"Was he a big hulk of a man dressed in a dark suit that doesn't fit him? He's bald. Sunglasses that he never takes off, only sets them on his bald forehead?"

"That could be him."

"That's him. His name is Anton Mueller."

Adam was certain that he did not know the man. He did look vaguely out of place, a man who did not fit the surroundings. If there is such a thing as an academic look, Mueller did not have it. The fact that he wore a gray, ill-fitting suit was odd. Except for deans and vice presidents, few men wore suits on campus. The more Adam thought about his impression of the man, the less he liked having been watched by him.

"And you say you know nothing about him?" Ryder's tone was quizzical, as if Adam should.

"I've never before seen or heard of him."

"Anton Mueller is one tough customer. He was William Henry Schwann's personal bodyguard. Schwann has an obsession about security. You don't want to have Mueller on your case. There are rumors. For years, wherever Schwann went, there was 'The Little Prussian.' That's what some call him."

"You just lost me. Who is 'The Little Prussian'? Do you mean Schwann?"

"He's one, too, Prussian, I mean, but not the right one. No, I mean Mueller. He's now in charge of security at The Evergreen

Institute. You'll find him there, except when on an errand for Schwann."

"You're going too fast for me—Schwann's man, The Evergreen Institute, me being shadowed."

"You got it. There he was, sitting at the back of the science lecture hall, listening to you talk about *Sorex vagrans*. Now you tell me: Why is that man, that imported East German bullyboy, listening to you talk about shrews? Other than the fact that he has the temperament of one, I can't imagine."

"Are you sure it was Mueller?"

"Oh, I'm certain! He is one that you don't forget. I first saw him two years ago."

Ryder told how he had been sent to cover a conference on Alzheimer's research held at The Evergreen Institute. It turned out not to be much of a story. Dull reviews of amyloid buildup in the brain, prions, and the rates of progression of the disease was all it was, quite dull. Out of boredom, Ryder passed the time watching Anton Mueller. He had taken a special interest in seeing every reporter's credentials and lectured them not to stray from the immediate area of the meeting rooms without escort. It made no sense, but was not worth arguing over. Another reporter quietly told him that Mueller was not one to cross.

"Don, it does not add up to much. Can the man help looking the way he does?"

"Doctor, I notice things. I am a reporter. Remember? On the plane, that creature was seated three rows back."

"I did not notice."

"Well, I did. At first, I thought he was with you. But it made no sense to provide you with security, did it? That's when I decided to change seats with another passenger. I wanted the chance to talk with you."

"I'm still not sure that I see where all this leads. I certainly do not warrant a minder."

Clearly, Ryder was pleased with himself. Chasing down rumors and suspicions was his red meat. Before setting out that morning, he had called his editor just, as he put it, to touch bases. He wanted an explanation of why there was so much interest in a reclusive scientist no longer affiliated with a major university. The editor mentioned The Morgan Prize. He admitted that it might be a bit of inside baseball, something of interest to science buffs and few others. But, the editor had his orders from on high. Get an interview and cover the award ceremony in San Francisco. Finally giving in, Ryder asked the paper's morgue to fax him all they had on Dr. Adam Grant.

"I wanted to tell him bullshit. But I let it go." Ryder dropped his voice to a whisper. "I called my brother-in-law. We're not close, really, but he happens to be a computer analyst at Schwann and Company, a contract worker. He's a financial type, numbers mostly. Last Christmas, when I visited San Diego, he told me that his biggest problem working for Schwann and Company was their mania for centralization and security. Everything about Schwann's holdings and investments is confidential and restricted. He was given access codes to do his work, but only after signing a confidentiality agreement. He hates that sort of thing. So he told me a bit about the companies. Schwann has his hooks in so many. The man has made his fortune off of government contracts to construct nuclear facilities and manage them. In the last few years, he's been buying up generic pharmaceuticals, grabbing patents and such. His interest in print media is limited, but concentrated in high tech cities.

"My brother-in-law tells me that the analysis he did for Schwann and Company on the money they've poured into that institute, you know, The Evergreen Institute, was supposed to show a return by this time, only it has not. He told his superior that the company should pull the plug on it, if the motive was to see a return on investment. He was told it was none of his business to offer opinions, just financial facts. That sort of pissed him off. I suppose that's why he told me about his work for them. He does not like secrets. So, yesterday, when I got to Albuquerque, I called him."

Adam listened patiently, but looked at his watch. He did not want to appear disinterested. He liked Ryder. The man was not dull or stupid. If there was a point, though, Adam wished he would get to it.

"To make a long story short, he accessed some financial projections dealing with the institute. This morning, I called him back to touch bases. He tells me there is a file. It's restricted. Brother, what Schwann knows about you! It reads like that old TV program, 'This is your life.'" Ryder pulled out a printout from his briefcase. "My brother-in-law downloaded the stuff. I went to Kinkos to print this out. You've been a busy man, Doctor."

Ryder pressed his point about the detail in the file, the need for it. Then, he changed the subject abruptly to a company called Genetrix, a centerpiece of Schwann's interests.

"I've never heard of Genetrix. I assume it's a pharmaceutical."

"Not long ago, on my own, I looked into the patents held by Genetrix and lawsuits for antitrust, patent infringement, and lobbying for licenses that involve the company. None of the legal actions against Genetrix has been successful. There are a good number of them, but they never go anywhere. Genetrix is a force to be reckoned with. Genetrix holds patents. It does not develop drugs or conduct clinical trials. It lobbies the FDA for exclusive rights to existing generic drugs. You would not believe the profits involved."

"Now, it comes back to you, Doctor. You have something they want, something he wants. Odds are that you won't have control of whatever it is for long. That explains Mueller. And, forgive me for saying so, it also explains The Morgan Prize. As I see it, the award is meant to influence you, to control you. They paved the way through grants from The Evergreen Institute. Now, they plan to exploit what you have. Genetrix will seek control through patents. It has no interest in the drudgery of research and clinical trials? That's for those who think they are doing good. As for The Evergreen Institute, it funds some research, but that has not paid off, not as planned, according to my brother-in-law, that is."

Adam's impulse was to argue that Ryder was making too much of it. It had never occurred to him that anyone could be so designing, so predatory. Ryder believed that Herman was not the prime mover. Schwann was the spider in wait, spinning his web in which Adam was becoming snared.

Adam was due at The Evergreen Institute. Now, however, he wanted nothing more than to get on a plane. He was shaken, and he did not like it. The feeling of vulnerability, of being used, was new to him.

Ryder reached across the table and put a disk and printout beside Adam's cup. "It is all on this disk. It will tell you things about yourself that even you don't know. They have kept a close eye on you, indeed they have."

Feeling nauseous and uncertain what to say or do, Adam picked up the disk and papers. "Don, I want to talk with you more, but I'm out of time. A driver is waiting to take me to the Institute."

"I'll be around, Doctor. You take care. That place smells like a swamp."

"Thank you." Adam stood up, feeling none too steady on his feet. He bent low over Ryder's ear. "I can't tell you how much I appreciate this. I will need time to sort this out."

Adam left the dining room and headed toward the front desk. Seeing the institute's waiting driver, he said, "Give me a minute; I need to ask the front desk something. What is your name?"

"Ronald, Sir. My name is Ronald."

"Ronald, I will only be a few minutes." Adam quickly returned to his room to retrieve his briefcase with his research disk in it. Foolish, he thought, to leave it out of his sight. Ryder's revelations indeed had an effect on him.

The institute was close by, and he did not have much time to think. As the driver turned left off Ashby Avenue, Adam opened his briefcase. His disk was there next to the one Ryder had just given him. With effort, he shook off his sense of nausea. He wished he had time to access Ryder's disk. Time had become an enemy. To the left, half a block ahead, he saw the brick Tudor front of Hardesty's home. "Driver, pull into that driveway on the left."

"Sir, we are running late. My instructions are…"

As he slipped his research disk into his breast pocket, he told the driver, "I insist. I need to cancel a lunch date. It won't take more than a minute."

He lied, not that it mattered. What the driver did not see was important; what he might tell his superior did not matter.

<++++++++++>

At five paces the automatic door opened. A long, aspirated hiss of escaping air flowed past him as he stepped inside. The electronic eye over the door whizzed as it moved into position. Damp, cool air enveloped Adam. A second set of doors opened, with another surge of damp, cool air. The letters etched on the glass door read "The Evergreen Institute." Another electronic eye whirred into position. Adam ignored it. A thin, pale, middle-aged man stood near the reception desk. As the glass door opened, the man stepped forward, right hand extended, a fixed, impersonal smile on his face. It was impossible to see the man's eyes behind his thick, tinted glasses. The man's thin, tight smile exposed his poorly aligned teeth.

"Good Morning, Dr. Grant. I am Dr. Gustav Hessen. If you please, the Director is expecting you."

Dr. Hessen motioned toward the elevator. His sweeping gesture implied that Adam was receiving the full Evergreen treatment. On each level, Hessen stopped the elevator to point out the offices lining the halls down the corridor to the left and right. He took special pride in every detail, with a satisfied grin that exposed his misaligned teeth.

"Everything is here, you see, everything. We keep an orderly campus, do we not? And, of course, there is our guesthouse, The Manse, on the grounds. It is not the Claremont, I must admit, but…"

Adam smiled noncommittally. So, Dr. Hessen is aware of my lodging preferences, Adam thought. He also wondered what lurked behind those coke bottle lenses. Adam decided to keep his observations to himself. But could he put on a good show of ignorance? He did not know.

For all appearances, the administration building was as Hardesty had described it. The main building resembled a drum, circular in shape, four stories, with a hollow center atrium. It resembled an above ground bunker, except for the windows. Windows also faced the interior open atrium. Dr. Hessen drummed on about the wonders of the building. Adam saw only a monotonous donut-like edifice that sufficed for architecture.

On the fourth level, Dr. Hessen ushered Adam past a half-circle of offices. At the far end of the corridor was the executive suite. Herman's taste was visible at every turn. The building itself was a self-contained, physical environment—uniform, utilitarian, and vapid. The corridor walls were painted in varying shades of gray. At regular intervals rubber plants or neon palms in large stainless steel pots, all uniform in size, interrupted an otherwise monotonous pathway of the muted gray linoleum floor. The drab captive greenery, abused, neglected, and dulled by indirect light, reminded Adam of the desert in a moon's half-light.

Entering the Director's outer office, Adam saw Herman standing at the door to his inner office. His smile resembled Dr. Hessen's, except that his teeth were straight and even.

"Welcome. Come in. Welcome and congratulations." Herman put special emphasis to the word "congratulations." He bent forward slightly, his hand out to meet Adam's. "The Morgan Prize is welcome news indeed! It's such an honor for our humble institute to have one of its own chosen."

"Please, Herman, you make too much of it." Adam mustered a tight, strained grimace.

"Yes, well...Heavens, you certainly have earned it."

Herman was visibly sweating. He gave a sidelong knowing look to Dr. Hessen. "You have met my deputy, Dr. Hessen, of course. He's my right arm. The science end of things is his department. He keeps the staff on its toes, so to speak." He pointed to Miss Adams, "My private secretary, Miss Adams. If there is any little thing you need while you are in town, tell Miss Adams. She will see to it."

Adam withdrew his hand from Herman's and turned to greet Miss Adams. "You are Marcy Adams? We've spoken a number of times on the phone. I am very pleased to meet you."

"Why, thank you, Dr. Grant." Caught off guard by Adam's knowing and using her first name, she blushed. "I am happy to at last meet you, also." She thrust out her hand, which shook a little.

"Do you prefer to be addressed as Marcy or as Miss Adams?"

Herman looked surprised. Miss Adams was smiling. He could not recall her ever having smiled. Though in truth, he seldom looked at Miss Adams in a way that suggested that he saw her as a person.

"Please, you may call me Miss Adams. Or, if you wish, Marcy, just Marcy."

"I will call you Marcy. It is a fine name. Is it a family name?"

"My grandmother's middle name was Marcy. When I was young, I was her favorite."

"It is good to meet you, Marcy. I apologize if my late arrival has caused you any inconvenience."

"Pay it no mind, Dr. Grant. It's nothing out of the ordinary."

"Please, call me Adam. After all, I do feel that I know you. You have always been so helpful when I have needed something. I am sure Herman values you highly." For his own reasons, Adam laid it on a bit thick, watching Herman and Dr. Hessen's reactions from the corner of his eye.

Shifting nervously in place, Herman interrupted. He was anxious to get on with business.

Dr. Hessen again extended his hand and then excused himself.

Adam settled deep down into Herman's couch as Miss Adams brought in the coffee and cookie tray. She pointed to the Fig Newton's. "I remember that you said you like them." As she poured his coffee and set the Fig Newton dish beside him, Adam patted her hand and thanked her.

"Herman, I do apologize for messing up your plans. Until Cynthia told me, I did not know that you had planned a lunch yesterday. You may have said something to me earlier, but it simply did not register."

Herman waved his hand dismissively. "Think nothing of it. It's for the best."

It was an odd response from Herman, almost accepting, close to forgivingness. "How is our dear Cynthia these days?" Herman had never liked Cynthia. "Is she still ensconced in that drafty ruin she calls Woodmere?" He often took an oblique swipe at Cynthia when the subject of her lifestyle came up.

"You know how she is. She has not slacked off using those pills you and Father talk about. I wish she would, but that's the way it is. How is Father, by the way?" Adam wanted to change the subject.

Before Herman responded, the intercom buzzed. Herman accidentally pressed the speaker button. Adam heard Miss Adams' voice. "The caller is on line one, sir. He insists."

Fumbling with the buttons, Herman finally secured his line. "Thank you, Miss Adams, put him on."

Adam sat back, feigning indifference by sipping coffee and eating a Fig Newton. For as long as Adam could remember, Herman could use charm or be cold as ice, depending on his mood or what he wanted. Even his skin could match his mood, rather like a chameleon's skin. Toward Marcy Adams he was ever impersonal, cold, and demanding. Once Miss Adams put the caller on the line, he turned attentive and solicitous. Adam watched his performance, likening him to a cold-blooded reptile, his tongue licking the air and his lower lip. It embarrassed him to imagine Herman as a lizard. He feared that he could not hide his thought completely. He forcibly turned his mind to what Ryder had told him. But he could not think clearly, while watching Herman. He remembered his chameleon instead, a Christmas gift when he was ten years old. He and three or four of his classmates were each given one for Christmas. Two girls wore theirs tethered to their sweaters by a golden chain and collar. They enjoyed waiting for reactions from their classmates. If one of the girl's fingers got too close, the lizard scampered up her neck and into the girl's hair. Far from their native Madagascar, none of them lived for long. They belonged to the trees and leafy jungle floor. No good came from being staked to mohair sweaters and the careless handling of ten-year-old girls.

Herman's voice rose, agitated and apprehensive. Had he forgotten that Adam was present? "All right, then, what else is the matter?" He looked up. "Adam, please forgive me. A minor problem has come up."

"Don't mind me," Adam said, fixing his gaze on his distressed half-brother. "Take your time."

Herman fell back in his chair, the phone glued to his ear. Perspiring now, he licked at the droplets collecting on his upper lip. Herman's tongue was extraordinarily long. He licked the beads of sweat and listened, trying to disguise his protestations at the same time. A minute passed, Adam kept very still, pretending to doze. Herman's agitation and his sweating increased. Adam continued to pretend to doze, to take no notice of Herman's state. Herman struggled to contain himself. After a long minute's silence, perhaps two, something snapped in him.

"No! That is not what I want. I do not want that. Do you hear? I don't care what...it's my decision...not your concern." A short pause ensued. "You must understand. I have someone in my office just now." Without another word, Herman hung up the phone. He leaned against his desk to catch himself. Except for Herman's heavy breathing and the crunch of leather as he squirmed, the room was eerily quiet.

"Do forgive the interruption. At times subordinates can be over zealous."

Adam weighed the moment. With Herman off balance, Adam used some of the intelligence Ryder had given him. "Herman, your security here is pretty tight, isn't it?"

"Well, yes, of course. It is a sign of the times. Why do you ask?"

"On entering the building, I tried counting the security cameras."

"Why would you?" Herman wiped his brow. "Yes, we have security." His tone was defensive.

"I assume that visitors, like myself, do not go anywhere without escort."

"Adam, any secure facility operates along the same lines."

"Perhaps some security is called for. I concede that much. But don't you think that an over-abundance of it can stifle the environment scientists prefer to work in?"

Herman tried to make light of Adam's concern. With effort, he slowly rose from his chair and motioned toward the office door. "Let me show you around. See for yourself how well things are run here."

For the next hour, Herman showed Adam around, boasting of the institute's achievements. Adam listened and pretended to be impressed. However, a different picture formed in his mind. The Administration Building, designed by some "renowned" architect was the largest building. It dominated the entire complex, implying its functions took precedence. From the scale model of the complex that Herman showed him, Adam made a mental note of Building 2, the computer center. Building 3, the annex to the computer center, was labeled security. Building 4, directly across from the Administration Building was identified as "The Research Center." Adam tried to estimate how many labs it could hold. Hardesty, who had attended two symposia sponsored by the institute, had told him that half of it was auditorium and conferencing space. Hardesty was not impressed. At the back of the complex were two other buildings, each two stories tall. For reasons Adam did not fathom, Herman ignored those buildings. If there was more research activity on site, these two hulks had to be involved. Overall, the balance was wrong, all wrong. There was too much security, too much administration, and too little space for research.

<++++++++++>

Entering the kitchen, Bayeta smelled coffee brewing. It was noon. Martin, having finished his morning routine, was sitting at the table. He was on edge and avoided eye contact. Alberto was sitting beside him. He was deeply fond of Alberto, but had difficulty responding to Alberto as a man. It was equally impossible to treat him as a boy, which in so many ways he remained. His condition forced him to depend on others for his care. The most ordinary act, like supporting his own weight as he walked down the hall from his bedroom, was painfully taxing. The doctors had done all they could to slow the progression of his disease. Adam, with the doctors' approvals, had designed a regimen of growth hormones and enzyme supplementation. It appeared to have some benefit. But, there was no certainty to any of it. Alberto insisted it did him good.

To Martin, any action was reason to cling to hope. His feelings went deep. To Bayeta, though never to Adam, and certainly not to Alberto, Martin admitted that he felt guilt. Alberto looked to him, as much as he did to Bayeta or Adam, for help in coping. He desperately wanted encouragement, some glimmer of hope that a way forward was at all possible. A Navajo, Martin admitted to being uncomfortable in the presence of disease. Evil existed in the world as much as good. How, then, was he to cope with his sense of guilt, a condition alien to him? Guilt was *a bilagáana* affliction, not part of his culture. White man pathologies only added to a world out of balance. At the base of Martin's consciousness, of late, was some unnamed imbalance, a mysterious, unseen, malevolent outside force.

Bayeta sensed the intense disturbance in Martin's demeanor. She wondered what the root of it was. She watched him each time he came out of the laboratory. She had known Martin all his life, had known his mother and older sisters from childhood. Martin was a simple man, one not prone to brooding. He did not possess the will or frame of mind to carry about inside of him the dispositions of two cultures at once. What was it that bothered him of late? It was as if a dark, forbidding hole had opened up inside of him.

In silence, Martin reached for his coat and stepped toward the door.

"Martin, did you help Alberto into the kitchen?"

"Yes, he wanted vanilla yogurt with strawberries. I told him they would only give him a bad stomach."

She turned to Alberto. "Do you want to sit a bit longer with me or are you tired?"

"Yes, I am tired. I want to sleep now." His words were almost inaudible, too thin to disturb the air.

"I'll take him to his bed," Martin offered. "Then, I have a chore to do in town."

"Will you be gone long?" Martin acted as if he had not heard. "Will you be back in time for dinner?"

"I will be back by nightfall. Don't wait dinner on me."

Martin helped Alberto to his room and returned to the kitchen. "Flagstaff took a lot out of him."

Bayeta's mind turned to what Adam had said, if, when, Alberto's heart began beating irregularly. The medicine was laid out on the hall table outside his room and in the kitchen. If Alberto drifted into shock or was breathless or chilled or disoriented or showed any of half a dozen signs of distress, she was prepared. She was prepared, she told herself. At thirteen, helping to nurse her great grandmother, she knew her duty, what must be and what could be done. At ninety-six, the matriarch of her clan faced her slow, painful death stoically. The family, except for Bayeta and Grandmother, feared contamination. Bayeta did what had to be done. George Slim, her father, had told her what must be done, but he could not help, so strong was his own dread. If the patient were a man, maybe he could have helped. He promised to drive to Ganado to ask the trader to come. That much he would do. The old woman, known to the trader as Dezbah, had brought her rugs to Mr. Hubbell to sell. He always treated her well. When her time came, she reassured her granddaughter, that the trader, a *bilagáana*, a good man, would do what must be done.

Now at Rimrock, everything needed was sterilized and ready, however inadequate any of it was. Alberto had come to fear the trips to the clinic. Alberto had come to believe hospitals were where people went to die, not survive. If he was to die, he wanted to die at home. Bayeta believed that Alberto still clung to hope. It helped to keep his spirits up.

Bayeta heard the Land Rover start up. Martin must have been sitting in it for minutes, brooding. His manner in the kitchen signaled a need to talk, to tell her something. But it was awkward for him to talk to her when he was depressed, and impossible with Adam. Martin was never comfortable talking about his smallest concerns. He would brood for days before Bayeta could pry anything out of him. Whatever it was this time, it had to wait. With Alberto asleep, time at her loom would clear her mind.

Smoothing out her kneeling rug, the one her mother had given her, she settled down before the loom. She took up the balls of re-spun bayeta and another of indigo from her basket. The initial band, which she had already woven to begin the pattern was three inches high. It was a band of bayeta with two oblong blocks of indigo integrated into it. She would repeat the same pattern for the band to follow, then would come three white bands separated by two indigo bands. In her mind, it was just so.

Bayeta settled in, folding each leg under with her soles turned upward. To build up the weave, she worked from right-to-left, east-to -west across the open warp. The width of the weave necessitated building up segments in "lazy lines." One section at a time would form before she needed to move to the left to continue. She set about building up the second band. The pattern, being horizontal, with each transition from one band to the next distinct, had to be straight and true. No margin of error was possible.

As she wove, it pleased her that the first two bands were emerging as straight, even lines and that the blocks of indigo set straight edged on the bayeta background. Deep indigo was the color of the universe before heat and time. The bayeta, red and luminous, was as the sun's glow over the earth of the fifth world.

For hours the house remained still and silent, except for the muted sounds of Bayeta threading yarn through the warp, tamping on the weft strands, sliding the batten, and pulling the heddle rod. Other soft, faint sounds played at the edges of her consciousness. A packrat crossed the threshold of the open patio door, saw her, and darted across the floor tiles, its tail scraping the whiskbroom leaning against the wall. She sat watching until it retreated back to the open patio door and disappeared. Her grandmother always said that packrat was very holy. It was, Grandmother insisted, Hosteen Packrat who brought corn, beans, and squashes to The People, having traded for them with the Hopi.

If only, Bayeta thought, there was another weaver present. She cherished being in the company of other women who wove, who talked about family. Two women might work at the same loom, exchanging ideas how best to make the design come into being. Bayeta missed the unity of purpose and being that came with sitting beside her mother at the loom. Yet, Mother seldom talked while she wove. The act itself spoke for her. Not from words did Bayeta learn, but from her mother's example.

Born in 1920, Ninaba had lived through hard times. The Great Depression was especially harsh on the Navajo. By then cash, what little could be mustered, was the medium of exchange for basic necessities. Ninaba grew up knowing that a woman's loom meant the difference between having little and having nothing. It had become ever so much more important after the Navajo walked away from Bosque Redondo in 1868. The years of captivity had exposed Navajos to the white man's economics. The Anglo medium of exchange served to mummify and petrify the very soul of desert life. Cash became a brutal tether, harsher than any act of prejudice or brutality. For a Navajo woman, the loom was her refuge and salvation. It served to sustain and preserve some sense of life's design and purpose.

Warmer days would soon arrive, and Bayeta could set the loom outside. Widow Tumecho and Johnny Kabito's wife, Marie, and Marie's sister, Lily, had promised to come and weave with her. Three or more looms set to work on the patio would make for a perfect summer. The afternoon shade would be at the northwest corner, with the promise of warm mornings on the patio. Widow Tumecho's hands had failed her, stiff and gnarled from arthritis. Still, she was sure to come to watch and talk of old times. She missed her lost Manuel and sons. She would talk of the good times, life before the hard time. It mattered little to the others that her fingers had too little patience or feel for the loom. Lily, too, had promised to come, but probably wouldn't. In November she had married a white man, a town man from Lupton. Young and filled with modern ideas, Lily was living between two ways. She was a cashier at a supermarket making enough money to help buy what she and her new husband wanted. Her husband's job alone was not good enough to make ends meet. Lupton was far away. Yes, she liked to weave, she had said, but had too little time. For her, weaving was time consuming and part of the past.

Bayeta reached for her favorite batten, one made of scrub oak and worn smooth from long use. Each time she held it, she examined the warm color of the grain, the patina that comes only from long use. To her right she placed the fork, the one made of ironwood. It was handy for building up the rows of lazy lines, alternating between the batten and the fork. Both were made by her father, the batten once her mother's. These two, her “familiars’, she trusted to guide her hand true and firm. Her unease over Martin slipped out of consciousness. Her hands became one with the wool and her tools. The thin thread of time in the moment was insignificant, lost.

Friday stretched from noon and beyond. Time was bound up in lengths of weft yarn laid down, the number of tamps, the pulling of the heddle rod. The warmed studio floor tiles reached up to embrace the air in the room. The sun in transit slipped past zenith's hour, its westward track embracing *Tseyi*, a place where linear time could be ignored. The loom, Bayeta, and sunlight were one. As her fingers stiffened, she rubbed and rested them in her lap. “Before me, I wander in beauty. Behind me, I wander in beauty. Above me…”

Alberto slept through the long afternoon. His body was gathering in what measure of strength it could muster. Before the sun abandoned Rimrock, he would wake. His mind, not his body, would tell him he was hungry, hungry for food, hungry for company, hungry for time.

<++++++++++>

Adam had never before set foot in the Kosmoi Club. The moment that he did, he disliked everything about it. When it opened ten years before, he was still at Berkeley. But, what he knew of it then did not amount to much. Jonathan Hardesty likened its membership to a medieval social cartel. Undeniably, the architecture loomed massive, faux cloistered stone and antiqued glass paneling of another age. Although three stories high, it seemed to crouch menacingly on the ground, its gray façade like a lizard's skin. The north face opened out onto a walled formal garden strewn with Romanesque statuary and manicured shrubbery. The atrium was lined with Doric columns resembling the Cryptoporticus of Diocletian's villa at Split. Oriented east to west, Adam surmised that the setting sun streamed through the length of the walkway at sunset. In the main dining room, Moorish arches supported a domed ceiling of chipped terrazzo tiles depicting hunting scenes and a pastoral harvest in a neverland landscape. High above, the central panel resembled The Abduction of the Sabine Women, the chipped marble tiles rendering it in grotesque caricature.

Herman, obsequious Herman, took Adam's arm and pointed to the rear of the dining room. "There's an indoor pool, steam room, saunas, and massage room. I often stay here when too tired to drive home."

"You must feel right at home here, Herman." Adam made an effort to avoid sarcasm. Herman was plainly proud of the place. Let him have his moment. Adam smelled the air stealing out from the direction of the baths. Pungent and humid, it bore the scents of chlorine and human sweat. Adam instantly understood why his father favored the Kosmoi. Thick and odorous, hot steam offered transient relief to his rheumatoid frame.

At the table reserved for them, men approached to greet Herman and his guest. Herman brightened. Toward each man, Herman knew just how much to tilt his head, how long to hold the man's hand, and the tone to use in greeting—depending on status. Adam could but admire such stagecraft. When it came to such details, Herman could be at his ingratiating best. He maneuvered, postured, and stroked each man according to his rank. Adam could only guess at the years of practice and observation it took Herman to recognize and respond appropriately to his superiors, and to his inferiors. When sober, Herman was indeed an adept at such social nuances. Today was a performance for Adam's benefit. Herman was desperate to show that here, within the rarified environment of the Kosmoi, he was in his element.

"Ah, here comes Lionel Cooper. Shale oil and Colorado mining made his family's fortune. He's now in pharmaceuticals. I find him pleasant but dull." Adam pretended not to hear. Herman stretched out his hand. His wide grin showed half the teeth in his mouth.

"Lionel, it's good to see you! Thank your lovely wife again for me. The party was perfect." They exchanged formal pleasantries. "Have you had the pleasure of meeting my brother, Dr. Adam Grant?"

"Dr. Grant?" Lionel Cooper gave Adam an intense look. "Ah, yes, the Thursday edition of the Chronicle had a piece about you. Great stuff you scientists are coming up with these days, great stuff, Doctor."

Adam took the man's hand, noticing the soft and palsied feel of it. He looked into the man's eyes, two pale, lifeless, vacant orbs of cold steel. "You flatter me, Mr. Cooper. Herman has told me nothing of you, except that you are in pharmaceuticals."

"From what I gather you are an independent researcher. No university bureaucracy to burden you, I'm told, a rare accomplishment, wouldn't you agree—a breed apart, the gentleman scientist. In my day, we had our share. Now, however, science must hold out its hand for public and corporate funding."

"I try to stay clear of entanglements, sir." Adam cared little how the man took his remark. It was enough that Herman heard. Herman blushed and showed signs of nervousness.

"You will excuse us, Lionel? The rest of our party is arriving."

Lionel Cooper gave Herman's arm a squeeze, waved, and turned back to his table.

Herman had said nothing of their father joining them. As Adam took Alexander's hand, Herman motioned to the waiter. He needed a drink. "Adam, what are you drinking?"

"It's too early for me." Herman insisted, motioning that the waiter needed his response. "I'll have a glass of white wine with lunch."

The waiter turned to take Alexander's drink order.

Alexander averted his eyes, as if examining the room. "Nothing, thank you." With that, the waiter bowed and left.

Adam had caught the tight-lipped response from his father. It was unlike him not to have a drink before lunch, he thought. Alexander, as Adam studied him, looked tired, aged, not at his best.

When Hessen joined them, more pleasantries were exchanged as the menu was studied. Adam sipped his water as if it was strong drink. Salads were served with the waiter going through the pepper mill ritual. Herman flagged the waiter for a second round of drinks. Adam knew that he would be on his third double in another five minutes. Did it matter? Nothing of substance would come out of this lunch.

"Have you lived in the states long, Dr. Hessen?"

His accent was thick, a convoluted admixture of Bavarian and Lowland Flemish. "Ya! Five years now."

"I take it, then, that you trained in Europe."

"Ya! I come from Leuven."

"From Leuven, Belgium, then?"

"Ya, Katholieke Universiteit Leuven."

Adam was taking the measure of the man. "I correspond with Merck, there. Do you know him?"

"I work in his laboratory, maybe three years. Then, I come to institute. Before dat, I work three years for Genetrix."

Herman had feigned disinterest in the exchange between Adam and Dr. Hessen. But, at the mention of Genetrix, he gulped down his martini, half choking on it. He was visibly sweating.

"Dr. Hessen is a very accomplished biochemist, Adam, a fine addition to our executive staff. But we're not here to talk about Dr. Hessen, are we?"

"I find it interesting that your right-hand man is from private industry, Genetrix, I mean. Of course, from what I know of Genetrix, which is nothing, I assume there's a connection between what Dr. Hessen did for them and what he now does at the institute. Would I be right?" Adam did not wait for a response. "I was impressed by a paper in 'Cell' by Merck, on his work with synthesizing hormones. Is Herr Doctor Hessen also working on hormonal interactions?"

"Ya! I work on serotonin. It constricts heart muscle. Constrict, is that the word?"

"Ya, it is the right word, Dr. Hessen. I had assumed that such a complex amine as serotonin had been pretty much worked out. Is there something new, something your work adds?"

Adam knew there was not. Hessen now recalled the paper, lauded it as insightful. Adam knew it to be a rehash of the known active properties of serotonin. Adam connected Hardesty's assessment: Hessen, he had said, was a humorless, thick brain. At the university Hessen had been given a course as an adjunct. Hardesty had observed his class and was not impressed. The man's lecture was straight from the textbook without amplification or insight.

Herman made repeated efforts to interrupt the exchange between Adam and Hessen. Having no grasp of biochemistry or microbiology, his attempts were futile. Alexander was another matter. He was not so limited by physics not to know enough to participate. Adam could not fathom, however, why he kept silent.

Dr. Hessen rattled on. Adam only half listened. He added a detail here or a nod there to keep the man talking. Nearly blind behind his thick, institutional glasses, he had a mastiff's face to match his disposition. He responded well to praise. His "Yas!" were getting under Herman's skin as he retreated ever more deeply into his martinis. He grunted as if he understood a word being said about neurotransmitters. Alexander leaned far back in his chair and stared intently at The Rape of the Sabine Women hovering above his head. He fingered the rim of his glass, generating a steady, high-pitched ring from the wet rim. Oblivious, Hessen soldiered on.

Somewhere between a tortuous description of the properties shared by tryptophan and serotonin, Hessen erred. A first year graduate student might make such a mistake. Adam let it pass. To correct Hessen would force an extended exchange. Time was short and this monologue only delayed the hidden agenda Herman had in his mind, before, that is, his last two or three martinis.

"Tell me, Doctor, as assistant director what is it that you do?"

"Deputy Director," Hessen quickly corrected. He straightened visibly as he said it, smoothing the front of his vest and tie. He leaned stiffly forward and planted his elbows firmly on the table, a warning sign of what was to come. He grinned, showing his widely spaced crocodile's teeth. His ill-fitted partial bridge looked discomfortingly misaligned. He sucked in between sentences to adjust it. The litany of his duties at the institute required repeated aspirated pauses. He was proud of his oversight authority of research. No research was initiated without his review and ongoing oversight. Even independent researchers supported by outside grants came under his jurisdiction, he proudly pointed out.

Hessen continued to drone on. Adam nodded at regular intervals. "Don't be fooled by the glitter and chrome, Adam," Hardesty had told him the night before. "It's a mirage, smoke and mirrors. Nothing much really goes on there." Nothing Hessen said, or anything Herman implied, bolstered the claim that real science was conducted on institute grounds. "Adam, it's a swamp fit for crocodiles and slithering things, no more," Hardesty had said.

Within the torrent of words from Hessen, Adam picked up that the budget was over twenty million, with a staff of about one hundred. Few of the scientists on staff were permanent or full-time.

"Tell me, Dr. Hessen, how many are doing basic research at any given time?"

Herman jerked his hand involuntarily, his spilled glass rolling across the table. Calling out loudly to the waiter for a towel, he had not noticed that nothing but ice was left in his glass. The last bit of patience Herman had kept in reserve had abandoned him. Alexander met Adam's stare with a look of resignation. Whatever the business was that Herman had wanted to broach with Adam melted away, as surely as the stray ice cube that had escaped notice beside his pale white-knuckled fist.

Dr. Hessen droned on, oblivious of Herman's clumsiness or his palsied gesturing at the mess he had created. The narrow slits of Hessen's eyes, blurred behind those coke-bottle glasses, gave no hint that he was aware of anything beyond his recitation of the wonders of serotonin.

To break the monotonous litany from *Herr Doctor* Hessen, Adam at last waved him off and turned to Alexander. "Father, do you still hunt?"

"Yes, I hunt if the prey is worth the expense. I'm due to safari next month in South Africa."

"Then, you do not feel too old to stand the rigors?"

"What rigors? It's a goddamned game reserve. They even have air-conditioned cabins."

As the table was cleared for coffee, Herman awkwardly gestured for a refill of his drink. Adam and Alexander settled into an uncharacteristic conversation, one that was casual, almost relaxed. Hessen and Herman sank back in their chairs, sullen, alone, left to their own thoughts.

"It depends on the prey, Adam. The prey is the thing."

Adam nodded agreement. "My wife's people were great hunters, you know. They hunted in order to survive. Many animals were sacred, however, such as coyote and bear. They were never hunted."

"Yes, well, the bear is an admirable beast. Myself, I've never hunted bear. They are loners, you know, loners and unpredictable. I prefer herd animals. As for the coyote, he's clever, but a lowly beast. He'd just as soon eat carrion as take down his own food. Rather like some people, I suppose."

Adam gave Alexander a long, penetrating look.

"The moment of truth comes for us all, Adam. The hunter and the hunted must be properly matched. Otherwise, there is no order or reason to their relationship. For the hunt to be fair, the when and where of the encounter must not be known until the moment of truth."

Adam nodded, holding his father's gaze for a long moment, until the aging hunter looked away. He understood what his father meant, subtle as it was. Herman was overmatched, and he'd come up empty handed.

"Never underestimate the opportunist, Adam. He is ever at the edge of things, waiting for the right moment to seize advantage."

"Yes, Father, I know that. Coyote may not be a majestic animal, but he is wily, intelligent, and patient. He is a survivor."

"As you say," Alexander said, as he gave Adam a penetrating, almost fatherly look, "he is a survivor."

8

Cope's Rule

Alexander's uncharacteristic comment showed signs of a rare subtlety. His quiet demeanor could not have surprised Adam more. He had sat observing without interruption, as Adam pretended to listen to Hessen's droning. He ignored Herman's increasingly black mood. Adam could not fathom why Alexander had allowed the stage-managed lunch at the Kosmoi Club. Had he anticipated Dr. Hessen's display of puffery? As for Herman, he was out of his depth, drowning.

Dr. Hessen continued to tout his accomplishments. With drink in hand, Herman was unable to control the flow. Nor could he have. Most things scientific were but babble to him. At one point, with Hessen distracted, Alexander had put his right hand on Adam's arm. "How long has it been? I count twenty-five years since you and Sanderson rented that house near campus. You could have moved in with me. Well, I suppose you knew I would try to talk you out of majoring in biology."

"There was never any question, not since I was fifteen. Uncle John had a lot to do with that. He would have made a really good biologist. You never knew him."

"Why did you come to Chicago? You had other options. You never told me the reason."

"Chicago was Mother's idea. They offered me a full scholarship. I would have been happy to stay in Albuquerque, even without a scholarship. But Mother insisted."

"You've always had the desert in you, something I have never understood."

"Anyway, Mother knew that I needed to leave home for college. She saw it as a test, how I would grow and change in the world beyond. If I could stand up to Chicago winters and you, she said, then I could handle anything. Cope's Rule, don't you agree?"

"What is that you say?" Herman said, as he straightened in his chair.

"Father and I were talking about Cope's Rule."

"Cope's Law, what is that, something important?"

Adam laughed and swung his arm in a wide circle encompassing the entire room. "We were talking about Cope's Rule, Herman. It's not a law, just a posited principle."

"Don't be patronizing. So it's a rule and not a law. I still don't see the point!"

"Look about you, Herman. Smell that odor coming from the steam room? Listen to the prattle of those men heading for the steam room. After downing a four thousand calorie lunch, there they go."

Herman's hair stood up on the back of neck. "What are we talking about?"

"Herman, if you stand next to one of the regulars you can smell the swamp on his breath."

This only further exacerbated Herman's distress. Adam, however, pressed the point deeper into Herman's alcoholic brain. "I have a paleontologist friend, Loren Cather. He always explains Cope's Rule to his students. Cather's specialty is reptiles, extinct reptiles. If he were here, he could easily classify every relict, cold-blooded giant plodding his way to the swamp back there."

"Adam," Alexander leaned over to whisper in his ear. "Tell him so he can go pee. Please."

"Herman, Cope's Rule is a concept in evolution. In the 1800s, Cope fancied the idea that organisms have an inner urge to evolve, to reach a higher level of existence, bigger size, if you will. It is in a species' blood to strive for perfection. It may not apply to you, though."

"Goddamn it, Adam, I wonder if we are related at all."

"We are half related, Herman, half related. But don't worry. Cope's Rule doesn't apply to you."

Alexander gripped Adam's arm. "Don't goad him, not here."

"All right, Herman. You deserve a better definition."

But, Dr. Hessen interjected. "Cope's Law is a general principle that body size increases in an animal lineage as it evolves. Thus it is so, perhaps, to pass the change on to his progeny."

"It's not a law, Hessen." By now, Adam had dropped the Doctor in addressing the man. "It's a rule, a discredited one at that. Still, if you persist, try comparing the body sizes of Alexander, Herman, and myself. Do you see? Herman cannot help being the family runt. That's why he favors a place like this. Here, men come to take the bath of renewal. They are desperate to believe they can enhance their ability to survive. They are so trusting in their epigenetic fantasies."

Adam's comment was as much for Hessen as it was for Herman, having exhausted his patience with the man's ignorance. Pointing to the massive front entrance, Adam said, "Herman, you think this place is sacred, don't you? Men come through that door trusting that they are at the apex of evolution. They lumber towards the swamp, desperate to escape the threat of desperation and failure. Isn't that right, Herman? Don't deny it. You know them well enough."

Herman clenched his hands together and stared at Adam. How could he know, in the state he was in, that Adam saw the Kosmoi Club for what it stood for. Ironically, for all his wanting, Herman did not fit in. He lacked something, that inner assurance that without question he belonged. He was but their instrument. He served their ends, not his own. Deep down he had to know it.

Alexander understood where Adam's barb was truly aimed. He chose to let it pass, unwilling to surrender the momentary truce he shared with Adam. Why object? After all, the characterization fit Herman. To take exception would only cancel out the one true exchange he had had with Adam in years. He wanted to hold on to the moment. He had of late, if only for his own purposes, come to regret not being a more caring parent for Adam. Advancing age was pressing down on him, hard and relentless. The emotional void it fostered created a cold feeling of defeat deep within his consciousness. He wanted to believe that things could have been different. Reason told him otherwise. The die was cast long ago, before the twins were born. Herman was another matter, another matter entirely. He hated Herman. The child, Herman, had clung to his pant legs, had always craved attention and reassurance, deserved or not. He saw in Herman something of himself, the worst element.

The waiter cleared the table and offered refills. Adam cleared his throat and stared in Herman's direction. Their eyes met. Adam decided the moment had come, as Herman was focused on his drink.

"Herman, I came for the conference. You know that much. Second, I have finished all the research that you have supported. I am finished with it. Our account is, so to speak, settled in full."

Herman was caught off balance. He did not expect an open breach with Adam. "Well, um, yes, of course, we need to review your work. I mean...well, just now, you see, my people also desire an update. I mean, well, not that there are concerns, you see. To keep things going here, well, our benefactors, those who sponsor our endeavors, naturally want to see results. I'm sure you understand. After all, they have a vested...well... I mean we all need to show... to show how valuable our efforts have been. I'm counting on you to continue to add to that. I mean..."

"Herman, I have accounted for all eight research projects. They've all been published in top journals. My work on pituitary and endocrine functions, which you supported, is complete. We should be able to resolve loose ends while I am here. Nothing more is needed."

Herman looked puzzled. "What I need...you must understand, right now, The National Institute on Aging, Andrus, The Rockefeller Institute, they are getting all the headlines. Dr. Hessen keeps me fully informed of, well, you know, the stuff that has real pay off. And, and...I know that you have something more, something big, really big to contribute."

"Herman, every contractual obligation has been honored."

Hessen interjected, "Come now, Dr. Grant. We know you have made great progress on another project. You come here to announce a breakthrough. That is true, Ya?"

"Is that what you think? Keep in mind that your funding never covered all my work. What I choose to work on with respect to aging is my own affair. It has nothing to do with your institute." Adam's stern, definitive tone caught Herman and his deputy completely by surprise. It had not occurred to either that Adam would resist their persuasions with an outright refusal.

Alexander was sitting far back in his chair, smiling, his legs stiffly extended in front of him. He was mindful of his instruction from Schwann. However, he remained silent. Herman twisted agitatedly in his seat, knocking his martini glass to the floor. It broke into pieces. He was too agitated to notice it. Alexander kept his gaze fixed on Herman, who was beyond caring how drunk he looked. Dr. Hessen made a guttural noise to deflect attention away from Herman, but without effect.

Adam waited. How far would Herman go to press him? Obviously, Herman had some inkling of his longevity research. A jumble of words spewed from Herman. Without one word from him, one hint, or one reference, Herman and Hessen knew more than they had any right to. How was it so?

Herman launched into an embarrassing torrent of words, banging repeatedly on the table, using words like responsibility and obligation. But Adam kept his eyes squarely on Hessen. If his work was compromised, Hessen was the one to understand its implications. Herman was too stupid.

Continuing his harangue, Herman insisted there were legitimate claims. Why, he asked, did Adam think the institute was so willing to send him all that lab equipment? What about the electron microscope? That was just one example of an investment, he insisted. Where would Adam's research have gotten, if not for all that equipment? Herman's arguments devolved into a jumbled torrent of noise and scolding.

But Adam kept his eyes on Hessen. He was not to be drawn in. Twice, Adam pointedly looked out the windows and the columned portico leading to the street. He watched a uniformed driver standing at the ready beside the institute's limousine. Two idle taxis waited at the curb. The means to disengage was at hand. Adam pushed back his chair and stood up. "Father, can I drop you?"

"What do you mean," Herman sputtered, "drop Father where? Where are you going?"

"I have an appointment. Our business here is done. Don't you think?"

"But you can't leave, not until..."

"Can and am, Herman. I'll call you later. By then, perhaps, you will have calmed down." Herman lurched from his chair to confront Adam. His rummy complexion had turned ashen. The blood had drained from his head and extremities.

Alexander rose from his chair. Turning to Adam, he said, "If you would drop me off at the house, I'd appreciate it." Herman froze, uncomprehending. "Thank you for lunch, Herman."

Adam smiled and pointed to the exit. "Of course, it's on my way."

As he got into the taxi's back seat with his father, Adam looked back. Herman had not followed. The taxi veered into traffic.

"Driver, turn down University Avenue. I'll tell you where from there." Adam asked Alexander what Herman expected from him.

"You should know that yourself. Word is that you have accomplished something that is too big, much too big, for them not to want it. Herman thinks it is his due. He has to have it."

"Turn right at the next block, driver." The taxi turned. Alexander pointed, and the taxi stopped at the curb. In a whisper, Alexander said, "I've already said too much."

"Are you a party to this? Are you?"

The old man nodded solemnly and got out. He turned back and handed Adam a hastily written note he took from his coat pocket. Eying the driver, he whispered, "Schwann means to bring you to heel. Be careful, be very careful." Adam pocketed the paper without reading it. He looked up at an old man who could not help himself. "Thank you for the warning."

"It is the best I can do. Say nothing of it if asked. Please."

The last thing Adam needed now was a fit of paranoia. He needed space, time, and distance. But that would have to wait. He was expected at the conference. There, he could try to put aside the embarrassing spectacle of the Kosmoi lunch, if only for a few hours.

<++++++++++>

Watching a beloved one slip slowly, steadily, painfully out of life was the most agonizing experience Adam had ever endured. Alienated from his own father, Adam had become very attached to Uncle John. He admired John Grant, who had no children of his own, and looked to him for guidance. Uncle John delighted in giving his time to his sister's children. That summer, 1960, John spent weeks walking the desert with Adam. He was an encyclopedia of lore on the life cycle of plants and animals, and how they adapted to the harsh demands of a dry, outwardly inhospitable environment. He found beauty in every corner of nature, no matter how arid or sun scorched. Beauty and nature are one and the same, he often said. Not even the death or desiccation of an animal or plant was ugly. As long as it was in the nature of things, nothing in or of the desert could be anything less than beautiful. He took pleasure watching a kangaroo mouse search for nesting materials. He could discern the difference between sand tracks of a bull snake and a sidewinder. He knew where to look for a cactus wren's nest, the hole of a burrowing animal, and a rock that sheltered a scorpion.

For all the depth and complexity of his knowledge, John Grant was a simple man. Life was not complicated to him. He had no tolerance for the claim that nature was uniquely designed for human dominion. Nature was an interwoven tapestry of interdependence. It was compelling and immediate. He taught Adam to recognize the cycle of life and death in each plant and animal they encountered.

Near the end of that summer, 1960, Adam walked in on John taking his medication. He realized that much of John's teaching applied directly to his own fate. There were so many pills. At once, the weekly trips John made to campus alone, at nine on Wednesdays, took on palpable meaning. "Yes, I take a lot of pills," he admitted without hesitation. And the weekly trips, Adam asked? "Oh, I get an injection and a blood transfusion," John said matter of fact.

With Eleanor's consent, Uncle John outlined his condition. He had a good bit of time left, he said. Cynthia cried. Shaken, Adam insisted that there must be a cure. The University Hospital doctors were hopeful, John said. There were new, experimental treatments, Adam argued. Was he getting the best treatment?

He smiled and shook his head. "No one wants it to end. Death is a payment come due. It is the price we pay for life itself." He hugged his sister and continued, "I tell you this: If I do die sooner than the doctors say I might, or with more pain, I accept it. Life is the gift. One should not insist how long it must be. Making each day count, that is most important."

At the time, Adam rejected his uncle's ready acceptance. Anger and denial only clouded one's thinking. John became his constant companion, his guide. He needed John in his life. John knew so much about rock lizards and pronghorns. He could tell just by the feel of the air if rain was coming, with a riotous bloom to follow. He had done things that a fifteen-year-old could only dream of.

"Adam, don't be sad. I have lived a good, full life. That's more than most can say. We'll still go up to Taos and fish for trout. We'll hike in to Keet Seel and Betatakin. I'd like that."

"That place is just a ruin. Mother took us there, once. It's a long trail in. You need rest to get well. Next summer, when you are well again, we can go then."

"Adam, I'm not going to get well. This thing inside me is not going away. Plutonium, I can't do anything about that. What I can do with the time I have is to live it. I want to go one more time to see how people lived a thousand years ago. I still wonder why they left so hurriedly, leaving clay pots with food still in them right there on the ground. Corncobs still lay about exactly where someone dropped them. We can see all that and tell them that they are not forgotten. We can touch the ground and tell them it was good, that their life was good. Nothing ever really dies, not completely."

That fall and into the winter, John and Adam were inseparable. Fishing 'the box' along the Mora was the best it had been in years. Restricted to fly fishing, how John believed one should take a brown trout, they worked the deep pools where big ones lurked, catching and releasing.

Adam's memory of John was brightest when he thought about early morning's spent hip deep in the frigid waters of the Mora. John Grant was wholly absorbed in the moment when he laid his line out across the water, his gray cowboy hat dotted with hand-tied flies. He had a smooth, easy arm, knowing intuitively where to cast his fly, settling it softly on the current's turn and letting it drift flawlessly within striking distance of a four-pounder. Watching his uncle at one with the river, Adam often forgot to watch his own line, letting it drift into a sunken log only to snare.

They did not make their walk into Keet Seel. Snow came early that winter. By March, John died. He died at home surrounded by those he loved. Never married, he left what he had to Eleanor and the twins. Adam cherished the two trunks full of nature books John had left him. Cynthia had not wanted any of them. John could not give her what she needed, a father as companion. He tried but could not disguise his ignorance about the things that mattered to teenaged girls. He never failed to ask Cynthia to come on desert walks or trips to the Mora. Cynthia envied the time Adam had with John, but would not go with them. Years passed before she admitted that John never discouraged her from coming on their outings. She did not care for the desert. She did not want to fish, insisting, "What's the sense in catching a fish only to release it?" John accepted each "no thank you" Cynthia uttered. Try as he did, he could not make her feel accepted.

It was thirty years since John's passing. Again Adam was confronting an impending death. He loved Alberto as much as he had loved Uncle John. Alberto's unalterable decline pressed down on him, as did the frustration he had felt with John's passing. The memory of Uncle John's grace and acceptance brought him no comfort. Alberto's fate was a different matter entirely. Still, he could not avoid seeing Alberto's chin tremble with each new sign of decline. Alberto's habit of sniffing air as he struggled to walk down the hall to the kitchen was not about what was cooking on the stove. It was the ash and dust floating in the air. Uncle John, too, near the end, sniffed the air against the pain. His hands had shaken uncontrollably, just as

Alberto's now did. The difference was in what life had afforded each man. Uncle John had outlived so many friends. The beach landings and mortar barrages on Guadalcanal had taken many of them, men younger than Alberto. At age fifty-three, still vital, Uncle John had laid his life down, ever the good soldier. He had stood his ground as long as he could, fully committed to life. He regretted one thing, the years he had worked with plutonium at the Hanford plant. The pay was too good to pass up. The war's end had brought with it the promise of a bright, energy-rich future. Nuclear power was the future. Breeder reactors were promoted as the key for turning non-fissionable uranium-238 into plutonium. It would be years before scientists admitted how difficult and dangerous was the process. Technical problems, high temperatures, and the ever-present possibility of a meltdown kept success beyond reach. John came to understand that scientists could be blinded to the dangers of "tickling the dragon's tail." He had known men who handled plutonium with rubber gloves. They saw it as just so much gray, heavy matter. He had felt the heat of the metal himself, handling it and wondering what made it so.

Now Alberto's life was slipping away, and Adam was not at his side. Adam had to make this trip. Part of him was grateful for the few days he would avoid Alberto's questions. He could not but feel that he had somehow failed Alberto. Unlike Uncle John, Alberto would never don hip waders and fly cast into a deep, trout-rich pool along the far reach of the Mora.

<++++++++++>

For Bayeta weaving had little to do with art and everything to do with living. At present it provided relief from the tangle of abstractions and cares. Tamping down a line of yarn, she was focused only on counting sheds. The foundation bands of bayeta red and indigo were making for a fine beginning. When completed only Adam would know how much it meant to her. Only he would know that it was true to her purpose. Other weavers, weavers she respected, might see the integration of bayeta as representing the earth bound up within the four sacred mountains. They might speak of how such symbolism amplified their appreciation. But it was her inner vision alone that mattered.

Weaving such a web was a challenge of every muscle and thought from beginning to end. Given its planned width, it was best to build up two bands at a time by building lazy lines. This demanded precision. Each horizontal band must hold straight and true for the entire 76 inches. No division of mind between the loom's need and her other duties could be permitted.

She worked without pause as the sun lowered in the sky. She could feel the firm, true strength of the warp yarn's tension, the firmness required to tamp down the weft. The batten with which she worked the re-spun bayeta pleased her. Bayeta yarn had found its place on Navajo looms before Bosque Redondo. The reworked English flannel was stripped and drawn out into new yarn, strong and enduring. No other yarn quite held such a deep, brilliant, and enduring red, certainly none with its unmistakable subtle bluish cast. A practiced eye appreciated the nuanced hue of crushed cochineal beetles used in the dyeing process. She alone now worked with bayeta yarn. Her Great Grandmother had planned well in saving the heirloom bolts for her.

Other weavers may have desired to work bayeta into their weaves. But, no more vintage, century old baize cloth was to be had. They would admire Bayeta's work, but not imitate. Each weaver nourished her own tradition and means of distinction. Each weaver found balance between expression and the restraint of tradition. Bayeta belonged to *Tseyi*. A Ganado weaver's pattern and color equaled in merit. It was just so for Nazlini, Two Grey Hills, Burnt Water, and Crystal weavers. The beauty way found expression in many forms. Bayeta did not ask her loom to be superior, only true to its spirit.

As she worked in each strand of weft yarn, she emptied from her mind the cares that weighed upon her. Education and travel had shaped her life with rich texture and knowledge. Yet, her identity held fast to her roots. Maturity had given her insight with which to identify her needs. What her Navajo side needed was grounded at *Tseyi*. Her worldliness was not abandoned, only framed within the four sacred mountains of *Dinétah*. When she was born, her mother had buried her umbilical cord at Crystal, in the Chuska Range not far from Rimrock. Thus anchored to the earth, no pull of the world beyond could overcome her sense of place. She had spent years living and coping in the world at large, but her sense of place was on the reservation. She had no need to abandon one skin for another.

<++++++++++>

Adam had yet to find that finely woven balance that sustained Bayeta. His life had not anchored itself to place, not since leaving Albuquerque for college. Albuquerque meant much to him, but it did not draw him like a magnet. His mother and uncle had died there. He lost his first love there. Loss, the memory of loss, did not anchor him. Science had long provided the grounding for his life. Beyond Bayeta and Alberto, like-minded scientists were his kin. He did not allow doubt to become his "*ignis fatuus.*" In experiments and proofs, he found reason to strive.

Bayeta, unlike Adam, did not trust that science could free humankind of ages-old fears. She had an intuitive sense how scientific advances too easily confused means and ends. Science tested the boundaries of the unknown before considering "what then?" On the day she first met Adam, he forgot himself as he talked of his work, and she sensed an imbalance. He had been engrossed with unraveling an imponderable, paying no attention to the "what ifs". The quest itself interested him, not application or consequence. He reveled to be the first to glimpse a new thing. But once examined, he moved on.

When the lab at Rimrock was up and running, Bayeta once asked him, "Are you searching for some kind of 'philosopher's stone'?" She remembered her classics professor calling such quests that. Was there danger in trying? "Oh, Bea," he had said, "I am not chasing after the Ring of Ogier or Medea's brew. That's the stuff of medieval fairy tales. I want to find the means to extend life, not reshape it."

The matter might have been left at that. Adam, however, often massaged the idea of life extension when pressed by a friend or colleague. "Is there a mritasanjivani plant out there?" he would ask. "Maybe it is rooted in exotic soil and waiting to be discovered. Call it an atavistic impulse, if you insist," he once told Sanderson, "You have to admit that it is possible."

Bayeta only half-believed that Adam was making light of it. She could not fully fathom his need to know, a need that bordered on a burning intensity that at times all but consumed him.

<++++++++++>

Bayeta put aside her work for the day and thought about Adam's trip. Could the award, The Morgan Prize, lure him away from Rimrock? For her, the question of place had been settled. The Place of Emergence was near Rimrock, to the north. The wellspring of existence for her people was the Place of Emergence. There, all life emerged from the lost fourth world below. The fifth world, here, was where harmony and beauty were to be found. Nothing essential for a good life remained undiscovered. Pythagoras the Greek, with his absolute conviction that truth is beauty and beauty truth, could not have found richer soil for his utopia. At the rim of *Tseyi*, the present order and harmony of her life was her mritasanjivani. She examined her day's progress.

"For a good weave, daughter, the wool must be clean and strong. The loom will tell you when it is right," Ninaba had repeated often. "Let your hands guide you. Do not force it." Ninaba would pat her shoulder when she looked uncertain and say, "With your fingers, let beauty find its way to the loom. It will come." Satisfied, Bayeta smiled at her work.

Once, Bayeta asked Adam if he believed in limits. "In a way I do, yes. Science is constrained by the limits of observation and comprehension at any given time. But that is all." If that is so, she pressed, where did he want it to lead him? "To the day, Bea," he had replied, "when all live by a new measure, a new standard of measurement for the span of life."

"You are not concerned what that might do to the world?"

"No." His answer had been immediate and unequivocal. "I am a scientist, not a philosopher."

"I wonder," Bayeta said with her eyes intensely focused on him, "why you ignore philosophy."

Adam could see where she was heading. "Everyone wants to live longer. It isn't something one needs to look to Aristotle or Socrates to know."

If Adam harbored any doubt about the benefits of longer life, he did not share them. Alberto did not deserve his short, painful life. Adam had worked long, grueling hours—days, months, and years—to come to the threshold of success. He felt guilty at seeing Alberto's hopeful smile, how his body was bent and twisted with pain. Progeria had done its work too well. He could not help Alberto. But, success was a kind of expiation.

Alberto stood at the open door to her studio in his nightclothes. In the air, with his finger he traced the line of the panel she had just finished. "I can't wait to see it done." His shallow, rapid breathing floated unsteadily on the cool air of her studio. An involuntary spasm ran through her.

"You have slept well?" He did not answer. His breathing was raspy, labored. She imagined the effort it took him to make the journey from his bed. "Come sit with me. I'll help you."

With his slippers scratching at the floor with each small step, she guided him to the couch near the loom. It was late afternoon. Before noon sunlight infused the studio with a warming glow. Bayeta liked best working at the loom when an early sun bathed her studio in clear, crisp morning sunlight. In such clean, crisp light the loom hovered, shining in anticipation to fulfill its purpose. By noon, with the earth hurtling eastward toward evening, a soft light quieted the hours. Bayeta often wove until mid-afternoon, the time when lengthening shadow spoke of the need to rest, of her need to rest. Now was such a time.

Bayeta held the deep indigo wool in her hand. Before her loom, Alberto glimpsed what Adam found so precious in his wife and companion. She was beautiful beyond description. Alberto sat down on the couch unsteadily next to her, leaning against her right shoulder. He fingered the sheepskin throw rug beneath him. His mood was subdued and silent, absorbed with his own list of "what ifs." What if he could live long enough to marry? What if he could have children? What if he was disease free? What if Bayeta… He had so many "what ifs."

Bayeta loved Alberto as a son. Since his coming to live at Rimrock, he had become transformed, no longer the confused, fretful boy. He was now a young man filled with curiosity and an insatiable appetite for the new. It pained her to know that at age twenty-two his spirit was trapped inside a brittle, decaying shell of ravaged flesh. "I'm like an old piece of toast, dry and crumbly," Alberto once told her. He described his state with stark precision. This disturbed Adam and Bayeta. Though he feared death, the burden of pain was almost too much for him to bear.

The doctors in Flagstaff admitted that Alberto's bitterest self-descriptions made them feel helpless. One had treated two other progeria victims over the years. He had some inkling of the psychological dimensions of the disorder. The progression of the disease often drove the patient to the edge of panic, compounding the pain and debility. "We do our best to keep the patient hopeful," he had said. "Fill Alberto's time with happy memories. Brooding can trigger a panic. A patient's sanity can fail before the body itself gives out."

Alberto had said that his own startle reflex, with each spasm of pain, was the worst. Each telltale sign of his heart racing as it stumbled toward arrhythmia could bring on panic and disorientation. The doctors had done their best to help Alberto cope with such inevitable moments. He must try, they told him, not to let pain overwhelm his knowing that such moments pass. He must remain calm and not panic. Alberto would nod unsteadily and look away. "What do they know," he had told Martin on the drive back from Flagstaff on Wednesday.

No matter how well he controlled his fear and held back an increasing sensation of arrhythmia, Alberto knew he was alone when it came upon him. It was his heart that raced, heaved, and convulsed. He alone had to battle the pain and not surrender. "No, not this time, not this time."

The doctors privately admitted to Adam that they wished for the less traumatic, if not less cruel. Alberto might, without warning, slip into semi-consciousness, followed by deep sleep. In such a state he would feel no pain. It would be hard to watch. But, they offered, the end would come quietly.

Alberto understood that one of two extremes awaited him. He was no fool. Even so, he did not want that final day to pass in comatose slumber. Before Adam had left for California, he helped Alberto walk out on to the patio after dark to watch the stars. Sirius, the brightest star in the night sky, was clearly visible. Adam pointed to it, calling it a dwarf star. The moment he said it, he realized he should not have.

Alberto squinted, pretending to see the star. "That's how I want to go out. I want to shine like that, just once." He raised his arm in the general direction of the Dog Star. "I want to shine, shine bright. Then, I won't mind it when I grow dark and still. I will blink out and just go."

Adam gently hugged Alberto and carried him to his bed. The boy-man felt so light, almost airy in his arms. Adam could not help but think of what would be required when the day came. Alberto would be laid to rest, his grave heaped with spring flowers. His spirit would occupy every corner of the house, reluctant to depart. Putting him on the bed, asleep, Adam could not suppress the specter of Alberto's passing. West of Rimrock, over the rise of hill toward the setting sun, a small stone marker would be put up after four days. Alberto insisted that was what he wanted, something simple, something that belonged. It would not do, Bayeta told Adam, to tell Alberto that she had reservations about a grave being sited near Rimrock. It would be one more place neighbors avoided.

Bayeta saw how Alberto squinted at her loom. Sight was failing him. She convinced him to have his meal propped up in bed. As she helped him back to his room, holding on to him at the waist, she thought how he would never feel the ordinary sensations of a young man's mature, competent body. Bayeta reviewed Alberto's list of "what ifs." There were far off places to visit—a tropical rain forest where monkeys scampered above in the branches, where coatis darted at the foot of giant fig trees. He dreamed of spying a jaguar creeping over the forest floor's gloom at dawn. What if he was an archeologist like Sylvanus Morley or Hiram Bingham? He might discover the lost ruins of an ancient civilization. He might find a second Machu Picchu with its own Intihuatana, the sun's hitching post. Llamas would feed out of his hands! His list of what ifs was long. It was rich with passion and extravagance.

Awake, he was propped up in the bed, picking at his food without interest. Alberto's diet was now limited and bland. Nothing tasted good to him. Bayeta nibbled at the food trying to make him interested, to see that it was not so bad. But what did pureed fruit and minced meat taste like? Silly putty and pity paste he called them. His mood turned petulant. Lost in thought, Bayeta felt Alberto's gnarled fingers softly touch her blouse's sleeve. His hand shook. "Adam, I…I want…I need to see him. When will he come home?"

"He will leave San Francisco Tuesday morning. Before nightfall, he will be home."

"Is he going to be famous? Maybe he will be too busy to come home."

Bayeta leaned closer and hugged him. "He is famous enough. He does not care for that."

"Other people care about that, don't they? Isn't that what being famous is?"

"Yes, I suppose that is one way to put it."

"He will be famous because they all want what he can give them."

"We'll see. We'll have to wait and see."

Alberto yanked on her arm. "But I can't wait."

Bayeta felt his rebuke. Alberto had some understanding of what Adam had accomplished. How many times had Adam explained to him how aging, normal aging, is a natural part of life? Adam saw it as a process of adaptive regulation. And yes, even the fittest body experiences apoptosis on a daily basis. Lymphocytes in the human body die each day. Nature tries to keep things functioning and in balance, but time is limited even for the fittest. "With most people, as they age, disease invades with increasing frequency. Vital parts wear out. Repair and replacement fail. In you, the clockwork became accelerated. If only there was a way to slow that clockwork down. Then, well…we'll see."

Alberto's body told him how rapidly his body was winding down. When Alberto first came to live with Adam and Bayeta, it was different. He believed there was a chance that his body could find a kind of symmetry for its growth, change, and maturation. It should take many decades, with senescence and death far off. But, of course, that was fantasy. The normal rules of progression did not hold for him.

Once they had settled in at Rimrock, many local children came to visit. They did not look upon Alberto with pity or undue curiosity. But little by little, things that hurt crept into conversations. Maria, Widow Tumecho's granddaughter, complained to her sister, Juanita, that her breasts were not becoming big fast enough. Little Tommy Yazzie bragged about his batting average. He was the best hitter in the under thirteen boy's division. Juanita was always arguing with her sister about who could skip rope the longest. None of this was meant to make him feel bad or inadequate. Nonetheless, he noticed every distinction between their lives and his.

Before Alberto was three years old his hormones had sent out confused, flawed, and premature instructions. His growth in height had slowed. He would never measure up to the scratch marks that lined the doorjambs of ordinary households. Normal children gained in height, weight, and function. He withered. In any group, his role was that of spectator or listener, not as participant. Alberto's most desperate longings could not be satisfied. His list of "what ifs" only grew.

"To hell with this food," Bayeta grumbled between her teeth. "Alberto, I'm going to take away this food. You and I will dine on tapioca pudding topped with raspberries. We'll have fresh baked bread with chokecherry jam. I'll make hot cider with a cinnamon stick."

Alberto looked surprised and was thoroughly pleased. A thin, tight smile stretched across his face. Tapioca tasted of exotic South American rainforests. Cinnamon smelled of adventure and intrigue in the far off Spice Islands of Indonesia. Yes!

<++++++++++>

The taxi dropped Adam off at the Oakland BART station. He enjoyed the crush of strangers on the train. He felt embedded. He relaxed and put the lunch spectacle behind him. The last eighteen hours had disoriented him. Now he needed time to think. Herman and his associates had designs on him. Mr. Schwann, thus far only a shadowy figure, was somewhere in the picture. But for now, he assumed, he could stay clear of him.

Walking west on Market Street and then up to Geary and Taylor, Adam found the Hilton Hotel. He braced himself. The lobby was crowded with attendees. He took the escalator to the third floor where the registration booths were located. On the way up, he diverted his eyes, not wanting to be recognized. Glancing at badges, he recognized some of the names. Dr. Olafson from Svenska University was holding court for a cluster of young doctorates on the second landing. Ronald Masterson, an acquaintance whose work he had recently reviewed for The Cell, walked by without looking up. Adam didn't want to talk to Masterson. On reaching the third level, he heard someone call out his name. It was Marion Webb. Adam waved. "Let's have a drink, later," she said in a loud voice. He nodded. Privately, he had no intention. Dr. Webb, a former colleague, would try to pump him.

He stood in the pre-registration line for A through G to pick up his badge and a program. It was nearly three in the afternoon. The line was short. He took the packet with the program and abstracts and was handed his printed badge. "There is also a message for you. Let me get it for you."

With the message in hand, Adam stepped away and removed the ribbons attached to his badge. The red ribbon identified presenters. The blue ribbon was for fellows. These would only draw unwanted attention. He still had time to listen in on a round table discussion on mutagenic nucleoside analogs. Another abstract interested him, recent work on anti-tumor applications. He also needed to find Hardesty. Making his way to the Sacramento II Salon, familiar faces drifted by. Some waved. He kept his pace and sped by.

For the next two hours, Adam sat and listened to papers on adenine and thymine nucleotides. They could have applications for developing antiviral drugs. By 5:00 PM, he decided to walk through the exhibits area. There he picked up a brochure on new electron microscopes. He would have to pack up and return the SEM model the institute had lent him. A higher power TEM would do nicely, if he could afford one. Still, he was used to seeing specimens intact. He wanted a demonstration before the exhibits closed for the day. As he approached the Phillips booth, he heard Hardesty's voice.

"Adam, I was hoping to find you."

"Jonathan, have you had an interesting day?"

"Let's find somewhere to talk." Hardesty looked to be on edge.

Adam spotted a sign at the rear, and motioned for Jonathan to follow him behind the curtain to the Exhibitor's Lounge.

"Won't the exhibit people object?"

"Just behave as if we belong. No one will say anything."

They took a table at the back. Jonathan spoke in a hushed tone. "I did as you asked. I picked twelve individuals, solid people, and downloaded the data disk you gave me. Here's the list."

Adam handed the list back without looking at it. "Jonathan, you keep the list. Can I assume that you sent it as if from me, without identifying yourself as the sender?"

"I used a computer at the library and did not identify myself as the source."

"Good. It is best that they think that I sent it. Since I don't know who they are, and I don't want to know, not for now, then I can't be compelled to divulge their names."

Jonathan put the list back in his pocket. "I trust each one. The note simply told them that a summary would soon appear in *The Cell* and in *Science*. Is that what you wanted?"

"Yes. The research can't now be locked away or suppressed."

"You mean…" Hardesty looked around without finishing his thought.

"Someone is behind Herman. At lunch, he lost it. He and that Herr Doctor Gustav Hessen made a spectacle of themselves. Herman believes that I owe him, which I do not."

"Just so you know, I put my copy in a safe place. I did not have time review it in detail, but I believe from what I have read that it is all that you say it is."

"The research protocol, results, and conclusions are all on the disk, as is the raw data."

"You mean all of it?"

"Jonathan, what is not there is the detail of how to transition from *Sorex vagrans* to humans. Treatments and regimens will come later. For now, the research and findings are for them to sort out."

"I take it that you made no mention of Alberto."

"Let the data speak for itself."

"All that stuff with the oversight committee may come back at you."

"The more noise the better. Don't you agree?"

Jonathan looked worried. Adam changed the subject. "You would have enjoyed watching Herman and Hessen. I referenced Edward Drinker Cope's Rule, and Hessen jumped in with both feet."

Jonathan laughed. "Cope has been dead for a hundred years. What was it about?"

"I was making a point that evolution generally proceeds from comparatively unspecialized forms to more highly developed, complex ones. It went right over Herman's head. Father appreciated it. After all, he is the runt's father. That's when Hessen jumped in. He blithered on in Lamarckian terms, as if a single organism can affect its own evolving. If I hadn't cut Hessen off, he would have launched into the wonders of the homunculus."

"Hessen is the sort to believe that tradition and good breeding is in the blood."

"Anyway, I left Herman in need of a transfusion."

"What was it Darwin said?" He paused to recall the exact words. "We may look with some confidence to a future of great length…All corporeal and mental endowments will tend to progress toward perfection."

"Well, he didn't have the Kosmoi Club members in mind. Darwin would have also reminded us that, "Of the species now living, very few will transmit progeny of any kind to a far distant future."

"When is your talk?"

"Monday afternoon. I did not know the time until I scanned the program's addenda. Have you heard of this reception Herman is hosting at The Evergreen Institute?"

"No. All I've heard is that the award ceremony is to coincide with the president's address. They are laying it on thick, determined to make a very big deal of the occasion."

"You've been asked to make some opening remarks?"

"In spite of the objection of a nominating committee member, I have."

"Good, and I insist that you come with me to the institute's reception tomorrow."

"I've not been invited. They are pretty strict about who gets in or out of that place."

"Jonathan, you are my guest. If they have a problem with that, we will both walk out."

"That collection of medievalists will fascinate you to no end."

"I'm hungry. Can you have dinner with me?"

"Do you want to go now?"

"Yes. I didn't eat much at lunch. Let's go to the Four Seasons Restaurant at The Clift. It's just a block up the street. No one will bother us there.

Dinner was an opportunity for Adam to put Jonathan's legendary powers of deduction to work. Since arriving late Thursday night, Adam had tried to piece together a confusing and disjointed train of coincidences. Jonathan had given him some insight. Adam felt a bit foolish for being so naïve about The Evergreen Institute.

"Now I remember. You've always liked The Clift."

"I stayed here when I first came to California. It was expensive, but those first few days were perfect. I'd sit in the bar staring up at the faux Klimt paintings on the walls and imagine what my future might be. I've had a soft spot for the place ever since. Crystal and I stayed here when I brought her out to California. She did not see the place quite the way I do. We did not stay long."

"She knows what is good for you. The desert is open ground for you, with no boundaries."

"Most people think of the desert as a lonely, desolate place. They see it as pounded flat, eroded, dried out. Desert people do keep close to water and mountain passes where they can escape from enemies. Wind, rain, and sun challenge life at every turn. Adapt or die is law.

Bayeta says it is more a matter of finding and maintaining balance. Without that, all is lost."

Jonathan, satisfied to sip his wine, listened. It felt good to relax. For the moment, nothing more needed to be done. Jonathan laughed at Adam's description of the Kosmoi—strong odor of chlorine, wisps of steam escaping from the doors to the steam baths and pool beyond the dining room. Then, he took a deep breath and asked again about Alberto.

"He's at home with Crystal. The other day he told her that he has pterodactyl blood in his veins. I had read him a letter from Loren Cather. He's found another one of his gliders at his shale site in Wyoming. As I read Loren's description of the fossil to Alberto, he interrupted me. He claims to know how a pterodactyl must have felt. He said that he, too, has a leathery skin and is clumsy on land. But when a pterodactyl glides out over an ancient inland sea, what wonders he must see below."

"Alberto sounds like a romantic."

"He is that. He tells me that he knows what must have gone on inside the brain of Cather's fossil. He insists that the pterodactyl knew his end was coming. That's why the thing took flight out over the inland sea as far as the winds would carry it. It tired and fell into the sea rather than having to live longer unable to fly. It preferred becoming a fossil."

"How did he figure that?"

"Oh, I took him on a visit to see John Sanderson three years ago. John has this print of Icarus in his living room. So when I told him about Loren's find, he said the beast must have been just like Icarus. He lectured me that was the only way Cather could possibly have recovered an intact skeleton of the creature. Otherwise, it would likely have died on land and been eaten."

"That is perceptive."

"Yes. But he was really telling me that he wants to be like that pterodactyl. He wants to imagine, just once, what it feels like to slip the bonds of earth, to soar high and see the world below as it really is. He's never been in an airplane."

"You are going to miss him terribly." Jonathan had never seen the boy. He knew of him only through Adam's eyes. Even so, he could sense the boy's spirit, his keen interest in things. He also believed that Alberto had given Adam and Bayeta something precious, an understanding of the meaning of family, something far more substantial than living only as a couple.

The waiter poured coffee, and Adam excused himself and went to the men's room in the lobby. As he returned he heard a woman's voice, "Adam Grant? Is it really you?"

The woman stood at the entrance to the dining room. In her late seventies, still attractive, she could easily be mistaken for Barbara Walters. She was well dressed and wore expensive jewelry. Adam had passed her on his way to the men's room, but had given her only a cursory glance to avoid bumping into her. Now, he looked. Did he know her? He drew a blank, but held out his hand.

"Let me see, how long has it been?" Her smile was warm, genuine. "My God, it's been ten years, Marianne!" His memory had clicked into place.

"Thank you for remembering. Yes, it has been a long time."

"You do still live in San Francisco, don't you?"

"Naturally, dear boy, where else would one choose to live?"

"You look as ravishing as ever. Do you see much of Alexander these days?"

"Occasionally, that is when he's not plotting something or other. We keep in touch for the boys mostly. They mean the world to me."

Alexander's first wife was third generation San Franciscan, a blueblood. It had always struck Adam as telling that neither of Alexander's wives took his name. Marianne had kept her maiden name, Cockroft. When she married Alex in 1935, she was pregnant with Herman. No Cockroft would bring a bastard into the world. John Marion Cockroft, her father, would not have stood for it. After a suitable interval, an amicable divorce was obtained. Each went their separate ways. Alexander met and married Eleanor eight years later. Nonetheless, Alexander had more to do with Herman's upbringing than he did the twins. For him, Herman being the firstborn, was his rightful heir.

Adam finally grasped the reference to the boys. "I haven't seen Herman's boys for five years. How are they?"

"They're my only grandsons, you know. I am very fond of both of them. I love them desperately. Tell me, how is your wife? I forget; is her name Crystal?"

"Yes, it is Crystal Bayeta. We celebrate our tenth soon."

"That is a good name, Adam. It sounds like cut glass, clear and bright."

"She was born in a small village named Crystal."

"I remember now, she's Navajo, a lovely woman. I never looked that good."

"Marianne, it's nice to see you, but I am dining with an old friend. Could I call you?" He looked toward the interior of the restaurant, anxious to resume his talk with Jonathan.

Marianne stood very still, waiting for Adam to notice. She wanted something of him. An unexpected meeting this was not. Although Adam barely knew her, he liked her. He saw her as an impressive woman, someone of character who looked straight at you and yet had an easy manner.

"Adam, I do need to talk with you."

"If it is important, of course we can. Would you like a drink?" He motioned toward the bar.

"I'd like that. I have something to tell you. In return, I want you to help me."

Adam took her arm and escorted her into the lounge. As she sat down, he excused himself. He needed to speak with his friend, Jonathan, he told her.

Jonathan nodded as Adam returned to the table. "I saw her, Adam. Is it important?"

"I don't know." He did not sit down. "I have the sense that it is. Do you mind? I'll split the bill with you and then see what it is she wants. She's Alexander's first wife, Marianne."

Jonathan smiled. "I am due at the business meeting, anyway. I can just make it."

"Thanks."

With that, Adam returned to the lounge.

Settling into the booth, he noticed how little she had changed in ten years. She still had a coquettish air about her, the way she looked at men. She was a woman who dealt in subtlety and coded sexuality without effort. When she wanted something from a man, any man, the unspoken cue served her best. Adam did not know her well, but liked this woman.

"How did you find me? And don't tell me this is just an accidental encounter."

"I could say that it's just by chance. I do come here often for afternoon tea."

"It's long past the tea hour, Marianne. How did you track me down?"

"I didn't, not really. Oh, I heard that you would be at the Hilton for this conference of yours. Herman called Carol and told her how you walked out on him at lunch. It was not difficult to guess that you would be at the Hilton. You are news, you know. I took the chance that I'd find you."

"Then you followed me here?"

"Well, it is not quite like that." She paused to sip her drink, giving him her look. "Did you see that ugly man who entered the bar after us?" Adam turned his head to look, but Marianne motioned for him not to. "I recognized him. He's Herman's man at the institute, that creature. He's always lurking somewhere about. Herman calls him his chief of security."

"Do you mean the man they call Mueller?"

"Carol calls him 'The Little Prussian.' Absolutely hates the man." Marianne stroked the collar of her sable wrap and leaned forward to whisper. "I saw him in the hotel lobby. I watched him. I knew he would find you. And that is what he did."

"I want to know what you know of Mueller. But first, tell me what you want of me."

"Thank you, Adam. Fair is fair. Herman is my only son. I don't pretend to understand what made him turn out to be weak and corrupt. Maybe it is something I failed at. I don't know."

“Marianne, maybe nothing you could have done would have made any difference. He is missing something inside. If anyone is to blame it is Alexander. A son needs a loving father.”

“You turned out fine. He was your father, too.”

“Be that as it may, the immediate question is what you are concerned about.”

“It’s not about Herman.” She was struggling to control her emotions. She reached into her purse for a handkerchief. “It’s about the boys. They are such beautiful young men.”

“You mean Linnus and Vann?”

“They are my only grandchildren. I have such hopes for them. Lately, Carol can’t do a thing with them. As for Herman, he doesn’t even try.”

“What is it that has you concerned about them?”

“Neither one has a job. Vann dropped out of college before graduating. He spends all his time chasing women. Linnus is a nice boy, just twenty years old. But he’s turning into a drunk. He’s in and out of trouble with the law. He’s been arrested for drunk driving three times. I can’t expect that my influence will keep him out of jail if he gets arrested again.”

“What about Alexander? Can’t he help?”

“Oh, he does try talking to them. That is, he talks to them individually, so as not to embarrass the other. But, Adam, that’s all he does, talk. They don’t listen.”

“How do they get the money for the kind of life they are leading?”

“Herman writes checks. Or, they go to Alex. I’ve refused to give them any more money.”

“What is it that you think I can do?”

“You are their uncle. Maybe *you* could talk to them. Maybe they could be persuaded to go and stay with you for a while. They have to be gotten away from here to straighten out their lives.”

“Marianne, I’ve not even seen the boys in five years. I am almost a stranger. If they won’t listen to their own parents, or you, or Alexander, what can I do?”

"Adam, you are the one real male in the family. You've always been the one Alexander believed would shine. Oh, it's true that he never understood you. But he is not stupid. Lately, do you know that he sees his life as wasted? He tells me old age has taught him that he was wrong about so many things."

"I don't understand. You divorced Alexander in 1941. Do you really know him?"

"Adam, I never really stopped seeing your father. Maybe it is terrible to admit it, especially to you, but I never stopped seeing him. I just did not want to be married to him."

What Marianne said struck home. If he had been more perceptive as a young man, he would have put together the number of times Marianne visited Chicago while he was an undergraduate. There, when he saw the two of them together, he thought little of it. After all, they had a son between them. Herman's welfare had to be the reason for their meetings. But, for the moment, this was not something he wanted to know more of, or cared about. Marianne's concern was the future of her grandsons.

"If I see the boys, while I am here, I can invite them to visit. Maybe the desert would be good for them. But I have to say, I doubt that either of them will even consider it."

"That's fair enough. It may be enough that they know you care. They admire you, Adam. They think of you as the one sane person in this whole family. Linnus calls you "the Wunderkind." He's always asking Herman about you. It makes Herman mad, you know, that Linnus looks up to you and not him. He gets all puffed up and reminds Linnus that he heads up a major research institute, while you have run off to the wilderness to lick your wounds."

"I am not licking my wounds, Marianne. As for being the in the wilderness, I…"

"Adam, please make time to see them. Talk to them."

"I will try."

"That is all I ask of you." Marianne dabbed her eyes with her handkerchief. "Thank you."

Adam surveyed the room as he finished his drink. In a darkened corner at the far end of the bar, there sat Anton Mueller. Above his head was a faux painting of "The Embrace." Mueller looked completely out of place. Or, did he? The painting was, after all death's embrace."

"Marianne, you were going to tell me something about this Mueller."

"You should know about him. Carol comes into town every couple of weeks. We have lunch and shop. She doesn't have anyone else to talk to. Herman is drunk most evenings. He talks. She listens. Well, he rants. It's not like he actually talks to her. So, she talks to me. He's always scheming. About a week ago, in the middle of one of his rants, he took a phone call from a man named Martin. Herman completely forgot that Carol was in the library with him. Carol told me it is not the first time this Martin fellow has called. Carol overheard Herman tell this man that if you did not turn over some thing, she did not hear it all, that his life would be over, that your life and reputation would be in ruins. He means to do you harm, if you…"

"Thank you, Marianne. You don't need to tell me more. I can fill in the details."

"Will you talk to the boys?"

"Of course, I am in town until Tuesday. I'll try to have lunch with them at the Olympic."

"They like the Olympic Club." She paused and touched his arm. "Will you be all right?"

"You mean with Herman?" Adam smiled. "I'll tell you something funny. Once, he could have had it for the asking. About two years ago, I needed more funding. Then, he could have gotten an agreement out of me. Well, I found a way without his help. Since then, I have made certain. No loose ends remain. No Evergreen involvement. They supported other work, but not this, my best effort."

"What will you do now? Can you just pick up your marbles and go home?"

"Alberto, our ward, is very sick. He has progeria. It cannot be arrested or reversed. All we can do is make him as comfortable as possible. In a way, I owe my success to him. His condition made me focus and redouble my efforts. Last spring, I realized how mature he has become. I enjoy being with him. Seeing him deal with his fate made me want to succeed for those who can benefit. I did not tell Herman one word about it. Herman is too much of an elitist to care."

"I know that you've done everything you can for the boy."

"He's not a boy. He is a man"

"How much time does he have?"

"He has a week at best, not much more. He's asked me to see to it that something special is buried with him. Bea helped him to choose. He also wants a stone marker. It is to read, 'The world is too much with me; Not getting or spending, it lay waste to my powers.' It will be hard to put up that marker. He wanted so little from life, so little." Adam fell silent. Marianne finished her drink. He looked to see if Mueller was still there. He did not like knowing that he was being followed.

"Do you mind picking up the tab? I need to make my way out without that man following."

"Not at all, dear boy. Let's order another round, as if you are in no hurry. Then, go to the restroom and not return. There's an exit door next to the left of the bathrooms. That should do."

Adam motioned to the bartender. "Barkeep, we'll have another round, please."

Adam walked at a slow pace to the door leading to the lobby, feigning nonchalance. He could make out from the corner of his eye the shadow of the man in a dark suit sitting at the far end of the bar.

Adam slipped out into the early evening without being noticed. Walking down the street toward Union Square, he breathed deep. The air was crisp and cool. It was nothing like the humidified indoor vapors he had been breathing most of the day. He felt free to be out in the breezy air of San Francisco. It felt good to be alone—alone, anonymous, and not followed. He walked east, Union Square behind him, not knowing where he was bound.

9

Through the Opened Door

Twice in two days someone told Adam that he was being watched. He felt vulnerable and compromised. It was disturbing, infuriating. But telling Herman off would accomplish nothing. He would lie and insist that Adam had an overactive imagination. It would also alert Herman to the fact that Adam had made a connection between Mueller and Schwann. Donald Ryder had left little doubt of that.

"It's time to be careful and clever," Adam said aloud as he quickened his pace down the street. Crossing Union Square, he stopped at a park bench to retie a shoelace and to look back up the street. Friday night was in full swing. Diner's stood outside Kuleto's, waiting for a table. On the corner of Post and Stockton, a street musician played his violin. Adam slipped into the crowd gathered around the violinist. He listened to the music and scanned the way he had come. Was this how a stalked animal feels? He did not like the sensation one bit. The traffic lights at the corner changed. He crossed to walk down Post to Market Street, trying to shake off the feeling of being pursued. The night air was crisp and fresh.

He remembered the first time he had watched an animal's response to being pursued. He had stalked a small lizard exposed on a rock near his home. He had crept up very slowly, watching the lizard's eye track his approach. Lizards fear what they do not recognize. Frozen in place, only its eye blinked, its body tensed for sudden flight. The standoff ended when the lizard sensed that to hold his ground was not an option. Faster than Adam's eye could follow, a split second of time, the lizard scrambled across the sand and out of sight.

As he walked, he began to think about his next step; he knew that he needed to act unpredictably. Mueller would expect him to act predictably. At the conference, he would be reasonably secure so long as he kept to crowded public areas. The Hilton was a rabbit's warren, cavernous, with many exits, elevators, and escalators. Getting lost in the crush of attendees would be simple enough. If he spotted Mueller, he could slip out a door or lose him in the crowded corridors. Not one to draw attention, Mueller would back off and pick up the trail later, Adam guessed. If noticed, Mueller might act like the lizard sunning on a rock—in wait for the chance to act.

Adam reasoned that he would be most vulnerable Monday, at or after the awards ceremony. He did not like the waiting. Until then, he would use the time to cobble together his acceptance remarks. How much dared he say about his achievement? In the program's separate printed addendum someone had included a tentative title for his talk: "Human Aging in Evolutionary Context." Who had presumed?

The Awards Committee Chair, signing the letter congratulating him, had added a postscript: "At your earliest convenience, please call." Adam gritted his teeth. It was the exact phrasing Dr. Hooke had used five years ago. Then, it had helped Adam decide to resign from the faculty. Hooke had made Adam's research an issue by taking it before the Ethical Standards Review Committee. He had insisted that Adam's research might lead to clinical trials using human participants. Adam had had no such intention. But Hooke was adamant: Adam's research would not be authorized. It meant turning over to a committee the power to decide what to explore. Adam knew that his views on cell metabolism, malfunctioning organelles, and the process of autophagy would be picked to death.

But all that was ancient history. Why was Hooke now a key player in the awarding of The Morgan Prize? Adam and Hooke had never got on well. Hooke habitually made enemies of junior members of his department. They were "too dependent upon leaps and bounds, sudden breakthroughs," he would say. He hated the "serendipity factor." Hook detested "the loner," any scientist who insisted upon control of his own work. What, then, had changed in five years? Adam knew better than to trust that Hooke had changed. More to the point, what designs did Hooke have on him now?

Walking down Market Street toward The Embarcadero, Adam sifted through the events of the last two days. Clearly, Herman knew more than he had a right to know. What was his source? Was it Martin, as Marianne had hinted earlier? How might Herman have compromised his assistant? Then, there was Mueller, that shadowy hulk. Donald Ryder called him "Schwann's man." Ryder was also a bit of a mystery. Yet, Ryder had confided what he knew, and his assumptions. Finally, there was Herman's performance at the Kosmoi. Adam had never before seen him so desperate, so unhinged.

Adam came to a standstill at the corner opposite the Hyatt Hotel. Why had Alexander acted so strange, almost fatherly? When lunch descended into farce at the Kosmoi Club, Adam's impulse was to confront Herman. Hessen's display had made that impossible. Alexander's maneuverings also confused the moment. Then there was Marianne intercepting him. She, like Ryder, had seen Mueller shadowing him. There was Mueller, sitting at a corner table in The Clift Hotel bar. Another piece had yet to fall into place: What connected The Evergreen Institute to Dean Hooke? Hooke was his old inquisitor and now Chair of the Morgan Prize committee. Hardesty had said that Hooke was a Genetrix consultant. As for the institute, its advisory board included Thomas Vaughn, Basil Valentine, Robert Boyle, and Jean Rey, among others. Adam knew of each man. He did not like what he knew of any of them, believing them third-raters. More than one fed off the work of doctoral students and post-doctorates, claiming first authorship to their efforts. Such connections spelled what, trouble?

On crossing over to the Ferry Building, the dots connected. If Hardesty could see it so plainly, why had it taken him this long to see it? William Henry Schwann was the majority stockholder of Genetrix. Schwann was a financial backer behind The Evergreen Institute, conceivably the major one. Schwann was Anton Mueller's puppet master. Schwann had sent Ryder to report on him. Schwann was his father's source of consultancy work. Schwann, Schwann, Schwann!

As the connections came into focus, a fainting sensation forced Adam to breathe deep. He was now alert, every muscle in his legs jittery, ready for flight. The night before, in the bar, Hardesty had said, "Adam, he's a God-damned puffer! He's after one thing, your *elixir vitae*, your Red Dragon. Can't you see that? He's got to have it." Both had drunk too much wine and Adam was only half listening. Now, however, Hardesty's words came flooding back, ringing true.

Entering the Ferry Building, Adam looked at his watch. To avoid further entangling himself, he needed to seize the initiative. He could just catch the last ferry to Tiburon. Rushing to the ticket booth, he saw passengers walking onto the ferry. With ticket and change in hand, Adam ran up the ferry's gangplank, the last passenger of the day. He could breathe fresh salt air for the next forty minutes and enjoy the skyline of San Francisco receding astern.

On second deck, Adam bought a cup of black coffee and Fig Newtons at the snack bar. He found a free bench and stretched his legs out on the seat across from him. He counted a dozen dim stars overhead. At Rimrock, the same stars would have appeared an hour ago. The cool evening's air felt good, fresh, and clean. San Francisco receded as Tiburon neared. He felt at ease suspended between the two. Leaning his head back, he was suddenly tired and closed his eyes. "I just need to get through the next couple of days, just the next…"

"Excuse me," said the young man on the bench across from Adam. "You are Dr. Grant, aren't you?" He had a book in his hand, a textbook, and a backpack was beside him.

"Do I know you?" Drowsy and unfocused, Adam shook his head and rubbed his eyes. The student had an easy, confident look about him. "Ah yes, you do look familiar, but I can't place you."

"Forgive me for disturbing you, Doctor. When I saw you sitting here, I figured this is my chance to apologize for the prying questions at Dr. Sanderson's symposium."

Adam sat up and stiffened, as he focused on the young man. The mention of Sanderson placed the student for Adam. "Wilson, isn't it?"

"Yes sir."

"Of course, you are here for the conference." He laughed at his own deduction.

"Dr. Sanderson said I should be sure to catch the award ceremony."

"Well, I may bore them."

The young man laughed and leaned closer. "I'm finishing my Ph.D. at UNM. I'm through in June. I have two interviews at the job placement service. One is with the Berkeley Structural Genomics Center. I'm hoping to make a good impression, and not bore them."

Adam smiled. He had picked up on Wilson's ironic sense of humor. "That sounds promising. What kind of position are you interviewing for?"

"Computer specialist with knowledge of protein sequencing and structural analytics. That's pretty much what I've been doing for two years for Dr. Sanderson. I think I can handle the work." He spoke with confidence, tinged with expectation.

Harold Wilson impressed Adam. At his talk, Wilson had asked about longevity research. The question was general, but it did catch Adam by surprise. While the other attendees emptied the lecture hall, he and four of the other graduate students in Sanderson's lab had lingered at the lectern. They asked Adam more about shrews as test subjects. They had never heard of shrews being used in experiments. "We just assumed that you used white rats, Doctor," one of the students said.

Wilson looked puzzled. "May I ask you about shrews? I mean, what made you decide to work with shrews instead of white rats or cats or dogs? You mentioned their metabolism and number of litters each year, but still, I've never heard of shrews being used in experiments."

Adam replied, looking for a way to briefly respond, "It is their expected lifespan that is the most important factor. *Sorex vagrans* may be a primitive mammalian form, but it shares many useful adaptive traits that are also found in humans. However different we are from shrews, most basic adaptations are shared. Aristotle even developed a psychology of shrews."

"Yes, but what proved that they could be useful in research?"

"Three days ago, I did a post-mortem on one of my Alphas. Alive, he weighed exactly five grams. That does not sound like much, does it? Anyway, he was a very adaptive creature. Shrews occupy the greatest variety of environments on this continent, more than any other mammal. Just as amazing, he ate an amount of insects, snails, and worms equal to his own weight each day. Can you imagine a rate of metabolism like that? He is active at any hour of the day or night, always on the hunt for food. At the time of death, this little fellow weighed four grams. Keep in mind that *Sorex vag*rans is not the smallest of shrews. I was quite fond of Alpha 11, a fine specimen. He was well groomed, aggressive, and a healthy eater. Whenever he noticed me, he'd scurry to the edge of his cage and scratch at the air, as if waving to me. Near the end, he was losing vital tissue at an incredible rate. He died of a massive heart attack and loss of blood circulation to the brain. Old age overtook him. Can you imagine my reaction examining that brain, a speck on the end of my scalpel? It was under two-tenths of a gram, including the optic nerve and olfactory bulb. The average human brain weighs about thirteen hundred and sixty grams. His heart was so small that I had to use a microscope to see the coronary damage. That pump is a marvel of evolution capable of beating two billion times. That is about the number of beats of a human heart over seventy years. One hundred million years of evolution separate us, and yet there it is: A heart not so unlike our own. The biggest difference is size and how fast it beats."

"Do you mean our heart is like the shrew's heart?

"It is similar, yes. As for size, a shrew's brain is seven thousand times smaller than that of a human. But what it does with its brain is adapt and survive. In the wild, every action is directed by the need to eat, evade predators, and reproduce. Metabolism is so high because of those needs. Does that brain think beyond the immediate moment? Who knows? So long as nature provides a stable niche, it will thrive. If the environment changes, shrews may well evolve and send out new forms of mammalian species long after our species has disappeared through catastrophe. It has done so before."

"You don't believe that shrews will inherit the earth, do you, Doctor?"

"In nature anything is possible. Given enough time and the forces of change, say a few million years, new forms of mammals are more than likely to evolve. New species will radiate out from the present lineages. Some will feed on grasses and seeds. Others will become flesh eaters. We came from meat-eating Homo erectus. Our seed eating progenitors died out what, a million years ago? Ask yourself, what would we have become if we contented ourselves with seeds, nuts, and plants? Would we possess less neo-cortex? What if we developed big brains organized in a different way, to meet different challenges? Would the structural differences make us less capable of abstract thought? Would we be a less aggressive species? Can you imagine an intelligent primate without nuclear bombs?"

"It sounds like what you said yesterday, that stuff about man being incomplete."

"I don't mean 'man' in the narrow sense. In *The Uncompleted Man,* Loren Eisley reminds us not to see the future as fixed, static, or predictable. Out of all the life forms on this planet, only humans threaten the future of all life.

"We could blow ourselves and everything else up."

"That's possible. Some believe that physics is our era's fiend. Remember, Shakespeare's Macbeth said something like, 'We have more than once juggled fiends, counterfeit realities.' "

"Would you also include biology as a science juggling fiends?"

"Harold, biology is also capable of 'tickling the dragon's tail.' The difference is perhaps more one of means, not ends. Underneath the polished veneer of the life sciences, we still harbor an atavistic curiosity in 'The Greene Lyon' and 'Red Dragon.' Of late, I have begun to understand that."

"Thank you, Doctor. I am looking forward to Monday. And, thank you for clearing up the question we had about Alphas versus Betas. Now I see why I won the betting pool."

Adam gave Harold Wilson a confused look. "I'm sorry, what betting pool?"

"Oh, we forgot to bring it up yesterday. On Wednesdays we meet as a study group, the graduate students, that is, in the lab. About six weeks ago we saw a printout message from the server that aroused our curiosity. Since then we've kept track of the online traffic every Wednesday on the Alphas and the Betas. It was routed to "Circle One". We figured out that the data contained animal identification codes, elapsed time in days from birth, and general physical condition at death. And, we guessed that the Betas were controls." Wilson was correct. "Anyway, a dollar betting pool was started up. How many Alphas would die in relation to the Betas."

Adam now understood why so many graduate students showed up at the talk. They had developed a guessing game on the longevity curve between the two groups, not knowing it was shrews in question. Without knowing the import of it all, their curiosity had been peeked.

"Let's go inside, I'm feeling chilled." The boat was due to dock in fifteen minutes, time enough. As they walked into the main cabin, Adam sat down and motioned to Wilson to sit across from him. For almost five minutes, Adam sat looking squarely at the cabin floor, trying to absorb the full import of what Harold Wilson had revealed. On occasion, Adam used the link to leave John a note, or use the mainframe's computing power. That was the extent of it. It surprised Adam that students saw and monitored emails. But, he had never emailed a site labeled "Circle One." He had no idea who or what "Circle One" was.

With the silence between them becoming awkward, Harold Wilson said, "We would never have read those messages, if it weren't for whoever was at the other end pressing a wrong command."

"That's all right, Harold. I am grateful that you told me. Now I understand something I did not know, had no idea of."

Harold did not reply, sensing that Adam was preoccupied with his thoughts.

"When do you go back?"

"I'll go back on Wednesday. I'm staying with a friend in Kentfield. She's picking me up. If I get that job in Berkeley, we can be together more."

"Good luck, Harold. By the way, the stuff we talked about…"

"You mean those computer messages? I promise. I won't say a word."

With the ferry at the Tiburon dock, Adam walked with Harold Wilson to the street.

"Thank you, Harold. Goodnight."

Adam left Harold on Main Street next to Sabella's Restaurant. It was a short walk to The Tiburon Lodge. With luck, they would have a vacancy.

<++++++++++>

Lengthened shadows and cooled air had softly settled into the corners of the studio. In her bones, Bayeta felt the sun retreat. Lighting a lamp, she examined her progress. She had laid down two identical panels of bayeta with blocked indigo embedded in them separated by a thin line of solid indigo. The next alternating bands of three white and two indigo, would be simpler. Every band would be three inches wide. Nineteen bands in all would enforce a smooth, even progression from bottom to top.

For the present, she set the bayeta yarn aside, calculating that there was sufficient yarn for the central segment of five parallel bands of indigo blocked by bayeta, with the tenth band solid indigo. The bayeta yarn, spun as finely as the white and indigo, made the task one of seamless integration. As milled, re-spun yarn it held great strength and durability. It felt good to the touch, strong, durable.

It had taken days to unravel the baize flannel strips and spin them into yarn. Only with the first segment completed, did she confirm her choice as the best possible. Its warm glow gave definition to the indigo blocks framed within. The contrasts of indigo to bayeta and white to indigo were simple yet compelling. She sought harmony in each shift from one band to the next. The eye would rest most at the transitions between colors. Most of all, the bayeta bands defined the web.

From the opened door, an unsteady voice called out. "Is it time? I am starved to…" His voice trailed off. Bayeta put down her tools and turned. It had taken so much effort for him to make the journey from his bed to her studio.

"Are you praying?"

"Yes, Alberto." Her eyes rested on the open warp strands. "Pray with me?" She cleared her throat, fighting back an impulse to wipe away a tear.

> "In old age wandering on the trail of beauty,
> For them I make.
> To form them fair, for them I make.
> For them I make."

Listening, Alberto leaned against the door's frame. Her soft voice floated on the cool air of the studio. She prayed in Navajo, knowing how Alberto enjoyed its sound. A soft-spoken tongue, Navajo made vowels sound pure, clean, and short, full of silent consonants. The unpracticed ear could miss so much meaning and intent. Glottal stops snipped at the air in distinctive, elegant constructions that Alberto heard as exotic, pure song.

Bayeta sat with Alberto in the kitchen, ignoring his fidgeting. She did not want to embarrass him. He needed to make toilet and resisted admitting it. He disliked being helped. Without speaking of it, Alberto put his spoon down. She helped him down the hall to the bathroom. "I'll read to you, when we get you all snuggled up in bed. But first, I must check on the lab."

Martin was late in returning. She would need to read the checklist and feeding schedule to make sure nothing important was left undone. It would take fifteen minutes to insure that the feeding trays still had food in them. That was the important detail, one that she did not relish. Shrews, to her mind, had a disgusting diet. Alberto settled back on his pillow and nodded that he understood. He never questioned the need. Nothing was more important to Alberto than the success of Adam's research.

"You will tell me how they are doing, won't you?"

"Of course I will. Now, you rest for just a little while. I will be back to read to you."

On entering the dimly lit lab, Bayeta picked up the checklist attached to the logbook and scanned it. Everything looked to be in order. Before Martin had left, he had cleaned the cages and filled each food dispenser. Martin had recorded precisely how much food was in the feeders as of noon. Most of the dispensers looked half-full. Thankfully, replenishing them could wait.

Before turning to adjust the light dimmer, she looked to see that no equipment was left running, except for the recording devices and the computer that monitored every aspect of the lab. Not so much as a Petrie dish was out of place. Then she heard the printer engage, which was unusual. The computer monitor on Martin's workbench lit up, and a message appeared, three lines. On the off chance that it was from Adam, Bayeta looked. It lacked address or greeting, only a request to transmit. She thought it odd. Adam never sent files via the internet. It was a rule never to do so.

Bayeta saw more printout scrolled on the floor from the printer. With Martin gone to Chinle, what was this? She read the message, "Send file now." The same message appeared a dozen times. Who wanted a file? Who kept sending the same message? If Martin were there, he would have responded immediately. That would have been the end of it. No one else would know. "Oh, Martin, what have you done?" Bayeta thought and read the printout again. Then, she left it exactly where she had found it.

A deep sense of loss crippled her face. For the time being, there was nothing to do but go back to the house. As she walked to the kitchen, she heard the car's motor. Martin had returned. Hungry, he would smell his food kept warm in the oven. He would sit down, eat, and tell her that nothing extraordinary had happened during the day.

Minutes passed before Martin entered the kitchen. She took the lasagna from the oven and poured him a glass of orange juice. Both avoided eye contact. Nor did she speak, occupying herself with drying the few dishes in the drainer. Her silence told him that something was amiss. Picking at his food, he spoke in Navajo, his eyes on his plate. "Hastin Gani, The Mexican's son, died today."

"No! Oh, please no." Bayeta knew Hastin Gani well, a young man. "How did it happen?"

"I was at the house when he had the accident. By the time I got to him, it was too late." Defeat was in Martin's eyes. His hands trembled. "We could do nothing."

"You must not feel responsible, Martin."

"He was a careful man. He was always careful with the horses and that tractor of his. But it happened anyway. The tractor turned over, crushed his chest. Why? He had no enemies. He was a hard worker, a good man. He was not one to make trouble for others."

Hastin Gani had visited Rimrock only four days ago to ask Martin to help him build a new room onto his house. Maria was pregnant, her baby due soon. Maria came, too, to sit in the kitchen and talk. She was proud of her children, three under ten years, and now a new baby to come. Hastin Gani was a good man. He worked hard. It was touch and go, Maria admitted, but with time and more water, her husband would make things work out. They had many sheep.

"The ambulance took his body to Ganado. He will be buried by nine o'clock." Martin put his fork down. "I cannot eat, not now." He made no move to get up from the table.

She said, "In the morning, can you look after Alberto?" Martin nodded that he could. "I will go to Maria at first light. Please get some lamb out of the freezer for me. I will cook food to take."

Neighbors and family from miles around would begin to arrive at dawn. They would come to cry with Maria and the children. Her outfit now had no adult male. There would be much to do to help her manage. She had a hundred and fifty sheep, too much for a widow with young children. Bayeta stood up and looked around the kitchen. With so many people coming, it was to be a long day and people would be hungry. She put on her apron and got the skillets out of the pantry.

"How is Alberto doing?"

Bayeta looked out the window, as if searching for something. "He won't tell me what he feels, not directly. When I helped him to bed a little while ago, he handed me a piece of paper." Bayeta picked it up from the table. "Thoreau, The Twilight Years," she said and laid the paper back down on the table. With effort she gained control of her voice and read, "Give me the old familiar walk, post-office and all, with this ever new self, with this infinite expectation and faith, which does not know when it is beaten. We'll go nutting once more. We'll pluck the nut of the world, and crack it in the winter evenings…I will take another walk to the cliff, another row on the river, another skate in the meadow, be out in the first snow and associate with the winter birds. Here I am at home. In the bare and bleached crust of the earth I recognize my friend."

She handed it to Martin. "Look, he even copied the reference, XVII 273-75 11/1/1858. He copied it months ago."

Martin studied the quote. "He does know, doesn't he?"

"One minute he acts like a child, impulsive and optimistic. Then, I find something like this. It tells me how old beyond his years he can be." She took the paper back and with extreme care, put it with her list of to-dos. She smoothed out the curled edges.

"It is his epitaph. I will tell the stone mason to inscribe it just so when the time comes." Martin put his plate in the sink and turned to go. Bayeta set a skillet on the stove. "Martin, when I return from Maria's, I want you to drive into Chinle."

"What do you need?"

"Find the elder, the one called Chanter of the Sun's House. He was born to *Kinyaa'aanii*, Towering House People, and for *Todich'ii'nii*, Bitter Water. He is very holy. Johnny Kabito will know where to find his family. Have Johnny take you to him. Chanter of the Sun's House is to come here. He is to hire assistants for a Night Chant."

Martin's expression was one of surprise and confusion. It had been years since such a ceremony was performed in the area. He was skeptical of curing ceremonies. People died of tuberculosis, old age, pneumonia, and alcohol. Tractors and rock slides killed people. Medicine had its limits, but it also worked. He could not say the same for the old ways. Alberto might want to believe. But he was in no condition to withstand the strain. Knowing that he was near death, would people come? Would the Chanter agree to conduct a sing?

“Crystal,” Martin almost never addressed her so, “Alberto’s paper is touching. But isn’t a sing going too far? The singer will insist he sweat and take an emetic. He can’t bear the strain.” Martin continued to raise concerns. Bayeta folded her arms and waited for Martin to run out of reasons. At last, argument failed him.

“Tell Chanter of the Sun’s House,” her words now precise and calm, “tell him the patient is not sick of the body. Harmony must be restored. Tell him black and dangerous magic is at work. He must be prepared for this. The patient has been touched by a *yee naaldlooshii.* He is *’a’ztóǫ́,* moth crazy. Her words were heavy with regret.

“No skinwalker used corpse powder on Alberto. Why do this?”

Bayeta fixed her gaze on the approach of night beyond the kitchen window. The moon was breaking free of the darkening ridgeline to the southeast. “Martin, please, you must do what I ask.”

Martin lowered his eyes to the floor and stared at his shoes. He knew then that the singer was to come for him, not Alberto. “When is he to come?”

“Ask him to come Wednesday afternoon.”

Bayeta quietly stepped behind Martin and rested her hand on his shoulder. He did not move a muscle. Her touch was tender, patient. He knew that touch so well. It was his mother’s touch when he was a boy, not accusing and not excusing. This matter was about restoring harmony in her home. He could not refuse. Bayeta withdrew her hand, turned, and walked softly down the hall.

Alberto was asleep; his breathing was shallow, irregular, an effort of will holding on tenaciously to his fraying life’s thread. His bedcovers were twisted about him, a sign that he was in the grip of a restless and fretful dream. Silently, she leaned over the bed to adjust his blankets.

Retracing her steps, she went back to the kitchen. Martin was gone. Until there was a good cry at Maria’s, she would not touch her loom.

<++++++++++>

The Tiburon Lodge did have a vacancy, a second-floor room over the inner patio. Adam paid cash, took the key, and walked across the street to the supermarket. He needed a toothbrush, razor, and deodorant. He would buy a fresh shirt after getting off the ferry in the morning. Macy's was in a direct line on his walk up Market Street. A symposium at 11:00 a.m., Saturday, featured two of Hardesty's former graduate students. Their papers would deal with mRNA and the rate of synthesis of enzymes by repressor proteins. Hardesty would be there. Adam had another favor to ask of him.

It was getting late, after 10:00 p.m. in Arizona. He knew she would not sleep until he called.

Bayeta answered the phone on the second ring. "Adam, is that you?"

"Yes. I miss you, dear. I miss Alberto. How are things there?"

"I have bad news." Adam detected defeat in her voice. She sounded on edge, not her usual self. "Is it Alberto?"

"He slept for most of the day. But he did get out of bed on his own and walked down the hall to my studio. I had to help him back to bed, though."

Feeling helpless and inadequate, he listened. Bayeta was bearing the full burden. "What if…?"

"Adam?"

He was guiltily thankful that she had not finished her thought. "Yes, I'm here."

"I have something I must tell you." An awkward silence followed. "It's about Martin. I found something in the lab, a printout message." She again paused, waiting for him to respond.

Finally, Adam broke the silence, echoing her tone of defeat. "You don't need to tell me, Bea, I know. One of John's graduate students told me about the e-mails sent from my lab."

"What should I do? What do you want me to do?"

"What can be done? In a couple days it won't matter. Try not to worry."

"Adam, you've made up your mind. I trust you know what must be done. One more thing: When you return there will be many people coming to the house. Do you mind?"

"What I care about is Alberto and getting through these next few days."

"Have you had your talk with Herman?"

"Well, I put off telling him anything."

"Why? Do you mean...Does he understand what you intend to do?"

"Have done, Bea, have done." Adam did not want to worry her unduly. She should not know what Jonathan Hardesty had done for him. Telling her would only make her understand how much of a threat Herman might pose. "Bea, don't worry. I've taken precautions."

"Adam, I do trust you. Do what you must."

"Bea, things got pretty confused at lunch. I could not tell Herman, not in the state he was in."

"What about those messages, the ones meant for Martin?"

"He could not have given away anything of real value. He has had no access to the details or analyses of the therapeutic regimens. Even what I gave Hardesty lacks key components. When the time comes, I will..." His words trailed off.

Bayeta pressed him. "Are you going to settle things with Herman?"

"Herman has no right. It is not, never was, a part of our arrangement. I took pains to isolate his grant-based research from the other. I kept good records, too."

"When will you see Herman again, Adam?"

"There is a reception at The Manse on the institute grounds. It is supposed to be in my honor. If I do not show it will cause a row. For the moment, Herman won't do anything rash."

"I wish I could believe that."

"Bea, I have to go. I need to call Alexander before it gets any later."

Adam needed to talk to his father. The two had hardly talked in almost five years. Bayeta never liked the man. Even so, she believed alienation from one's kin was not a good thing. Nothing good came from ill feelings toward a parent.

"Will you call me to come pick you up at the airport?"

"John wants to lend me a car to drive home. Did you say that people are coming?"

"I'll tell you everything when you come home."

"I love you. I'll call Monday, after the award ceremony, if not before. Goodnight my dear."

<++++++++++>

Alexander rolled over in bed and picked up the phone. "Damn you, Henry," he cursed. The phone slipped from his hand. For an hour, he had fought with his covers and tried to ignore his aching knees, left arm, and neck. Half awake now, he considered what to tell Schwann. Dare he insist? Could he tell Schwann that it was no good? Schwann never tolerated explanations, even good ones. He expected Schwann to bully and make threats. No doubt Herman had told him that he was of no help at the Kosmoi. Being weak, Herman would shift blame. "Damn Herman," he muttered.

As he recovered the phone from the floor, he almost knocked over the nightstand. "Look, can't this wait?" But he heard only the dial tone. He punched up his pillow and slumped back down.

At the ragged edge of unconsciousness, Alexander saw Norman Urakami's face. That face had only of late inserted itself into his recurring dream, the dream he could not shake. It was an innocent face, not the least inscrutable as Alexander's xenophobic turn of mind demanded. He had not seen Norman Urakami in thirty years. But there he was, in his dream, there at the front stairs of Eleanor's house, hat in hand. He stood there with others, men Alexander had known—Oppenheimer, Compton, Lawrence, and Bethe. They all stood there—silent, waiting, waiting. Something terrible was about to happen. But, no, Dr. Norman Urakami could not have been there. He was interned at Manzanar.

In 1945 Alexander had assumed that Norman Urakami was not even still an American. After all, the government men had picked him up at the Berkeley lab in 1942 and driven him away. How strange it was, then, nineteen years later, almost to the day, to be standing there looking down at the man? Alexander, one of Teller's "termites", a cold war apprentice on the "The Super" project, could have nothing to do with such a man. Dr. Urakami could not possibly understand the need for a weapon one thousand times more powerful than the A-bomb. Given his way, Urakami would abolish atomic weapons. What foolishness it was for the likes of Urakami to obstruct

"Adam, I tried to tell you in the car. But, courage comes but once. I could have told you then. But I don't know if I can now. I don't know if I can..."

"Look, I need to know. Frankly, you implied too much as it is. You consult on nuclear power. You have long had dealings with a nuclear plant construction firm owned by Schwann. But what the hell does any of that have to do with me, or what we discussed?"

"Adam, I've just had a bad dream. Let's not go into this now. Look, I can tell you this much." From the silence that followed, Adam assumed that Alexander was putting his thoughts together. If pressed too hard, Alexander would freeze and shut down. Whatever he would admit over the phone would not be the whole of it. Out of blind habit Alexander never gave up all that he knew.

Then in a blizzard of words it came, three minutes of it without pause. Alexander outlined the extent of Schwann's interests, especially Genetrix. With pharmaceutical plants in eleven countries, Genetrix alone accounted for billions of dollars in annual revenues. But unlike the majors, Genetrix specialized in exclusive marketing concessions for generic drugs. Genetrix marketed a dozen drugs for immune-suppression therapy, as well as technologies for enzyme immunoassay. One such drug was Ambulent, prescribed for patients complaining of depression, restlessness, sleeplessness, or joint pain. Ambulent was addictive. And, like Prozac and Vicodin, once approved by the FDA, little regulation or follow-up investigations of patient use were undertaken. Such drugs were said to work for some patients. Would doctors prescribe them, if they did not work at least some of the time? Schwann, Alexander admitted with a bitter tone, liked to say that if a Genetrix drug failed a patient, it was the patient's fault, not the drug. It was always the patient's fault. That's what lawyers were for, to establish blame and avoid expensive settlements.

Schwann had no interest in bearing the expense of research, clinical trials, and a decade long expense of FDA approvals for new drugs, at least not until recently, not until he focused on Adam.

"Jesus Christ, Adam, I've given you more information than I should. Don't ask me for more."

"You still work for Schwann, that's it, isn't it?"

"Don't, please don't ask."

Adam regained his balance with difficulty. "Will I see you at the reception?"

"I will be there. Herman called this afternoon to insist. He's in a terrible state. Be careful with what you say, won't you? And, please, not a word about Genetrix. Please."

"I am thankful that you told me this much. I suppose you mean well."

"It would only set Herman off. He's too unstable just now to reason with."

"I have never known him to be stable."

"Adam, don't be snide. He is my firstborn, you realize. I had such hopes."

"You are right, of course, no sense beating up on him now. I will try to do as you ask."

"Until then…"

Adam hung up the phone. Now he knew more about where things stood. It was not enough, though. Herman or Schwann, or both, would force the issue. They believed that they were destined to control the outcome. Chances of putting them off were rapidly evaporating. Something unexpected was needed if he was to gain the initiative. Time, however, was not on his side.

<++++++++++>

Before the alarm went off at 5:00 a.m. on Saturday, Adam had already given up the pretense of sleep. He dressed and made ready to leave. In the early hours before dawn, he had struggled to draft his remarks for Monday. He did not intend them to be provocative or memorable, and an award ceremony was not the ideal setting to announce his success. Adam was also annoyed that Dean Hooke had asked to preview his speech. As chair of the selection committee, Hooke's request was reasonable enough. Still, five years had not dulled the irritation Adam felt over Hooke's insistence that the university had the right to approve and oversee his research. Adam had resented Hooke's insinuation that extra controls were called for in his case. It was an old wound, and Hooke no doubt intended to rub more salt into it. Since it was still early morning,

Adam felt no obligation to respond to Hooke's lunch invitation. Later, he could feign ignorance and say that he had not gotten the message. Hooke would have to be satisfied with a draft copy of Adam's remarks that he would leave at the Hilton for him later in the day.

The first ferry was due to depart Tiburon at 6:30 a.m. He looked up to see no more than a handful of faint stars over the Golden Gate and to the north. Urban settings all but banish the stars. From every direction, he could hear the mechanical noises of human activity. Silence, too, had been banished. The smell of coffee coming from the lobby overwhelmed the scent of lilac and jasmine planted along the walkway below his room. Away from Rimrock for three days, he missed it terribly. At home the smell of desert penetrated and soothed his senses, no matter the time of day. If he could not sleep, he often sat out on the patio and watched the moon track across the dome of night sky. The house, nestled deep in the red rock country of *Tseyi*, was a reality unto itself. Bayeta had chosen the site with deliberate intent. It was surrounded on three sides by sheer sandstone walls. In the reflected light of the moon, he could almost count the eons laid down by a once vast inland sea, before the human coming.

His present sense of displacement surprised Adam. The desert had become embedded in his mind, more completely than he had imagined. He missed Bayeta sleeping beside him, the feel of her warm body when he rolled over in the night. She usually awoke first, before first light. If his hand was resting on her thigh, she patted it before rising. If he became half-roused, she would wait until he fell back to sleep before rising. Soon, the smell of fresh coffee would wake him. Years of living quietly had taught him that the desert was a place for life in the light and on open ground. Night was no time to be abroad. Bayeta was amused the first time Adam told her that he intended to use shrews in his experiment. Shrews were night creatures. "It is good your laboratory doesn't have windows. That would only confuse the poor beasts." Adam appreciated Bayeta's humor.

Disembarking from the ferry, Adam walked up Market Street, the morning sun at his back. He had eaten a muffin with his coffee on the ride across the bay. Life in the moment was good. He had forgotten how invigorating a ferry ride could be with the Golden Gate half shrouded in fog and sailboats plying the waters between Tiburon and the Alcatraz reach. Today, sail surfers were on the water in force, darting out from the Marina District beach, slicing their way between sailboats. Watching them refreshed his spirits.

Adam realized that if he arrived at the Hilton before lunch that he would run into people wanting to talk about The Morgan Prize. He did not want that. The President's Address was set for 3:00 p.m. Monday, along with the award ceremony. The preliminary staging irritated Adam. It allowed no opportunity to freely discuss his work with those colleagues who mattered most to him.

Entering a coffee shop near Union Square, Adam smelled bacon. The tables were covered with red-checkered tablecloths. A row of booths lined the windows. It vaguely reminded him of Rose Bia's Cafe, but in Rose's the men spoke Navajo, and they talked about the weather and livestock prices. Here he overheard snatches of conversation about baseball and what City Hall was going to do about the hookers that were on every street. Woven into the sounds of dish clatter, Adam overheard Smitty, the counter man, complaining about how he was being cheated on his monthly Social Security check. He told George, his patron, that at age sixty-nine he earned too much as a part-time cook to get all that was coming to him. George had little sympathy for Smitty. He commented that after forty-four years at a desk, he'd been laid off at age sixty-three. His company had gone belly up, and with it his pension. Two more years, and he might have been okay. Now, he didn't know. Adam finished his coffee and ordered another coffee and a toasted bagel to go.

On impulse he took a taxi to the Palace of Fine Arts. He had not sat on a park bench in years to take in a San Francisco morning. He remembered Jonathan Hardesty's story about the Palace of Fine Arts and how his father often took him there to sit by the reflecting pool and feed the ducks. It was as good a place as any to sit and think.

Jonathan was right. He had ignored the social and economic consequences of extreme old age for a mass population. How might his research impact the future? Did he know anything about what the world would be like full of very old people? His ambition had been to succeed at solving a problem of pure research. Consequences had not entered his mind. What did he know of the daily struggles of people like George and Smitty? How would so many in their advanced years provide for themselves, or be provided for? Was it right to expect them to live longer, but in poverty?

Leaning back on the bench, Adam watched the ducks waddle up from the bank toward him. Jonathan had said that he and his father always fed the ducks, probably from a brown paper bag like the one Adam was holding. Generations of these ducks had been born, lived, and died since Jonathan's childhood, but that did not make handouts less precious to them, not on a clear, warm morning like this. At a safe distance, each duck eyed the bag with his bagel in it. One duck in particular stood its ground, his eye fixed on the bagel. A Muscovy duck, he imagined, perhaps Stalin's relative, one of Jonathan's favorites.

"Come on, come and take it." Adam sprinkled crumbs on the grass, which prompted a stampede of ducks.

"Hey, you! Can't you see? I'm trying to sleep here!"

The disembodied voice was coming from behind. Adam turned and saw a body stretched out inside a very large, refrigerator-sized, cardboard box beneath the branches of a twisted, overhanging pine. The box looked crumpled and worn.

"You can't see me, is that it? Never mind! I'm here, sure enough. You're trespassing."

"Excuse me?" Adam now saw a head. "I didn't mean to disturb you."

"It's been a long night, Mister, and you're trespassing."

"What do you mean trespassing?"

"What do you call it, coming here at this hour and waking innocent folk?"

"I just needed a place to sit and think."

"Sure, you look the type." The sleeping bag struggled to a sitting position, a face sticking halfway out. "Yeah, you're the type; mid-forties I'd guess, well-off, and got a lot on your mind. So you can't sleep. You come to talk to them birds. Maybe you figure they have answers."

"I was just giving them a bite of my bagel."

"You got any left?"

"Do I have any of my bagel left?"

"What you got on it?"

"Cream cheese."

"No sense wasting a good bagel on ducks. They eat better than I do." With that the woman—up to that moment Adam had assumed he was talking to a man—unzipped the sleeping bag and got out. She sat down on the other end of the bench and eyed Adam. Adam slid the bag with the half bagel toward her.

"Thanks, I need breakfast." She took a bite and made a gesture to straighten her hair. "I wasn't always like this, you know. I suppose you got kids."

"Yes. Well, he's not my child, he is my ward."

"Fancy, ain't we! You're married. I can see that. I was married once. I was young then. I was young and had lots of problems, just like you. Now I got nothin' and no problems." She eyed his paper bag. "Hey, you got coffee in there?"

Adam slid the bag across the bench.

"Well, thank you. Now I got somethin' to wash down that dried-out bagel with."

Adam looked over his shoulder at the box and the empty sleeping bag.

"This is my spot, see."

He also saw a turned over shopping cart with a plastic bag of empty soda bottles and clothing in it. Beneath the tree limb was a half-gallon water bottle and a black garbage bag.

"The cops don't come for two more hours. So long as I'm gone by 9:30, they don't care. That's when tourists start showing up." She noticed Adam looking at the garbage bag. "I keep the place picked up. Two, maybe even three dollars a day, just from them cans and bottles. Seventy-two."

"Seventy-two, what is seventy-two?"

The woman brushed back her hair again, as she finished the bagel and turned her face to him. "You were thinking how old. I know that look. I'm seventy-two."

He watched her sip his coffee. She watched the first rays of the sun advance across the Doric columns and roof of the Palace of Fine Arts. The Fates, bathed in sunlight, watched the two of them.

The woman began to talk non-stop. She talked of working. She was once a beautician. She talked of her life's savings lost in a stock fraud. She cursed her four children who did not care that she begged on the streets and picked up aluminum cans in order to eat. Twice last year, she said, the pneumonia bug had got her. "If I'm lucky, it will get me again and soon."

"Why do you say that?"

"Hospital, if I get it, get the bug, I mean, they put me in the hospital. I get three squares as long as I'm in there. It's my vacation trip."

"You could die."

She laughed, exposing her bad teeth. "One less butt for the cops to kick, that's all."

He wanted to get up and excuse himself. He smelled urine and strong body odors. But, Adam remained seated, learning about the life of Katherine Elkins, one-time beauty shop owner and operator. Life was once good. It was good so long as she worked and made money, she said with bitterness. But then, "that crooked stockbroker" relieved her of her savings and her future. Self-employed most of her life, she still collected a minimum social security benefit.

"It goes for food and a flop until the sixteenth of the month, more or less. Then, it's back on the street." For two weeks a month, she said with exaggerated pride, "I'm Katie, the lady of the Palace." Having exhausted the topic of her life, she turned to Adam. "Why are you here?"

"I needed a place to think."

"You could pick a hundred places nicer." She pointed toward the Golden Gate Bridge.

"A friend of mine used to come here on Sundays with his father and feed the ducks."

"You never fed ducks with your dad, did you?"

"How did you know?"

"Beauticians know things. You can't style hair for forty-five years and not know things."

She looked at Adam for reaction and lit a cigarette. Adam looked intently at her. Her hands shook. The lines on her face were deep. She had thinning hair and a goiter on her neck. Adam could guess how Katherine Elkins' life would end. On a cold rain-soaked night, alone and without anyone to hold her hand, she'd slump over on a park bench, perhaps this one. In the morning a policeman would nudge her and tell her to move along. She'd not respond. A tourist or two might stare for a moment and then move on. Who would know her story, her struggle to survive?

Katherine looked squarely at him. "Not now, maybe in the fall. I might even last 'til winter."

"How did you…?"

"Easy. You look educated. You're the type that wonders about people dying. Maybe you think too much about people dying. Life won't touch you, not like it has me."

"Why do you say that?"

"You don't have kids like mine. I don't blame anyone. See. It's just how things are. If you got work, you got things. If you get old and got no work, you got no place, nothin'. Old people ought to be put down like dogs that can't hunt no more. That's what the queen's doctor says."

"What do you mean?"

"You know, the Queen of England. She's got this doctor who says old people need to be killed."

It was true. The queen's physician had openly proposed that a state-run program of euthanasia be put in place. It was a purely utilitarian argument. No one took the proposal seriously. Nor did anyone voice outrage. It was, the papers implied, just a case of bad taste.

"I got one winter left, maybe two. They'll find me laid out cold, like day-old Thanksgiving turkey. Meantime, what I got is pain and stares. Punks steal what little I got, except this bench. Now I got to go to take my cans and bottles to recycling. And you, you got to do what you got to do."

She grinned at him, Adam wondering how many times had she talked like this. Who else came to sit on her bench? She did not mean to embarrass him. What she wanted, what she needed, was human contact, even if the cost was to bare her burdens.

Adam put two ten-dollar bills on the bench and walked on without looking back. She might have refused had their eyes met. For a few minutes the bag lady had made Adam forget his problems. His were nothing compared to those of Katherine Elkins. What did it matter how desperate Herman was? Harsh words between them were nothing new. Now, whatever Herman said or did would make no difference. Come Monday those who wanted to translate his research into a means to extend life would be welcome to it. He would be free to move on to a new challenge. Listening to Katherine Elkins tell her story helped him realize how little The Morgan Prize meant to him. He had not sought it. Others had decided for their own purposes. Ryder and Hardesty had helped him to see that. Poor Herman had tried his best to possess or control something he did not understand. What could have made him believe that Adam would turn it over to anyone he did not trust or respect?

In the taxi to the Hilton, Adam thought about what the old woman said about her own death. "My obit in the Chronicle will say how some old bag lady died on this bench, died of natural causes. At my age they'll say it was natural causes. What do they know about natural causes? What hurts is not the dying. We all got to go sometime. But I never figured to be buried alone, you know. That's the worst of it. Like a fool I signed over my plot. My husband and me paid out for twenty years to have it. Then, when I didn't have money to pay for Harold's funeral, our oldest son loaned me the money. I gave him them plots, you know, for collateral. Well, I had no way to pay him back. So, he just goes out and sells them without telling me. Harold was cremated. Me, his mother, he tells me how his needs got to come first. He's got his own family to consider. He says my bones won't never know the difference. Me and my Harold was Catholic, you see. Burning was not for us, no way."

<++++++++++>

The taxi let Adam out at Macy's where he went in to buy a shirt. Walking into the Hilton, he was too late for the panel he wanted to hear. He did not care. At the door to the third-floor meeting room, Adam spotted Hardesty.

"Ah, there you are. You missed a good presentation, Adam. The new stuff on repressor proteins is really good."

Adam smiled. "It will end up in print if it is that good."

"True. But I know you. You hate to wait."

"I'll count on you to send me a synopsis."

"By the way, I received a hand-delivered invitation last night for the reception."

"I asked Marcy Adams, Herman's secretary, to put you on the list."

"I wondered about that. I did not imagine Herman Cockroft would include me."

"I also asked Miss Adams not to tell him."

"They can still turn me away at the gate, you know."

"We'll be together. They will just have to take us as a package."

"Have you thought what this reception will be like? Herman must have an agenda."

"I expect a lot of boring talk. From what I gather, it will be mostly institute staff, directors, and an outsider or two." Adam paused. "Oh, yes, Alexander is coming."

"Adam, Herman will try to use the occasion to commit you."

"Perhaps, but surrounded by all those people, Herman has to be on his good behavior. Later, tomorrow or the next day for sure, he'll try something. His last pitch has to be soon."

"Is it wise for you to include me?"

"Jonathan, it is paramount. I need your moral support."

"You just want me there to watch how things go down."

"You have always been a more detached observer. If things get complicated, I may be too engaged to watch my back. You, however, will be my Chateaubriand's cat."

"Ah, I am to pretend to sleep in the window, while you commit verbal warfare, you mean."

"Precisely. Sparks might fly."

“Will you come by the house first?”

“Could you pick me up at The Claremont?”

Jonathan nodded.

Adam left the Hilton fifteen minutes later and returned to The Claremont. He needed to work more on the draft of his remarks for Monday. At the Tiburon Lodge the words simply had not come out right.

On the BART train to Berkeley, Adam remembered that he had seen Alexander carrying a copy of a biography of Michael Faraday at lunch. Alexander had an obsession for biographies of physical scientists, Cynthia once told him. They were a source of inspiration for the lab devices he designed. Adam knew little about Faraday, the metallurgist who developed the first dynamo and posited the laws of electrolysis. Jonathan had once salted a lecture with the story of Faraday’s refusal to accept the honor of becoming president of The Royal Society. “I must remain plain Michael Faraday to the last…” he had proclaimed to the deputation of scholars pleading that it was his duty to accept.

Faraday’s refusal was a lesson that Hardesty had admitted he ignored when he was awarded the Nobel. He had followed Newton’s advice and accepted every honor. As a result, he did no good science for almost three years afterward. The attentions and distractions took up his time and inflated his ego. “Beware Swedes bearing gifts,” he had told the class. Adam wondered, “Was that Alexander’s intent?”

A little before six o’clock, Adam finished his draft, naming it ‘Evolutionary Constraints and Human Aging.’ For a title, it would have to do. He had taken pains to avoid including an admission that he had a personal motivation. That could invite questions about Alberto and the role progeria played. His audience might not find his view of evolutionary theory related to the quest for extending human life. Evolutionary theory was not new to them. But they would expect something “interesting,” not a review of plowed ground. Adam was tempted to approach, subtly, the assumed reasons why Dean Hooke and the committee had chosen him. His audience should know that Hooke and others had their own motives, and chose to promote certain interests. Adam was certain of it, though he did not have the proof. Hooke was not one to want to see him shine. The man was vain, envious, and calculating. No, for Hooke to have a hand in the award meant that he had something to gain.

At six o'clock, the phone rang. "Adam, are you ready?" It was Hardesty.

"Where are you?"

"I'm in the lobby. Oh, by the way, I just ran into Donald Ryder."

"Right, I almost forgot that he's staying here."

"He asked me to tell you he is in the bar. Do you want to talk to him?"

"Yes, if you don't mind. Give me five minutes."

"Ryder said he has a story to file."

Adam thought he could let Ryder file what he already had as THE story. But was that being fair? After all, the man had been a valuable source of information. He deserved more.

"Jonathan, you don't mind do you, if I take time to talk to him?"

"Not at all, I'll wait in the lobby. It is best if you see him alone."

Entering the bar, Adam saw that Ryder had picked a spot where they could talk with some privacy. As he approached, Ryder motioned to the bartender. Adam declined.

"Thank you for seeing me, Dr. Grant. I brought a draft of my article. Would you like to read it and comment before I file it?" Ryder held out his five-page draft.

"I trust that you did not misquote me." Adam did not reach for the document.

"It's not my most inspired, I admit. It's mostly a rehash of what you've done over the last ten years, a profile piece. I put something in about The Morgan Prize and past recipients. There's also a bit in it about your interest in progeria and aging in general. I resisted adding the 'pill of immortality' bit."

"Thanks, Donald. As I told you, it is nothing like that in any case."

While Ryder sipped his drink, Adam looked around to make sure of their privacy. "Look, after tonight's event, things might become confused. I may have a face-off with my half-brother. He assumes that his institute has some claim to my longevity work. Frankly, when I realized, thanks in part to you, that Herman has been trying to get at my research, I knew something was up. And this Mueller has been following me. I think now it is wise to keep my intentions vague. As long as others think I am clueless that they are out get what they want, by any means, I can maneuver and work around them."

"Forgive me for asking, Doctor, but why attend that reception? Is it to keep them guessing for as long as you can? If so, remember you are on their home ground at that place they call The Manse."

"I see your point. But I have to see for myself just who the players are. Second, unless I stir things up a bit, I can't maneuver. Tell me about The Manse."

"It is positively gothic. They use it mostly for receptions and director's meetings. It existed long before the institute was built; it was once the home of one Raymond Lull."

"It does not fit in. Why didn't they tear it down?"

"Oh, but it does fit. Raymond Lull lived in it until he died. He called it Miranda. The story is that he came to America in 1869. He somehow landed a contract with Union Pacific to supply coal from property he owned in Wyoming. He supplied coal from Carbon and Rock Springs. He branched out into mining copper and quicksilver near New Almaden. He made yet another fortune in the China trade by exporting wheat. By 1889 he retired and built Miranda. He became a recluse and something of a mystic. They say the old crocodile died drinking medicinal alcohol. He was found dead in his workshop, a sort of chemistry lab, really. He'd been experimenting with making perfumes and patent medicines under a different name. He was quite a character. A codicil in his will stipulates that Miranda had to be left just as it was, just as you see it today. The new owners had to honor the provision of his will. As you walk in the front door, stop and read the brass plaque. It speaks volumes about the people now running the place. I wrote a story on Lull years ago, a quirky piece I did for a history magazine."

"Thanks, I will look for the plaque. May I ask how you know about the guests, the directors?"

"A good reporter has his sources, you know."

"I expect you do. But, I have to go. We'll talk more. I have a story for you."

"If it is that good, I wonder if my paper will print it."

"Let's trust events to take a hand."

"Until then, Doctor."

Adam shook Ryder's hand and left.

Jonathan was waiting by the exit door of the hotel. He indicated the young uniformed driver, the same one who had been sent for Adam on other occasions. Pointing to Hardesty, Adam told the driver,

"You can lead the way or follow us. That way we'll arrive at the same time and place. That should satisfy your boss." He was tempted to say "handler." But why cause the young man more misery?

At the institute's gate, Jonathan flashed his invitation at the guard. The guard insisted that no one named Jonathan Hardesty was on his list. "Either you allow us to proceed immediately, or we will turn around and leave. Dr. Grant and I are a package. I assume that ***he***, at least, is on your list."

The guard grimaced and reached for his phone inside the guard station. After a moment, he gave a tight smile. "Follow the limousine. You do not want to become lost on the grounds."

"That can't happen, can it?" Adam eyed the guard, how his neck muscles stood out. An involuntary jerk, a nervouse tic, of the guard's head caught Jonathan's eye. "Are we having fun yet?"

"Soon, my friend, I'll be back on my own ground. I can last that long."

"First, let's see how it goes tonight."

"I agree. Let's go pinch some blue noses." For the moment, however brief, both were in the mood for a bit of mischief. It took the edge off the serious business before them.

Parking the car at the end of the driveway, Adam and Jonathan walked slowly up the walk to The Manse. The evening's spring air felt warm and dry. Both men breathed in deeply, braced themselves, and looked up at the first star to blink on, no doubt the planet Venus.

At the entrance Adam pointed to the plaque. "I promised Ryder to read it before stepping through the open door." It read:

"Oh wonder!
How many goodly creatures are there here!
How beauteous mankind is! Oh brave new world,
That has such people in it!"

Jonathan shrugged and gave a knowing wink. "What has this brave new world to offer?"

Herman stood at the threshold, a tall drink in his hand. "Good evening, Adam." Someone Adam did not know stood beside him. Hardesty, however, knew the man and looked away.

"And Dr. Hardesty, how good of you to join us. Welcome." Herman made a move to take Adam's arm. As he did, the stranger stepped to Adam's right. Hardesty again winked at Adam and followed.

"Adam, this is Dr. Bacon. He's done marvelous things with magnetic resonance imaging and optics. You'll want to get to know him better." Adam had expected that Herman would put on something of a dog and pony show. But even for him, this was a bit over the top.

Herman wasted no time in making himself the fool. Plain courtesy demanded that Herman acknowledge Jonathan, a Noble Laureate, no less. However, he pointedly acted as if he did not see him.

"Tell me, Dr. Bacon, are you on the staff here?"

"Heavens, no! I am on the faculty at Oxford. When I do come to the colonies, I still regard your lovely land as a colony you know, here is where you will find me. The institute's facilities are superb!"

"How nice it must be for you. By facilities, what do you mean?" Adam already knew that there were no MRIs or CAT scans on the premises. To what facilities was Bacon referring?

Herman excused himself. He needed a refill. Was Adam drinking champagne? Anything?

Adam used Herman's momentary absence to size up Dr. Bacon. He was a short, stout man, with a ruddy complexion. His clothes were expensive, if poorly fitted. The golden chain attached to his vest pocket was striking, an anachronism long out of fashion, even for an Oxford don.

"What brings you to Berkeley, Doctor?" Hardesty gave the man an intense look.

"Ah, yes. Well, you see that man over there in the corner?" Bacon nodded in the direction of a man standing alone at the far end of the room. "That is Dr. Flamel, a former student of mine. He has published a great work, a truly seminal one, if I may say. I am to introduce him at the conference."

"Then you are here for the molecular biology conference?"

"Forgive me, no. I meant the International Philosophic Society."

Adam looked puzzled. He had never heard of such a society. Hardesty, standing to the side of Bacon, turned to give Adam a knowing look. He would draw Dr. Bacon into talking about the International Philosophic Society, while Adam watched Herman. The men Herman was talking to he recognized. He saw Thomas Vaughn, Basel Valentine, Robert Boyle, and Jean Rey. He looked for, but did not see, Alexander. Through the open front door came Dr. Hessen. Jonathan nodded to Adam, as if to say "Ecce Homo." Alexander followed, with Marianne on his arm.

With everyone present, Herman waved for all to follow him into the library. Herman's face was ruddy and sweaty. He remarked that this was the room in which Lull entertained guests. "He once said that no dispute of fact should ever be left half consumed when references are near to hand."

How apropos of Herman, Adam thought. He had no intention of leaving The Manse with his business with Herman only half consumed.

Vaughn, standing beside Herman, asked Adam about his current work. Adam ignored the question. "I just met Bacon. He's English, as are you. Are you familiar with his work?"

"Of course, internal illumination is cutting edge technology these days. But I don't go so far as Bacon to suggest there are seven states to the body's internal experience. Any system based on a fixed number is to be questioned, wouldn't you agree? Maybe there are only five states, or perhaps nine?"

Adam pursued his point. "Where do you come down on the matter?" Vaughn looked puzzled. "Are you a lumper or a splitter?"

"Ah, I see what you mean. Yes, I am definitely a lumper. One must treat the body as a unified whole. Imaging technology will take us there. Don't you agree?"

A waiter appeared with a tray of champagne glasses and moved about the room.

"Gentlemen and Dear Lady," Herman said to bring the group to attention. "On behalf of The Evergreen Institute it is my honor and pleasure to propose a toast. To our esteemed visitor and grantee, I give you Dr. Adam Grant, winner of this year's prestigious Morgan Prize."

A round of applause followed. Herman finished his glass and motioned for the waiter to refill everyone's glasses. As the waiter poured, Herman again raised his arm for silence and resumed his introduction.

"My brother, Adam, has many accomplishments. His early work on the regulation and production of hormones is still regarded as ahead of its time. With the support of The Evergreen Institute, I am proud to say, his daring advances in fractionation techniques have contributed to further unmask the secrets of the cell. Biologists now isolate and identify many functions of proteins based on Adam's pioneering work. In the coming days we are certain to learn more about his accomplishments, which will remind us that nothing is forever beyond the reach of science."

Herman lifted his glass and drank it down. Adam surveyed the room, meeting each pair of eyes. Jonathan was the only one not smiling. Adam pretended to sip the champagne.

Herman could not have spoken in more contrived terms. Herman's toast inferred, no declared, that Adam had earned his keep, by way of the institute's largesse. It offended Adam, but he let it pass uncontested. Herman had not directly mentioned his longevity work. For the institute's funding, Adam had produced eighteen published papers on the isolation and synthesis of newly described hormones, all regulator-enforcers as he called them. It was a solid record, innovative, and a respectable output. Still, none of it warranted The Morgan Prize. Herman had to know that. He could not be that stupid.

"Thank you, Herman, for the kind words," Adam said. "As I entered the front door this evening I recalled that this house, The Manse, is said to have quite a history. That plaque at the door, does it not say, "Oh wonder! Oh brave new world! That has such people in it!" As I understand it, Raymond Lull called this house Miranda, after Prospero's daughter, who took Ferdinand as husband. Those are her words. Prospero, her father, responded: 'Tis new to thee.' "

Adam paused for a few seconds and continued, "I feel that way now. The Evergreen Institute is indeed new to me. For five years, I have kept to my desert retreat, so to speak. I do my work there, at Rimrock. My wife, Bayeta, is my Miranda. I have been free to do my work above the tempest. But now, as you see, here I am, confronted by the tempests of your brave new world."

There was a hint of unease on Herman's face. Some of those present shifted uneasily at they stood.

"When I first came to Berkeley to study and learn from Dr. Jonathan Hardesty," Adam raised his glass to Jonathan, "molecular biology was my all consuming passion. It became my brave new world. When I left the university, I fancied myself a kind of Prospero. The Evergreen Institute gave me the means to continue to practice my art without constraint or distraction. Yes, I am grateful that I did not have to drown my book, or put out the candle, or ring the bell when I departed Berkeley. Many others have had to. At the time, I was accused of insisting that research be without oversight, without limits. It was heresy, the university administration said, to define my own objectives and pursue them without restraint. My work has been solitary and at times tedious. The age of individual scientific pursuit may be all but extinct. I do thank this governing board for providing grants for some of my work. I have, I believe, fulfilled your expectations and the terms of the grants awarded to me. Now that the work is complete, I can look back on our association with satisfaction. Thank you."

Without pause, he continued, though a faint, restless stir seemed to invade the mood of the room. "On Monday, at the award ceremony,

I will speak for the first time about my other passion, work I have followed independently. I do hope that you will listen to what I have to say. Until then…"

Adam did not finish his words. Aware of the silence that gripped the room, Adam looked at Herman. His face was ashen. With a fixed grin, flesh drawn tight and rigid against the bone, Herman looked to Alexander. After an awkward pause, a sudden wall of noise erupted. Who had heard Jonathan's coda to Adam's last words? "On to Naples," he had said and lifted his glass.

Thomas Vaughn raised his voice, "Why no, Dr. Hardesty, we met in Geneva last year, at the International." The man had obviously had too much to drink and had not been listening.

"I remember," Hardesty responded, grinning. "You wore black. I wore white. You opposed the draft on guidelines for independent recombinant DNA research. I supported it."

"You were too harsh about such dangers posed by large, properly managed laboratories. It's the independents one has to concern oneself with."

Jean Rey, to Vaughn's right, overheard. "There's a place for the free agent. My own metallurgy laboratory accepts no outside funding."

Vaughn momentarily forgot himself. "Pure puffery, of what practical use is antimony?"

Valentine, pointed to the drapes. "Do you see those drapes? The fire retardant in them contains antimony. Almost every plastic you can name, from aircraft interiors to upholstered chairs, contain antimony. It's in carpets, tape, paint, computers, and television housings. It is a most useful metal. I've made a fortune on stibnite mining and its uses in industrial processes."

"And so you have." Vaughn feigned indifference. "And you, Dr. Hardesty, what have you to say for the uses for antimony?"

"Well, let me see. Cleopatra used antimony as eye makeup. In medieval Europe it was used to induce vomiting. What more is there to know about it?"

"Seriously, Doctor, there must be any number of ways antimony works in the body."

"In very small doses, it can stimulate metabolism. But, it can also damage the liver."

Gustav Hessen leaned forward to join in. He had twice attempted to interrupt, only to have Vaughn wave him off. "I have used it with good results, good results indeed."

"You used it to interfere with cell division, not promote it," Hardesty retorted.

"Precisely!" Hessen's chest visibly puffed out, he on the verge of pressing his point.

Boyle made a small hand gesture toward Vaughn and Valentine, enough to quell the argument. Hessen turned to Adam, trying to ignore Boyle.

"You may prefer that we wait until Monday, Doctor. But certainly we here deserve an advance summary, wouldn't you agree? After all, the institute shares in your success."

Adam occupied himself with sipping his drink, choosing not to answer. Adam knew that Boyle advocated the "wear and tear" theory of aging. He alone would have an informed grasp of the current literature on aging processes. Boyle's theory, however, focused on raw morbidity data, not cell level processes. What did he know of the role of stress at the cell level? A tortoise could live to be 250 years old. The mayfly lived but one day. Each creature's programming had its own internal stress diathesis. Where was the evidence of differential stress levels in a morbidity table? No, it did not matter what Boyle thought. Adam fingered the rim of his glass. He half thought to respond with some vague reference to corticosteroids and catecholamines. But no, they were at best peripheral factors.

"I'm sorry, Dr. Boyle, what were you saying about the wear and tear?"

Herman grunted and made an attempt to recover a semblance of being the good host. "Forgive all this talk, Adam. I'm sure we can find a lighter subject to occupy our evening. Later, we can talk? Just the two of us, I mean."

"I prefer to wait a day or two.

The evening devolved into superficial snatches of polite conversation. Hessen, predictably, was the exception. He labored to impress Hardesty with his ideas about immunologic processes and aging. He kept on about the role of the thymus. It is, after all, vigorous in the young and atrophied in the aged, he insisted. Alexander, to Hardesty's surprise, tried to deflate Hessen. Hessen, at last, fell silent, worn down by the lack of enthusiasm for argument. But when brandy made the rounds, Hessen, rather than accepting defeat, turned petulant.

"Tell me, Dr. Hardesty, why are you here?"

"My dear Dr. Hessen, I believe you have had a bit too much to drink,"

"Why, whatever do you mean?" Hessen's face flushed with indignation.

Adam grabbed Herman's arm to restrain his interference. "Jonathan is my guest."

"He is your familiar you mean. At your side at all times, is he?"

"Herman!" Alexander intervened. "I suggest you tell Dr. Hessen to shut up."

"Well, of course, yes, we've all had a little too much wine."

Hessen emptied his glass and surveyed the room. "I beg forgive."

Alexander turned away and engaged Jonathan in conversation, looking surprisingly at ease. Seeing the two engaged in something of a truce, if only for the evening, pleased Adam.

"I confess to it, Jonathan. I envied you. For a long time, I thought of you as having apprenticed my son to your own selfish interests. Even your politics infected him. But, I know now I was wrong to resent you."

"Alexander, Adam always had his own mind. He learned all that I had to teach." Jonathan grinned, seeing that Adam had heard. "Well, almost."

"You held something back, then?"

"No. It is just that he's a hard one to teach about limits. He still doesn't grasp the limits of science. Science will not solve all our problems. Indeed, it may create more along the way."

"He's very fond of you."

"Do you know when I went to Stockholm, I was flattered to be thought of as the quiet, tough-minded enzyme sleuth. I had opened a door or two into the cell's mysteries. For this, I received the Nobel. At the time, I didn't understand just how unprepared I was for the notoriety to come."

"You've had a great career, Jonathan. You have earned all that has come your way."

"At the time, I didn't grasp the essence of science as ethos. I had only mastered knowledge and method. What I had failed to appreciate is that science is a unique community, in which one must keep one foot planted in the laboratory and the other in the world at large, society itself."

"Lately, even I have come to glimpse that fact."

"Have you?" Hardesty leaned back, a look of surprise coming over him. For as long as he could remember, Alexander Terman had topped his list of Teller's cold warriors, his favorite example of science gone over to the dark side, where ideology ruled reason.

"When I was young, I read Aristotle and dreamed of becoming a citizen in a free society. We Estonians almost never dared to dream such a thing. I believed that England was the new polis, a republican society. I believed in '*Omnia in Unum.*' "

"And now, you believe that America has a strong physics and weak sociology."

"You could put it that way. Physics is a house divided. Who knows, maybe Oppie was right. It is not good to be oblivious to the consequences of invention."

"Science has often forced social and political change. We just find it so hard to own up to it."

"Look around this room. Real science is in the minority here. What you see is anti-science. It has always been a problem. Goethe rejected Newton's optics, saying that the microscope and telescope distorted the human scale and confused the mind. In Germany, Goethe was hero. Newton was rejected. What do you see when you look down that microscope of yours, Jonathan?"

"Every time, I become a little less certain of what I think I know, of what I see."

"I wish that were so with my son."

Jonathan gave Alexander a long look. "Isolation makes for a different optics. In my Nobel speech, I quoted Humphrey Newton, Isaac's brother. He said of Isaac, '…at spring and fall of the leaf…he used to employ about six weeks in his elaboratory, the fire scarcely going out either night or day… What his aim might be I was not able to penetrate into, but his Pains, his diligence at these set times made me think he aimed at something beyond the reach of human art and industry.' "

"Ah yes, it is a cautionary tale, to be sure."

"I did not spend all my time in the laboratory. For that matter, neither did Newton."

Alexander looked over at Adam. "What about my son?"

"He reminds me of Albert Claude. Adam is a fan of Claude."

"I don't understand."

"I'm not sure I do, either. Except to say that Adam is facing a dilemma Claude glimpsed. He once wrote, 'We have entered the cell, the mansion of our birth, and started the inventory of our acquired wealth.' Hardesty paused. 'The cell is very much like a mansion; rich, elegantly made and maintained, full of half-explored corridors and rooms. For you, the issue now is whether to let someone else set the value of what it is you have found and inventoried.' Adam has to make up his mind. Either he sets the value of his work or others will by controlling it."

As Hardesty cited Albert Claude, Alexander watched Adam talking to Herman. "Can Adam permit others to set the value of his discovery? Should he?"

"In the wrong hands, it can fund great mischief." Jonathan's tone was somber.

"Jonathan," Alexander pressed Hardesty's arm, "help Adam to decide his course."

"He alone must decide. If asked, I will tell him what I think."

"Please." Alexander gripped Jonathan's arm until it hurt. "I don't want to see him end up like Timothy Andrews. You know what happened to that poor boy."

Jonathan stared at Alexander. Of course he remembered the incident.

On January 15th, the young biochemist had been fired from The Evergreen Institute. That night, after drinking too much in a bar on University Avenue, Timothy Andrews returned to institute, intending only to clean out his desk of personal affects. Angry words were exchanged with the guard at the gate. What happened next remained unclear, even to the present day.

Two days later a sheriff's deputy found him lying on the side of an unpaved road up Mt. Diablo State Park. He was incoherent. He had four cracked ribs, and his right hand was broken in three places. Both of his eyes were swollen shut. When he recovered enough to be interviewed, all he would say was that he had been in an accident. No damaged car was ever found. The news accounts quoted the sheriff as being skeptical. Mr. Andrews' injuries were inconsistent with the accident story. If he had gone over in a car, he most likely would not have survived. Days after the first report of Timothy Andrews' ordeal, the story disappeared from view. So did Andrews. There were rumors, nothing substantial. No one seemed to know what had become of him. One rumor was that he was working in a research lab in Hungary, or was it Poland? Who knew?

As if the air had simply evaporated from the room, the spirit of the gathering collapsed with the shaking of hands and saying goodnight. Marianne and Alexander insisted that they drive Herman home. He was in no shape to drive.

At the exit gate, Jonathan gave the guard a close look. "I wonder if that is same guard who argued with Tim Andrews last January."

"What are you talking about, Jonathan?"

Oh, it's nothing, just a bit of gossip Alexander told me. It does not matter."

At the door to The Claremont, Adam thanked Jonathan for driving and said goodnight.

10

The Apprenticed Will

Bayeta awoke an hour before first light and dressed. It was to be a day for tears and grief. The People would make their way to Maria's home. Women would bring food. Men would see to the livestock and finish plowing the cornfield to prepare it for planting. The children needed looking after. Maria Klah's future was everyone's concern. Maria had held such hopes for a good future. After years of struggle and pain, she deserved it.

At age twelve Maria had almost died from a lightning strike. Although young, she was old enough to know better than to stand under a tree in a thunderstorm. But she had worn a new dress that day even though she was herding the sheep. She was proud of her first full dress made of soft, light blue velveteen with a red cloth belt. Her father had yet to see her in the new dress. How grown up she looked. She did not want to spoil everything by getting it soaked.

A lightning bolt struck the cottonwood tree she was standing under, splitting the trunk and killing two sheep outright. Her older brother, Tall Boy, found her. He could not tell if she was breathing. He carried her back to the hogan, two miles over wet, slippery rock. In the weeks that followed, Maria slowly recovered. But the headaches did not go away. She could not concentrate on schoolwork or the household chores. Without being asked, Tall Boy took to herding the sheep. Her mother did all she could to ease the headaches, but Maria languished, lost weight, and suffered nausea. A patient woman, her mother wove from dawn to dusk each day for two years. Much money was needed for a sing for Maria.

Bayeta remembered how desperate Maria was to be free of her pain. On the second day of the sing, as she entered the Hogan to witness the ritual, Bayeta had tried to suspend her doubts about the power of traditional medicine. She had been exposed to the wider world and western medicine. She felt compromised in the midst of her own people. She had come for Maria's sake.

The *hataalii* was an old man, someone Bayeta recognized. When he had visited her parents, months before on a similar mission, he had carried many small leather bags strung on a leather string on his shoulder. Curious, Crystal Bayeta had asked him what was in them. He had smiled, opened one, showed her a red powdery substance, pigment. Such pigments were used to make a drypainting used in a healing ceremony. She tried, but could not suppress a skeptical look, to which he smiled.

"Not all that heals comes in medicine bottles of the white men," he said. "I have seen a web from your loom, many times, even when you were little and put your loom beside your mother's. You make beauty from the wool of sheep, a sacred thing. I, too, bring beauty into being, with these pigments."

The *hataalii* stood at the west corner of the hogan behind a newly completed drypainting. Maria bowed her head as the *hataalii* blessed the drypainting with white cornmeal. He sprinkled cornmeal at each corner, from east to south to west to north. He instructed Maria to do likewise. Her hands trembled as the corn meal sifted softly through her fingers. Maria stood to the north of the drypainting, took off her jewelry, and her clothes, except for her skirt. The Chanter and three assistants began to chant. The *hataalii* shook buffalo hide rattles.

Maria stretched out her hands and arms stiffly at her sides. With great care, two of the assistants applied body paint to her chest, her arms, her hands, and her back. The sound of chanting rose and fell, hypnotic and solemn. It filled the space within the dim hogan, a palpable aura of sound indescribable to Bayeta. More paint was applied to Maria's legs and face and lastly to her feet. Her big toenails resembled the heads of two black snakes. Out of breath, desperate for air, Bayeta stepped back and fled through the doorway covered by the buffalo hide. In the light she stood listening to the chant, stood as if hypnotized. To this day she could not explain what had come over her. She returned inside. It had taken all the courage she could muster.

She never spoke of what had happened next. The chanter and an assistant helped Maria to sit down squarely on the drypainting. She faced east, her legs straight out. Time passed. Without moving her body, Maria fixed her eyes upon an invisible point beyond her grasp. Pigments from the images of the sacred beings in the drypainting were pressed against her skin. Maria took pollen into her mouth. Bayeta closed her eyes, overwhelmed. The chanting continued. Shadows moved darkly against the hogan walls, east to south to west to north. Bayeta felt faint, unable to move her arms or legs, unable to retreat, unable to breathe.

The ceremony for the day ended with Maria walking out of the hogan, her face radiant. She took in four deep breaths as the late sun streamed across her face. She wore an offering of turquoise and olivella shell in her hair. Since that day, Maria never stepped from her home without the offering in her hair. It protected her from lightning and things unseen, snakes, anything that moves in zigzag ways. From that day forward, Maria was free of headaches and believed her life would be a happy one.

On the four days following, Maria had entered the hogan each day, a new drypainting complete for her to sit upon and be sung over. The people talked of her demeanor, how it was just as it should be. Bayeta had listened with respect and unease. Kinfolk smiled at her each time she emerged from the hogan. They sensed her doubt. She had been away at school too long and talked like a *bilagáana*. She spoke of things they did not understand.

Bayeta knew well how life and work in Albuquerque had taken its toll on her Navajo identity. Each passing year she had felt it slipping away. At the sing for Maria, it struck home. Her people did possess their own sense of power and substance. To glimpse it, she had only to look into Maria's eyes each time she came out into the light from the ceremonial hogan.

In the years that followed, having been sung over, Maria recovered her balance. Life was hard, but the family managed. Modest as it was, Maria took pride in her family's outfit that clung to the barren sandstone rim west of White Butte. They tenaciously endured the harsh winters, some so bitter that at times new lambs froze to death before Maria or Tall Boy could find and bring them into the hogan for warmth. But they never doubted the coming of spring. Then, when the spring rains had sunk down into the sandy bottom of Monument Canyon and the trail firmed up, they packed up and moved down to their summer hogan, a mile downstream from Widow Tumecho's outfit. Summers in the canyon were the good times. Men rode their horses and tended the gardens. Women wove and gossiped.

At nineteen Maria had married Hastin Gani, a quiet man, a good man. He worked hard and did not drink. No neighbor ever heard him raise his voice, even when others complained at the Chapter House that Maria's sheep were too many, were eating up too much grass. Maria let them say what they would. Hastin Gani stood by her, as did his kin. Both families were proud of Maria, "the one who stood up to lightning." What could they do to her that lightning had not already done?

Now, with Hastin Gani buried, Bayeta's concern turned to Maria and her children. She remembered how transformed Maria had looked at her sing. Before, her nerves had been edgy. She had looked worn and pale. But at the ceremony each time she emerged from the ceremonial Hogan her eyes had softened a little more. It was plain for all to see that she was at peace.

Bayeta wrapped the meat and packed it into two coolers. With the lamb chops and mutton for stew ready for transport, she set aside two bags of flour, baking powder, salt, five two-pound cans of Folgers Coffee, and a tin of sugar. More should be done, but this much would have to do for the moment. Many women would already be there, ready to cook, weeping. They needed something to do while they cried and waited for more family and neighbors to arrive. Later, if needed, Bayeta would send Martin for more provisions. He would come, too, as Hastin Gani was his friend. She would attend to Alberto when he did.

Piling the coolers and boxes into the back of the Land Rover, Bayeta paused to look to the eastern horizon. First light, somber gray, was advancing, melting away the stars and giving form to the land. House Made of Dawn greeted the Klah clan this day. Hardship had come to the family. Bayeta said a prayer for the peace of her own home to suspend her anxieties. Until she returned from Maria Klah's, all else would have to wait. Martin would care for Alberto until she returned. He also had the lab to tend. What must be done would be managed until Adam's return.

With sun breaking over the eastern ridgeline, Bayeta turned south onto the dirt road. The eastern flank of White Butte in the distance was newly clothed in the colors of day. On each side of the road the greening hues of piñón and juniper danced upon the red earth. Rocky outcrops stood proud, red-brown and tawny-yellowed sentinels. Bayeta slowed at the first straight stretch of rutted road. " '*Sa'ah naagha éi Bik'eh hózhǫ,* " she whispered. She spoke each syllable right and true, so as not to betray her sadness for the day ahead. "'*Sa'ah naagha éi,*" long life, had deserted Hastin Gani. She cried and gripped the wheel hard. At the last turn Maria's two-bedroom manufactured home and the hogan came into view. The hogan, now used only for ceremony, stood thirty feet to the south, a wisp of smoke winding up from its stove hole. A snatch of wind stirred, bending the sage and rabbit bush along the edges of the sheep pen. What would happen to Maria and the children, now that Hastin Gani's wind was gone?

At the far end of the sheep corral two dozen cars were parked in a disordered assembly, looking like bone dice thrown down on bare ground. There would be many hands to help with the food. Bayeta slowed and eased her way into the compound. Her face muscles softened at the sight of the women coming to greet her, their eyes full of tears. Bayeta let her own tears fall. It is good to cry, Maria's folk would tell her, good to feel the pain. Maria's husband was a good man. No one would speak of his misfortune, only his good. It was just so.

Bayeta heard cries coming from within the hogan. As she cried with the women beside the car, she waited for a kinswoman of Maria's to receive her. The early morning air was cold and unsettled. It was unusual for a cold wind to stir up after dawn. But this was an unusual day, a hard day.

The men stood in a circle inside the open space enclosed by the jumble of cars and trucks. Tall Boy was with them. He saw Bayeta and tipped his hat. For the present they would keep to themselves. They had much to talk over, much to decide. How best to help with the sheep and finish plowing the cornfield for planting? What to do about the half-finished addition to the house, the room for the new baby? In daylight, the open framing looked forlorn, a bare skeleton of a dream unfulfilled. The men would finish what Hastin Gani had so well begun.

The door of the hogan opened. Maria stood mute, wrapped tightly in a shawl against the cold. The first rays of sun silhouetted Maria's figure. She was still a young woman, fine figured even with her swollen belly. Bayeta walked to her and embraced her. Maria's face was drawn tight and stained with tears. As the shawl fell from her shoulders, Bayeta saw that her long, silken hair was freshly brushed back. Her mother was caring for her. Bayeta reached out to touch her right cheek, seeing that the ever-present turquoise and olivella shell offering was not in her hair. Maria quickly grabbed Bayeta's hand. "Someday I will wear it again, but not now. I cannot."

"I come to cry with you. A good man is gone. My heart is heavy. Will you come to my home when you are feeling better? We will sit and talk. If it is good, we will weave together."

"I would like that. But I am getting heavy and cannot sit for long."

Bayeta looked down at Maria's womb. She dared not ask if Maria had a name for the child. "Come to Rimrock soon. Many people will be coming. I need to buy sheep to feed them."

"I have three young ewes. They have been eating much sage and will taste good. I do not need them to make more wool."

In better times Maria would have sold the older, less tasty adult ewes. But now the money was needed. It was also true that the ewes would bring in less. Bayeta understood the difference.

More cars and trucks arrived. A handful of men came on horseback. Hastin Gani had loved horses and racing them. All the men would talk about horses and farming the land as white men do. They would not speak Hastin Gani's name or of his misfortune.

"Maybe it is not good to use that contraption," a young man said. An old man complained, "They break down and cost money to fix. You got to feed them gasoline all the time." The men knew that the field to the west was but half plowed. The tractor lay there still, on its side. No one would touch it. Tall Boy would go to Ganado to talk with a John Deere dealer. It would not be top dollar, but the price would be decent. The buyer would come to haul it away.

It would be a long time before Maria looked out on that field, even with it plowed. She would take the children and sheep to the summer camp early this year. Tall Boy would tend to the field of corn. It did not matter so much now in any case. Her strength had to be put into dealing with loss, not gain. In time, perhaps, she could look at that field again and hope.

By mid-morning, Bayeta saw what more was to be done. Martin Atsidi Chon, her cousin, was of the Towering House People, *Kinyaa' áanii*. He'd been too long alone and needed to begin a new life fresh. Maria was about his age and her clan ties did not conflict with Martin's. There was also the matter of what he had done to Adam. It was best that he leave Rimrock.

The first morning filled with tears and regrets ended. Bayeta loaded the empty ice-chests into the Land Rover. Maria came out to say goodbye. A hundred people remained. They knew what must be done for Maria and the children. The men talked of when to plant the corn. Some remained skeptical. The drought was likely to continue. Tall Boy settled the matter. It was good to try.

"Maria, I will send Martin to help Tall Boy. His people are *Kinyaa' áanii* and his father *Biih Diné é Táchii'nii*."

Maria took in a deep breath and looked toward her children playing. "They are good people."

"He is a good man, Maria. We will miss him."

"With his help my brother will finish the baby's room."

"Come to Rimrock in three days and bring three sheep."

Bayeta returned home and gave Martin the list of needed supplies he was to get in Chinle. She reminded him that he must talk with Johnny Kabito. Kabito would know where to find Chanter of the Sun's House. The old man moved about, often was hard to locate. Winter was the season for sings. The chanter might be exhausted from so many engagements. No matter, Johnny would know where to find him. He was to say that the daughter of George Slim needed him. He had once performed a sing for George Slim. Knowing that Crystal Bayeta needed him would be enough to persuade him.

Bayeta knew that Chanter of the Sun's House, on seeing Martin, would know that he did not look well. The old man had wise eyes. He had learned from Flapping Mexican, an apprentice to Bogeesyason, the Missing Tooth Mexican. Bogeesyason, too, was *Kinyaa' áanii*. The circle was complete. He would come without delay, as Martin was his kin.

Watching Martin drive off, Bayeta picked up the message from Adam and read it again. Martin had heard the phone message and put the handwritten note on the hall table. It read: "Things are sticky here. Herman has been spying. I have yet to tell him what I will do. Call you later. Love, Adam."

The buzzer in the kitchen sounded. Alberto was awake and needed her. Emily, the part-time helper, had already arrived before Bayeta returned and had mixed a pitcher of Kool-Aid for him. As she prepared a food tray, Bayeta scanned the clear, open southern sky beyond the kitchen window. The far reach of the Defiance Plateau was in the distance. There, Maria Klah and the women cried. By day's end, the late sun would dry their tears and the hardest day would end. Streaming into the kitchen, the sun's rays felt warm and clean. She needed to feel something warm and calming. The terracotta tiles at her feet were warm to the touch. She took her sandals off.

The distraction of the sun's warmth on her face lasted longer than she realized. She focused with effort on what needed doing for

Alberto. Did she hear him coming down the hall? It was hardly possible, yet she listened for the scrape of his sandals on the tiles, for his breath gasping at the stilled air. She was now used to hearing his approach, the soft scraping of his bedclothes against the wall, his weak voice calling out. He would stop once or twice to catch breath and then continue his labored journey calling to her, "Bea…Can I?" "Bea," he would say, "I want to sit in the kitchen to eat. Can I?" But today, she heard no such plea, no sound of his approach.

She carried the tray with Kool-Aid and Lorna Dunne cookies down the hall. "No more Fig Newton's," she called out. It was a lie. The acidity was not good for him.

Bayeta wanted Alberto to feel as much of a sense of normalcy as possible. His lips bore their familiar, thin, bloodless smile, his mask of hope. He had been unable to walk farther than half the distance down the hall. Bayeta set the tray on the stand outside her studio door and went to him. With deliberateness, unwilling to betray a hint of panic, she put her arm firmly around his waist and helped him to the couch in her studio. The sun's rays had moved beyond the patio, yet it was still warm. The room was alive with dust dancers spinning, rising, and falling at the slightest disturbance of the air. Alberto's skin felt cold to the touch. Martin had kept the curtains drawn in Alberto's room to shut out the glare of midday. With Alberto settled down on the couch, she went to get his sunglasses. Returning, she fluffed up a pillow to make him more comfortable. Retrieving the tray in the hall, she handed him a half-filled glass of Kool-Aid and a cookie. In the moment he looked contented, at peace.

"Adam will come home soon?"

"He won't be long now."

"He will not go away again?"

Bayeta sat down beside him to hold his glass. "I know you miss him. He had to make this trip to give a speech, an important one. Then he will come home."

"Will he tell them about me?"

"They might not understand."

"Why?"

"They are scientists, not doctors. They might not understand."

Alberto was silent for a long time. At last he asked, "Can I stay here?"

"What a question. You will always be with us."

"I mean here, on the couch. I am tired and…"

Bayeta smiled and took his glass. He was looking at the loom, the weave's beginning. "You can rest here as long as you like."

"I like it here, when you are weaving."

"I will not weave today. It is not a good day for doing so."

"Please, I like to hear it sing."

Hastin Gani weighed upon her mind. Until a good cry was had, she would not weave.

But for Alberto the house was often too quiet, too silent, except for the sound of his own breath, the rustling of his bed-sheets, the almost imperceptible hum of lab equipment, and the intermittent puffs of the lab's air compressor. Alberto wanted to hear the sounds of life, the sound of her loom. To him, it was music, the music of life, life being lived. Outside, the spring had yet to quicken. The desert was slow to stir with new life until the earth absorbed the sun's warming embrace.

Within a minute Alberto fell asleep. It was this way with Alberto of late. He would be alert one moment only to lapse into deep sleep the next.

Bayeta walked out the sliding door of the studio. The afternoon sun clung to the far end of the patio. To the north and east, light bathed the serrated Chuska peaks. Her father had been born there amid the mountains he called "The Goods of Value Range." The backbone of his world stretched north to south along that range, dividing the land of red rock canyons to the west from the dull browns and empty desert spaces to the east. George Slim took some pride in being called a "wild" Navajo. The white man's world did not impress him much, except for sugar, Folger's coffee, and cigarettes. For years, he had used little sugar and smoked no cigarettes. He was born to *Tódích'il'nii* (Bitter Water Clan), one of the four clans created by Changing Woman. He had never seen that great ocean to the west, home of Changing Woman. But, he knew it was there, a place one could visit, if one chose. For a wife, he chose well. Ninaba was of the Jemez Clan (Coyote Pass People) from *Tseyi*. Ninaba's father was of the Tall House People, *Kinyaa' áanii*. They knew the ways of planting, of settled living. George Slim joked of having the best of two ways to live, horse-stealing and raising corn. Within "The Goods of Value Range" and east of the *Tseyi* rim, The Place of Emergence was close at hand. He once said that to see his daughter weave told him that she, no matter how much white man's education she had, would always be "a good Navajo woman." If he could see her loom now, she thought, as she walked about the patio, he would know that this weave would be her best. He would not need to be told that the bayeta yarn she was using brought the four sacred mountains to the beholder's mind. He would know, too, that the play of indigo on a bayeta background signified Red Rock Walls Crashing. He would know it. He would know that this web was meant for Adam, was meant to protect him from the cold winds of winters to come.

Alberto's coughing brought her back to the present. What her father would know slipped from her mind. She stepped back into her studio to find Alberto still asleep. He was such a dreamy young man, a young man trapped within an aged frame. His wind was faint, at the edge of night. As she silently closed the sliding door, she heard the car. Martin had returned.

<++++++++++>

Waking from a restless night of little sleep, Adam had room service send up a breakfast tray. He would have preferred to go down to the dining room for a hearty Sunday brunch, but the prospect of being recognized discouraged him. He could avoid any calls, having told the night clerk to hold them. But such a tactic would not hold up for much longer. How to occupy his time? A brochure on the desk gave him some ideas. He could visit the zoo. Or, he could wander about campus, not that the thought of drifting about his old "digs" gave him much pleasure. It would remind him of how good it once felt to be a teacher. No, that would not do. There was the Botanical Garden. How long since he had sat in the cool shade of redwoods? Something very tall, old, and enduring, that was what he wanted to occupy part of his day. No science, no distractions of the moment.

"I'll write a letter to Alberto. So many things I want to say to him," he thought. Adam regretted not being more open with the boy about his feelings. So much was implied between them, but not spoken.

Stopping at the front desk, he asked the attendant for his message slips. One was from Sanderson saying only that he was looking forward to dinner. Hardesty's message confirmed that they should meet at the Hilton at the late afternoon symposium he was moderating. The third message was from Herman: "Must, absolutely must, see you today, at the earliest possible time."

Adam was relieved that he had insisted to the night clerk that they take his messages. He had not wanted to have to hear Herman's desperate voice, his whimpering, his endless pleading.

"Excuse me, Miss," he motioned to the attendant who had given him his messages. "Did anyone stop at the front desk asking for my room number, or if I was here?" She thought for a moment. "No, but I can ask Brian; he's been on duty since six."

"Yes, sir," the young man named Brian said as he walked over to where Adam stood at the counter. "There was one man, at about seven this morning, I think." Adam asked what he told the man. "I informed him that you had left instructions not to be disturbed. He looked a bit put out."

"I see. Did he leave his name?"

"No. I asked him, but he would not leave one. He sat in the lobby for an hour. Then he walked out. I've not seen him since."

"Please, it is important. Can you describe the man to me?"

"Oh, let me think. Yes, he looked to be in his mid-fifties, bald, about my height."

"I think I know whom you are referring to. He wasn't wearing an ill-fitting suit, was he?"

"Now that you mention it, yes, it did look like that, well, a bit. It was grey, I think."

Adam looked about the lobby, but did not see the man. He knew it probably had been Mueller.

Using the house phone, Adam rang Ryder's room. He was in.

"Would you do me a favor?"

Ryder said yes without asking what it was. "I'm about the leave the hotel and won't be around for the better part of the day. When you are at the Hilton, I assume you plan to be there, please keep an eye out for that Mueller, or anyone of his sort. Would you?"

"You don't need to ask. Of course I will."

"Thank you. I'll try to find you there later in the afternoon to touch bases."

"Fine, between sessions I'll be in the lobby bar."

"I'll look for you there." Adam rang off and returned to the front desk.

"One more thing, if you please," he said to the desk clerk. "I don't want to have to deal with someone who is looking for me. Is there a back way I can take?"

"If you like, you can go through that door," he pointed to his left. "It leads to the service corridor. From there, it leads to the back entrance for staff, on the east side of the building."

"That will do nicely. Thank you." Adam checked the small leather case he carried to make sure he had his wallet, a pen to write with, and the brochure for the Botanical Garden. "One last thing, if anyone asks for me, tell him I am in, but that I left instructions not to be disturbed."

"I will put a notice in your box, sir. Have a nice day."

The two-mile walk from The Claremont to the Botanical Garden gave Adam time to clear his mind of distractions and focus on what mattered most. Twenty minutes later, he turned onto the Centennial Drive. Since it was still early, the car traffic was light. Visitors to the garden would not begin to arrive much before 9:00. Still, he had to remain careful and listen for oncoming cars, as there were no sidewalks. He also had to dodge a dozen bicycle riders. He had forgotten that the hilly roads above the campus were a favorite of bike enthusiasts, especially on Sundays.

After paying his admission, Adam checked the brochure map for directions to the rhododendron and dogwood areas. The booth attendant had said they were at their peak and should not be missed. Adam appreciated the thought. He had not realized how much he missed flowering plants and shrubs that were not native to the

Arizona desert. It amused him to remember his mother trying for years to grow a rhododendron at their home in Albuquerque when he was growing up. Every year she would ask that the garden shop carry them, only to be told that if she wanted, they could order one for her. She insisted. They ordered. It came. She planted and nursed it every spring and summer, doing her best to acidify the soil and keep it damp. But at the first hard freeze of winter the poor things died. New Mexico was no place for the rhododendron, no matter how much she tried.

After drifting about for an hour and a half, Adam made his way to the Redwood Grove. It was Sunday and still early in the day. He had the grove to himself. An open, concrete amphitheater in the midst of the grove was a perfect place to sit and draft his letter. It had troubled him that every time he phoned the house, Alberto was asleep. Alberto would want to know about his trip, what he saw, and whom he saw. Alberto knew that it was a conference where scientists discussed research, debated, and argued. He believed that Adam would argue for more attention being paid to those suffering like Alberto. Adam began his letter:

"My Dear, Dear Boy,

I am writing this letter for you while sitting in a grove of redwood trees near the campus of the University. When Bea and I lived here, before you came to us, we used to come here a lot. It is a wonderful place, a botanical garden. It is quite different from where we now live. Well, not so different in some ways. There is a very nice area for desert plants, ones you will recognize. But no, this is not canyon country. Most people who come here probably have never seen real rock canyons, or watched red-taileds soar overhead, or spied on a six-point buck lurking at the edge of the cottonwoods by the streambed. But you and I have. We will do so again as soon as I return. It won't be long.

"Did I ever tell you about redwoods? There are times when I forget just what we have yet to imagine together. Close your eyes and imagine now. A redwood tree can grow to over 300 feet into the air. At its base it can be 40 feet around. A redwood tree is just about the biggest living thing, ever. It begins life from a seed that is the smallest of all conifer trees. They are always green and never lose their leaves, not like cottonwoods do. What is also amazing is…"

Adam was about to say what is amazing is that a redwood tree can live for thousands of years. But, that could hurt Alberto's feelings. Mention of how long people or anything else lives would only remind Alberto of what was to be denied him. Later he would finish the letter. Handwritten and in an envelope, he would deliver it personally to Alberto, when he returned to Rimrock.

Adam felt terribly tired once he put the unfinished letter away. The weight of care and the uncertainty of what the coming days would bring bore down on his consciousness. Odd, he thought, to feel so exhausted, as if he had not slept in days. He would find a phone and call Bayeta, tell her…

"Sir, sir are you all right?" A tall, young man in khaki and a broad brimmed straw hat was shaking his shoulder. "I don't mean to disturb you but…"

Adam squinted at the glare in his eyes from the sunlight streaming through a narrow gap in the canopy above. He struggled to right himself into a sitting position. "I must have dozed off."

"I did not want to disturb you, but…"

"Yes, I must have dozed off for a minute or so."

"It was quite a while, actually. I came by two hours ago to check on the clean up job that was done after yesterday's wedding ceremony. You were lying there just as I found you a minute ago."

"Thank you for waking me. I had no intention of dropping off like that."

Adam gave the man a sheepish, embarrassed grin. "Yes, well, I better get cracking then."

Adam walked back to the gift shop and called for a cab to pick him up at the main gate. He guessed at how long he had slept on the concrete bench. The crick in his neck told him it had been long.

"Where to, mister?" asked the cab driver as he eyed him from the rear view mirror. "

"Take me to the Hilton."

"Which one is that?"

"Oh, I am sorry. Yes, take me to the Hilton in San Francisco, the one near Union Square."

<++++++++++>

Hardesty had suggested that Adam meet up with him at the symposium, between 4 and 5. Sanderson would join them later at the restaurant. Adam arrived just as the session was breaking up. On their walk to Chinatown, they talked about the reception at The Manse, and what Jonathan had observed. At the corner of Bush and Grant Streets they stood and talked about his father and what he had said.

"I could not believe Valentine! He went on and on about 'free radical theory,' as if it was news. Alexander kept goading him by bringing him back to it repeatedly, pretending that it interested him."

"Unstable atoms interest him." Adam was being flip, but he had a point. "The idea that an element or molecule can inhibit or accelerate a reaction has always interested him. Free radicals he believes in, anything oxidative. At his age he worries about anything that affects bodily functions."

"Valentine kept going on about megadoses of Vitamin-E. He driveled on endlessly about what he called 'the scavenger role' it performs inside the cell."

Something in Hardesty's account connected with what Adam had picked up at his end of the table. He stood at the curb, trying to recall it. "I saw something yesterday, quite by accident. In the taxi, when I gave my father a lift from the Kosmoi Club, he had a copy of McKusick's *Mendelian Inheritance in Man, Volume 1*. It was stuffed like a huge brick in the side pocket of his briefcase. Seeing it surprised me. When I took it out to ask him about it, I saw the paper he had used as a bookmark. It was inserted in the page on Cerebral Vascular Amyloid Peptides, underlined and highlighted. He made light of it, but I did see it. The paper was a lab report, a summary of his DNA profile. He had underlined a reference to Chromosome 21. The word hybridization was scribbled in the margin.

"Did you ask him about it?"

"No, it relates to prion proteins. I was reluctant to."

"He offered no explanation?"

"He just shook his head and stared out the window. Getting out of the car he smiled and whispered, 'Don't worry, it's early days.' "

"You should talk to him."

"I don't know if he will talk about it, let alone admit it."

"He was very sharp at dinner, even witty. He more than held his ground with Valentine and Vaughn over oxygen being THE elixir of life. He babbled on about how all functions of respiration derive from the body's ability to utilize oxygen. Alex kept pushing them to explain. Neither of them expressed their views clearly. It boiled down to 'combustion theory.' "

"Was that when Hessen got into the act? I heard him say something along those lines."

"Jesus! What a character he is. By the way, where does Hessen come from?"

"An institution for puffers, I imagine."

"No, seriously, where is he from?"

"He studied at Leuven. That is about all I know."

Hardesty thought for a moment, then he said, "If he did, it was not with Merkl. Merkl would never have put up with the likes of Hessen."

Adam smiled, "Hessen believes that you lack of imagination."

"He said that? Well, he said that you showed little interest in the institute."

"As if there is much of anything there to be impressed with."

"Alexander overheard Hessen and told him to shut up."

"I'll have to thank Father for that."

"Alexander also told Hessen that you are interested in the wonders of the cell, to the mountainous chain of existence." Hardesty waved his arms over his head, as Alexander had done in saying it. "Quite a compliment, I thought. Hessen had no clue. It was quite a performance."

"I haven't forgotten your admonition, Jonathan."

"And which one is that?"

"Newton: '...much better to do a little with certainty...than to explain all things.' "

"Ah, but you do, you do sometimes forget that there are limits, Adam."

"I know that. It's been on my mind these last few days. Up to now, I've been focused on near term goals. I have ignored the implications of what they might lead to."

"It takes some a lifetime to realize that. At least you are now asking the right questions."

Walking into The Red Dragon, Jonathan's favorite Chinese restaurant, Adam asked about Sanderson. Hardesty said he was to meet them at the restaurant, but had to check into the hotel first and touch bases with a colleague.

"Thanks for coordinating things."

"He did say that he's bringing a friend to dinner."

"Who is it?"

"He's a biologist at the National University on Taiwan. John's been corresponding with him. I think he's sounding out John about a visiting appointment at UNM."

"In that case, I hope you're right about this being the best Chinese restaurant in town, Jonathan. He or she is sure to know if it is or not."

"His name is Liu Xiang."

A line of people stood at the door waiting for a table. Jonathan gave his name at the desk. "I'm afraid we're in for a wait, at least forty-five minutes."

"If John's a bit late, it won't matter so much."

Jonathan began to ask Adam something, but broke off. "John, I didn't see you."

Sanderson waved. "I thought I'd keep very still and see how long it took you."

"Blame it on my steamy glasses. Anyway, I am glad to see you. Adam tells me you're getting tired of being chair." He noticed the man beside John and smiled at him.

"It's a thankless task," John said. He turned. "Please forgive my manners. "Jonathan Hardesty, meet Dr. Liu Xiang."

Jonathan extended his hand and motioned. "And this is Adam Grant."

Adam held out his hand and smiled.

"I am very happy to meet you, Dr. Grant. Talk at the meeting is all about you. I am honored."

"What talk? I am only here to give a few brief remarks, nothing remarkable."

"It is said that you have a major—how do you say—something up your sleeves?"

"Well, Dr. Liu, as you can see, there is nothing up my sleeves." Adam stretched out both arms.

"Forgive me for speaking of it."

"There is nothing to excuse, Dr. Liu. I just wonder why all the talk."

"They talk about your work on aging. Of course we Chinese are most interested in this. May I say that we, too, have such interest for thousands of years?"

"If I'm not asking too much, may I ask whom you spoke with?"

"Dr. Thomas Vaughn. Do you know him? He has written a book, *Secrets of the Cell*."

"Yes, I am acquainted with Dr. Vaughn. He's fond of quoting Bacon, as in '…you may deceive nature sooner than force her.' I do not happen to hold to his theories."

"I, too, think as you. His book is, how do you say, written with too much old wisdom?"

Adam caught Liu Xiang's wink. "Too few facts can lead one to too much old wisdom."

Hardesty interjected. "We could choose another restaurant. The wait is another half hour."

Liu Xiang looked surprised. "That long? I do something. I know the family."

With that, Liu Xiang stepped to the front desk. A brief exchange in Chinese was overheard. The waiter, all smiles and bowing, motioned for Liu Xiang and his party to follow.

"I come to restaurant when in America. The food is very good, very Chinese." Dr. Liu laughed at his own joke.

They were seated in a private dining room on the second floor, an impressive view of The Embarcadero and Bay Bridge beyond the windows. Liu spoke to the waiter, gesturing and returning the waiter's bow. "If you permit, to begin I have ordered dim sum and hot plum wine."

"Thank you, Xiang, that's great. Do you prefer being called Liu or Xiang? I do not wish to…"

Dr. Liu politely interrupted Adam with his hand. "Xiang is given name. Liu is family name. Xiang is good to call me, Dr. Grant."

"Adam is good, too, just Adam, Xiang."

"Also very good! We are good friends now. Yes? I shall call you Adam."

The mood about the table was a change from the tension of the last few days. Adam was in fine form. Hardesty and Sanderson caught up on each other's lives. And though Xiang hesitated at first, he easily fit in and called everyone by his first name. It was a concession on his part, as familiarity often came slowly to a man like Dr. Liu Xiang. He moved in and out of the talk about the table seamlessly, deferential and familiar as the moment called for. For an hour, hot plum wine flowed. Xiang kept the carter's tongs busy serving one dim sum delicacy after another. Soon, a large platter of mu shu pork and roll-ups was brought out. He had taken pains to ask everyone's preferences. But since everyone expressed complete satisfaction in designating him their guide, he ordered everything in Chinese.

"Ah," Xiang explained, on hearing a good-humored complaint that they were beginning to feel stuffed, "now we come to the best. This fish is very special. Li Chao Kuin, the cook, is a magician!" As he spoke, the headwaiter took the lid off the large, oval silver platter and placed it in the middle of the table. "Li's most special preparation—sautéed halibut cheeks in ginger and garlic," the headwaiter proclaimed.

"Oh, to be in the hands of a true adept," Jonathan rejoiced. Hot plum wine was having its effect. The concerns that had consumed them for days evaporated, if only for the evening. Hardesty poured the last of the third bottle of plum wine into his cup. "I shall sleep like a log tonight."

Hardesty turned to Xiang. "Do you know, Xiang, my former apprentice is also something of a magician? He lives in Navajo Land, where they call him 'the wizard of Rimrock.' "

"I am two times honored." Liu Xiang bowed. "May I inquire? What is this Rimrock?"

Adam raised his glass. "Rimrock is my Miranda, my fortressed isle of solitude. There, I live and conjure. The Navajo are my wife's people. Rimrock is surrounded by desert and beauty."

"You are in exceptional spirits tonight," said Sanderson. "Feeling the wine, are we?"

"And why should we not? Are we not friends out for a toot, a quiet howl?"

Xiang looked pleasantly confused. "But Doctor, Adam, I mean, what is Rimrock?"

"It is a remote corner of Arizona, on the Navajo reservation."

"You see Xiang, Adam's home and laboratory are in the desert. His wife had the permission from the Navajo Nation Council to build. He and his wife have not lived in Berkeley for five years."

"You must have wife permission to build house? How is this so in America?"

"Well," Sanderson interjected. It was best if he, not Adam tried to explain. "It is not really Adam's house; that is, he does not own the house. His wife, Crystal Bayeta, is Navajo, a Native American. She has the right to build on Navajo land. Her right comes from her being Navajo. So, when it was time to build their home, it was her wish to live at Rimrock with her people.

"And, you, Adam, in their eyes, are you a wizard?"

"It's just that some local people don't like to see me at the rim of Monument Canyon, a place not far from Rimrock. I sometimes park my car there to look at the canyon. To them, it is an unlucky place. When they see me there, they say that only a wizard stands at the edge of such a chasm for so long. It is dangerous, they believe, and invites bad things to happen."

"Adam, I am hearing talk of making people live longer. It is some kind of magic, is it not? Always, we Chinese have interest in immortality. The emperors had many magicians at the royal court. They sought the Red Dragon. It is odd, is it not, that we are at the Red Dragon restaurant?"

John, anxious to shift the conversation, chimed in. Xiang, however, was not easily deflected. "All Chinese seek chu-sheng. My father's uncle, he was a seller of traditional medicines. He had many, many recipes for long life. He had much knowledge. He lived to be very old."

"I assume that you are also interested in such matters."

"I am Chinese. The great lords and princesses were buried with much gold and much jade. It is said that gold and jade preserve the body from decay. In life, they wished to drink the waters of life, the waters of long life." Liu Xiang was warming up to his subject. "Many medicines are two thousand years old. But now, it is said, the right gold for making such medicine is not to be found. That is the problem. Such knowledge is lost. Plain gold will not do."

Xiang was outside himself, speaking with pride of family and tradition. "A magician, the favorite of Wu Ti, told the emperor that he would make the proper gold from cinnabar. He did so. His divine gold was made into utensils for eating and drinking. Wu-Ti wished for long life, and he was very afraid of death."

Adam leaned forward. "And, did he live a long life?"

"The Emperor Wu-Ti, it is said, died before he was eighty years old."

"Then it is not so good."

"On the contrary: Such a secret requires many sacrifices. Seven Han emperors before him died from taking the 'pill of immortality.' "

"You mean they actually drank gold?"

"It is so. They believed it was the proper gold. One cannot be certain unless it is tried." Everyone but Liu Xiang grimaced at the thought. Xiang continued, "I, too, hope to find the way. Chu-sheng exists. It is only our poor eyes that do not see it."

"Maybe it is a plant, some herb yet to be discovered?"

"We Chinese believe in Xing and Ming. Xing is one's nature. Ming is one's destiny."

"I don't follow. What do you mean?"

"I am a scientist. And so, I believe our destiny is inside the cell. I am Chinese. Xing can be what you call rule of nature. We cannot be outside nature. Ming is other, the path each human must take. Each human, alone, must consider his destiny and choose his nature's path."

"It is all about nature and experience taken together then."

"It is as you wish. Science deceives and manipulates. Is that not so? We Chinese obey nature. Also, we honor the wisdom of our ancestors. It is good to swallow a hen's egg on New Year's Day to vitalize one's body for the whole year."

"As a scientist you don't believe in that."

"Perhaps the egg is more than an egg. An egg is a beginning of what is to come. Do you not see DNA in your microscope and see the floor of life and all that moves upon it to know what is to come?"

"You do have an interesting way of putting it."

Xiang was having them on a bit. For the rest of the evening, talk focused on issues of sequencing and bond formation of amine chains, studies that related to Liu Xiang's work. It was midnight when they paid the bill and walked out into the fog that had descended upon the city. Adam remembered that he had promised to call Herman. It was now too late to call. Sanderson and Liu Xiang said good night and walked south on Grant toward the hotel. "A walk in the night air," Xiang chuckled, "may we live to be a hundred years."

Waiting for a cab, Hardesty broached the topic that had been under the table all evening. The cold air had sobered him. "What are you going to do about Herman?"

"Herman's precious institute does not concern me."

"I think he knows that by now. He can still make trouble."

"As you have aptly put it, and so has Ryder, the threat is Schwann." Hardesty asked if Bayeta had an opinion.

"She has, as she will be affected by all of this. We talked on the way to the airport. She worries how unstable Herman is. She has been more concerned about Herman than I was. In her way of putting it, subtly I admit, a life's thread can be too finely drawn and pulled to its breaking point. Herman's, I think she would say, was woven with uneven fibers. Self-serving ambitions will pull him apart. She speaks of it like that, rather than come right out. Still, I get her point."

"Can you placate him in any way?"

"Nothing I do will make any difference."

"Yes, I can see that. Perhaps Herman has gone too far to accept failure."

"He's fifty-five years old, desperate to hang on to what he has."

"You have decided what to do next." The comment was an affirmation, not a question.

"Let's get this cab." Adam hailed a yellow cab approaching. "What you sent out for me to those you chose will do its work. They will not be able to resist weighing in on it, even accepting that I have held back some key elements. From this point on, it is out of my hands."

"Perhaps, Adam, perhaps. They could take a wait and see approach, for the present do nothing."

"In any case, I think my work is protected. After the award ceremony, I may release more detail. Once that is done, no institute or drug company will be in a position to exploit it without my permission. The patent applications have already been filed."

"Are you sure you want to do it this way?"

"What other way is there?"

On the bridge across the bay, Adam dozed. He was not used to plum wine. One more day, he told himself, just get through one more day. He was grateful for Jonathan and John. He could rely on them unreservedly. Come morning he would deal with Herman. Then, Herman would have to deal with Schwann, the force behind Herman. Adam did not know Schwann, but he feared him.

<++++++++++>

Sweat from his fevered forehead had soaked his pillow. He needed more time, he begged, "I can. I will bring Adam around." The sharp metallic click in Herman's ear made him drop the phone. His hands shook. Nausea from his acidic stomach forced him to stagger to his feet. He reached for his car keys without turning on a lamp. He had been drunk and exhausted when he fell asleep two hours before. He was still dressed, with his shoes on. His swollen feet and pinched toes made him stumble.

Herman walked about the house, his nerves on edge and his head aching. The rooms were dark and silent, more like a tomb than a home. In the study, he fumbled in the dark for the garage door remote. He had to get out of the house, get beyond Schwann's reach, if only for an hour. "I'll drive somewhere, maybe think of something." Up Mt. Diablo road, he told himself. The park road at this hour would be deserted, a quiet place above the glare and confusion surrounding him. At the summit, William Henry Schwann could not reach him. There, he could think of what to do.

Fleeing his house was sudden, a desperate spasm of panic. He had lost control of events. Adam's behavior had showed that things really were out of his hands. Herman had willingly served Schwann, was his secret intermediary. What had it gotten him? Had there ever been a time when Adam would take his calls or respond to e-mails unless he wanted something? He was not stupid. Every slight was an insult, was Adam's way of underscoring his dislike. If only he had been smart enough to have insisted five years ago to an exclusive right to Adam's work. Then, with Adam desperate for funding, he could have gotten him to agree, Herman told himself.

"The man between, I am, with no real power. Well, there it is—I'm a failure." Now, at last, he realized how much he hated Schwann. "He's thrown me over. Mueller's now the one to get him what he wants. Jesus, god in heaven, I hate that man," Herman screamed as he ran a red light.

At Bear Creek Road Herman headed east toward the Briones Reservoir Dam. He was sweating and needed to stop the car, get out, and breathe fresh air. At the dam, he watched the water flow over the spillway. It was like watching his own plans simply flow out of his hands. He looked up the road to where it climbed into the open expanse of hills and meadows of mixed oak. That was where Mueller's man drove Tim Matthews and left him for dead. His stomach muscles tightened as his nausea returned. Herman imagined himself watching the young man being beaten up. He, Herman

Cockroft, had looked the other way as the man's life was being ruined, ruined for nothing, nothing at all.

Two minutes later, again driving, Herman swerved sharply toward the drop off. Panic gripped him, told him he was being followed. But he saw no car lights. But Mueller could drive without lights. Mueller could be out there, anywhere, behind him.

At the Alhambra Valley Road juncture he stopped. What if he went right? Or left? If Mueller was behind him, this was his chance to spot him. "He will see that I am trying to lose him. He wouldn't like that." Herman drove on looking for a place to turn around. There was none. Mueller, Mueller, Mueller, he kept thinking. "Good God, I've got to get a grip!" Herman's fevered brain blamed Schwann, blamed Adam, blamed his own weakness.

He drove north on Alhambra Valley Road. For ten minutes he drove with but two cars passing him, small luxury models too extraordinary for Mueller. Nauseous, he turned off at a vista point and got out. He needed air, needed to fight off the shakes, needed to get a grip.

"Vaughn, Boyle, they're all against me. They want to replace me." Herman spit the names out. "Mueller's just the enforcer, a bully. What a fool I was to let Schwann put Mueller inside. Strong-arming made things worse. God, I hate that man! Now Vaughn and Boyle are Schwann's chosen. I'm out. They are in." Herman swung his arms wildly at the dark beyond the headlights. "Father knows Schwann is going to replace me. I did everything for that man, and this is my reward. He is going to pitch me out! How do you like things now, Father? Your first-born is to be pitched into the pit. Why, why is this happening to me?"

Herman sat down on wet, dewy ground. He watched the incoming marine layer blink out the lights of San Francisco row-by-row. Schwann knew everything. Genetrix stock had risen twelve percent in four days. Herman's broker had made the move too clumsily. Schwann must have seen the sudden uptick in trading. The Marsh Clinic stock, another Schwann holding, was dropping just as rapidly. Schwann had to know that someone was dumping it.

Genetrix rose in lockstep by the same margin. "Jesus, what if my broker is in his pocket, too? He's told Schwann what I am up to!"

Herman had taken his gamble, certain that Adam would come around. Once Genetrix controlled and marketed Adam's discovery, a product to extend the life of millions of people, he would make a killing. What if Schwann later found out it was he who manipulated the stocks? Too late then, he'd do nothing. Why would he? It would cost him nothing. Others could have snatched up the shares, not just Herman. Delivering Adam would have made all the difference. That had to be worth a great deal to Schwann. He could leave the generic drug market behind him. Yes, of course, it was never about the money. Money was simply the means to his ends. Power was Schwann's elixir, not money.

Herman had reasons beyond money as well. No more doing Schwann's bidding. No more frigid, crabby, blueblood wife. No more days trapped behind a desk. No more worry about his good-for –nothing sons. He'd set up trusts for them, get them out of the house, be rid of their sorry asses. "I just want out. Can't you see that?"

Herman was shaking again, tears obscuring his sight. "Adam, I want out. Can't you be decent to me for once in your life? I always hated you, you know. Father always brags about his Trinity twins. You were the smart ones. You are his legacy. Me? Father never needed me. Not me, not me, not the one who needed his love.

Until the debacle at The Manse, Herman had held on to a thread of belief that Adam could be brought around. Adam should have long forgotten that minor exclusionary clause in his grant agreement, the one excluding his work not specified in the grants. Herman blamed the lawyers for that. They saw it as a give-away. Hutchinson-Gilford Progeria Syndrome, something mentioned but once, was of no interest to Evergreen and certainly not to Schwann.

"Give him the damn clause," Schwann had said. "Let him tinker. No pharmaceutical wants a thing to do with it." Herman had no concept of what it was. Adam said it was an autosomal recessive disease, whatever that was. Herman was certain no one was interested in anything of the sort. So, why bother?

For five years, Adam produced results. His work resulted in useful applications. He had never asked for rights to the resulting licensing agreements. The links between companies in England, Belgium, and Germany—Schwann's companies—would it have made a bit of difference?

In the state he was in, Herman had no memory of driving to the summit of Mount Diablo. For all he knew, the car had driven itself. He was standing there, in the predawn fog, shivering. He felt the damp, cold air suck at the heat of his fever. The thought of Vaughn and Valentine only served to intensify his chills. He wondered: Which of them would now become Schwann's familiar? Which one had rushed out of The Manse the night before to tell Schwann how miserably he had behaved?

Herman could hardly believe how unraveled things had become. Everyone was against him now, not just Adam. Carol had locked her bedroom door. Schwann accused him of involving "the goddamn press." He had done nothing of the kind. No press had been admitted to the institute in weeks. What was Schwann ranting about? What story had he killed before it was printed? How was it possible that a "hack" reporter, as Schwann called him, had got that close to Adam? What was he supposed to be, a mind reader? Did Schwann say, "You are finished?"

Herman took a liquor flask out of the glove compartment and poured a double shot. He needed fortification against the cold, against Schwann. The whiskey plunged down to his gut like hot molten steel. He staggered with pain searing his ulcerated stomach. He sweated, shivered, and paced in front of the car, its headlights still on, casting his long shadow into the oblivion beyond. Completely absorbed in finding blame for his situation, unable to admit his own failures, he took another drink. His stomach again wrenched and twisted from the pain, driving him to his knees. He flung the emptied flask into the bushes. Adam was not his problem. Mueller was out there somewhere, lurking in the dark, Schwann's "Little Prussian," the fixer. He would carry out Schwann's wishes and dispense retribution.

Every nerve and fiber of his body was now poised at the ragged edge of flight. Herman started the car. He had to get away. He must escape, must abandon everything and everyone. He had gambled and lost. What was left but to run? Father, too, had failed him. He'd seen how Alexander behaved at the Kosmoi. There he was, the great man, treating Adam as THE favored son. Everyone had seen it. It was Adam he really cared for, not him, not Herman, the ever-obedient son.

At the left turn onto Shattuck Avenue Herman still felt chilled from standing at the turnout on Mount Diablo summit. He was calm now, almost sober. "God, I hate my brother," he said, pounding the steering wheel so hard that the horn blared as he crossed the intersection. His fevered brain saw a hundred eyes staring at him, intense, accusing glares. "God help me. I'm being watched! They are all against me." But his words were no longer intense, not even desperate—only cold and resigned. At a stoplight, he wiped his sweating palms on his jacket. "Yes, must get a grip." Two blocks farther on Shattuck, another light changed to red. He wiped his brow and looked at his hands. They no longer shook uncontrollably. "None of it is my fault, none of it."

Before the light changed to green, his fever returned and intensified. Last Sunday's sermon came to mind. He regularly, "religiously", attended church. But he did not believe. On Sunday the sermon had meant nothing to him. But now it crowded in on his consciousness, the whole of it. He had once wanted to believe, wanted to be possessed of an inner spirit that could save him. The minister had stormed from the pulpit, "All men must have the will to submit their souls to the mystery of faith." The minister was absolute. He used the word "must" as a weapon. Luther's admonition demanded belief. "In all other creatures God is known by his footsteps only. But in man, especially in Adam, He is known truly and fully; for Adam is seen that wisdom and righteousness, and knowledge of all things, that he might be rightly called a microcosm, or little world in himself; for he understands the heavens, the earth, and the whole creation."

"My god," Herman cursed, "even he believes in my half-brother!" Herman privately hated the minister. He was a Schwann man. Yes, of course he was. When in town, Schwann attended his church and listened to his sermons. Yes, he was Schwann's man, too. Carol had a hand in this, she and her goddamn father. Both Carol and her father insisted that the family attend the Lutheran church. It was of no consequence to them that the Reverend Frederick Wise was forever ranting on evil. Every soul was "*De Servo Arbito*." Who was Herman to doubt it? Did he not accept the promise of predestination? It was for the elect to rule on earth. They alone held the keys to the kingdom. Herman had tried to believe in purification by fire. Alexander believed and trusted in the power of cleansing fire. Herman doubted, however, that his father was speaking of Luther's kind of cleansing fire. A physicist and European émigré, he could be so cryptic. "Cleansing fire, is it?" Herman was past caring what his father thought of the purified souls. "For as in the furnace the fire retracts and separates from a substance the other portions and carries upward the spirit, the life, the sap, the strength, while the unclean matter, the dregs, remains at the bottom, like a dead and worthless carcass... will separate all things through fire, the righteous from the ungodly..."

Herman had so wanted to believe, but it was no good. He was "the unclean matter, the dregs, remains at the bottom..." Why should he submit to any such fire? Let the Lutherans have it. They deserved it. Mueller was Lutheran. Schwann was Lutheran. So was his wife. How many times had Herman seen them sitting together in church, their eyes watching him?

If there had been a time to act, it was drained away, had run out. Every hour of his existence felt the presence of Schwann and his dangerous impatience. Adam had not come round. Everything was lost. Ten years he had served Schwann, always apprenticed to his ambitions. He had groveled and done the dirty work. Why? Schwann was not really a man! He was an avaricious conglomeration of evil.

"Willing fool that I am," Herman admitted, "I promoted The Evergreen Institute as a generous dispenser of grants for promising research. Every precaution was taken to insure that no one paid attention to how research findings found their way to Genetrix or an affiliated company. I did my part."

"She made me keep going to that church, Father. I could have cared less." At fifty-five Herman hated religion, hated the pretense and the futility of it. What had religion done for him? He was shackled by its conventions and to a woman who offered no intimacy, no tenderness. Nor did his sons love him for all his caring. They believed it was enough to be destined for salvation. That would explain their wasted youth. Why behave according to rules? Vann Arnold spent his days drinking cheap wine and pursuing women. Linnus was fat and getting fatter. In and out of scrapes with the law, he, too, was drunk most of the time. How much can any father stand?

Ten years ago things might have turned out differently. The institute was just the vehicle for Herman to display his talents for organization. Within months the buildings rose up on the Black Hills site. Herman was in his element. Publicity and praise came his way. At first the institute attracted scientists who were impressed with the promise. The aftermath of a national recession and scarcity of grant monies made his job all that much simpler. Everything seemed to work out perfectly. It had been a good start. Ten years ago Herman had hopes.

However, Schwann, with his money and control of the board members, began to shape the goals of the institute. At first, Herman did not pay a lot of attention to the maze of shell entities that provided funding. He cared only that the money was there to use. Not until it was too late did Herman ask questions. By then his only course was to accept the funding with gratitude.

If only Adam had come around. Of course Schwann had penetrated Herman's lies. Yes, Mueller's men had lost Adam's trail in the confused crowd at the Hilton. But, Mueller had picked up the trail at The Clift. Losing him again had doubly irritated Schwann. Mueller was now free to bring Adam to ground by any means he deemed necessary.

Schwann's call before the reception at The Manse had left Herman sweating from every pore of his body. Having failed to deliver, he had stammered, "But…" His alcoholic brain had at last failed him. Mueller had told Schwann that Adam had shaken free of his minders. He could not be located. "But it is running to plan. Believe me," Herman had pleaded. "I tell you everything is fine!" Schwann would hear none of it. The phone went dead. He had cut Herman off without another word. Herman pleaded on, oblivious to the fact that he was talking over a dead line. "Everything is going to be fine. He is here now. We are talking things over. In an hour I'll have…"

When the attendees began arriving at The Manse, Herman was almost beyond caring what would happen. His plan was destroyed. So, why should Adam fare any better? Let Mueller have his way. Who was there to stop him?

As he drove through the thickening fog, Herman resolved what he must do. He needed the papers from his safe. Monday was Carol's day to stay in. She would spend her morning with her needlework. Their sons, what did they matter? He'd not spoken to them in days. It would take only minutes to get the papers he wanted, the stock list and account numbers. He would not pack a thing. If Carol saw him, what did it matter? Of course, she'd tell Marianne, and Marianne would tell Alexander. Schwann would know, and Mueller would be sent. They were all against him. But he would be gone. He would get away before any of them knew of his intentions.

It was after 1:00 a.m., Monday, when he returned to the house. Carol was in the drawing room, still up. He thought it odd that she was working on her needlepoint at that hour. She did not look up or greet him. At the door to the drawing room he said, "It's late. Aren't you tired of working on that?"

Carol ignored his question. "Your dear brother called two hours ago."

"Yes? Did he say where he is?"

Carol continued with her stitching.

"What did he say?"

As she bit off the end of her thread and looked up. "Read your bible, Malachi 4:6."

"What?"

"He said, and I repeat, read Malachi 4:6. He sounded serious, so I wrote it down for you."

Herman went into the library where he kept a facsimile of the William Whiston translation on his desk. The house felt cold to Herman, a dead thing. Except for a hall light and the reading lamp on his desk, his part of the house was dark, filled with black corners and smelled of dead air. Herman opened the bible. He often fingered through his bibles, especially this one. Bibles, old and rare ones, had always fascinated him. He counted thirty-two in his collection. The Whiston was a private translation by the very man who succeeded Sir Isaac Newton at Cambridge. That he, Herman Cockroft, owned such a volume was proof of his taste in things that mattered. How long had it been since he had examined its pages? Faith had nothing to do with his passion. Rarity alone mattered to him. He possessed something other men did not.

How much time passed with Herman staring at the page? It could have been long. The hall clock struck four times. Minutes had stretched into hours. A glass of brandy was at his left elbow. By the third glass, Herman knew what the passage meant. He had used it against Adam many years ago. He grinned harshly. Adam had turned even Malachi against him. Destiny had taken a hand. Though his speech was slurred, and the brandy glass emptied, Herman read the passage out loud. "And he shall turn the heart of the fathers to the children, and the hearts of the children to their fathers, lest I come and smite the earth with a curse."

Herman recalled with bitterness how Alexander had behaved after the reception. He said nothing to Herman, not even goodnight. He gave no sign that he would once more help to make things right. It was too late for things to turn out right. Adam made that plain enough in telling him to look up Malachi. He could have picked any book of the Old Testament, a stern and uncompromising litany. Adam had indeed shown his mind, cunningly. One can never trust the faith of the father. He leaned over the page, spilling a last drop of the brandy on the first verse. He tried to wipe it up with his sleeve. "For behold, the day cometh, that shall burn as an oven, and all the proud, yea, all that do wickedly shall be stubble. And the day that cometh shall burn them up, saith the LORD of hosts, that shall leave them neither root nor branch." Herman repeated the words "neither root nor branch" through his tears.

Herman lurched backwards, his empty glass falling on to the floor. He felt the heat of an oven in his brain. The final reserve of hope imploded within him. What was left to him? Nothing. Why go on with the charade?

Down the hall in the "knitting room" as she called it, Carol Cockroft put her needlework down. It was later than she realized. The clock struck the quarter hour. A dull noise came from the library. Herman was still in there, drinking, she thought. She got up and walked into the hall. The house was quiet now, almost peaceful. Had she stopped to consider it, she might have found the idea of peace in her house as an odd visitation. It had been so long since peace within the house was conceivable. She mounted the stairs, anxious to get to her room before Herman appeared at her bedroom door to complain that he was out of scotch or brandy or whatever he was drinking these days. In the state he was in, he was sure to want sex. That was the last thing he would get from her she vowed, the very last thing.

11

Whitman's Brain

Adam's first encounter with shrews was at age fifteen, camping with Uncle John. A shrew by nature is a wary beast, his uncle said. One had to be lucky to see one at all. Spending the night on the desert floor in a sleeping bag was the price to pay for a chance encounter. Uncle John had a special means to coax shrews into the open. Before sunset they trapped six scorpions. Uncle John helped Adam tie a string to each scorpion's tail and stake them in a large circle, each one just beyond the claws of the others. Then, the tethered scorpions rushed toward the center of the circle snapping their claws the air. Were their actions aggressive or defensive? Uncle John could not say. Their frenzied behavior, he was certain, would draw out the shrews.

At full dark Adam crouched low in his sleeping bag behind a rock for hours, trying not to move a muscle. Flashlight in hand, he tried to breathe without making a sound. He listened to the scorpions clawing and snapping, menacing their opponents just out of reach. Before dawn, he woke suddenly. As Uncle John had promised, something interrupted the steady, angry rhythms of claws clicking. Adam heard something, a high-pitched, triumphant scream? It was unbearable not see what was happening. Fumbling with the flashlight, he heard new sounds—rubbing, rapid and faint. Adam inched his hand out of the sleeping bag and aimed his flashlight. His heart was beating fast, and his hand felt sweaty. For what felt like an eternity, he hesitated. Would he see anything? He flicked on the light. There it was in the open, a frenzied blur gnashing and crunching a scorpion. He heard it. He saw it—a shrew caught in the open with a dismembered scorpion's tail between his paws. Temporarily blinded by the light, the minute, furry assassin stood his ground. Its eyes stared defiantly at the glare of the flashlight. An intense, high-pitched scream followed. In an instant of time the beast was gone.

Adam had faced his quarry for only a second or two, three at most. But in that span of time he had witnessed nature as few have. Later, Uncle John told him that his encounter was just as Francis Bacon had written. He quoted exactly, "...even in mere natural things you may deceive nature sooner than force her." Adam had deceived a shrew, not forced it, and so was rewarded.

Thinking back on the encounter years later, Adam understood Uncle John's admonition. It was not wise to disturb or force nature in order to encounter it. Yet, Adam still regretted sacrificing those scorpions. In daylight, he had examined the killing ground. Except for the stingers tethered to strings, nothing was left of the scorpions.

"He lives fast and dies young," Uncle John had said. Later, Adam looked up the heart rate and life span of the shrew. "Someday, I might need to know this," he told himself.

<++++++++++>

It was a little before noon on Monday, and Adam still did not feel fully prepared to stand before an audience at 3:00 p.m. He told the cab driver to let him out at Union Square, deciding to walk the rest of the way to the Hilton and using those few more minutes to think of final changes. He thought that something about consequences of unintended outcomes might be a good addition. Hooke, his old adversary, never liked that sort of thing. Adam knew the man favored applied research, and always looked to "capturing" corporation grants and developing "shared" partnerships. Hooke wanted to commoditize the university. Although it was years in the past, it still rankled Adam that Hooke could be so dismissive to any other point of view.

"Yes," he thought aloud, "I should leave out the excerpt from *The Uncompleted Man*." He admired Loren Eisley's thinking. It would pain him to leave it out, but he was not in a mood to defend the point, if pressed. He would keep Eisley's admonition, though: "Under the spell of such oracles we create not a necessary or real future, but a counterfeit dream from within ourselves, through purely human power upon reality." It would serve his purpose, though the temptation to quote something else, something Eisely's had taken from Macbeth. It sorely tempted him: "And be these Juggling Fiends no more believ'd...that keeps the word of promise to our ear..." Even scientists could so easily be tempted by the voices from the shadows.

Entering the Hilton, Adam checked his suitcase at the bell captain's podium. He thanked the bellman and said that he would retrieve it later. He saw someone point him out to two men. The men did not look friendly.

"Have you checked out, Sir?" The bellman looked nervous as his eyes focused on the two men now standing near the podium. Seeing the bellman distracted, Adam did not reply.

"Are you Dr. Adam Grant?"

"Yes, I am Adam Grant."

"I'm Lieutenant Kestos, Berkeley Police Department, and this is Detective Barnes." Neither policeman extended his hand. The lieutenant gave Adam his card as identification.

"How can I help you, officers?"

"I think it best to talk in private."

Adam looked about the lobby. "Will the lounge do? It looks empty."

The officers followed Adam into the lounge at the east end of the lobby. There was an empty table near the back. As they sat down, Adam asked, "So, officers, how can I help you?"

"Were you at The Claremont last night?"

"I was. I checked out a little while ago. I don't see why that should be of interest to you."

"Please, Doctor, just tell us your movements from last evening to now. It will make our inquiry so much simpler." The lieutenant leaned stiffly forward in his chair. He looked to be impatient.

"All right," Adam said, "I got up early to work on a draft speech, had coffee, went down to the lobby to have my draft printed out by the concierge, checked out a little after 11, and took a cab to Union

Square. From there, I walked up to the Hilton. Here I am. Is that precise enough?"

The Lieutenant's smile was thin, strained. "We just need to place your movements."

"Is that necessary?" Adam was becoming impatient and irritated with the questions.

"In this case, yes. You had dinner in Chinatown, is that right?"

"I understand routine, Officer, but where is this going; why the questions?"

"We need to confirm your movements. Once we've done that, Doctor, we can focus our investigation elsewhere. Did you eat dinner with a Dr. Jonathan Hardesty?"

"Yes, I had dinner with Hardesty and two other friends.

"We have already confirmed that."

"I have a lunch appointment. Since you're not about to tell me anything, I'm not going to..."

"Doctor, explain your movements since returning to The Claremont last night. We can then erase any doubts as to your involvement. And yes, we already know about your lunch date." Lieutenant Kestos cleared his throat. "You'll be late for that, I am afraid."

Adam began to get up from his chair to leave.

The Lieutenant motioned for him to sit back down. "You see, Dr. Grant, we discovered the body of Herman Cockroft a little before nine o'clock this morning. He was your brother, correct?"

Adam's face went white. He felt dizzy. "Half-brother, he was my half-brother." He looked confused. "Are you sure? What happened? Are you sure we're talking about the Herman Cockroft?" His voice was almost pleading, only half-believing.

"Forensics is still on scene. We won't know much more until they are done."

"Where did it happen?"

"In his study," Detective Barnes said. His tone bordered being snide, almost rude. "A 45 caliber pistol was on the floor, near his right hand. The blood spatter suggests suicide."

"He shot himself? Herman shot himself? I don't believe it. He detested guns. I doubt that he owned one. Carol would never have permitted one in her house. No, I don't believe this."

"The ME will determine the cause of death and the circumstances," the Lieutenant said.

Adam sat mute, trying to, or unable to, digest the news.

"Do you have any idea why a man like Mr. Cockroft would commit suicide?"

Adam shook his head.

"No note. One might expect one, in cases like this. His type usually leaves a note."

"Are you saying there is doubt about how he died?"

"As I said," the lieutenant responded, "we'll have to wait on that for the ME's report."

"I see. What about his wife, Carol, and his two sons?"

"She discovered the body this morning when she came downstairs. I believe Dr. Alexander Terman, his father, your father as well, I take it, is with her now." Without pause, the lieutenant continued, "You did not get on well with your brother."

"What makes you think that?"

"Oh, you know how some families are. His wife, naturally, is distraught. In her present state of mind, she said something about you being the cause, that you are to blame. She showed us a note from you, said that it was the reason."

"I sent him no note."

"Well, Mrs. Cockroft insists it is from you. We did find a note. It was on the desk."

"I did phone yesterday, late. I gave her a message for him, but that is all."

"Then, you do you remember giving him a message."

"Yes, of course I do. I gave it to her over the phone."

"What was the message?"

"It was personal." Adam's tone was defensive.

"With a death like this, nothing is personal. Tell us what it was about."

"It was a biblical reference. Herman has this thing about bibles, had, I mean, an obsession, really. I sometimes prodded him with one. As you have guessed, we were not close."

"What was it, the substance of it, Doctor? Be specific."

"You must have read it. I assume that you saw that it is in Carol's handwriting."

"It is, but we still are not clear what it means. Why don't you explain it to us?"

"Lieutenant, I will willingly give you a statement accounting for my whereabouts. As for any other information bearing on our relationship, that is, was, between Herman and me. I prefer not go into it. We had professional disagreements. That is all. I can't see how that matters now."

"Humor me, if you will. What was Herman supposed to have understood from the note?"

"It is from Malachi in the Old Testament, that the wicked shall burn, that nothing will be left from the evil that men do."

"And that bit about turning the heart of the fathers to the children, what is that about?"

"I was telling Herman not to count on Father in the disagreement we were having. Herman expected Father to persuade me. He often tried that tactic. For once, I thought that he put too much trust in such loyalty. Maybe the argument we had did unhinge him a bit, I don't know."

"If suicide it is. I've never had a case where the question of one's loyalty was the cause."

"Didn't you say that it was suicide?"

"Was your brother, I mean your half-brother, right or left handed?"

"Lieutenant, what possible difference…?"

"Doctor, was he left or right handed?"

"Ask his wife, Lieutenant."

"As you wish, we can ask the grieving widow, if you insist."

"He was left-handed. Does that satisfy your curiosity?"

"Only in part," Detective Barnes said. "You see, the bullet entered Mr. Cockroft's temple just above his right ear." The detective pointed his right index finger to his temple.

"I don't see your point."

"If you are going to use a gun to kill yourself, you'd handle it like everything else. Herman Cockroft would have used his left hand and pointed the gun at his left temple."

"I see."

"The ME will tell us if and how he did it, if he did it."

"And if they cannot confirm suicide, what will you do then?"

"Treat the death as suspicious, a probable homicide, Dr. Grant. That is why, you see, we need to verify your movements from eleven last night to nine this morning. Once that is done, we're done."

"Except for one thing, Herman will still be dead."

<++++++++++>

At the Berkeley police station, Adam answered questions about his whereabouts in detail. They had already talked to Jonathan Hardesty. Detective Barnes conducted the questioning, while Lieutenant Kestos consulted with the forensics lab. By 2:30 p.m. the officers told Adam they were finished with him—for the time being. The inquest would be held on the coming Friday.

"I won't be here, Lieutenant."

"You won't be here for the funeral? Mrs. Cockroft has told us it is planned for Friday."

"Lieutenant, I have a very sick boy at home. He's dying, to be precise." Adam turned away from the two policemen. He shut his eyes tight to suppress tears and turned back to face his interrogators. "I must be there for him. I've already been away too long. As awkward as it may be, I can't be in two places at once."

"I was not aware that you have a child, Dr. Grant."

"Technically, I do not. Alberto is my ward, has been for five years. He has a terminal illness and very little time left."

"I am sorry to hear it. What, may I ask the nature of his illness?"

"Old age," Adam blurted out, instantly regretting it.

Lieutenant Kestos gave him a strange look. He didn't want more complications than what he was already facing.

"What I mean, Lieutenant, is that Alberto, a young man, suffers from a very rare disorder called progeria. He was born with it. The signs of progeria are premature aging, loss of function, and ultimately death by about seventeen. Alberto is twenty-two. He has outlived every expectation, but now he is out of time. He will, in all likelihood, die within a week or two, if not days."

"I see." Lieutenant Kestos paced behind his desk. "I'll give it to you straight, Dr. Grant. Forensics says Mr. Cockroft died between one and two. Figure thirty minutes one way or the other. Except for a couple nasty details, it points to suicide. But, you see, I don't like details. Suicide is never cut-and-dried. The man was alone, supposedly, no note, pieces of physical evidence still to account for."

"I don't quite get your "nasty details" characterization."

"While I am waiting for the ME's final report and the coroner's recommendation, under the circumstances, I should insist that you remain available until this is settled one way or the other."

"What possible reason could you have for considering me a suspect?"

"I did not mean to imply that you are. But, you didn't like your brother. You argued. I am told that you argued over something important, something that could be worth a great deal of money. Money, you must admit, is often the root cause of homicide."

"Or suicide, wouldn't you agree," Adam retorted.

"Yes, of course. It can be so in either case."

"Who told you all this? Who implied that money is a factor?"

"The interim director of The Evergreen Institute told us, a Dr. Thomas Vaughn."

"Well, I tell you this: I am under no obligation to The Evergreen Institute. I owe them nothing. Herman, while he lived, may have thought otherwise. But that is neither here nor there."

"I take it that you wish to return to New Mexico?"

"Arizona. I have a reservation for a 9:00 a.m. flight to Albuquerque on Tuesday morning, tomorrow, that is."

"I could insist that you remain in the area as a material witness. Even if it is suicide, until the inquest is held, I have grounds."

"Witness to what? I just spent the last two hours explaining that I have nothing…"

The lieutenant was interrupted by a phone call. He listened but said little. Adam did not want to appear interested but he did hear a name, Anton Mueller. Lieutenant Kestos put the phone down. "Yes, I have confirmation that you were at The Claremont. You made two phone calls, one at 11:23."

"That being the case, I trust that we're done?"

"Yes, I would say so. For now, we are done. If you do take that flight on Tuesday, do keep me informed of your whereabouts. We may have to subpoena you for the inquest. You have my card."

Outside the police station, Adam hailed a taxi. He had just enough time to make it to the Hilton to look for Jonathan. He considered going to Herman's house to express his sorrow to Carol over Herman's death. But what could he say to her? Did he feel partly responsible? He had given Herman a terrible time. Carol likely knew of their confrontation at The Manse and would be in no mood to see him. Would Herman's sons be there? Marianne had asked him to talk to Linnus and Vann Arnold. But this was no time for that. Now, there would never be a time for it. He regretted not acting on Marianne's request. Of the Cockroft clan, she was the one person with character, the only decent person of the lot. Would she understand if he was not at the funeral? It struck him that she probably would, knowing, as she did, that Alberto was in such a precarious state.

As the taxi passed by the university, Adam saw a lively demonstration in front of Sather Gate. Some things never change. The young faces, the placards, the picketing line, and an older man with a bullhorn—possibly a faculty member—brought back memories. So, he thought, resistance to the powers that be, it still happens in the open. Not knowing their issue, he wished them well. Adam shut his eyes and tried to rest. The two hours with the police had drained him.

By the time the taxi reached the Bay Bridge tollbooth, he had dozed off, still remembering his first day on campus, September 1966. Another student standing outside Dr. Hardesty's office door had pointed him out. Adam had stepped forward, blocking Dr. Hardesty's way, and introduced himself. The professor was not the least put off by his boldness. He always liked meeting new graduate students, he said. He wasted no time in asking Adam about his draft status. Adam knew only that he was listed as a 4. “Good. One of my students died in Vietnam in June. He was 1A. What a waste.”

That first day on campus Adam knew little about Vietnam. Hardesty had grabbed his arm and led him through the crowd to the makeshift protest. Adam was excited to be standing with a professor in front of the crowd. Dr. Hardesty stood tall and intense, his lab coat flapping in the wind like an avenging angel. He held up a specimen jar that he’d been carrying in a sack. It looked like a brain suspended in clear liquid. Hardesty spoke of French colonialism, broken promises, and the insanity of American involvement.

Dr. Hardesty’s voice boomed out clear and forcefully across the plaza. “This is what can happen to any young man we send to Vietnam!” With that said, Dr. Hardesty threw the jar to the ground. The glass shattered on the steps in front of him. The brain, what looked to be a brain, bounced down the steps and rolled away over the walkway. A shocked silence that followed. Then, Adam heard camera shutters clicking. Frenzied questions erupted. Hardesty grabbed the megaphone.

“A dead brain possesses no more dreams, no more hopes, no more ideas, nothing. Think about that! What if that brain could have become the next Walt Whitman? War is nothing but the death of the future and the death of our young men. It is death to our society.”

Three uniformed campus police rushed forward. They took Hardesty into custody and led him away. Adam stepped back. For the first time he knew why he did not want to be drafted. He did have a deferment, but he had never before fully understood why it was essential. Then, he felt guilty knowing that others, those without a deferment, might go to war and die.

The next day, Dr. Hardesty had called him into his office as he walked by in the hall. “Did you like the protest?”

Adam nodded that he did, feeling hypocritical for it. He didn’t know quite what to say. “Smashing the jar like that really got to them.”

"That was just a bit of theater. Professors are not supposed to incite students, not supposed to get involved. The faculty senate wants to censure me. But I'm tenured. Anyway, it was just a rubber toy suspended in water. But for one moment they believed it was real. The point was made."

"You said it could have been Whitman's brain. What did you mean?"

"He saw and wrote about life being in everything, even leaves of grass. To be alive, to create, to build, and to honor life should be the highest good any of us can aspire to. If he were alive today, he would have led the protest. Walt Whitman was a war resister."

"What if you had used a real brain?"

"His brain was shattered to bits, you know. What a pity that was."

"What do you mean?"

"Walt Whitman's brain was kept in a jar for years, one not unlike the jar I used yesterday. Occasionally, someone took it out to study, as if they could see in it what it was that made him a genius. People once believed that bigger brains were smarter brains. Well, sooner or later it was bound to happen. A laboratory assistant was clumsy and dropped the jar. The brain shattered into pieces on the floor. Think of that, the brain that once distilled every emotion into poetry was destroyed. That was THE brain that had written *Leaves of Grass!*"

"But, by then it was just a specimen, right?"

"Mr. Grant, you surprise me. Yes, it was a specimen, but what a specimen. The Dean has written a nasty letter about my endangering people by smashing glass on the walkway. I don't think he understands the meaning of symbols at all. I can't change how Dean Hooke thinks. But, if you are going to be my student, I expect you to use symbols, use them for good. Otherwise, I can't teach you. Abstractions clarify what we see at the end of a microscope, you know. One must understand, use, and appreciate the power of symbols. Otherwise, one cannot hope to become a scientist."

"Sir, we're here," the taxi driver said, breaking Adam's reverie. "Thirty-five dollars."

Adam shook his head and reached for his wallet. His dream of his first days at Berkeley, when life was simple, sank back into memory. Then everything lay ahead of him, not behind. What he did keep uppermost in his mind as he stepped out onto the sidewalk was Hardesty's injunction about symbols. It was mixed in with the detective's description of Herman's brain being spattered on the back of a leather chair. Detective Barnes wanted Adam to picture it in graphic detail. Herman's blood and gray matter had stuck to the illustrated bible his head rested on, the pages stained and glued together. That his brain and blood stuck to the pages of a bible impressed Detective Sergeant Barnes.

Barnes had asked, "Did that bible have special meaning, Dr. Grant?"

"It did to Herman. But now, what does it matter?"

"You never know about these things, details like that always mean something."

With five minutes to spare, Adam made his way to the Grand Ballroom on the third floor. As he entered he saw that there was standing room only. Dean Hooke and members of the selection committee stood on the dais, talking in an agitated manner. Realizing that he had misplaced his badge, Adam stood at the entrance door. A guard gave him a stern look and barred his entering.

Hardesty spotted Adam and grabbed Sanderson's arm. They rushed over. Yes, they said, the police had interviewed both of them. Neither man could find the right words to say to Adam about what had happened.

"I just left the Berkeley police station. It's tragic."

"What did they tell you?"

"Not much. You probably know more than I do."

From the stage, near the podium, Dean Hooke was waving to him to come forward. Adam nodded and turned back to Hardesty and Sanderson. "We must talk as soon as..." The background noise of the restless audience was so intense that his words did not carry. With his prepared remarks in hand, Adam began to walk up the aisle. The guard stepped briskly in front of him. Hardesty intervened.

"No badge is necessary for the honoree. You do understand, this is Dr. Adam Grant."

As Adam stepped onto the stage, Hooke rushed over to shake his hand. He said the news about Herman was terrible, such a loss, terrible. "He will be missed, yes, terribly missed."

Thomas Vaughn grabbed Adam's hand. "I am so sorry about Herman. Have you talked to…?"

Adam cut him off with a word, "Later."

Dean Hooke took his place at the podium and fumbled with his notes. "Terrible, terrible, but we must soldier on."

"It is best if you do not make mention of any of this in remarks," Adam insisted.

"I was not planning to," the dean spat back at him.

Ignoring Hooke, Adam turned to Vaughn. "Until two days ago, I knew nothing about the institute's role in awarding The Morgan. Still, I'll gladly take the prize money."

"That was Herman's doing." Vaughn looked irritated, angry. "If it were up to me…"

Adam kept a fixed grin as he spoke. "Well, it wasn't up to you, was it, Doctor?"

Vaughn said under his breath, "I will say nothing more of it."

Hooke led Adam to his place beside the podium and pressed his arm. "I'm afraid the media have every right to be here. But if they ask about, well, you know, Herman."

"Perhaps you can manage it, so there are no questions at the end?"

"That would be awkward." Hooke hesitated. "However, under the circumstances, I suppose we must." Hooke cupped the podium's microphone and looked back at Adam. "I'll try to manage it."

Adam replied with a tight, forced smile, "I would be grateful for it."

Hooke began his remarks by launching into a list of Adam's academic and research achievements, without, for once, a hint of sarcasm. Of course, if he had known in advance what Adam intended to say, his introduction might have been much different. Smiling, Hooke wound up his introduction and turned to applaud Adam as he stepped forward to take the podium.

"You are very kind, Dean Hooke, thank you. I want to thank the members of The Morgan Prize Committee for honoring me with this..."

Acknowledging past support from The Evergreen Institute, Adam went on to mention Herman Cockroft as if he was indeed in the audience. He did not refer Herman as the late director. Nor, did he call attention to what had happened. With the preliminaries over, he eased into the heart of his remarks.

"When I began to explore how cells determine when to divide, how long they remain viable, and the process of cell replacement in the organism as a whole, Albert Claude served as my guide. In his Nobel Lecture, in 1974, he said, 'We have entered the cell, the mansion of our birth, and started the inventory of our acquired wealth...' " Adam paused for a moment, then continued, "In the present, today, this inventory is well along. We have been busy sequencing the genome. Claude would remind us, however, that this is not enough. He saw life at the cell level. The cells create and maintain us, they provide our will to live and survive, search and experiment, and struggle. That this will lies within, Claude had no doubt."

Adam continued with his view of life's limit in relation to theories that seek to explain it—the biological clock theory, genetic cross linkage theory, error theories, the theory of free radicals, homeostatic imbalance theory, hormonal theory, immunologic theory, and stress theory. All, he said, play some part at the organismic level. Nothing should be, or can be, ignored. Finally, Adam returned to Albert Claude's insight. "Within the cell an unparalleled knowledge of the laws of physics and chemistry reside."

As he spoke, Adam looked to Hardesty, who smiled. He knew what Adam was about. The cell knows itself, Adam was fond of saying, and possesses foresight of its future. He believed that the cell possesses a precise and detailed knowledge of its potential for differentiation and growth, that it transmits information to elements within itself and to other cells about its own status, as well as potential. Biologically speaking, humans are, he insisted, highly organized and efficient colonies of cells in action, governed by a shared will to survive and maintain function. To gain any measure of control over the messages between cells, and within the cell itself, enzyme functions are the key. It is enzymes that transmit commands when malfunctioning organelles need to be replaced. The process of autophagy is required to insure viability and function. The really exciting thing, Adam stressed, is to understand what occurs in "the space between the nucleus and the cell wall." There lies the true frontier of the cell. To confirm this, he had chosen the common shrew, *Sorex vagrans*. Yes, he admitted, it may amuse his listeners. But, he said, leaning forward at the podium and smiling broadly, a shrew had indeed shown him the way.

Adam restated the research question he had posed years ago, the methodology used, the experimental results, and the conclusions he believed were incontrovertible.

"So there you have it, ladies and gentlemen. I began with two hundred subjects, divided equally between controls and subjects. Of the one hundred treated animals, eleven *Sorex vagrans* are still alive at day 1448. That's 3.967 years, twelve days short of the four-year mark. Two years is this creature's normal life span. Every subject exceeded that limit. None died short of a 120 percent threshold beyond the normal span."

Adam described his treatment protocol only in passing. More would be revealed in June, both in *The Cell* and in *Nature*. Adam paused to drink water from a glass. "I must inject a word of caution. My protocol requires a lifetime regimen. The younger the individual to be treated, the more effective and profound will be its effect. For those who believe that intervention late in life can have a significant effect, I say this: You do not understand cell function. It can have little effect on an aged organism." This drew a nervous reaction from Hooke and the committee members seated on the stage.

"I wish to conclude my remarks with a personal note. Some of my work, work not related to my aging project, received generous support from The Evergreen Institute. I heartily thank them for the grants that allowed me to explore a number of basic questions about cell functions. However, and I wish to be clear on this point, that my research on life extension was in no way supported by the Institute. I felt it necessary to pursue that initiative without obligation to any authority, funding or otherwise. I realize that there are those who…"

The audience all but drowned out Adam's words. Dean Hooke and two of the institute directors rose from their seats.

"Sit down, gentlemen! I am not finished." Adam's blunt admonition had effect. Dean Hooke sat back down. The Evergreen Institute directors walked off the platform.

"I have been told that The Evergreen Institute is in part funded by a multinational pharmaceutical corporation known as Genetrix. At no time did I intend for my work on aging to be turned over to The Evergreen Institute or any such company. To the contrary, I intend to make my results widely available. I alone hold the patents. Perhaps it is naïve of me, but I seek no monetary reward."

"I leave you with this cautionary tale. Loren Eisley wrote, 'I came down across stones dotted with pink and gray lichens—a barren land dreaming life's last dreams in the thin air of a cold and future world.' For myself, I want to believe that such a fate is far, far into the future, if ever. Life is precious, and we all deserve to gain a longer measure of it. Not the few, not the privileged, not those with wealth alone should possess the means. Life extension must be freely and generously given."

All at once, hundreds of people rose from their seats and were wildly clapping. Hardesty and Sanderson rushed to the foot of the stage. Everyone was applauding, except Dean Hooke.

While the attendees applauded, a barrage of questions came from the media at the foot of the stage. "Are you saying there is a connection between The Evergreen Institute and The Morgan Prize?" A microphone was thrust in his face. "Does the death of your brother, Herman Cockroft, have something to do with this?" "Do you think it is suicide?"

Adam stepped off the stage. "Let's get you out of here." Hardesty took his arm.

Adam turned to Sanderson. "John, would you mind? Here is the claim check for my bag. Would you retrieve it? Meet up with us at The Clift." John took the stub.

Adam and Jonathan pushed their way to the service elevator behind the curtains at the back of the stage. Dean Hooke, surrounded by reporters, was yelling at the top of his lungs for order. In the confusion, Adam and Jonathan were not followed.

On the street outside of the hotel, Adam said, "I need a drink."

"Jesus, when did you learn to throw grenades like that?"

"Was it you who once said, "When you take a stand, don't use half measures?"

"Adam, you certainly have a unique way of going about it."

"I learned from the master."

"Ah yes, you remember my protest days."

"How could I forget?"

"It was a stroke of luck that we were able to get out of there without a mob on our heels."

"Luck had nothing to do with it."

Jonathan looked puzzled. As they waited for the light to change, he asked, "Did you have an idea he would try to take charge?"

"The reporters expected to corner me in there. They were there only because of Herman's death. I was not so naïve as to assume they cared a fig about The Morgan Prize."

Jonathan had a wry look on his face. "You intended to goad Hooke and the others with your words at the end. You knew what would happen, how you could take advantage of the confusion."

"I did not know, but I hoped. It turned out better than I hoped for. Here we are—headed uphill with no one in pursuit."

"When the police interviewed me, I was tempted to accuse Schwann and Company of being at the root of Herman's death. I overheard one of the detectives say something about Anton Mueller. I could not hear more than a few words, just enough to realize they had some thread along those lines. Maybe Herman's death has unintended consequences. Jonathan, you are quite right to think it. I am not so sure that was not his intent."

"Do you believe he did commit suicide?"

"How do I know? But if he did, it certainly does shake things up."

"What are you going to do now?"

Entering the bar off the lobby of The Clift, Adam pointed to a table near the back of the room. They ordered and waited for John Sanderson. Within a minute or two, he appeared with Adam's bag.

"Thanks, John. We ordered a beer for you."

"Adam, what on earth are you going to do? You can't return to the Hilton."

Jonathan looked concerned. "Can you leave town? I mean are you free to leave?"

"As far as I know, the police have made no demands that I stay. They may have implied it."

Sanderson asked about the coming Friday.

"You mean must I stay for the funeral?"

"Well, it will be expected. Your absence might provoke more questions."

"I don't think the Cockroft family cares whether I stay or leave. Carole will be relieved. She thinks I had something to do with it."

"The police are working on the assumption that it was a suicide?"

"I don't know. I have the impression that Lieutenant Kestos thinks otherwise."

John shifted nervously in his chair. "How can it be anything else?"

"Detective Barnes, made a big deal about Herman being left-handed. He described to me in some detail how the bullet entered Herman's right temple and exited through his left ear."

"What has that to do with anything?"

"Try holding a gun in your left hand and shoot yourself in the right temple." Adam raised his left hand to his right temple, as if it represented a gun. "It can be done, according to Barnes. But suicides use the hand they write with. It is a detail that does not fit."

"Adam, perhaps you should..."

"You are right. Jonathan, would you see if there's a cab at the front of the hotel? John, do you have the keys to the car you offered to loan me?"

John handed Adam the keys and a parking lot ticket. It's in Lot B, row 10."

"Thanks. I need to get going. When are you flying back to Albuquerque?"

"In the morning, I'll stick around this evening to see what I can learn."

"Thank you, again."

"Few will believe what you said about The Evergreen Institute and its links."

"Some will. Well, a few will. You were right all along, of course." Adam shook John's hand and embraced him. "I'll be off, then." Adam and Jonathan shook hands and said their goodbyes.

As the cab driver took his bag, Adam told him to take him to the airport.

"Which airline are you flying, sir?"

"Just take me to the Southwest Airlines, please. Make the best time you can."

"This time of day, rush hour, you're looking at 40 minutes, easy. I'll try to shave it a bit."

Adam settled down into the back seat, the weight of the day and a sleepless night descending upon him. What he had set out to do in San Francisco had not turned out as he expected. Herman was dead. He had spoken his mind, but wondered if any of it had its intended effect. He was leaving a trail of confusion and unanswered questions behind, so many "what ifs." He did not regret the confusion. Herman, however, was a different matter. His death had set in motion things he could only guess at. His father, Marianne, Carol, the rest of Herman's family would wonder why he left town without a word. The police would want to talk to him again. What about Anton Mueller? What might William Henry Schwann do now? Would those Hardesty had trusted follow through with what he intended? They now had his results, except, that is, the formulary and the details of treatment schedules. It would have been too risky to share those all-important parts, at least as yet.

Adam sat back in the taxi and stared at the traffic. What mattered to him now were Bayeta, Alberto, and Rimrock, nothing more. Alberto needed him. Bayeta needed to see his resolve to settle the issues he faced. In all likelihood Rimrock was beyond the reach of

Schwann. With his mind settled, he dozed off as he watched to jumble of cars and trucks thread their way south.

Herman's death did occupy part of his consciousness. But he could not bring himself to regret refusing Herman. Poor, desperate Herman had not been true, was so desperate to be part of something he only dimly comprehended. He'd been used, abused even. Adam was certain he had not abused him.

With the airport minutes ahead, the full weight of the day pressed down on Adam. It had been a long day, a long, hard, tragic day.

12

Rite Of Passage

By Monday morning, Adam's absence was making Alberto desperately anxious. So many things crowded his mind, important things he had to tell only to Adam. Bayeta asked, but he insisted, "I can't tell them to you." For reasons she could not share with Alberto, she, too, was growing desperate. Could she cope if Alberto took a turn for the worse? Even with Martin present, could she cope? Every phone call from Adam ended with "When can you come home?" If Alberto was awake when Adam called, he would ask, "Is his speech over yet? He will come home now, won't he?" Now, with the afternoon sun setting, she could say, "Yes, he will be on a plane in the morning."

"What time is it?" His voice was hollow and so pitifully faint that Bayeta did not quite hear. She tried to make him comfortable on the living room couch. She had made a fire earlier, before carrying in Alberto. It had warmed up the room and the scent of mesquite was strong. Alberto stared into the fire, his eyes red from the strain. He ignored the cookie and warm cocoa set out for him.

"Do you want me to read to you for a while?" He said yes. She picked up the book he'd been trying to read and turned to the bookmarked page. He had not touched it in four days. Robert Frost was his favorite poet, a fact that made Bayeta feel a knot in her stomach.

He said, "Please, *Nothing Gold Can Stay.*"

She read aloud, consciously doing her best to make her voice smooth and flowing, somehow indefinite.

> "Nature's first green is gold,
> Her hardest hue to hold.
> Her early leaf's a flower;
> But only so an hour.
> Then leaf subsides to leaf.
> So Eden sank to grief,
> So dawn goes down to day,
> Nothing gold can stay."

Alberto dozed off as Bayeta read the poem. She was grateful for that and wiped her tears. What of hope could he have found in those lines? Adjusting the blanket about his neck and chest, Bayeta heard a car cresting the rise to the west of Rimrock. Martin had said that he would stay at Maria Klah's overnight and return before noon the coming day. Tall Boy needed his help, and he could not say no. She was glad of it. He would have time to think and not have to avoid her like a shamed creature. He would be there to share Maria's grief with her. A beautiful young woman still, Maria regained her shape after each child's birth. She cared how men looked at her in a dress. Vanity, perhaps, but why should she feel shame in that? Martin was sure to take notice. Nature and need would take its course.

Who was it out on an evening like this? The car's engine did not sound familiar. In the desert every mechanical sound is distinctive and has its place. Bayeta was used to the Land Rover's sound and could tell long before Adam did when it needed servicing, or if the tires needed air, or if the front-end alignment was shot. No, this car had a well-tuned hum to it. It definitely was not a neighbor's car. No one within thirty miles possessed so well cared for a vehicle.

Alberto opened his eyes. "Is it Adam? He's come home!" He tried to sit up.

"Don't get up. I'll see who it is. You be still."

Bayeta went to the kitchen door and opened it. Her eyes slowly adjusted to the darkness. Eight o'clock was no time for a neighbor to visit. The threat of rain had held off all day. Rain meant slippery roads and flash flooding in the low-lying washes. Who would risk being caught out at night in the rain? She stood inches behind the eaves, adjusting her eyes to the dim. The dense, roiled look to the west did portend rain. She felt the first tentative drops; a hard rain was but minutes off.

"Mary? Is that you? What on earth brings you here at this hour? Has something happened?"

Mary smiled and waved her hand reassuringly. "That last thirty miles is quite a drive. I swear that I hit every last rut. I don't suppose they are planning on paving it anytime soon?"

"Pavement only brings strangers. If one can make it over that dirt obstacle course, then he belongs. Come in. Alberto is anxious to see who it is."

Mary followed Bayeta into the living room and kneeled at the foot of the couch. She smiled at Alberto and gently patted his blanketed feet. "I just had to come see you. Bea tells me you are doing so well."

Alberto smiled, but said nothing. Mary could see for herself how drawn and weak he was. She turned to Bayeta and talked as if she and Alberto were having a conversation.

"Yes, I have come to see you, Alberto. Besides, Albuquerque is too lonely with John away." Alberto settled his head back on his pillow. Sleep again overtook him. "Yes, you rest now. In the morning we can sit and chat."

Bayeta went to the kitchen and returned with the coffee tray. "Can you stay for a couple days? Did you bring a suitcase?"

Mary said, "I can."

"While I put Alberto to bed, get your bag from the car before the rain gets worse." Bayeta lifted Alberto into her arms. "I can manage," she told Mary. "Go and get your bag and pour us some coffee."

Mary and John had no children but were still trying. Time was running out for her. She watched Bayeta carry Alberto, a grown man, to his bed. It was so painfully unnatural. As an anthropologist she was used to being the detached observer. Mary felt helpless. It saddened her beyond tears. At lunch last week, Adam reminded Mary and John that Alberto had lived beyond all expectations. He had been blessed with added years. That had to count for something. But Mary knew that the benefit of more time, with its accompanying pain and decline, had a bittersweet edge to it.

Bayeta returned. The warmth and glow of the burning logs had made the room a quiet and peaceful space. Neither one spoke, content to drink coffee and watch the piñón logs hiss and spit resins up the chimney. Sweet and smoky, the incensed air set the mood. Finally, Bayeta said, "I used to sit with Mother watching a fire dance. She'd say that Coyote, the wily one, brought fire to our people."

"I must tell you what has brought me."

"You will tell me when the moment is right."

"Crystal, have you talked with Adam today?"

"No. He will call tonight. I expect him home late tomorrow, hopefully before nine or ten."

"Has no one called you?" No one had. "It's not like him to not call you by now, is it?"

Bayeta spoke as she stared into the fire. "Things are a bit extraordinary at the moment." She smiled, "I am glad that you came. In fact, I know that you've always wanted to be present at a sing. I am planning one, The Night Chant. Can you stay for a week or longer?"

"If you like, I would be happy to stay."

"Good. I have sent for the *hataalii*. I expect him Wednesday or the next day. If he agrees that the time is right, people will gather here for the sing."

"Do you mean that it is to be here at Rimrock?"

"Yes, if the *hataali* agrees." Bayeta gave Mary a knowing, amused look. "You are surprised?"

"It's not that. I mean… Well, I don't quite know what I mean."

Bayeta poured Mary more coffee. "Many will come. You will find it good to be here." Mary smiled and settled back with her coffee. "Now, no more delay. What made you come all this way?"

Bayeta stood up, but Mary waved for her to sit back down. Mary leaned forward, the firelight illuminating the stress lines in her face. "John called about noon. I don't quite know where to begin." Mary closed her eyes to concentrate. "Let me see if I can keep things straight. John called. He said the police had interviewed him. They had not been able to talk directly to Adam. They wanted to know about Adam's whereabouts last night."

Bayeta stiffened. In a slow, deliberate tone she told Mary that Adam had dinner with John and Jonathan last night. Bayeta had kept her hands in her lap, but now was tightly gripped the folds of her skirt.

"Anyway, John answered the detective's questions. They kept asking, where was Adam, where? The police had yet to find him."

"Why are the police looking for Adam?"

"John said that they needed to confirm his whereabouts between eleven-thirty and one or two that morning. They believe that's when Herman died, sometime between those times. He died from a gunshot to his head in his home. It happened in his study."

"Herman? Herman is dead? Shot?" Bayeta's voice was unsteady, confused, but her eyes remained fixed, firmly, on Mary's.

"It could be suicide. John says that they have not yet made up their minds."

"This is awful!" Bayeta stood, wringing her hands and looking about the room. "I didn't like Herman, but I would never wish bad things for him." After a long moment's silence, she stood and stared into the fire. "What do they want of Adam? He had nothing to do with this."

"John says it is all so confused. Herman's body was not found until this morning. Carol found him in his study." Mary stood up and took Bayeta's hand. It felt cold, as if Bayeta had been outside in the night air. Impulsively, Mary felt Bayeta's pulse. It was steady, not racing. "Crystal, I am sorry to bring you this news. Maybe it sounds odd, but I have the feeling it does not surprise you. Forgive me for saying so."

Bayeta patted Mary's hand. "The truth is, while I would never have imagined it, I am not all that surprised, not really. Herman, I believe, was a desperate spirit, a man uncomfortable in his own skin. Adam often said that Herman was self-absorbed, a prisoner of appetites that he could not satisfy. I did not know him all that well.

For five years we lived within two miles of their house, but except for a couple of times each year, holidays, we had little contact."

Bayeta paced before the fire. "If Herman did shoot himself, there must be something, something that happened, that he could not cope with. I've seen men on the reservation with his look, men drunk on whiskey, men whose ambitions were beyond their reach, unable to cope. Unless he was so desperate that he saw no way to go on, he would not have done it."

"You are saying that he was a desperate man."

"Yes, from what I know of him. Adam distrusted him because he wanted to possess things and have control of other people. He never gained possession of the people close to him, though. He even tried with Adam. Nor do I think Carol liked him much. She complained that their sons were all but strangers to him."

Bayeta stared into the fire, watching the dance of flames licking at the air. There was more she could have said. But this was not the time for it, if ever. Immediate matters weighed down upon her.

"I learned two days ago something that I wish I hadn't. It's not important now. Herman's death, I fear, does involve Adam indirectly." Bayeta sat back down on the couch. "I think I need to sit. My knees feel weak." Bayeta was about to speak about Martin, of his betrayal, but thought better of it. It was for Adam to deal with, without involving others. "Forgive me…"

Mary interrupted, saying that John's second call was what made her come.

"John called back about 2:45, his time. The Morgan Prize ceremony was scheduled for 3. John was in a rush to meet up with Jonathan for the ceremony."

"Did John ask you to come?"

Mary smiled and took Bayeta's hand. "Not directly. In any event, I wanted to come."

The phone ringing in the kitchen interrupted Mary. "I am glad you came." Bayeta excused herself to answer the phone.

From the hallway Bayeta motioned to Mary. "It's John. He says that Adam tried phoning, but the line was busy." She turned back to the phone. "John, John, slow down." John's voice sounded at once both agitated and relieved. Yes, he said, Adam did make it to the ceremony. He accepted the award and spoke. It was a stunner, John said. And yes, Adam left no doubt that The Evergreen Institute has no claim to his work. He promised more would be forthcoming. Bayeta turned to Mary, telling her that John had yet to mention Herman's death. She handed the phone to Mary.

"John, this is Mary."

John could not contain his excitement. "Jesus, you should have been there! Adam hammered the Pharmas. Science must commit itself to discoveries that are necessary, he said, and of benefit to all. The audience, especially the younger ones, seemed to understand completely. They stood up and applauded for at least three minutes before he was able to finish his comments." Bayeta was listening on the hall extension. Mary asked, "What about Adam?"

John, his excitement rising with every sentence, continued, "Crystal, you would have been so proud of him. Dean Hooke, you remember him, he looked as if a truck had run over him."

Bayeta listened, unsure if it meant that Adam intended to step away from the firestorm he had created or pour more fuel on it. Did he not yet see how naïve he was? His research, his kind of research, was free of consequences only so long as it did not lead to profitable application, to ends to which others might exploit. John was not so naïve, but had he made Adam see it?

"John, tell me, where is Adam? He has not called me today."

"He took a cab to the airport at 5:00 p.m. He was going to try and get the first plane out. I loaned him the keys to the Mustang. When he gets to Albuquerque, he'll head straight home."

"Do you think he can get a plane out?"

"I don't know. The forecast is for heavy rain from here to Texas. The TV news is reporting long delays and cancellations at San Francisco International."

"If he can't get a flight out, is there a chance that you will see him?"

"Crystal, I don't know. The news here is full of Herman's death. They still have not ruled it suicide. Adam said that if he did not leave, they might insist that he remain available."

Mary interrupted, "They are certain Adam is not involved, aren't they?"

"I think so. They know that Adam had a running argument with Herman. They are interviewing everyone. Some uncomplimentary things are being said. The Evergreen Institute is stirring up rumors, which are getting wilder by the hour. In the evening paper, Thomas Vaughn, who was appointed the interim director today, hints at contract violations, infringement of proprietary rights, that sort of thing."

"Does Adam's leaving complicate things?"

"Who knows? Anyway, it can't make much difference in the long run, Crystal."

"Why do you think that?"

"After Adam left, Jonathan and I walked back to the Hilton. There was a hell of a scene with the reporters who wanted to interview Adam. They were not at all interested in the award. They wanted something juicy to spin about Herman's death."

"Adam would not have talked to them about that, John. They would have gotten nothing."

"Donald Ryder from the San Diego Times was there. Adam would have talked to him.

Bayeta interrupted, "Who is Ryder?"

"Sorry, he's a reporter Adam met on the plane coming out. Jonathan knows of him, says he's a good egg. The thing is, he's the one who pointed out Anton Mueller, an unsavory character. According to Ryder, Mueller has been following Adam for days, since our lunch at the faculty club, that is."

"You can't be serious. Who is this Mueller? Why would he be following Adam?"

"He was the bald guy in a grey suit sitting alone at a corner table. Ryder told Adam that Mueller is some sort of security chief at The Evergreen Institute. Well, that and that Mueller in reality is a henchman of sorts for Henry Schwann. Lots of rumors follow that man."

For an instant Bayeta imagined that she had actually seen such a man. One's imagination can play tricks. Yes, there was something at the lean edge of her memory. It was not the image of a man in the dining room, however. It was of a man walking slightly behind them on the walk between campus buildings. Had he stared at them, looking neither right nor left?

"John, Mary is going to stay here for a few days. Can you come, too?"

It was agreed. John would reschedule the departmental meeting for Thursday and come.

Bayeta let Mary talk more with him as she went to look in on Alberto. John agreed to tell Mary's department chair that she could not meet her Wednesday class. She would e-mail him an assignment for her students. Could he bring her the camera equipment she needed? Of course he would. There was some disagreement about their neighbor, Al Bender. John wanted to ask Al to keep an eye on the house while they were gone. Mary did not want to obligate him. But in the circumstances it made sense. Neither one again spoke of their concerns for Adam.

After seeing to fresh towels and an alarm clock for Mary, Bayeta made a new pot of coffee. Though exhausted, neither was ready for bed. Mary asked to see the weaving Bayeta was working on. With the coffee pot and cups in hand, Bayeta and Mary went to the studio. Mary settled herself on the couch across the room from Bayeta's loom. A table lamp at the far edge of the room and smoldering embers in the fireplace cast soft shadows on to the loom. If Alberto woke, he would want to be with them in the studio. Bayeta poked at the fire, agitating it until vigorous flames rose up, casting a warm glow on the weaving in progress. Dust mites drifted and swirled on the unsettled air of the space between. Mary's practiced eye surveyed the completed bands.

"You are using bayeta yarn in this weave. Such beauty in the making, is this for Adam?"

"Yes, this is to be a very special web."

Mary resisted asking about the meaning implicit in her design or her choice of colors. Bayeta would tell her in good time. "It looks to be strung in the old way, I see."

"If I were to use metal tension hooks and milled dowels, it would go faster. It might also make it easier to lay down straight weft lines. But this way draws out the full nature of the yarn."

"I don't know how you do it, Crystal."

"Practice, since I was a little girl. In Albuquerque, I kept at it. The loom is my familiar. It tells me who I am."

Mary understood that in Albuquerque weaving had helped her friend remain grounded. She looked to the small weaving on the wall next to the door, one she had seen many times. It was Bayeta's first web, almost three adult hands wide. A simple, lustrous red bayeta diamond floated in the center of a background of soft white un-dyed wool. "It is perfect, Crystal."

"Grandmother worried that it was."

As in so many things, her grandmother believed "perfect" to be a danger. One should never claim perfection. Grandmother had seen no warp showing beneath the weft. Her mother, Ninaba, had also praised her effort. Of course, young Crystal Bayeta had indeed much more to learn. Before it was finished, Grandmother made her undo an inch of the weave and put an escape line in. It was necessary in order to free the spirit trapped inside. It was hard to undo it and weave it back again, Grandmother told her, but do it she must.

Mary walked to the door to examine the weaving closely. She'd never seen it in such soft, warm light before. Bayeta pointed. "Look very closely at the top. See my escape line. It is there, to the left, only one thread's thickness."

Mary wanted to feel the history bound up within those threads. The weaving hinted at an old and enduring legacy with its bayeta yarn that stretched in a straight line back to Bosque Redondo and before that time. Daughters, mothers, grandmothers, great grandmothers were bound together through it.

"Some girls sell their first web. It is a custom. I kept mine. Mother told me that I would make my husband an even better one when I grew up. She always thought ahead. When Grandmother cut my little web from my loom, she did not know that I heard her tell mother that she worried for me."

"Grandmothers always worry, don't they?"

"Have I ever told you about the time I was sung over? I was thirteen. On the fifth morning of the ceremony, all I could think of was that I could sleep once the sun came up. I got up from the west corner of our summer hogan with my ears still ringing. The singer was chanting a Blessing Way song. The men and boys were singing, and I heard the deer rattle. Mother told me it was natural to feel pain, the cramps. She said a woman is like the moon: Every twenty-eight days she shines and is full. But the day comes, she said, when you are old and the pain does not come. At dawn the boys chased me to the east as far as the sheep corral. Auntie Yazzie was right, they always let you win."

"Your father said that you had trapped Adam, or was it that he snared himself? I don't remember. He said that it was destiny, was so because you ran too fast for boys to catch you."

"Father likes to put it that way. He would say *bee 'ódleehi*, like trapping a bird."

"Adam was the pursuer. I could see that from the beginning."

"Perhaps, but I knew from that day when I was thirteen, that when the time came, I would be the one to choose. Like the Squaw Dance, I had the right to choose. A man would come to my door. I would choose him or send him away. At the sing, I understood that it was up to me to run fast and not be caught like a bird. So, I ran fast. I kept saying over and over, 'May I be lively. May I be healthy.' When I reached the corral gate, Martin, my cousin, caught up. '*Yázhi amá, Yázhi amá'*, he called out. From that moment on, I became a 'little mother.' Twelve years later, when I saw Adam, I knew it was no time to run."

"You still want children, don't you?"

Bayeta had never before spoken of wanting children. She stood with Mary, remembering that long ago dawn, how the women helped with cutting the sweet, spongy corn cake, enough to feed a hundred people. It was hot and tasted good. Out of the dawn mist her people came to take a piece. Everyone spoke to her of her long and happy life to come.

"At the wedding I took him to, I walked right up to him, Mary. I said, 'This dance is for me, Dr. Grant.' That's what I said. He never had a chance. Like Father said, it was like *bee 'ódleehi*."

Mary was charmed. "It is a mystery to me, how we know when and who to choose."

"I just took hold of him and looked straight into his eyes. He was ripe for it."

"Everyone saw that you two were meant for each other. But I do admit that it is also a mystery to me how you cope. Here you are in the desert, so isolated. I know that you want a quiet, orderly life. Harmony and balance are the essentials. But out here, lacking many conveniences, your life is so very complex." Mary had raised the matter of coping with surprising bluntness. Bayeta understood what she meant and accepted it as praise. Alberto's illness, the laboratory attached to her house, Adam obsessed with his science. Now, with the death of Herman and Adam's decision, what would tomorrow bring?

"Tell me about this new sing, The Nightway? You say that you are organizing it. I imagine it will surprise Adam. You must have sensed that trouble was brewing for him."

Bayeta did not think it the right moment to tell Mary that the sing was not for Adam. She walked to her loom and strung her fingers lightly across the open warp strings.

"It is not always easy to keep one's feet on the right path. I found my path when I made my first weave. I found it again at my puberty ceremony. I found part of it in college. Then, I found Adam. Mary, I've always believed that life should be lived with what is necessary and absolute in mind. My people sang for me when I was thirteen to teach me what it means to be a woman. When it was time, I found the man who could help me straighten out the path I would walk for the rest of my life. Even with the travel and being away for five years, Adam gave me the grounding I needed. Now, there are complications in his way, and they cannot be avoided. We will cope. Together, Adam and I will get through this. After all, I have Bosque Redondo in me. It is the Navajo in me that tells me so."

"Crystal, nothing throws you. I admire that."

"Oh, I lose my balance at times. We all do."

"I've never seen you lose your balance."

"You saw me struggle for years, Mary. You did not want to see it. You are *bilagáana*, but you have a good eye. Stress and challenge are part of modern life. We are all told to struggle, that we have an inner drive to create or to destroy. But I do not see struggle as a creative force. I try to keep my thoughts focused and avoid struggling against what I cannot change. I do what I must do."

"Crystal, I think I'm a good anthropologist. Most cultures believe that a sense of place gives people strength. You have that. But is this enough for you?" She waved her arms around the room, as if encompassing the desert beyond. "Is it enough for Adam?"

Bayeta slowly, tenderly strummed the taut warp strings of her unfinished web. She turned to Mary. "It is true that I have no child. I want children. I know that Adam does. You know how he feels about Alberto." She looked at the rain spattering on the patio. It was coming down hard. "I'm so glad you came. We should turn in. Tomorrow is going to be a long day."

Five minutes later the house went dark. The rain drowned out the sounds of gas venting from the laboratory. The north wing's hisses and purrs of automated functions were alien to the ages-old inventory of sounds unique to desert life. By dawn the band of dark rain would slip eastward.

Bayeta had planned carefully. Everything that was necessary would be made ready. And yet, she worried. Martin's behavior had unsettled the balance and harmony of Rimrock. Like a moth hatched inside the folds of a cherished blanket, deception had made a hole in the peace of Rimrock. It had to be mended before more damage was done. Another hole would soon manifest itself. Alberto's life's thread was coming all undone. No future for him would be tamped firmly into place. Too short, his thread would soon be cut away. If a woman, a weaver, died before her time, the unfinished weaving on her loom would be taken down by a relative with care. With prayer the web would be buried where no one could disturb its remains. Bayeta asked herself how she could bring herself to gather up and bury Alberto's spirit? Bayeta slept without rest. Why must life be laid down before its time? She grieved for Hastin Gani. Soon she would grieve for Alberto. A black rain beat against the windows until the hour before the dawn.

<++++++++++>

The gate agent put Adam on standby for the seven o'clock to Albuquerque, with one stop in Phoenix. The flight was overbooked, and a band of heavy rain was streaming eastward from the Pacific Ocean, causing delays and flight cancellations. Getting any plane east bound airborne did not look good.

With standing room only at the gate area, Adam stood and watched the TV monitor. A news bulletin scrolled across the bottom of the screen: "Los Angeles and Southern California experience severe thunder and rain." Las Vegas and Phoenix were both on the storm's track. The departures monitor listed only delays and cancellations for Southwest Airlines. The arrivals screen was no more promising. There was nothing to do but wait it out. Fifteen minutes later, at seven o'clock, the flight he was listed on as standby was posted as delayed. A service attendant rolled out a courtesy cart with sodas and bags of pretzels and peanuts.

On impulse, Adam decided to try America West. He walked briskly over to the next concourse. Yes, the gate agent said, they had a flight to Albuquerque, connecting through Los Angeles. The flashing green status monitor indicated that it was in the boarding process. Reluctantly, the gate agent agreed to check to see if another standby could be listed. Checking his screen at the podium, he insisted that only once all ticketed passengers were on board would he be able to call out names of those on the standby list. Adam smiled resignedly, "Thank you for checking."

Minutes passed without an encouraging sign. Adam turned to leave.

"Sir, there is one seat left in first class."

Adam pivoted briskly on his heels. "Yes! Absolutely!"

He produced his credit card and driver's license. Boarding pass in hand, the agent gave Adam a reassuring smile and rushed him down the ramp. "Forgive the rush, Sir, but if we don't get this plane out of the gate in the next couple minutes, they will put a hold on it. The weather is that bad."

Adam had no time to call Bayeta to tell her that he'd be home a day early. He found his seat, 1A. As he began to sit down, he spotted Donald Ryder smiling and waving at him two rows back. Adam asked the passenger next to Ryder if he minded changing seats. The young man said he was "only too happy to change." He wanted a window seat.

"What a surprise," Ryder said, looking genuinely pleased. Before Adam had fully settled into his seat, Ryder said, "When you left the podium, it was like an earthquake!" He quickly related some of the reactions of the other reporters present. Adam listened. Was Ryder fishing for a follow-up piece?

"How long did you stay around?"

"I left about five-thirty. It was best to get on my way before my editor got a hold of me." The stewardess took Ryder's empty glass. Over the intercom, the captain told the cabin crew to be seated. "Thank God, we've got a pilot determined to get us out."

"Don," Adam consciously addressed Ryder as a friend, "what happened to your story? In today's paper I saw nothing. I looked to see if you quoted me accurately."

"I'm glad you asked. It appears that the great William Henry Schwann told my editor to fire me. Naturally, my editor is sorry to cut me loose. No matter; it has been coming for some time. Lack of interest, he said, some such drivel. In a way, that is true. Science angles don't have as much traction as they once had. Half the stories I submit are not published. I'm not sorry to leave that paper."

"So, they killed your story. I really am sorry they fired you."

"Don't be. I'll get a six-month severance and a rave letter of recommendation. All I have to do is not go around bad-mouthing. I'll come out ahead, actually. Look, I'm flying first class. Trout season is almost here. Now, I have time to do what I want. Yes, I'll be fine." Ryder grew silent for a moment and looked intently at Adam. "I get the impression that you won't fare so well. You really hit them where it hurts. You got their money and a plaque out of it, though. I assume they'll get nothing for it. I don't think anyone has stiffed the likes of Schwann like that before."

"I suppose they cancelled the reception," Adam said with a hint of mischief in his tone.

"Well, not exactly. Dean Hooke wanted to cancel. I overheard Vaughn suggest that they reconvene the committee and strip the award from you. He already had another candidate. Hooke, though, said that either course would only make a bigger mess, make them look vindictive. He said that taking them to task as you did, especially if you keep the award monies, will backfire on you, 'biting off the hand that feeds' I think was his expression."

"What on earth gave Vaughn the right to pontificate in the matter?"

Ryder offered a reason. "He was involved in the Geneva conference."

"Yes," Adam finished Ryder's thought, "he wanted restrictions on independent research."

"Your friend Hardesty says he is tied in to Genetrix. That explains how he stepped in immediately to replace Herman Crockoft."

"I suppose he was a logical choice, given the players."

Ryder agreed. "The Times reporter asked Hooke if Vaughn might have a conflict of interest. Hooke evaded the question, insisting that Vaughn's research record qualified him to serve as director of a prestigious institute. After that the whole thing degenerated into a shouting match, with rapid-fire questions from the reporters. Hooke, with Vaughn in tow, made for the exit when questioned about Herman Cockroft's death. God knows why it took so long for that to come up."

Adam was anxious to be airborne, to be beyond reach. The sound of the jet's engines helped to sooth his fatigued brain. With Ryder momentarily at a loss for words, and before the aircraft cleared runway 22-Left, Adam retreated into a deep sleep. A dream, his recurring dream, possessed him. Well-dressed men paid to ride into the future, conveyed by one magnificent, steel-plated, electrified beast. The beast was always the same. It reared and sparked, dipped its massive, gray metallic head and plunged forward hard against its traces. "The work of the devil, that's for sure," an old man at the curb complained. The driver shouted out for all to hear, "You must pay. Pay or be left behind." Another said, "It was you, was it not, who threw that stone." The boy answered: "It was only a small pebble." The old man wryly smiled, "All is ruin because of you." Slumped down in his seat, his dream winding down, something new entered it. Its ending was now different. He heard a voice whisper, "On to Naples." In dream, Adam recoiled from the dry, stale air flowing against his cheek. The dream had slipped out of its well-worn track. New faces stared down at the beast—Vaughn, Hooke, Boyle, Herman, and Mueller, all waiting for the thing to right itself. "This was a means to our ends," they cried.

"Sir, are you all right?" The stewardess had her hand on his shoulder, nudging Adam to consciousness. He sat up, the stale smell of airline coffee in his nostrils. He could hear the plane's hydraulics whine. The pilot was adjusting the plane's trim and banking left toward the east. Yes, he told her. He had slept through both the landing and take off from Los Angeles. The stewardess offered to bring him coffee and a snack. Ryder, still holding his glass, motioned for a refill. Adam noticed. "I drink too much, occupational hazard. Well, I suppose that I have to change that habit, or drop the excuse."

"Fishermen need a steady arm to catch the big ones."

Ryder smiled and set his glass down. "Yes, I will go fishing."

"My Uncle John was a fly fisherman. With a hand-tied Mayfly or Spring Stonefly he could tease any brown trout out of any hole. Once, on Antonio Creek, just above Los Alamos, I saw him work this one hole for two hours straight. He didn't change the fly once. He could cast so as to double set that fly, making it land twice on the water. I've never seen anyone else even try that. Just when I thought there was no fish there, wham! A six-pound beauty took it hard."

"You must love him."

"Yes, I did. I still do. He was a good man who taught me a lot."

"He died when?"

"He died a long time ago."

"I'm sorry."

"So am I. He had more to teach me, I'm sure of it."

"Tell me about him." Adam settled back and sipped the coffee the stewardess had brought him. "Once we took a trip, just the two of us, to Alamogordo. On the way back we stopped at a small settlement called La Joya. He liked the name, the jewel. It wasn't much of a place, little more than a bend in the road on the eastern bank overlooking the Rio Grande. He used to stop there when he drove from Albuquerque to Las Cruces or El Paso. He said it had a mysterious feel to it, a place for ghosts and spirits. The first time he was there was in 1945. He was part of a platoon of soldiers on their way to Jornada Del Muerto. That morning by ten o'clock, it was already 100 degrees in the shade. At Joya, the convoy stopped for a smoke break. They were on a guinea pig mission, all those soldiers. That's what he called it. The scientists were going to conduct the first atomic bomb test. He did not know that, not then. Their captain said only that something big was up." Ryder looked surprised, knowing that Adam was speaking of Trinity.

"Ironic, isn't it? He had survived half a dozen landings in the Pacific. He saw buddies cut down before they got within yards of the beach. He had got used to the idea that he was already dead. He wondered how he survived so many bullets. As one who survived so much, he was sent back stateside as a trainer. That's how he found himself on the road to Trinity. The soldiers were told a new weapon was to be detonated. Goggles and face cream were part of the drill. Some thought that was a joke. The next day he stood waiting in a shallow trench, putting face cream on. He remembered laughing at the madness of the whole thing."

"Three days earlier Uncle John had asked for leave to be with my mother, his sister. She was due to give birth, and our father was not there. John didn't get leave, needless to say. So, at Trinity, at the very hour to the minute that Cynthia and I were born, John was in a slit trench a few miles from ground zero to witness a different kind of birth. Years later, his insides burning up from cancer, John laughed at his misfortune. Radiation had ripped through him as certainly as if it had been a Japanese sniper's bullet. If he had not been part of that detail, he would almost certainly still be laying down a mayfly with a double set cast on Antonio creek. Catching that six-pounder was a triumph."

"Was he bitter?"

"No, he was completely occupied with living. You should have seen him with that six-pound trout. Once the fish had exhausted itself, John reeled it in very gently, trying not to damage it. He had rare patience and a soft hand. Knee deep in the water, he coaxed that fish into his net and lifted it so gently to the bank. When he released the fish, it actually circled before him and slowly angled off to the deep pool. It was as if the fish knew that Uncle John meant it no harm, that it was safe."

"Truly a man who died before his time."

"I have always counted death as defeat. In a sense, that's what got me involved with life extension issues, with apoptosis." Ryder looked as if he had not understood. Adam gave Ryder an apologetic grin. "I'm sorry, apoptosis is not a word thrown about every day. Apoptosis is a fancy word for programmed cell death, that's all."

"Saints preserve me. And I thought it was the alcohol fogging me up."

Adam was entrained at the moment with his subject. "I had ideas, you see, about what made cancer cells different. Did they have a program that made them wildly proliferate? I did not get far with that. So I switched to studying how normal cells behave. All cells die, of course. The question is: When does a normal cell know it is time to die? What mechanisms must be understood if one is to alter the timing, the switching from on to off?"

"This afternoon, why didn't you speak about that?"

"That's what the bit on Albert Claude was about. He expressed it so clearly, how at the cell level there is planning, memory, and decision-making at work. To understand how a cell thinks is to begin to understand its behavior and its trajectory over time. Frustrating, isn't it? Everyone wants an exact, precise formulation for intervention—schedules and treatment dosages. They act as if aging is a disease to be treated. Rather, it requires a life-long regimen to promote fitness. To alter or mediate a cell's behavior, one must change its itinerary, not its nature. It is not alchemy. It is engineering."

Ryder smiled. "Tell me more about Uncle John."

As the plane held to a holding pattern over Chaco Canyon and waited for permission to begin a final approach, Adam told Donald Ryder about the time when Uncle John first became sick. At the time, he was working in Pullman, Washington. His war service had qualified him for placement in a job at Hanford. For almost fourteen years he worked at refining uranium into plutonium. When he got sick, he went to the Veteran's hospital for treatment. He was told they would take care of him. But once admitted, he saw how they shut away cancer patients in a remote wing of the hospital and kept them on morphine. He was in a ward with other wartime veterans. They, too, had gone through the hell of dawn landings on mined beaches, bullets whizzing by at one-foot intervals, and bamboo booby traps on every jungle trail. But they had survived. That is, they survived long enough to end their days on morphine drips. Uncle John did not want that. Instead, he moved to Albuquerque to be with family. His last summer in Albuquerque, he took Cynthia and Adam for an overnight trip to the Trinity site. He wanted them to see the place where his last military duty was performed. With the twins he stood at ground zero and spoke of the Day of Trinity and of their passage into life. Only later did Adam realize that for Uncle John the Trinity trip had been the beginning of his passage out of life. Adam turned to Ryder and interrupted his story. "In a way, my father, Alexander, is also Trinity's child. He was there in the command bunker when it went off."

"Life is full of irony," Ryder said

Adam continued, "The night before, we stayed in Alamogordo and ate at an Italian pizza place. It was crowded, and we shared a table with an Apache family. I still remember them—Mangus and his wife, Concha, and their four children. The other patrons would not sit with Indians. John wasn't like that. He just shook hands across the table, and we all sat together eating Italian pizza. They were Chiricahua Apache tasting their first pizza. Mangus was a descendant of Geronimo. He said his great grandfather, Geronimo's cousin, stayed with him right to the end. His people had fled into the Black Range to the west. That was in May 1885. Geronimo, Natchez, Chihuahua, and Mangus, the great grandfather, led one hundred and forty into the Black Range. Mangus, eating pizza, was proud of his great grandfather and his people. They rode into the wilderness with no food or rest for many days. They had no Italian pizza either, he said. Mangus laughed at his own joke. It was an all too familiar story. They were overtaken by soldiers and forced to surrender. 'Nothing good, only Florida and Alabama—bad places,' Mangus said.

"So, there we were in 1960, sitting with Mangus and his family, who had come to see for themselves what their ancestors had lost. Concha gave Mangus a sad look when he spoke. The only thing she said that night was that they had come to stay. She had not wanted to leave her home for a place like Alamogordo. Mangus reminded her that they did not have pizza where they had been living."

Ryder asked, "Did they like pizza?"

"The children and Mangus liked it. Concha only ate a couple bites. I do remember Mangus saying that he also wanted to eat deer meat and ash bread and was thirsty for yucca juice. His wife grinned when he said that. The girls blushed. One of the boys reminded him that deer meat was not on the menu. Mangus shrugged his shoulders at that and said, 'Tonight, we eat White Man pizza.' "

Ryder turned to the stewardess to order another drink. Adam chided him, "Why not try yucca juice and vodka for a change?"

The plane's engines droned on. Adam closed his eyes, the story of Mangus and his family still fresh in his mind. He remembered the eldest daughter best. The whole family had fascinated him, but she was the same age as Nancy Urakami and just as pretty. Then, Adam was still nursing hurt feelings over Nancy. In the fall he would see her at school every day. But he never again talked to her, even though they were in the same English class. Eating Italian pizza while sitting across from that girl, Adam felt things for Nancy. Mangus had noticed how his daughter furtively eyed Adam. And, he had caught Adam's eye as he told Uncle John that she was the real reason for the trip. Uncle John was someone with whom even a reticent Apache could talk. Mangus said that it was three years since her time. Late as it was, she would have a coming of age ceremony. For four days, near Sierra Blanca Peak, she would become dawn maiden and wear a dress of white buckskin. Her face would be painted with corn pollen. All who came would dance. The shaman would bless her, saying, "The sun…had come down to earth…Long Life!"

Mangus was probably not used to so many words, and never so with a white man. But that evening, eating pizza and seeing how his daughter eyed Adam, he saw the need. She was soon to carry in her hands the very dress that one day she would be married in, he said. And, when her last day of sun goes down to the west, she would be buried in the dress made of white buckskin. She was to have a full life, an Apache life. At thirty thousand feet over the Chuskas, Adam remembered the Apache girl whom he had met but once and Mangus, who ate pizza as he talked of his daughter finding her place. How Adam had admired the girl. She was embarked on the journey of her life, about to be accepted into her clan as a grown woman. No one would again speak of her or to her as a child, as one too young to make her way in life.

Adam also remembered the day when George Slim told Adam of Crystal Bayeta's *Kinaalda* ceremony, her coming of age rite. It was not that different from the Apache girl's ceremony. As a woman Bayeta would possess the powers given by Changing Woman. If Adam was serious about George Slim's daughter, he had to promise that whatever happened he would honor who she was and what she was. Adam had not yet dared to say it, but he knew. Crystal Bayeta possessed what Adam saw in his own mother: An ancient spirit with a boundless capacity for inner peace. Such a woman knows who she is and what she wants. Eleanor had faced every challenge in her path and made good of them. When Adam met Crystal Bayeta, he knew she was just such a woman. And, there was also that special something. She was capable of integrating two distinct life-way patterns into one coherent life. He knew that the first day. Weeks later, holding her in his arms on the dance floor, lightly and tenderly, he knew that he was bound to her. And, she was more. She was the promise of a new beginning for Adam.

"What was it like to visit Trinity?" Ryder's question brought Adam back to the present. "I've written about it and always wanted to go there, but never have."

Adam stared out the window lost in thought. Why now, why had his memory dredged up the memory of the Apache girl and that long ago trip to Trinity? With effort, he returned to the present.

"The thing that impressed me most was those strange bits of greenish glass." Ryder nodded. He knew about those bits of glass, fused sand. They supposedly looked like raw emeralds. Visitors could not resist picking them up. "Someone called them 'Pearls of Trinity.' Trinitite is the technical name. That day my uncle kept rolling them around in the palm of his hand. He said that he could feel the heat of a man-made sun coming from them. We were standing at the marker, the very spot where the first bomb was detonated. Uncle John said Robert Wilson had explained 'the gadget' to the soldiers. That's what the physicists called it, 'the gadget.' Wilson told them it would end the war in the Pacific."

It would have been a good thing, Ryder agreed, if the bomb had really been the means to end the war. Yes, he knew of Robert Wilson. It was Wilson who said Los Alamos reminded him of Thomas Mann's *The Magic Mountain.* It was a very strange book, Germanic and Faustian. He saw a connection to Trinity, though. Wilson and his fellow scientists had indeed come to participate in a rite of passage. The old physics was swept away, replaced in a blinding flash by the birth of an atomic age. As it was with psychiatric practice in *The Magic Mountain*, physics was destined to breathe rarified air at a great height. Its truths were not to be fathomed by mere mortals living in the world's flatlands.

Adam had asked Uncle John if perhaps it was not a coming of age for physics. Uncle John would not say, but instead he gave Adam his copy of *The Magic Mountain.* "Read it carefully," he said. "Look for the unanticipated within." Yes, he added, Los Alamos had been very like a sanitarium—remote and free of the trappings of ordinary life. All the patients at the sanitarium were reduced to a routine of daily nostrums and constant flirtation. They existed separate from the rest of humanity, special beings. They believed that they were initiates of a special knowledge. So it was for the scientists at Los Alamos, where it was easy to forget Einstein's caution: "We should be on our guard not to overestimate science and scientific methods when it is a question of human problems, and we should not assume that experts are the only ones who have the right to express themselves on questions affecting the organization of society."

"Jornada del Muerto is remote, the perfect spot to bring in the atomic age," Ryder added.

"It could have been any remote site. The Interior Secretary at the time overrode both Oppenheimer and General Groves. They had favored a mesa site north of Alamogordo, a place inhabited by Native Americans. But Harold Ickes had no intention of being one more white man to displace Indians. He was a true progressive. At Jornada del Muerto the Indians were long gone. The Spanish had crossed through it in search of El Dorado and wisely moved on. For over a century, miners searched for recoverable minerals, only to abandon it. When the army moved in to prepare the site for the bomb test, they found only a handful of ranchers spread out over hundreds of square miles of bone- dry desert.

"Uncle John said, 'God looked the other way when it was created.' He spoke of the Trinity site in the starkest of terms. The closest settlements, Troy and Carthage, were abandoned mining settlements, named for utterly devastated, vanished civilizations. Sand devils had scoured the barren surface down to a hard crust in the 120 degrees heat. In the gypsum-laden soil, plants sent roots down forty feet to get at moisture. Rattlesnakes and fire ants hid under rocks hot enough to fry an egg on. Scorpions, tarantulas, centipedes, lizards, and Gila Monsters patrolled the surface. For millennia, this tortured expanse of earth had been left virtually undisturbed; that is until the 'march of progress' claimed a use for it."

To prepare for the Trinity test, soldiers had secured and patrolled the restricted expanse. Their mission was to run the pronghorn off or mow them down with machine guns mounted on jeep turrets. The maze of monitoring test wires, which had been strung out over the desert, was constantly in danger of being severed by the pronghorn's hooves. Uncle John insisted that the first victims of the atomic age were the pronghorns.

"Before Uncle John took us to Trinity late that summer, my father visited. He was on his way to a new test site, Cape Thompson, in Alaska, another march of progress site."

"Was that the radioactive iodine experiment on Eskimos?"

"That's right, Iodine-131. They were to test how soldiers react under cold conditions. But the real purpose was Project Chariot. Edward Teller wanted to make artificial harbors using atom bombs. Father was involved with the preparations. I learned a couple days ago that was when Father first met William Henry Schwann. Ironic, isn't it? He was consulting for the military and for Schwann and Company Engineering. They wanted to use atom bombs ten times more powerful than the one used on Hiroshima. They went so far as to ship radioactive soil from a Nevada test to see if it would leach contaminates into the ground water. Of course, it would. What idiocy was that?"

"What else did you see at Trinity?"

Adam went on to talk about how Uncle John had received special permission to take the twins to McDonald Ranch, headquarters for the test. A young army sergeant accompanied them as a guide and to insure that they remained on the site for no more than an hour. The background radioactivity was still of some concern. At the ranch house there were pictures on a wall showing military police on horseback with guard dogs. The guide told how seconds before detonation animals sensed that something was about to happen. Horses became hysterical. Dogs howled. Pronghorns grazing on the flat pan of alkali wash fled, vainly trying to escape the blast that would vaporize them. A million spadefoot toads gave out one last mating song seconds before the blast and went silent. What primeval instinct told animals and not men what was to come? After the test, the desert was stained with ghostly impressions on the crusted over sands—carbonized tracings of antelope, lizards, snakes, and toads. The Albuquerque Tribune's afternoon edition reported that an ammunition dump had blown up, a prepared cover story. Gallup residents doubted it. A pilot flying a military transport plane 30 miles away at 10,000 feet reported that he thought it was the sun coming up from the south, so bright that it lit up his cockpit. The guide had pointed to the spot in the distance.

"Right about there is where Herb Anderson drove his tank in to scoop up hot samples. He was the first man ever to see Trinitite." The guide had picked up a sample and held it to up to the light. Just fused grains of green sand, he insisted.

Uncle John was not so dismissive. "Anderson reported his Geiger counter going off scale. He became a victim, you know. He died of beryllosis."

The guide had been impressed. Visitors typically avoided mention of death from radiation. It was perhaps impolite of Uncle John. But, unlike the young guide, Uncle John well knew the price some paid. He could have bared his chest, then and there, to show firsthand how radiation eats away one's flesh. He had worked with plutonium for fourteen years. Did the guide know that Edward Teller, standing to the west on Compania Hill, had passed out suntan lotion and bet that the yield would be forty-five thousand tons? That day many bets were made on "S-1", "the device", "the gadget." Later, Truman chose to call it "the thing." Whatever the name, the test was demanded, if only to settle the "battle of the laboratories." When used on Japan, the public was told it was to end the war.

Uncle John was drunk with history that day. He had read that Oppenheimer boasted to Teller that it would be many years, if ever, before a more powerful device could be created. Teller, however, already had fixed his mind on "the super." Fusion, he insisted, was the future, not fission. To Uncle John, the difference between fission and fusion could not have mattered to Louis Slotin. He had operated the guillotine, a nightmarish device set up in Omega Canyon. As a bomb assembly expert, he had been charged with measuring the critical mass needed for an implosion detonation of plutonium. His team made tests by dropping a "slug" of fissionable material down through the center of the guillotine assembly to measure the resulting chain reaction as it passed through the hole. With each trial, they increased the amount of radioactive material. They became committed to "tickling the dragon's tail" in order to learn the exact amount necessary to make the "gadget" go critical. At Trinity, Louis Slotin assembled the two halves of the plutonium core in the McDonald Ranch House. By then, he had become used to handling the components of the eighty-pound spherical core of gray metal, had become used to its warm feel as he handled them.

Later that summer at Omega Canyon, he repeated the guillotine experiment. A screwdriver slipped from his hand. In an instant, he realized the consequences. He immediately disconnected the assembly with his bare hands, absorbing 880 roentgens of gamma radiation. Then, he calmly went to the blackboard and sketched out the positions of every person in the room at the moment of the accident. Their lives, not his, hung in the balance. Nine days later, at the far edge of madness, Louis Slotin died. The coming Cold War had claimed its first victim. He was not to be the last victim of Trinity. As for Oppenheimer, the "father" of the bomb, he never returned permanently to his home, Eagle Hill.

As the aircraft banked and the engine pitch changed, Adam wondered what consequences might come from his research? Had he tickled a dragon's tail? He had never considered the possibility. Questions flooded his exhausted mind. Was he so single-minded that he did not see? He had dared to experiment because he could. If only he had Hardesty's good sense and restraint, he thought.

As the cabin lights dimmed in preparation for landing, Adam saw that Ryder was asleep. He had imbibed one too many. The pilot spoke from the cockpit, apologizing for the delay. The storm they had flown through, he said, had dumped three inches of snow on New Mexico's higher elevations. The landing might be a bit bumpy, but he promised to have the plane on the ground in twenty minutes.

Below fifteen thousand feet, the plane began to pitch and yaw as it threaded its way down through lightning and rain. As it banked left, nose down, the airport landing lights came into view. The stewardess in the forward jump seat mentioned to the other flight attendants that flashfloods were west of Albuquerque. She complained about having to drive home on the road near Petroglyph National Monument where the river could flood. Adam knew that Rimrock would be experiencing the same dark, cold rain. Alberto was deathly afraid of thunder and lightning. Thunder and hard rain on the roof would keep him awake. Bayeta, he was sure, would be in his room to comfort him.

Adam estimated the time it might take to reach home. Road conditions on I-40 would be no problem. But with no lights and faded or non-existent lane markers on the secondary roads, a night like this would be hazardous to drive. The gravel and dirt roads beyond Sawmill would be even worse.

The Boeing-737 set down hard. Ryder roused himself and sat up.

"What will you do now?"

"I really don't know. Not staying for the funeral will raise questions."

"Have you decided about what to do about your work?"

"I've been asking myself why I began it to begin with. When I designed the experiments, it was out of curiosity more than anything. I wanted to unravel an unknown. Now that I know how the lifespan can be extended, I realize that I haven't sorted out the real questions, ones I should have from the beginning. Who might want control and why? So many unknowns now confront me."

"We are not talking about immortality here, are we?" Ryder was not asking, simply stating the obvious question from what he knew of Adam's research.

"It will be most efficacious for the relatively young individual. It entails a prescribed regimen. Individual variation is a factor. The manner in which any one individual absorbs, makes use of, and disposes of proteins at the cell level is complicated. Just reading the information a cell gives off about its status, its timing, what it needs is complex."

"Herr Doctor, we're on the ground now. The lesson is over." Ryder gently pinched Adam.

Adam blushed. "I forgot myself for a minute."

Ryder laughed. "See what a bumpy ride on a rainy night can do?"

Adam again became serious. "I worked on this without telling anyone. Even my assistant, Martin, knows only the basic approach, the broad parameters."

“Then, no one else is in a position to control it, are they?” Ryder pressed Adam’s arm and gave him a look. “In any event, prepare yourself. They will come. You know that.”

“Vaughn or Valentine might try. Schwann, if you are right. Hessen is too dense to take any initiative. At the very least, it could get litigious.”

“I wanted to tell you earlier.”

“What should you have told me?

“At the aborted press conference Mueller was standing off to the side. He was there with two big, rough looking types. Dr. Hessen was talking to him, waving his hands about. Mueller nodded and took off like a shot with his two hounds at his heels.”

“When was this?”

“I’d say 5:15, maybe a minute or two later.”

“They could have had no idea I was headed for the airport. How could they?”

“They might have guessed. But if so, I bet that they are still at the airport.”

“I was ticketed on Southwest. I doubt that it got out. In which case…”

“Consider yourself lucky. They would probably search every gate trying to spot you.”

Exiting the baggage area, Donald Ryder walked out to the arrivals curb with Adam. He was going to stay at an airport hotel and drive to Los Alamos in the morning. Adam gave him the phone number at Rimrock. If he heard anything, Ryder promised to call. His sometime roommate in San Diego had agreed to pack up his stuff at her place and send it. He would miss her, but she was no six-pound trout, he said. The season was to open on Saturday, and he had a date with a mountain stream above Los Alamos. “Mayflies, you think?”

Adam shook his head. “It is too early. Try the Caddis.”

In the hard rain pounding the parking lot, Adam found Sanderson’s car. The cold and wet did him some good. He felt alert and fit to drive. As he waited in line at the exit, he listened to the radio. It was 1:20 a.m. The stopover in Los Angeles had caused the delay. He might not make Rimrock for breakfast. The weather forecast was for more rain and thundershowers until morning. He would drive nonstop to Gallup and stop for coffee. Beyond Gallup he'd have to take it slow.

On I-40 strong gusts of wind drove the rain hard against the westbound traffic. The car shuddered and veered to the right as each gust from the south hit it broadside. Visibility was no more than three or four car lengths. Hydroplaning slightly to the left, he slowed to 45 to regain control. Two semi-trucks, 18-wheel, long haulers, boomed past him at 75 miles an hour. He dared not go faster than 55. He was too tired to trust his reflexes. His sense of alertness on leaving the airport had worn off. He gripped the steering wheel hard and rocked to and fro in his seat to restore circulation in his legs. Straining his eyes, he cursed the miles still ahead of him.

Two hours and one hundred miles later, he saw the exit for Thoreau. He had leg cramps, and his left foot was numb. He would have to stop soon and walk around a bit. The problem was where to stop. West of Thoreau, he saw the marker for the Continental Divide, one mile ahead. He took the turnout and got out to stretch and breathe fresh air. A lone big rig was parked near the exit. Adam listened to the truck's diesel idling. The trucker was probably napping, waiting for daylight and for the rain to cease. The rain had let up some and felt good on his face. It helped to revive his senses. Stretching his legs, he looked north toward Hosta Buttes. He knew the buttes were there, at 8300 feet, but saw nothing. Chuska Peak was to the northwest at 8000 feet. Either summit would have done for Loren Eisley, he thought, suitable places to consider the uncertain future. Of late, Adam had thought more than once of Eisley's insight: "I came down across stones dotted with pink and gray lichens—a barren land dreaming life's last dreams in the thin air of a cold and future world." Adam took in a deep breath of moist, cold, thin air. Had Eisley got it right?

Adam was too tired to try to resolve anything about what lay ahead for him. His thoughts, as he drove, had settled nothing. He was certain, however, that leaving San Francisco when he did was the smart thing to do. It was as right as his leaving Berkeley five years ago. But should he have involved Hardesty? His feeling was that there was danger, undefined but palpable.

The dark time in a high desert is no time to settle such an issue, Adam admitted to himself. Near the low horizon to the west, a gibbous moon was slipping down below the black cloud layer, its pale light etching the outlines of the Chuska range. There, beyond the Chuskas, things would have to settle out. Adam stretched his legs and breathed in fresh, moist air for another fifteen minutes.

Back on the road, he passed the exit for Church Rock. The 4:00 a.m. news faded in and out on the radio. "On the international front…sources close to…treaty breakdown." In Chicago the Red Sox lost a double-header. Congress was in Easter recess. A traffic pile-up in dense fog on the George Washington Parkway had claimed five lives and backed up traffic for miles. Adam punched the buttons until he found an FM station, New Mexico Public Radio. The signal was weak. "Turning to regional news…found dead…Spokesman for the…reported that a well-known research biologist…missing …whereabouts unknown at this…" Adam tried fine-tuning the radio, but the news summary was over. The weather report followed. "Due to heavy gusts and rain, the Albuquerque International has suspended all..." The signal faded out. Adam tuned to KGHR, Navajo Public Radio. It was playing "September Song", by Willie Nelson. The car's clock read 4:18 a.m. Shaking his head, he realized that fatigue was again dulling his senses. He needed coffee. With the outskirts of Gallup ahead, he decided to stop at The Fruitland Cafe three miles farther.

At the cafe's door, Adam parked the car and made a run for it. The downpour drenched him. But it felt good and partially revived him. Standing in a puddle just inside the door, he heard a familiar voice. "Got you good, did it?" It was Melanie Quintana. "Twice in one week you come to see me. Keep showing up like this, and people will begin to talk."

"I just can't resist your coffee, Melanie."

"Sam, get this man a hot cup of Java." The short order cook already had two fresh cups poured. "Dry yourself off. Come sit with me." Adam smiled and shook himself. "You sure do look like a drowned rat."

"I feel like one."

"Say, I heard something about you. It was on the 4:00 a.m. news. You're missing."

"Do I look lost?" He looked around and saw that no one else was in the cafe. "Did it say that I'm a person of interest? I left California without saying goodbye."

"You never were one to stick around when things got dull. If you had, I might have caught you." Adam hugged Melanie and sat down with her in the corner booth. "Still, you do keep coming back for my coffee. Want something to eat?" Melanie knew without asking. Adam always ate her peach pie with his coffee. Of course, there were grounds at the bottom of every cup. Melanie believed that without the grounds, how was one to know the coffee was real. Truckers, her best customers, insisted that coffee was not coffee unless it was "twice-boiled."

Two truckers came in, talking about the road conditions to the west. The older one had just come from Flagstaff. "A real pisser out there, flooded out at Mentmore. You think they'll ever finish that stretch of highway?" Adam listened. He had planned to stay on I-40 as far as Lupton before turning north. Route 264 to Ya-Ta-Hey was the short cut to Window Rock. What especially concerned him now were the road conditions beyond Sawmill.

Adam thanked Melanie and tried to phone Rimrock. Melanie could see that he was not getting through. "Lines are down west of Window Rock. I can try for you later if you like."

"Here's the number." He wrote it down on her order pad. "Tell my wife when I left here."

"Will do."

"Thanks, Melanie, I appreciate it." Adam paid for the coffee and pie and started for the door.

"It will start to get light in another half hour. You'll be fine. Just steer clear of the arroyos if you see more than an inch or so of water running in them."

"I'll take care." Adam hesitated. "Melanie, tell me, what did you hear on the news?"

Melanie gave him a knowing look. "It don't make sense, saying you're missing." She turned serious for a moment. "It's too bad about your brother. I didn't know that you had a brother."

"He was my half-brother. We were not close." Adam thanked her again and headed back into the rain with a third cup of coffee in a paper cup.

Crossing the Santa Fe Railroad tracks, he headed north on highway 264 and entered the Navajo Reservation. He remembered again how Bea said she had felt when she and her mother would come to Gallup looking for her father. It was part of her history. The Treaty of 1868 had drawn the reservation line north of Gallup in order to reserve a corridor for the coming railroad. The treaty did recognize as Navajo land the Chuska Range, Canyon de Chelly, and much of the territory within the four sacred mountains, but not Gallup. When the Navajo drifted back to their homeland, they found the hogans in shambles, the peach trees cut down, and the cornfields barren. The People took to rebuilding their lives, existing at first on wild plants, prairie dogs, rabbit, and field rats. Ration Day at Ft. Defiance was a bitter acknowledgement that the *bilagáana* were there to stay. In time The People found their footing. The sheep herds grew enormous. Hunger and defeat became but bitter memories. Then came a double misfortune, the Big Depression and drought. The overgrazed grasses dried up. Winds carried away the precious soils. Summer flash floods washed more soil into the arroyos and down the Colorado River. It was the hardest time for her family. The struggle to survive finally became too much for George Slim. Too sick to work, in frustration and shame, his spirit broke. He drifted into Gallup seeking cheap whiskey and oblivion. His wife and young daughter had to cross the Santa Fe tracks to find him. Only their love, and their persistence, brought him back home and restored him to harmony.

It was after 5:00 a.m. when Adam entered Window Rock and turned at the junction onto Navajo Highway 7. He skidded making the turn. He'd already had one near accident a mile back. He was worried about the road conditions beyond Sawmill. Worse, Three

Turkey Ruin was gravel and dirt. Fatigue was gaining on him. The rain kept up. His coffee was too cold to drink.

He drove on, losing all sense of time. Dawn approached, momentarily reviving his senses. He smiled at the prospect of reaching home before sunup. But in the next instant, before he could react, the car skidded and plunged down an arroyo. A wall of water washed over the hood, momentarily blinding him. The force of forward momentum carried the car up the opposing bank to higher ground. The engine flooded out. He tried starting the car, knowing it was futile. Turning off the lights, he resigned himself to staying put. He looked about and realized that he had come too far. He should have turned off two miles back. If he had, he would not be sitting in a car with the engine flooded out. Exhausted and still shaken, he smiled at his mistake.

<++++++++++>

It was after six-thirty when the rain slacked off. Most likely, Adam figured, Melanie Quintana would already have called Bayeta. She would expect him home by seven. By eight, she would begin to worry. He could count on her to phone around to see if anyone had seen him. Adam found a car rug on the back seat and wrapped up in it. It was too early for anyone to be driving on this road in such weather. It was useless, but he listened with his ear against the fogged over window. To fight fatigue, he rolled the window down a couple of times to feel the chill air on his face. He lost track of time. Half awake, he listened to the wind driving a band of rain eastward. He tightened the rug about his shoulders and dozed. *Tseyi* was close, somewhere in the distance to the west. The last settlement he had passed was near a lake. If the rain would just stop, he thought, he could get out and inspect the car. He was anxious to see Alberto, to know how he... He slumped over on the front seat and fell fast asleep. Fatigue and delayed stress had finally won out. The steady patter of rain on the car made soothing background noise for his dream. His last waking thought was of riding horseback along the foot of the Chuska Mountains, The Goods of Value Range, as George Slim called them. George Slim was proud of his home on its slopes for the soils there were fertile and the view beautiful.

<++++++++++>

Three sharp raps on the car window brought Adam to his senses. He looked up to see a man's face staring down at him. In the soft morning light he recognized a familiar face—that of a Navajo policeman. He was a tall, slim man in a blue shirt and Levi jeans. Adam stiffly straightened himself and smiled at the man. He rolled his window down and looked around. He saw the Ford pickup parked on the shoulder. Adam greeted the policeman, "*yá'át'ééh.*"

The Navajo policemen gave Adam a knowing look. "It is a bad time to be on this road."

"It is that."

"This time of year one never knows about rain. Black rain this, but we need it." The Navajo policeman gave Adam an inquiring look. "You don't look stuck." He looked south, down the road. "I see you came through that water."

Adam nodded. "I did not see the dip until it was too late." Adam stepped out of the car and extended his hand. "I was headed home. The water in the arroyo flooded out the engine."

"I figured that. You also missed your turn a mile or so back."

"After I hit that arroyo, I realized that."

"The sign got washed out late last night. Lucky for you I came along to fix it."

"I am needed at home. I could not wait until daylight."

The policeman scratched his chin. "You're headed for Rimrock. That makes you the husband of Crystal Bayeta. Ninaba is the mother, and George Slim is the father."

"If you know George Slim and Ninaba, then you know they live close by."

"Crystal," the Navajo policemen said.

"Yes, that's my wife's name."

"I mean the village. You are south and west of Crystal."

"If I can get my car started, I'll go back to the turn-off. The road should be passable now."

"You can make it if the car will start, Dr. Grant."

"You know me." Adam took care not to pose it as a question.

"Everyone round these parts knows the husband of Crystal Bayeta of Rimrock."

"If I was not needed at home, I'd stop at Crystal to see my in-laws."

"Good people. I hear there's to be a big do at Rimrock."

"I've been on a trip."

"You will have much company."

"I'll see if the car will start," Adam said. He doubted it would, but he needed to try.

"That car won't start, not after all the water it went through. I'll get my cousin on the radio. He'll come and get it going. Meantime, I'll run you over to George Slim's place."

On the way they talked about rain and how much it was needed. Officer Clyde Yazzie said that Adam could have waited it out in Albuquerque or Gallup. Adam said that he should have, but he had to try making it home. "You made some big news on the radio, Dr. Grant."

"I'm sorry, what did you hear?"

"The Albuquerque news said something about a big award you got. They made it sound like you took the money and left San Francisco for parts unknown. Also, some question about how some relative of yours died the same day."

"As you can see, here I am. I'd prefer it, though, if you told no one."

"Those city cops will have to figure it out on their own. That business about your brother, that's between you and them."

Adam's momentary apprehension fell away. Clyde was indeed a policeman, but his manner suggested that he accepted Adam as not just another lost *bilagáana*. Crystal Bayeta's husband had in-laws close by, George Slim and Ninaba. That was enough to satisfy Clyde Yazzie about Adam.

The road to Crystal was rough. Fresh potholes did not make it any more navigable. Clyde apologized for the road. It was long overdue for a grading. Talk turned to family, which was inevitable. Clyde Yazzie was *Naakaii diné é*. He was related, on his father's side, to George Slim. Adam smiled, letting Clyde know that he understood. One way or another, most Navajo living in and around *Tseyi* and the Chuskas were related to one another.

Entering Crystal, Clyde parked his truck fifty feet from George Slim and Ninaba's door. The rain had diminished to a freshening, heavy mist. It felt good to get out and stretch. The moisture helped Adam feel better. They waited for Crystal Bayeta's parents to open the door and call out to them.

Two minutes later, the door opened. George Slim waved. He did not show surprise at seeing Adam. He smiled and said to Clyde, "Awful early for you to be bringing me a stray lamb, Clyde."

"I was just passing by, Grandfather. Some miles back, his car flooded out."

"Come in. Little Mother has a pot of coffee on the fire."

Adam entered their comfortable "manufactured" home and smelled the fresh coffee brewing on the stove. Ninaba smiled and hugged him. "I make biscuits. You look to need fattening up."

Adam told them that he had got into Albuquerque quite late. Clyde volunteered that Adam had missed the turn-off and tangled with the washed-out arroyo over by Luke Many Goats' outfit. George Slim nodded. Easy to get stuck there, he said. Ninaba said that they were getting ready to drive to Rimrock. They were busy packing up food before setting out. It was agreed, then. Clyde would have his cousin get John's car running and drive it over later. Adam drank coffee and ate Ninaba's biscuits. He was in good hands. She asked, "And the boy?"

Adam did not respond directly, but looked sad. "You will do for him what you can," she added.

"It will not be enough."

She patted his shoulder and smiled sadly, a resigned smile of acceptance.

If Alberto were strong enough, he told her, the two of them would drive out to *Tseyi's* rim. The rains had quickened the flowers to bloom. The yucca cacti were greening up. All would show well against the sand and red rocks, a sure sign of spring. Before leaving for San Francisco he had stood at the rim looking for scurf pea and wild geranium blooms. He had spotted hawkweed, primroses,

Jamestown weed, and blue-eyed grasses. Even at the edges of the last patches of snow stubbornly clinging to the talus slopes, green was taking hold. Renewal was near at hand. Alberto would want to see it all. In winter the barren expanse of snow cover and dulled red rock walls had made Alberto morbid and sullen. He spoke of the canyon walls as if they hid enemies in wait. He knew that they held a record of time. Time was something he had little of left. It was, he had told Adam, not fair.

To brighten Alberto's moods, Adam often took him to one special place at the rim where the two could sit and watch for signs of life in the canyon. In late spring and summer, below their perch and up the far talus slope, was a lush patch of green. It stretched for hundreds of feet, a verdant ribbon stretching out among the cottonwoods at the stream's edge. Mule deer often drifted among the line of trees, contentedly browsing. A magnificent six-point buck, the one with a slit right ear and scarred throat, would often stand as sentinel on high ground. Except for the autumn rut, he stood alone and apart. For four years, each spring, Adam had taken Alberto to the rim to watch that stag and his family. The buck's dusky form and shadow often slipped in and out of view among the cottonwood trees. His great ears were trained on the far rim where Adam and Alberto watched. If he caught their scent, he would scrape the air assertively with his six-point antlers. Through binoculars, they could see the glint of his eye, intense and alert to alien presence. He would stretch his long neck stiffly out and up and sniff the air streaming down and across the space between. He knew the smell of man. And when he sniffed, he stared straight, tolerating their presence so long as the distance between did not close. For Alberto to know that such an animal was at home in the fastness of *Tseyi* was a gift.

Each spring Adam had struggled to accept that it could be Alberto's last trip to the rim. Now, he was conflicted whether to take Alberto there, given his condition. Would Alberto insist? The pretense that this spring was just one more spring, not his last, was almost too much for Adam. Alberto knew, almost to the day, when the deer would again come to browse that verdant patch along the stream.

With the old Ford pickup loaded with staples, the three set out for Rimrock. The truck rolled and dipped, slipped and swayed, as George Slim navigated the road. With his head against the window, the image in his mind was of the toss of antlers splitting the air, the dark eye meeting his, the stag insisting, "More cannot be done." Adam let his thoughts of the stag drain away and dozed.

13

Wind Shifts

By 3 a.m. the storm's leading edge stalled over Rimrock, sheet lightning and black rain pummeling the desert floor. A steady drumming on the roof had made sleep impossible. There was nothing to be done but to get up. Bayeta walked through the darkened hallway, lightning flashes illuminating her path. The phone had not rung all night. She picked up the receiver and heard no dial tone. The wires are down, she told herself. No repair crew would venture out in this storm. She stood in the dark with the receiver in her hand. The uncertainty of not knowing when Adam would return had distracted her, was the reason that she could not sleep. He was not expected until early Wednesday, assuming that he would be on the 6:00 p.m. plane out of San Francisco on Tuesday. Still, John had called Mary to tell her that Adam had gone to the airport late Monday afternoon. Not a word since. Alberto kept asking, "When will Adam come home?"

Bayeta had done what she could to keep up Alberto's spirits. She kept reminding him of Adam's schedule posted beside his bed. He asked every time he roused from sleep. With effort she kept an outward calm. But sending for Chanter of the Sun's House had complicated things. Was she taking on too much? If Adam were home, things could be managed. She only half-believed that. Adam would confront Martin over what he had done. But she had already sent for Chanter of the Sun's House. Confronting Martin would not serve to restore him. Martin, being the singer's nephew on his mother's side, deserved to be made whole. A nine-night ceremony was needed to restore him. Hastin Gani's widow, Maria Klah, needed her life restored to harmony.

Bayeta sat at the kitchen table in the dark watching the red dot on the coffee maker. She made a mental list of calls to make when the phone came back in service. She had already called her mother last evening. Extra blankets, another barbecue grill, and some *ch'il gohwéhi* were needed. Many of the women preferred her mother's Navajo tea to coffee. There were so many things to attend to, and here she was without a phone. Chanter of the Sun's House would be resting up from his long winter of healing duties. She had to know when to expect him, tomorrow preferably. Would he agree that Nightway was appropriate? What preparations would he add to her list of duties? Would he ask her to provide special items? How many assistants were needed? What items could the assistants provide?

She would need to respond to his questions, respond with answers that would satisfy his needs. Chanter of the Sun's House was a "traditional", one who seldom responded to direct questions. It was impolite. Before addressing what was on her mind, the questions she had, he would talk about family and the hard winter. But who was to assist him? What items were needed? When to have the sing? He would take his time to settle upon what Bayeta needed to know. That was custom, but time was short. In spite of everything, the sing must go forward. Martin had to be put right. He had been alone too long. It was time he began to live correctly, with a wife and responsibilities. Maria Klah would help him return to harmony. Bayeta was certain of it, and anxious to see it so.

With the coffee pot in hand, Bayeta looked in on Alberto, who was still sleeping. She entered her studio and turned on a light. Pouring a cup of coffee, she examined her weave. The weft-line was now four hands high. She would soon need to adjust the loom to bring the open warp down to a comfortable working level. That required loosening the top dowel, lowering the warp, drawing the completed segment up the back of the frame and re-tensioning the top beam. She preferred not to wrap completed segments into a roll at the bottom. With the warp strung vertically, re-setting the warp tension demanded patience and skill. The weft, edge to edge, was 76 inches wide and demanded equal tension across the warp foundation. Adjusting eight tension brackets would be tedious. Reluctantly, she decided to wait until another few inches were built up before re-setting.

For an hour Bayeta lost track of time. With each pull of the heddle, she inserted the batten and drew the weft yarn across the opened warp. Working right to left, then left to right, she emptied her mind of concerns that had denied her sleep. The strong, obedient fibers—natural wool—felt good to the touch—smooth, almost oily. She had taken care not to lose lanolin content by washing the raw wool. With a length of yarn drawn through each shed, Bayeta tamped each new weft line and examined it for straightness. The house had drawn into itself. She wove in the soft light of a new dawn giving ground to full day.

A little past seven Alberto awakened and called out. Bayeta went to him and asked if he would eat something. He shook his head no, but with coaxing, he promised to eat a little later. He wanted to get out of bed, as it felt lumpy to him. He asked to rest on her studio couch and watch. It was what he wanted. She helped him make his toilet and supported him for the walk down the hall to the studio.

With Alberto settled, Bayeta sat down again at her loom. Before she tamped down the first weft line, she looked back and saw that his eyes were closed. He had a thin smile on his lips. She ran her fingers across the warp as one would a harp. Her fingers felt stiff. No matter, she told herself. If he opened his eyes and saw her weaving it would please him. She positioned her batten and prayed.

A smooth, steady rhythm took hold of her. But, she did not feel completely at ease. Hastin Gani's death weighed upon her. In the normal course of things, she would not weave until her grieving for Hastin Gani and family ran its course. But Alberto would not be with her for much longer. His need came first.

Seeing his head cradled against the pillows, Bayeta continued to pull the heddle, count out her sheds, and push on the shed rod. Holding the weft yarn in her right hand, she inserted her batten and pulled the yarn through. For an hour she built up one segment of a band and then another, each time shifting her position along the loom from right to left. She drew the yarn straight and tight before closing the warp and reaching for her fork. With each tamping, she listened to Alberto's breathing. Her ear told her when the tamping of her fork on new thread was firm and steady. Her ear told her how tenuous and shallow was his breathing, how strained from dryness was his throat and mouth. With each breath, the thinning thread of his life frayed a little more. She could not repress the thought that he would not live to see the weave complete. At last, her fingers tired. Having miscounted two sheds in as many minutes and retracing her work to correct it, she stopped. It was not good to weave with so much on her mind.

For the first time in hours Bayeta heard the hall clock chime. She had been so absorbed at her loom that she had tuned it out. The rain, which deadened sounds inside the house, had also stopped. She listened for and heard the faint, shallow rasp of Alberto's breathing. It was relief mixed with sadness to hear it. He was asleep on her studio couch, dreaming perhaps. She heard bare feet go by the studio door. Martin was on his way to the lab. Mixed in with the sound of rainwater dripping from the roof and into the catchment barrels, she heard sheep bleats and the rattle of a pickup coming to a halt outside. Tall Boy, with the four sheep Maria promised, had come.

Bayeta went to the kitchen door to greet Tall Boy, a fine looking young man. Like so many Navajo males, he was ill at ease in the presence of women not close kin. He was deferential to his mother-in-law and other women her age. He would not speak to Bayeta about his brother-in-law's fate. Talk of death would only make both of them sadder.

"Maria said I must bring the lambs over early." Bayeta nodded and offered him coffee. "I got to get back."

"I'll tell Martin you are here." Bayeta poured Tall Boy a fresh cup of coffee and handed him the sugar bowl. Excusing herself, she went to fetch Martin. He would be in the lab feeding the animals. Martin looked tired and was unshaven. He admitted that he had not slept well.

Tall Boy drank his coffee and asked Bayeta, reluctantly, who was to come and deal with the sheep. She thought for a moment and then admitted that she did not know. She would ask her father, George Slim, to handle it when he came. Tall Boy looked pensive and stiff, still gripping his cup to warm his hands. Finally, he spoke. "I will take the sheep to Widow Tumecho. That will be better."

Bayeta did not immediately react. Intuitively, she considered why he would think it preferable. Martin entered the kitchen. He had heard Tall Boy say that he would take the sheep to Widow Tumecho's place.

"He is right. It would be best to take them there." Bayeta agreed without having to speak of it. There was enough to deal with already, and the sound of animals that were soon to die was not a good thing. It would not do to have big birds circling Rimrock. Alberto might see them. When others came, they also would see the birds, a bad sign. Ten minutes later, standing at the kitchen door, she watched the men drive off. Tall Boy and Martin would unload the sheep at Widow Tumecho's and drive on to Maria Klah's outfit. Widow Tumecho would see to it that the meat was brought over when needed.

Mary entered the kitchen and said good morning. "I looked in at your loom again, Crystal. It is so big." Bayeta sensed Mary's confusion. Mary was most familiar with rugs and tapestries, saddle throws, and mantas,

"It is to be a *honalchodi.* They are not now common." Bayeta took a book from the shelf to show Mary. Traders often referred to a *honalchodi* as a Chief's Blanket. She did not like the term. Most people, rich white people, displayed it flat on a wall. "That is not how one should be used."

"It is to be worn."

"Yes, it is for Adam. It will cover his shoulders and hang just so." Bayeta made a graceful, sweeping movement, as if donning the *honalchodi* shown on the book's color plate.

"How did Alberto look to you?"

"Asleep. I think he is saving his strength for Adam's return."

Mary and Bayeta caught up on each other's lives over breakfast. In ten years of marriage to Adam, Bayeta's friendship with Mary and

John had grown strong in spite of how far away their homes. It helped, too, that John was a biologist. Whenever Adam and John were together, they spent hours huddled over the latest advances in research, methods, and laboratory procedures. Bayeta and Mary had their own interests to share. Mary was still trying to have a child. Mary talked about her last visit to the fertility clinic. The testing procedure was painful. She'd have the test results in a few days.

Bayeta listened intently. Adam had not asked her to consider being tested. Had he even thought of it? Why had the two of them not considered it? They did not use contraception, and Bayeta did not believe she had a "female problem." She did not know how much time she still had to conceive.

The phone was ringing. "Ah, we have a phone now!" The hall clock chimed. It was nine o'clock. "Good morning."

She heard Johnny Kabito's voice. He was a real talker, unusual for a Navajo man, especially when addressing a woman. He talked about weather and that the time for sings was winding down. She motioned to Mary. "Could you look in on Alberto, see if he is still asleep?"

Johnny Kabito had contacted Chanter of the Sun's House. The chanter would have instructions for her. His assistant would come soon, and determine what was needed. Was the hogan in order? Who would tell others to come? How many? Hearing Johnny Kabito relay so many concerns made Bayeta realize that the enterprise was more complex than she had reckoned. Was she rushing things? Nothing would be gained by moving too fast. But neither was delay in order. Martin needed to be brought back into harmony, and soon. Although Adam was not yet back and Alberto was gravely ill—so many imponderables to weigh—her impulse was to have the sing at the earliest possible time.

"Tell Chanter of the Sun's House to send his assistant. He can tell me what preparations and how much time they will take." She thanked Kabito for his help and hung up the phone.

"Mary, I just realized that it could be more involved than I thought to hold The Nightway. I must negotiate the timing with the singer. My father will help me with that. I've never done such a thing before. You can sit in, if the chanter allows it. Do you have to get back to Albuquerque soon?"

"Crystal, I'm happy to stay for as long as you want me. Graduate students can manage for a couple weeks without me. To attend the sing is a privilege, something I want to do."

"As my best friend, it is important to me that you share in this."

"I feel blessed. John has to be in Albuquerque. But I'm sure he'll understand."

"It's settled then."

Until the assistant arrived, or Alberto needed her, Bayeta and Mary had more time to chat with one another. For, though every fiber of her being was now part of Rimrock, Bayeta still felt the pull of her second nature, her need to belong, if only half so, in the wider world that Mary represented. Bayeta understood, too, that withdrawal from the currents of life beyond Rimrock had not served Adam well. Once he had been so embedded with the pace and stimulation of the academic life. Living in California had meant academic standing, research assistants, travel, conferences, dinners, even healthy disputations with rivals. She, however, did not miss those things. When she met Adam, she had been already stepping back from the trappings of academic life and urban life.

Mary talked at length about her hopes for a baby, boy or girl. Bayeta listened, not with envy but with her own hope softly kindled. Mary wanted the sense of renewal a child would bring to her life and to John's. John promised to add a bedroom to the house. She wanted John to give up being chair and return to full-time teaching and research.

As for herself, child or no child, Bayeta needed a sense of newness and renewal. The one difference was that Rimrock would always be home. Before Bayeta realized it, Mary left off talk of "what-ifs."

"Crystal, your mind must be elsewhere. I don't think you heard a word I've said for the last five minutes." Her patient smile was comforting.

"I'm sorry. You were talking about children, of having a child. My mind drifted off. It could be fatigue. I did not get much sleep last night, none in fact."

"Dear Crystal, I understand. We're all under a strain."

Neither spoke of the obvious. Nothing would be resolved until events took a turn. The outcome of Adam's work was still in the balance. Alberto's final days were upon them. Healing the pain that Martin was suffering under was needed. Maria Klah needed a husband. Her children needed a father. What would be the repercussions from Herman's death? If only Adam was back home.

<++++++++++>

For a short while, the house grew silent. Bayeta and Mary had exhausted their list of "what ifs" and, with effort, put them aside. Only the sound of the phone ringing brought both women back to the present. Bayeta answered. At first, she could not hear, so much static was on the line. It was John Sanderson.

"I am just leaving my office. What with so much happening, I've decided not to wait until the end of the week to come. Is Adam back yet?" Bayeta told him she had no idea when to expect Adam. John said that he was coming in any event. Bayeta turned the phone over to Mary.

A minute later, Mary hung up the phone. "He says that he can't leave Adam to deal with everything alone. He'll be here by late this afternoon."

Bayeta hugged Mary. "I am so pleased."

<++++++++++>

By the sound it made bouncing over the muddy ruts leading to the house, Bayeta knew it was her parents' old pickup. Anticipation brought her to her feet. Mary had been telling Bayeta that she wanted to help in the kitchen after taking a shower.

"While you shower, I'll see who this is." Bayeta knew, of course, but preferred to get her parents settled while Mary showered. Her mother would insist on taking charge of the kitchen. She would also take Maria and Juanita in tow when they arrived to help with the washing. When Chanter of the Sun's House came, her father would volunteer to negotiate. It was for men to settle such things. What a relief to have her parents there.

As the truck rolled to a stop Bayeta saw a third figure in the cab. It was Adam! How did he know how much she needed him just now? A rush of intense relief ran through her body.

At the kitchen door Adam embraced her tightly and gave her a long, deep kiss. Her parents discreetly busied themselves unloading the back of the truck. Bayeta blushed and fussed with her hair, once he had set her back on the ground. George Slim gave his wife a gentle pinch and grinned. "It is good," he whispered. Ninaba smiled at her daughter.

"Clyde Yazzie, Marie Tsosie's grandson, found him. His car flooded out in one of them arroyos."

"I got on the last flight out of SFO last night. John's car got me as far as the turn-off to Crystal before the high water got me. But, as you see, here I am." Bayeta punched his arm and buried her face in his chest. The tension that had been building inside of her for days instantly melted away. "You must be tired and hungry."

"First, I want to see Alberto. Then, I'll eat something. Is he awake?"

Mary came out to greet Adam and Crystal's parents. "He's not quite awake, Adam."

"Hello, Mary. What a surprise. I am glad to see that you are here."

"Alberto is in Crystal's studio."

"I'll go and see him now." Adam took three cups from the shelf and poured coffee, first for George Slim and Ninaba. "Is the phone still out?"

"A while ago ours was restored."

"Bea, put the answering machine on. Don't pick up unless you know who it is."

She nodded. "Go to Alberto, I can manage the rest." As he turned to leave the kitchen, she took the letter from the prep table and handed it to him. "You need to read Dr. Himes' letter before you see him." He saw the pain etched on her face. He knew the letter contained the final clinical evaluation. He read it and handed it back.

He made no mention of his need to check the lab. It was such a small omission, but it told her volumes. Something had changed.

<++++++++++>

Alberto awoke as Adam entered Bayeta's studio. He did not try to rise up from the sofa, but he smiled. He had waited days to ask Adam if he would keep his promise to take him to the rim, to his favorite place. The place he shared only with Adam.

"Only if you promise me that you will not to get too excited."

Last night's storm had moved on and a bright sun warmed the air. It took time to convince Bayeta. Reluctantly, she agreed. It would be worse to deny Alberto what probably was his last outing. Adam could take Alberto at noon and return by 1:30, no later Bayeta pleaded.

On the winds high above the canyon, the hawks soared, hovered, and dove. They did not remain aloft on steady circuits, as was their habit. The larger one, the female, made a steep dive toward the sheered edge of the canyon rim. At the last split second she veered up and away, screaming complaint. Alberto watched intently. Her red tail feathers caught the updraft from the canyon floor, and, effortlessly gauging the distance, she outstretched her wings and took full advantage and measure of the current of air. She was matriarch and mistress of the rim. Again, her piercing complaint scratched the air sharply. She dove headlong again, disappearing below the ledge. Seconds passed, then she came on, soaring up and over the far rim, bound east and away. The other hawk, a male, hovered above and waited. His feathers were dull gray and rough edged, a sign of his immaturity. He stubbornly held aloft, uncertain of his mastery of the agitated wind. His screech was plaintive, persistent. The matriarch ignored him.

"You see, Alberto," Adam said, "He's hungry. I don't think his mother is going to feed him."

Alberto was content. He was at the rim out in the sun and fresh air. He was propped up against a warm slab of sandstone with the sun at his back. Before their outing, Alberto had felt feverish. Once outside, however, he was determined to ignore it. He wanted to be out in the open. He wanted to be with Adam. He wanted to watch hawks. What mattered was to have choice still in his power and to not be denied something that mattered to him. The intense light, however, would soon prove too much.

Since returning from the Flagstaff clinic, Bayeta had confided to Adam, Alberto's mood was subdued. Dr. Hime's assessment was grim, a final acceptance of the inevitable. Nothing more could be done. A few days, ten, two weeks at the outside, was all he could say.

Alberto nodded off, while Adam stood beside him at the rim's edge watching the two hawks. Aware of human presence, it was rare for them to come so close. The matriarch made her fifth dive on the rim, not thirty yards away. Adam saw her flint-black piercing eye, her look a challenge. A bird of prey, she was not intimidated by human presence.

Adam thought of Widow Tumecho whose summer hogan was warming in the sun on the flat ground across from the stream below. She was never comfortable at the sight of large birds stationed overhead, birds that she was certain came from *Tsé Bit'a'i*, the rock white men called Shiprock. They waited for one thing, she said, and one thing only. It had been so for thirty years. The hawks, she insisted, had seen the tragedy. It was they who came down to feed before searchers reached that place of loss and sadness. The widow was absolute. Monster Slayer had made the big birds, owls and eagles, she insisted. He had made them from the bird monsters that once lived on *Tsé Bit'a'i*
and fed on human flesh. Monster Slayer was responsible for her loss. It did not matter to her what the *bilagáana* named it, or that they said that it was nothing more than an ancient lava flow driven fifteen miles up through the earth's crust. What could a *bilagáana* know of pain and loss? Hawks, eagles, and buzzards were all *atsá.* Making a fist, she'd say, "It clinches its food."

Alberto knew that those were Red-tailed hawks at the rim. Nonetheless, he chose to see them as peregrine falcons. Don Federigo would have seen peregrines, Alberto insisted.

Adam thought about Alberto's love of, near obsession of, the *Decameron.* On his nightstand, he kept his copy open to the story of the boy's death for want of a fabulous bird. He obsessively parsed every phrase of the story for meaning. Bayeta had hung a weave of hers above the nightstand, one she had exhibited in Albuquerque. He called it Two Red Hills. When Alberto saw the weaving hung, he asked Adam, "Will you and Lady B always live here?" He meant live on there without him. Of late, Alberto had come to call her Lady B, the great lady in the *Decameron* story. It made Adam uneasy, knowing how he clung to romantic fantasy. And, that the story was of a time of plague when young people sought refuge in the remote countryside. Alberto was desperate to believe his redemption was still possible. He saw Bayeta as lady-in-waiting and Adam as knight-errant.

"Yes, Alberto," he had told him, "we will always live here. Bea will pray each day at dawn, '*Sa'ah naagha éi Bik'eh hózhǫ*. Adam's halting pronunciation made Alberto smile. He did not understand the precise meaning. Adam would say only a Navajo could. "Don't tell Alberto such things" Bayeta had remonstrated. "He cannot go 'in-old-age-walking-the trail-of-beauty.' To say so will remind him of what cannot be."

Before Adam and Alberto had departed for the canyon, Bayeta had insisted, "Don't be long. Please. Father and I will be occupied with details for the sing. Things can't be rushed. Mary will help Mother in the kitchen. Juanita and Maria are coming to handle the laundry chores. Tall Boy will rope off a parking area. Martin has gone into Chinle to get Johnny Kabito and a truckload of firewood." Bayeta with her list in hand was in command mode. "Alberto is your responsibility."

Adam was content to give his full attention to Alberto. He would be no help with the planning for The Nightway. He was not, George Slim had confided, born to it. "Today, it is good for you to take the boy to *Tseyi*. The wind within you blows strong. The boy needs to share it."

It was the first time George Slim had spoken directly to his son-in-law of wind. Bea had told him how her father felt about such a thing. To him, wind was the same as soul or spirit. Every person had a "wind" within. It could blow too strong if one was not mindful of it. It was the wind within Adam that made him often stand at the rim of *Tseyi*. It was why others were uneasy at seeing him there.

There, an hour later, huddled against a warm rock, Alberto had fallen asleep. A stiff breeze flowed across the rim from west to east. Adam stood, bracing himself against the mass of air pushing on him at the hard edge of the abyss. With his right toe, he tested the ledge's limit. If fatigue or momentary vertigo overtook him, no one would hear his fall. From out of the sun, the matriarch swooped in close. His knees buckled from a sudden, reflexive rush of adrenalin. He backed away.

The hawk had cut short his review of the events of the last few days, uncertain if he understood his own intentions or motives. Hardesty had warned him, "Have you thought through the ends of the what you have sought?" Hardesty had no quarrel with Adam's decision to seek answers, or the means. Adam had good intent. He had always been good at setting out a course of research. It was the ends to which his research could be applied that had concerned Hardesty.

Again the hawk swooped down to stare deliberately at him. It was as if the bird was telling him that he must face reality and the consequences for exposing himself. In spite of the warmth from the sun on his shoulders, he felt a shiver run up his back. Someone was sure to come, he now fully realized. The advantage gained by his sudden departure from San Francisco was now diminished or exhausted. Schwann, Thomas Vaughn, someone would come. Ryder had said as much. "Did you know that Schwann and Company's corporate motto is '*Ars totem requirit hominum*'? Schwann is powerful and shrewd. He's a true adept at getting what he wants. He'll use violence if necessary. Perhaps now, nothing less will do for him."

Would it have been simpler if Herman were still alive? To spar with him could have given Adam more time, time to maneuver. But Herman's death complicated things. He regretted Herman's fate, but he did not grieve for him.

A thick vegetal smell, sweet and pungent, was on the wind carried up and over the rim. It was humid and warm, the gift of rain. Adam picked up Alberto and carried him to the car. The boy, half-conscious, let his thin smile speak for him. Adam had kept his promise.

The hall clock struck three as Adam carried Alberto to his bed. Yes, he admitted to Bea, they were late in returning. "We watched hawks. The Tumecho hogan was half in shadow when we left. Tomorrow, maybe we will spot that six-point buck and his harem. It felt and smelled like spring."

"Adam, he looks terrible. You promised to be back no later than two."

"How are your parents?" He acted as if he had not heard her complaint.

"Mother is napping. Father is outside. He and the singer's assistant are going over how to put up the temporary hogan. While I see to Alberto, you go and help them with the poles and tarp."

"Has Martin returned?"

"Yes. He says to tell you the beasts are fed. He and Kabito are stacking firewood."

"Good," Adam said. Bayeta gave him a long, anxious look. He knew why. He needed to have his talk with Martin, needed to settle the matter of his betrayal of Adam's trust. Adam, however, was not ready to speak of it, not yet, not then.

"I want him to help me set the tub up for Alberto. He wants a hot soak."

"Adam, you don't mean that, not on top of everything else."

"Bea, come into the kitchen for a minute."

She followed, her hands planted firmly on her hips. She knew that look he gave her. He was about to tell her what he would insist upon. In the kitchen, Adam explained.

"Dear, it's his skin. It is so dry and sensitive. He needs a good soak. You've seen the bedsores. A soak will help him sleep."

"You can't subject him to that."

"Martin will set the tub up in the lab. You pampered him while I was gone. Now, it is my turn."

"What do you mean by that?"

"You've been feeding him roasted marshmallows."

Mary came in as they talked. "John called. He won't be here much before seven."

Adam looked relieved. "Good, he and I can go over what happened after I left."

"Oh, he said a Lieutenant Kestos called at the hotel this morning. He's looking for you."

Adam knew that John would have said nothing to Kestos. "Mary, I'll call the lieutenant in the morning."

Bayeta nudged Adam and gave him a stern look. He was putting the call off. "Go, then, and set up the tub. I'll check to make sure that he is up to it."

It was important to Adam that Alberto believed that he still had a choice. He needed to be treated as an adult. He did not want what time left to him to be framed by denials. George Slim had said as much that morning. "When I go, daughter, give me up to fire. If it is a big fire, my spirit will rise high. I will die as I have lived." Bayeta was uncomfortable with talk of death. It made her leave the room hurriedly. She had heard it before, when he was sick with cancer.

Entering Alberto's room, she could see how taxed he was from the outing. His vitality was draining away by the hour, as a weaving coming off its loom prematurely. Sadly, his life had been strung from errant fibers. With a hand over her face, she left the room. If Adam persisted, how could she cope? She knew how foolishly men could act.

For an hour the house regained a semblance of normalcy. Mary sat in the kitchen reading and made up a plate of vegetables and onion dip for later. Bayeta napped. She did not object when Adam carried Alberto to the lab. Perhaps a warm soak might do him some good. Perhaps.

After the bath, Adam helped Alberto into his pajamas and plugged in the electric blanket for him. Standing by the bed, watching Alberto's eyes close, Adam could not remember the last time he opened the drapes to let light in. Alberto did not like drapes, complained that they shut out the world. But the sunlight now hurt his eyes. There was little reason for drapes at Rimrock, except when it was so cold outside that they served to hold in warmth. Looking at

Alberto's drapes, he realized how faded they had become. Once a solid, bright red, they had faded to bands of pink and dull rust. The rust hue reminded Adam of dried blood on a microscope slide. He would ask Bea to replace them.

George Slim was out on the patio putting the last of seven large, round pine posts in the cement perimeter holes of the five-sided concrete pad. Bayeta had planned well. The metal castings sunk in the concrete patio made it a simple task to set the posts in place. Such forethought pleased George Slim. Normally, the east corner of the patio was for all appearances simply a flat concrete slab. Bayeta had not been unmindful of her people's ways and had made space for a hogan, even if only a temporary one.

With the posts set, the custom-made tent fabric was ready to be stretched into place, in clockwise fashion with the opening for the door facing east. In minutes, with Adam helping, the men had the canvas stretched and tied in place. It took longer to tie down the convex crossbeams that formed the gently sloping roof. Each crossbeam was notched and numbered by the carpenter who had worked from Bayeta's set of plans. Adam helped to put the crossbeams in place. George Slim tied them off. Many a late summer afternoon had been spent under the open framing covered by the tarp roof, a perfect, open-air gazebo. The walls, however, had never before been put in place. In the hour after sunset, many were the times when they had sat warming bare feet on the concrete pad. Later, with a cooling breeze, dinner was served in the gazebo. Bea had indeed seen to Rimrock's every detail.

With the roof framing installed, George Slim retrieved the roof tarp from the patio shed and inspected it. It had a proper smoke hole. A separate attached flap would keep light out. Adam helped to stretch the tarp up and over the roof frames and secure it. The assistant stepped into the interior and inspected each seam. No light must come through them. He had earlier voiced skepticism, but now he said, "It is good."

Once he had gathered medicine plants, Chanter of the Sun's House would come. He was fussy about details, the assistant gently insisted, but, the "hogan made of cloth" would do. His last sing of the winter had been performed in a plywood hogan, its windows covered with black tar paper.

By late afternoon the massing clouds to the west swallowed the sun. With attenuated light and warmth, the stilled air brought a welcome pause in the preparations. George Slim was certain—more rain would come before morning. Chee agreed. He was not a talker. George Slim had known the singer's assistant from when he had first begun to learn The Nightway from Chanter of the Sun's House. "Twenty years is a long time to learn," George Slim said, appreciatively.

"It takes time," Chee agreed.

"Soon you will conduct a sing," George Slim said. It was not as a question.

"I am making my *jish*."

George Slim set his hands on his knees and smiled. Chee had spoken what needed to be said. His presence would add more power to the ceremony. His Bayeta had chosen well. Having two *hataali* and two *jish* bundles present was a good sign. Twilight and time for dinner had come. Watching the road, George Slim saw a car make the last rise. "Company's coming."

Two minutes later, John Sanderson shook George Slim's hand and commented on the rough road. George Slim laughed. "You got to have a four wheeler, not one of them city jobbies."

Bayeta called out. "It's time to wash up and come to the table."

"Bea, have you seen Martin?"

"He's staying over at the Klah place tonight. He and Tall Boy want to get a wall up."

Upon seeing John come through the door, Bayeta and Adam greeted him, as if he had just come in from a stroll. Mary would see to it that John was settled and washed up for dinner.

"I'll go get Alberto."

George Slim lightly gripped Adam's arm. "Show Mr. Chee where to wash up." Chee smiled and relaxed his shoulders. It was good not to have to ask. Adam led him down the hall.

Dinner was to be something of an occasion. The dining room was across the hall from the kitchen and adjoined the living room.

Absent company, the kitchen table sufficed. In planning the house, Bayeta had insisted that the dining room face south. On summer evenings, the dining room was the coolest room in the house. Tonight, however, fire burned in the double fireplace, heating the living room and dining room. Firelight gave the rooms a glow, and the wood gave off the sharp, sweet scents of juniper resin and pine pitch. In the center of the long oak table Bayeta had placed her favorite tapestry, one she had woven for such occasions. It was the only one of its kind that she had ever done. The table was set for eight to include Chee.

George Slim and Chee entered the dining room first. They waited for Crystal to indicate the seating arrangement. She entered carrying the soup tureen. Ninaba followed with a basket of fresh, hot, crispy fry bread. Hers was always golden brown and tasty, George Slim remarked to Chee with pride. Chee grinned broadly, looking discreetly in the direction of the basket. Adam brought Alberto in his wheelchair. Bayeta had removed a chair for him at the north end of the table. "Son" Adam said with emphasis, "you sit here tonight, in the place of honor." He settled Alberto in and motioned to Mr. Chee to take his place to the right of Alberto.

"Mother, Father, you are on the west side. Ninaba blushed, grasping her daughter's meaning. Tonight, she was to take Changing Woman's place, her husband that of the Sun. Ninaba often spoke of wanting to visit California. Changing Woman lived on an island in the Great Western Ocean.

John and Mary sat at the east side, Bayeta next to Mary. Adam sat at the south end, the gathering dusk at his back beyond the window. So seated, a momentary silence gathered about the table. The fire spat embers up the chimney, infusing the room with the scents of juniper and pine.

Alberto looked to be at peace. Tonight he was eating at the big table. Chee did not ask about Alberto's affliction. He had heard the talk at Rose Bia's Cafe of "the dwarf" living at Rimrock, the boy who was very old. He also knew that this was the house of Crystal Bayeta, she married to *tsétah,* "crashing rocks," the *bilagáana* wizard.

Bayeta passed the soup tureen to George Slim. Hot and steaming, it was his favorite, a pureed chili soup with turmeric and cardamom seasoning. With Ninaba's fry bread, it was a meal in itself. As the soup made it around, Mary passed the plate of roasted Poblano rellenos stuffed with cheese and a hint of fresh minced, sage-fed lamb, the perfect pairing with the endive salad. Adam saw Alberto eye the stuffed peppers.

"You will like it," Adam assured him. "They are mild and have goat cheese stuffed inside." Alberto was convinced. Even if he only tasted them, it was good to have them on his plate.

Conversation centered on food and ordinary things. George Slim would soon plant a new field of heirloom corn. Late rain was a sign that three years of drought could be ending. Chee occupied Alberto with accounts of birds he had seen at the rim. Alberto described a bird that swooped straight down at him. The hawk is a noble bird, Chee agreed.

"Yes, but these are falcons, Mr. Chee. They can go over 200 miles an hour. Don Federigo raised falcon's, you know."

Chee smiled and did not correct Alberto. Yes, both were noble birds. But he could not remember ever meeting a Don Federigo. No matter, the young man was so enjoying himself.

Bayeta brought in the platter with the main entrée. A sigh went up. She had prepared the saddle of venison with port sauce. Adam stood to do the honors, to carve the venison. Bayeta took up each plate and ladled port sauce over the meat. She added a garnish of reserved bacon and warm, lightly baked apple slices before passing each plate. George Slim and Mr. Chee behaved with rare abandon. It had been too long, George Slim would later tell his daughter, since he had tasted such good game meat. Bayeta had greatly honored him by her choice. "This old stomach gets tired of mutton," he told her.

Adam cut Alberto's portion into thin strips and moistened them with the sauce. He could see that he was tiring. His perfect moment would end in a minute or two when his reserves gave out. If only Alberto could marshal his spirits and try to eat. And, he did. The taste of venison was new to him. He was not to be denied. Later, Bea would say that she chose venison because it was so lean. If she had cooked fatty meat, Alberto could not have eaten any. And yes, she also did it for her father. He had not hunted for years. Adam promised not to tell him that it was New Zealand venison. George Slim held up his plate. He and Chee were ready for seconds. Bayeta served them while Adam took Alberto to bed. Sleep had overtaken him. But, he did have a smile on his lips.

Back at the table Chee spoke as Adam sat down. He had never tasted venison so good. He wanted to know what "port treatment" was. As Bayeta explained, he could not resist picking up the rib bone on his plate and sucking on it. She was very pleased that he enjoyed it so much. Conversation and good food made for a pleasant interlude for everyone. No mention was made of the sing to be held.

With everyone claiming to be stuffed, Mary went for the coffee pot. At last Chee set his bone down and cleared his throat. It was the moment to speak to Bayeta about the timing of the sing. George Slim had touched on the matter before dinner, asking if the timing might interfere with the time to plant corn. Chee had already mentioned, obliquely, that corn needed a good rain past May 1, if it was not to burn up. Chee's outfit was, he admitted, closer in altitude and meridian to that of Rimrock than it was to Crystal, which was up in The Goods of Value Range. Chee intended to move down into *Tseyi* by May 1 to plow and plant. The sandy bottom of Canyon del Muerto would by then be sufficiently drained. Talk of timing, however, had less to do with corn planting that it did the sing.

Setting an auspicious time for the ceremony had to be decided. May 1 was still a good while off. There was time for the sing, he said. Chee would sleep in the temporary Hogan that night. The answer would come to him as he slept. Then, he would drive to Window Rock in the morning and speak with Chanter of the Sun's House.

Earlier, before dinner, Bayeta had tried to convince her father that Chee would be more comfortable sleeping in the living room. Rain was due and with it wind. He could not get much sleep with wind and rain beating against the hogan.

"Daughter, Chee knows best. He wants to sleep in the hogan with the feather walls. It will speak to him. You have told him that the sing is for Martin. The singer is Martin's Uncle. Maybe the singer does not know, and thinks you want the sing for Alberto. The wind and rain will tell Chee what to say when he sees the singer."

"I did not think to tell Chanter of the Sun's House that."

"Daughter, you have yet some things to learn. When the hogan was put up, a wind came. Chee stood still and listened. The walls moved with the wind and spoke. Now, he wishes to sleep in the hogan. He will make a fire and listen. When dawn comes, he will know what to say." George Slim gave his daughter a gentle hug. He put a finger to his lips and Crystal Bayeta remained silent. "Chee must complete his *jish*. He knows what he lacks. Give him what he asks for."

"I understand, father."

"I think, maybe it is a comb. When I showed him where to wash up, he saw your loom. He does not know any woman who weaves as you. He saw bayeta yarn. He believed such a yarn exists only in old webs, like in a museum. He wants a comb from your hand, one that has touched bayeta yarn."

"I will give him my oldest one, grandmother's."

"He will see how long use has polished it. That will please him."

When dinner ended and Chee had put his fork and knife down with a clank to express his contentment, Bayeta sensed it was a good moment to speak of Chee's need.

"You sleep in the hogan tonight, I am told. At dawn, I will bring you coffee."

"Thank you, Little Mother. I will sleep well and listen. The wind will come into my ear."

Bayeta now had the full measure of the man. His manner was serious, finely tuned to his role. As a child, she had been told how First Man created a feather to be attached to his ear so that he could hear the words of the gods on the wind. What might the gods say this night to this man?

"It pleases me that you wish something from me." She led him down the hall to her studio. She picked up the comb, the one her grandmother had used most of her life, and held it out to him. Chee looked in her eyes for only a moment and then, took the comb with his right hand.

"Little Mother honors me. In two days I will make good use of this." He held the comb up to the light and examined it carefully. "I am well satisfied. You must keep it until I return." With that, he gently placed it in the basket with the bayeta yarn. Bayeta was not certain why he did what he did. But she guessed that as long as she kept the comb for him, it would be safe. It would keep the power that she and her grandmother had infused it with over the years of weaving in beauty. When he was ready to complete his *jish*, he would take it.

When they returned to the dining room, Mary did the honors of dishing out her fresh peach cobbler. John changed places to sit next to Adam. He had done his best to wait, but they needed to talk. Adam, however, kept his focus on lighter things as he ate Mary's peach cobbler.

"Mr. Chee, I hear that you like peaches." Adam had a mischievous look in his eye as he caught the man's attention. Of course he liked peaches. All Navajo like peaches.

"My great, great grandfather had many peach trees." Mary handed Chee a second helping, this time with a double scoop of Ben and Jerry's vanilla ice cream on top. "I hope you like it this way. I soaked the peaches with brandy."

The fire had burned down to a warm glow. Bayeta turned off all but one soft light in the corner of the room. The coffee pot made the rounds. A calm, pleasant silence took hold. Mary's cobbler and coffee, the glow of a dying fire, and good company made life in the moment complete.

After what seemed a long time, George Slim spoke. He remembered what Adam told him of John's hobby. He had never met anyone who rode balloons up into the sky. Did John fear being thrown out of "the basket thing" in a strong wind? Did he see ant people from so high up? Everyone laughed and enjoyed listening to John try to explain the difference between hobby and sport.

Conversation meandered in this vein for some time, including warm memories of good times together. Chopin was on the stereo. Soft and constrained, the music enhanced the dreamlike mood that had taken hold. Outside, rain was coming down, its tempo tentative, intensifying when random gusts of wind swooped down. The full force of a continent-wide wall of cloud stretched itself out over

Rimrock. Half an hour later, lightning seared the leading edges of the cumulous mass, and ozone-laden wind raked the desert. Brilliant flashes of lightning preceded long, agitated rumblings of thunder, the promise of black rain.

While Ninaba helped her daughter get extra blankets from the linen closet, Mary volunteered to do dishes. Chee insisted that he would dry them. Mary was pleased at the chance to talk with Chee. Her interest in him was peaked when the subject of his training to be a *hataali* was mentioned. With as much restraint as she could muster, she tried to get him talking without seeming overly inquisitive. He did not know that Mary was an anthropologist. He guessed as much. It did not matter to him, and he was not reluctant to talk about his years of training and preparation. Mary, for her part, did not step beyond the bounds of respectful conversation.

With the others occupied, George Slim went to sit a spell with Alberto, even though the young man was sleeping. Adam, anxious to go to his lab, asked John to come with him.

Entering the outer door to the lab, Adam handed John a fresh lab coat from the shelf by the door. He did it reflexively, without giving it a thought. Adam pushed against the sealed door. A whoosh of stale air flowed passed them. The smell of urine laced with the hint of Formalin made John pinch his nose. He focused his eyes on the test subject cages.

"Adam. Every time I see this, I am impressed."

"It served my purposes. With many things automated, Martin and I handle the routine maintenance and procedures well. I've had time to design the experiments and work up my analyses without much distraction. Martin was really good at handling the breeding program."

"What will happen now?"

"You mean, with the lab?" Adam looked about with a pained look. "Well…" He ran his hand over the empty counter in front of him and surveyed the cages.

"You can help. But first, tell me what happened after I left that fiasco of a ceremony at the meeting. You talked to people afterwards? What with Herman's death, the police asking me questions, that Vaughn taking over the Institute within hours of Herman's body being discovered, all I could think of was to get out of there." John said that Adam had done right by leaving as he did.

"After I left, did you learn anything I need to know?"

"That's hard to say, really. I had the impression that a couple of men Jonathan was talking with knew a great deal more than I did. They kept pressing him about something he had downloaded. Parts of the data were encrypted. They needed the key. Jonathan saw that I had overheard. He did not introduce the two, which I thought odd of him."

"John, I did not want to keep you out of the loop. It is best that you not know what Jonathan has done for me. He did me a favor. Keeping things under his hat was necessary." Adam wanted desperately to tell John all. The material that Jonathan had disseminated was proof that he had found the means to recalibrate the timing of cell division and how, with a regular therapeutic regimen, the lifespan of an organism, shrew or human. Once he had identified how, his experiments had turned to finding the right combination of proteins and amino acids involved. He wanted John to know everything but for his own safety it was best to wait a bit longer. John said he understood.

"My patent attorney has submitted applications. My instructions include a letter stating that the patent is not transferable unless explicitly authorized by me in the presence of my lawyer and Jonathan."

"You are afraid it could get into the wrong hands."

"Yes, I am. I now understand how powerful this man Schwann is. He is also dangerous."

"What that reporter, Ryder, says about Schwann and how he gets what he wants makes me believe he is dangerous."

"One reason I left so quickly was to confuse Schwann and his people, even Vaughn and that creature, Hessen. Also, since Jonathan was the one to send out my stuff, there is no paper trail to follow. If they can't get at me, they won't know where to begin."

John repeated his belief that someone would come after Adam.

"Of course," Adam admitted, "they might. I had that feeling tonight, listening to Chee talk about sleeping outside to listen to the wind. Funny, isn't it? He was talking about something totally different. All I could think was what the wind coming from California would bring to my doorstep."

"It's this weather, Adam. Wind has a way of infecting us all. Rimrock really is a place out of time. Christ, Adam, you are so isolated out here. You would be better off in Albuquerque. If nothing else, you need more security. There is an underutilized lab in my building. It is yours just for the asking. Our security is a damned sight more advanced than what you have here."

"John, I appreciate that. When you go back, take a set of disks with my research on them. Put them in a safe place, but not in your office. I've decided to strike the bell, close the book, and put out the candle. With your help, I am shutting down this lab."

"You don't mean to shut the lab down completely, do you?" John looked surprised and confused. He could not imagine Adam doing such a thing. Research was at the core of his being. If he did not have a challenge before him, how would he cope?

"John," Adam stood at his workbench stroking the edge with his hand, a habit of his to check for dust, "I have given this a lot of thought." He looked about the lab, but his eyes saw only the cages. "I know it has to be done. Now is the time. I can't put it off. You said it yourself, John. Someone will come. Tomorrow or the next day, someone will show up. When they do, I may not have time to decide or think what to do."

He pointed to the small, carefully wrapped package on the next table, the one by the door. "That's your set of file disks that I want you to take back with you." John nodded that he would do as Adam asked.

"It will take a few minutes to erase all the computer data files and corrupt the hard drives. While I do that, you can start at one end of the lab and shut down all the equipment. Unplug everything."

"If you insist on doing this, what about the freezer?"

"Martin took care of it. There are no more specimens to do a postmortem on anyway. Odd, isn't it? Before dinner, I had this impulse to come into the lab to check. I knew that no more would I examine dead shrews, but I felt the need to make sure."

Fifteen minutes later, the computer files were erased and procedures invoked to insure that data could not be recovered. The sounds of a working laboratory, which for so long Adam had taken for granted, fell silent one by one. The staccato clicks of relays stopped. The hisses and puffs of air under pressure ceased. The background buzz of ultraviolet lamps ceased. The only sounds left were the restless rustlings, scratching, scurrying, and whistling of the shrews in their cages. It was night, their active time. There was so much scratching and high-pitched whistling from shrews that had already lived beyond their natural limit. On each cage was a penciled notation, the same as entered in the daily log sheets. John examined the notation for some of the cages. One read 1470, another 1365. The ones on an opposite row ranged from 120 to 400. John scratched his head and counted on his fingers. "Adam, are these numbers, of elapsed days, right?"

"Is what right?"

"That tag indicates 1470." He pointed. "That translates to 48 months and 10 days, give or take a day or two. From what I can see, it looks to be in good shape."

"Ah, that's Lazarus. He's the longest survivor. Experimental subjects live well beyond two years, but Lazarus there, he is the oldest."

John scratched his head again. "You got this kind of result consistently?"

"It is not all that exceptional to find a common shrew that can live for two years. But to get a high percentage to survive beyond two years, that is what is extraordinary. Once I found the right formulary, the longevity curve kept increasing. It came just in time, I can tell you. I was not sure that I could succeed until I worked out the extended age gradient."

"Odd, isn't it, that such a primitive creature led you to the result you were looking for." John stood looking with admiration at the caged shrews. The rustling sounds of the search for food, for sex, for enemies filled the room, amplified by the silence of disconnected lab equipment beyond their wired cages. They had lived in a windowless, weather free, electronically enhanced, sterile environment all of their lives. For the first time, something had changed. Those closest to the two humans standing near their cages, rose up on hind legs, their paws gripping at the wire, heads shifting back and forth as they sniffed the air. Were they curious, anxious, or confused? Whatever they sensed, they were definitely excited. "What about them?"

Adam pointed to the makeshift, compartmented cages in the corner. "As Alberto would say: On to Naples!"

"Can you do that?"

"And why not? They have earned a bit of freedom."

"Some are already geriatrics. I find it hard to imagine a geriatric shrew. Would it be kinder to put them down?"

"Look at it this way: They served without consent. Imagine the thrill—for the first time in their lives to hunt freely, establish territory not confined to a wire cage, procreate, bear and raise young." Adam set the carryall cages on the nearest bench, donned thick gloves, and began patiently retrieving each animal and putting it into a compartment. They could not be put together, for they had not lost the instinct to compete or to dominate. Conflict was certain to rule. For the first time in their lives, it would be up to them to hunt their own scorpions and squeal in the night to proclaim their place in nature.

It was late and the rain had not let up. Even so, Adam and John carried the shrews to the Land Rover parked on high ground. There was a ridgeline running to the north beyond Rimrock, a perfect place for release. In silence, except for the confused, high-pitched squeaks, Adam and John drove out into the night. Each rut or sudden bump caused the shrews to scamper from side-to-side in their cages, sniff the night air, and scratch at the wires. Not since the Pleistocene had such a shrew roamed the Arizona desert. Two miles distant from Rimrock, Adam stopped and released one male and one female. Another fifty yards along, a second pair was freed. An hour later all were free, were on their own. Without hesitation each pair darted off from the circle of light from John's flashlight to find a crevice, a rock, or low spreading vegetation.

In the rain, they had driven as far as the Spider Rock at the confluence of Canyon de Chelly and Monument Canyon. They were strangely moved by the releases. Neither spoke a word.

In a hard driving rain, Adam and John returned to Rimrock and parked next to the kitchen door. John went into the kitchen to make coffee. Adam looked in on Alberto. As he passed the hall door leading to the laboratory, he turned his head away. Like the electrified beast that had for thirty years dominated his recurring dream, the laboratory was now a dark, silent, dead thing. Miles north experiencing their first challenges in rain and cold beneath a clouded sky, Adam's army of volunteers scurried for their own food and future on the floor of their undiscovered country.

With a fresh towel, Adam dried his face while John poured coffee. Both sat at the kitchen table relaxed, relieved. "The first time I saw a shrew in the wild I was fifteen. Uncle John taught me how to coax them into the open. We captured a bunch of scorpions and tied them out in a circle on strings. Before dawn, the shrews came for the scorpions. I couldn't believe my luck. With my legs cramping from having to crouch for hours of waiting, I had almost given up. I wondered if my flashlight would work. Would I shine it at the right spot? Just before I chucked it in, I heard them. I snapped on the flashlight and saw them for all of two or three seconds. In that moment, I had them. It was amazing. Then they were gone. Until tonight I have not felt quite like that since."

John warmed his hands on his cup. "Few of us have a moment like that, Adam." The two men embraced, friends who shared such a rare event. "I have to be back in Albuquerque by tomorrow night. If you like, I can make some calls."

"Thanks. I'll call that detective Kestos. If he calls you, try not to tell him anything."

"The departmental secretary screens my calls. I won't pick up, unless it's you."

"I will spend time with Alberto. Nothing else matters."

"If only to learn where things stood, you had to go to San Francisco. If you had not, someone would have come here. You would not have met Ryder. Hardesty would not have been in a position to help. You would not have seen your father, to say nothing of that crowd at the Kosmoi or The Manse."

"You are right. It forced a lot of things into the open. Now, there is this Mueller character and his boss to factor in. I could have been blindsided."

"For the moment, you have the advantage. They don't want this forced into the open."

"Herman's death, if it is ruled a homicide, may force them to act."

"Have you thought, what if they accuse you of something?"

"There will be rumors, even accusations. Did I use Alberto as a human subject? He lived here out of sight for four years. All that crap about my so-called disregard for controls and oversight could be dredged up again." He leaned stiffly back in his chair and set his hand on John's forearm. "I can make my case against any such slanders."

"They will try to tear you down, you know. They will use any leverage that they can."

"I can't worry about that, not now. I have taken some care. Every doctor's examination and the medical records are safe. My lawyer has copies. Anyone with knowledge of progeria will see that no harm came to him. Alberto has precious little time left. I will do what I can for him."

Adam stood up and walked to the window over the sink. Lightning lit up the sky to the south and west. He leaned heavily against the sink. "No one could have cared more or loved him more." He turned to face John. "It's late. I'm going to hit the sack."

Before turning off the kitchen light, Adam pressed the phone's message button. There were two messages waiting. "Ah, this is Detective Kestos, Berkeley Police Department. Please call me back at…" Adam pressed the delete button. The second message: "I'm going fishing. Talk to you later." Adam would have taken Ryder's call.

John said goodnight and walked down the dark hall to the guest room.

Slipping into bed beside Bayeta, Adam felt her hand reach out. She smelled of fresh mint and frangipani. He leaned into her warm, inviting body. He had been too long away from her touch, too long from the scent of her.

14

Blowing Sand

A shadow drew across Adam's half opened eyes. He sat up, looking intently at the old man who stood beside his bench. "It's not good to lie in the sun too long." Adam did not recognize the man, except by the buckskin pouch he carried. It was a *jish*, a big one. Adam had never seen one, except on display at a museum.

"The daughter of George Slim and Ninaba makes me come." He pointed to the erected hogan.

"I suppose it doesn't look much like a…"

"It is a hogan. It will do. Shape is important. It has a good door. It faces east. We can make a good sing in there." George Slim came out of the house to greet Chanter of the Sun's House. Adam had been told that his father-in-law would negotiate the details of the sing, when the man came.

"You are the son of Eleanor of Albuquerque. She was a good woman." The chanter looked to George Slim, who nodded. "I come to sit and drink coffee." Adam smiled and shook the man's hand. Seeing that George Slim was waiting to speak with the chanter, Adam went into the house, only to have Bayeta ask him to come back out to the patio with her. The chanter and her father were to set a time for the sing, and she wanted him to be a part of what was to happen.

Bayeta was concerned about the likelihood of rain. Would there be enough dry places to put everyone?

"We can put people up in the laboratory."

"Adam! I wish you had not said that." She looked embarrassed. Chanter of the Sun's House had heard. He stretched his neck and looked intently at the laboratory wing. "It is big."

Adam saw the chanter's expectant look as he rubbed his chin. "It's also air conditioned, heated, and has running water. The refrigeration unit works fine."

"Good! The house of *Tse-nis-na-sa* will make a fine place. In the first world, all The People were together. *Tse-nis-na-sa* is our brother. Many can use that place. I will burn sage in that place and make prayer. Then it will be good." He turned to Adam, "Thank you; Father of the *Tse-nis-na-sa*."

Crystal Bayeta looked dumbfounded. In five years all she had ever heard, if she heard anything, were rumors and innuendos. Her husband was called a wizard. Worse, some hinted that he might be a night witch, the laboratory his lair. There were *ch'į́įdii* inside. Neighbors often pointed to the wisps of escaping gases venting from the roof, certain they were dangerous vapors or worse. Now this holy man dismissed it all with humor. The singer called it a "house of shrews," nothing more. Chanter of the Sun's House squeezed her hand to reassure her.

"I will bless that place. We will burn incense. No harm will come to those who enter. People will smell sage in the air. We will walk around it four times and speak of good things. That is what we will do."

Adam excused himself. Alberto had been asleep for hours and he needed to look in on him. The very mention of Alberto's long sleep forced Bayeta's hands to cover her eyes.

<++++++++++>

Earlier that morning Bayeta had asked Adam not to allow Alberto to exert himself. The previous afternoon's bath and dinner had been more than enough excitement. Adam nodded, but she knew. He could not deny Alberto. Being spring, it was time to pick the lilies blooming. Alberto wanted to see the flowers.

"I must, Bea. He asked, and I will not disappoint." Adam had turned to Mary. "I have been instructed to pick a few. I once told him their botanical name, having looked it up. *Hesperocallis* is the desert lily. Alberto insists they are the most beautiful flower of all. He calls them the Evening Star. The Navajo once picked them and ate the bulbs. I will pick them again, later, for the service. They will still be in bloom when needed, he told me. That was hard to hear him say."

Bayeta reached out and squeezed Adam's hand. He suddenly excused himself, insisting he needed to get something before tending to Alberto.

John said, "He's going to take it hard, Crystal. When Eleanor died, Adam stayed with us for a few days after the service. He was like that then, too. Little things distracted him. He went to the old house and tended the flowers, filled her bird feeder, cleaned house. He was unable to focus on anything else."

"That was a long time ago, John."

"How often have you heard him talk about her? Adam never talks of loss or disappointment. Don't forget, I went to college with him. I know how he thinks. He keeps the past locked up inside him, never lets it out. As long as I've known him, he's brooded about Trinity. It's as if some sin rubbed off on him. A month before Eleanor died, she insisted that he take her to Los Alamos. She never liked that place. But she said she had something she had to face there, some unfinished business. He still regrets not coming to take her. If he had, he might have understood why it was so important to her. He's never forgiven himself." John looked to his wife.

"She called us, did you know? We drove her up there. We drove all around Los Alamos but never got out of the car. She just looked and pointed at things she recognized. That night after we returned, Eleanor stayed for dinner. She talked about giving birth, being abandoned, of living in Albuquerque and starting over. She talked as if the twins were still children. She called them her innocents. At the kitchen table she stood and put her arms about Mary. It was like she was a young woman again, talking to another woman of children, family, what was yet to come."

Mary had become uneasy with John's recollection. At any moment, Adam was sure to return. "Yes, he is acting like he did when Eleanor died. Now, he can deny Alberto nothing. He still feels guilty for not taking Eleanor to Los Alamos, for what they could have shared together. Like Eleanor, Alberto allows him to half-believe that death can still be somehow put off, if only a bit. Adam sees time as an uncertain variable. Isn't that really what is at the heart of it? Time is the variable in life that he is at war with. Eleanor told John that was Adam's blind spot, even as a child. She said that he always had this thing about believing time was flexible, changeable, a matter of willing it other than it is."

"When Eleanor died," Crystal responded, "Adam said that time had cheated. He was angry, believing that his mother was robbed of many years. His uncle's death affected him, too, in the same way. He's always believed death is something to overcome, if not forever, for a while."

Bayeta walked to the kitchen sink and looked out of the window at the morning sun and shortening shadows. "Yes, he wants people to experience a full and long life. Life is a celebration of sensation to him, that you know. When he hears of someone with so much promise and so little time, it depresses him. As for Herman, his death will not affect Adam in the same way. He thought Herman's was a wasted life. Life is like an exchange to Adam—good for good, less for less."

"How will he feel when Alberto…" Mary heard Adam's footsteps. "If you are going to make Albuquerque before dark, John, now's a good time."

He patted his wife's hand. "I'll get my bag." He kissed his wife and said his goodbyes

Adam walked John to the car, reminding him to close down the Rimrock computer link. He also gave John a small packet. "Please, put this in the provost's vault at school."

John nodded. "That, I will do." He hugged Adam. "Mary will stay for the sing."

"You know anthropologists, John. If there is ritual to see, she is not able to resist the chance."

John started the car and put it in drive. A few feet down the path, however, he stopped and turned the motor off. "Adam, you know someone is bound to come. You are quite alone out here."

"John, if I thought that for one minute, I'd insist that Mary go home with you today."

"Are you certain that you are not too exposed out here?"

"Odds are they think I am still in San Francisco. I did tell that detective I was leaving, though. He may have assumed that I meant after the funeral and the inquest."

"You were smart to get out of there while you could. Now, why not decamp for a bit? Come to Albuquerque. Out here you are vulnerable."

"People are coming, a hundred or more Navajos will be in and about the house. With the sing Crystal is organizing, what better security is there? I won't be able to walk anywhere without being seen. They will watch after me. They'll know if anyone shows up. They don't miss a thing, not a thing. No, John, we'll be fine."

"But can they really be of much help?"

"With a big crowd of Navajos, what can happen?" Adam said it with a wide grin. He was in good humor. They both laughed. "Call when you get to Albuquerque."

John Sanderson waved surrender and put the car in gear. As the car mounted the rise, the wind was gathering force, driving red sand across the hard, sandstone shelf of Rimrock, scouring it clean. The sky was empty. Adam smelled rain. He thought rain was sure to come after nightfall, tomorrow for certain.

<++++++++++>

An hour later, with Mary driving, the three of them set out for the field of lilies. Crystal stood and watched the car make the rise and disappear into the late afternoon sun. The field was only half a mile away, but to her it felt like an unattainable distance for one so frail. If only it was half the distance, just half.

Adam pointed for Mary to stop the car at the edge of the field. Hundreds of flowers swayed in the breeze. Full bloom was still days away. Mary said, "I see what you mean about these flowers."

"See how many of them are in one place. Some grow to three feet. The Navajos have no explanation for how so many can thrive in this one place. How did they get established? Amazing, don't you think? In spite of blowing sand reshaping the contours of the hillside, they come back year after year. The bulb tastes a bit like garlic. See that green stripe, how it sets off each petal?"

Alberto momentarily aroused and looked out his window. "Please pick some for my room." The wind was picking up, coursing through the expanse of budding flowers. They moved like waves breaking on shore at the far edge of a long buried inland sea. Adam got out of the car to pick some. Mary had only half believed the story of hundreds of lilies coming into bloom in the desert, unattended and not watered. She had to come to see them for herself.

<++++++++++>

With Alberto's deterioration intensifying, Adam fought to not allow it to bore into his consciousness. When Alberto slept, which was almost all the time now, Adam or Bayeta watched for signs of wakefulness. Earlier, while Adam had said his goodbyes to John, Mary had kept busy in the kitchen. Bayeta had gone to her loom, desperate to regain a sense of balance. What was to come next? Beyond the veneer of normalcy, they struggled to maintain. All were doing their best to distract Alberto's preoccupation with his condition. Mary feared saying or doing anything that was awkward. She was also apprehensive over John's involvement in Adam's affair. He would do anything in the world for Adam, even if it put him at personal risk. The irony, she believed, was that Adam and Crystal were now beyond caring or worrying about how Adam's work might alter their lives. In the present they cared only for Alberto and how to make him as comfortable as possible. Not one word was uttered about the morphine drip or his pills.

Sand-laden wind kept up its steady pace west to east. Adam stretched out on the weathered bench at the edge of the patio. He had cocked his head to one side to listen to the wind work its way into and through the temporary hogan set up the day before. His eyes were closed. He was at the edge of his unsettled waking dream.

He had already thought better of his plan to give Alberto a second warm bath. Bayeta's reasoning left no margin of doubt. Precious body heat, which Alberto might not be able to replace, would be drawn off. The deficit from exposure outweighed any temporary relief his swollen joints might receive. Yet, she did understand.

Adam wanted to give way to Alberto's stubborn will. It was Alberto's desire to be free of pain, if only for as long as the bath water warmed him. It was that or the morphine drip. To him, morphine signaled surrender.

The thought of a warm soak had another connection to Adam, one of another place and time. Then, eleven years ago, Eleanor had called to insist that he and Cynthia come home for a short visit. She needed to see them. How long had it been since Adam had taken time off from his research and teaching? Cynthia, of course, would come. She was two hours away by car. At first he put his mother off by talking about the advanced stage of his research. Wisely, he caught himself. Eleanor had asked without in so many words telling why. The snow on Sandia Peak, she had said, was only good skiing for another week. Later and it would be too late. Wasn't that reason enough? How could Adam refuse? Eleanor and Cynthia, though, were the real skiers in the family. And so, Eleanor saw to the cleaning of the cabin and stocking it with food. There was plenty of wood for the recycled redwood hot tub. Adam had had a local contractor install it, though he had yet to use it.

"When you come, Adam, we will sit in that tub and soak away our sins and catch up." Eleanor had always wanted a hot tub, "a bath of renewal." She insisted that no family should ever have to do without one.

That long ago March the three of them had four glorious days on the mountain. Each day was sunny and the temperature rose into the forties by noon. On the last night they sat in the hot tub talking about the skiing, the weather, and Albuquerque neighbors who remembered the twins. Many had sent their best wishes. Mr. Bates, one of their teachers in Junior High, still stopped at the front gate every few days and chatted, asking Eleanor how her brilliant brood was getting on. As a science teacher he took special pride in knowing that two of his former students were doing so well.

Adam and Cynthia had sat each evening in the hot, soothing waters, waiting for their mother to say what was really on her mind. Why had she ***needed*** them to come? She talked about her youth, favorite moments as the twins were growing up, Uncle John, and her life after they had gone off to college. So many friends who had enriched her life were remembered. It was on that last evening, when Cynthia stood up to get out of the tub, that Eleanor broached the real reason. She reached her hand out to grip Cynthia's arm and asked her to sit back down. She began by talking of past failures and disappointments. At thirty-one, she said, she was still naïve. She had met a man a decade her senior. He had a brilliant mind. His manners were that of a cultured European. He was involved in important government work at Los Alamos. The mystery of his work fascinated her. What with the war and his work, he had many secrets. Yes, he had been married. He talked of how science would free the world of fascism. She knew nothing of the Soviet Empire, but believed him when he said it was evil. She entered marriage believing that she could soften the hard edges of this intelligent, displaced soul. But the marriage quickly failed. At that, she broke off her account of those years.

"I have little time left, children."

Seeing their looks of confusion turn to disbelief, and then denial, she continued. "I have tried for four days to find the right moment. I wanted these days to be good ones for us, together." Of course, she said, there is never THE right time to tell one's children that one is to die soon. Sitting in a hot tub and soaking up its palliative heat was the best moment to tell them in a straightforward manner. Neither Cynthia nor Adam found it possible to respond with anything but denials. They insisted that other doctors, specialists, could better diagnose her condition. Clinical trials offered hope. Eleanor listened until both of her children ran out of words. Cynthia spoke through tears. Adam remained dry eyed, but could not keep from shaking. Eleanor smiled throughout, saying, "It's all right, children. It is all right."

Below the cabin two late skiers raced down the slope toward the edge of the snow line far below. There would be yet one more chance to ski in the morning and take a good soak in the tub before returning to Albuquerque. She had had thirty-four years, almost thirty-five, as the head of her family. It was, she insisted, a full and rich life. To be brought up short of three score and ten mattered little to her. She had lived through a great depression and war and had seen her children grow to adulthood. Through it all she had kept her sense of place anchored in Albuquerque, practiced her art, and run her gallery. She had, in short, lived a content and quite adequate life. She insisted it was "quite adequate."

Eleanor had been the root and stock of Adam's sense of family and of place. With her death and that of Uncle John, only Cynthia remained. His father was not part of the equation. Eleanor's fussing at him for not having a wife—no one to love—took on added meaning. She had worried about his "lonely bachelor life" for years. To her way of thinking, it was not healthy, not natural. He insisted that he had not met the woman who would share his life. Nor was he so naïve as to believe that one woman should have the perfect combination of all that he desired in a mate.

Cynthia was different. Early on Eleanor realized that her daughter did not share her attitudes or beliefs about marriage or science. Before she reached puberty, she announced that marriage was never to be for her. Through high school she kept to her stubborn claim. Physics was to be her life. Yes, physics, the thing that stood between her mother and father. She excelled at physics and math. It was a man's world, she admitted, but that was one more reason to pursue it. She had no intention of being a housewife or secretary. No one was going to stereotype her, she said.

When they returned from the cabin to Albuquerque, Adam had stretched out on the wood bench on the porch. He had yet to accept his mother's condition. She was central to his sense of who he was. What was he to do? His visits to Albuquerque had become infrequent due to research and teaching. Nonetheless, his being was tied to her, to her being there for him, in her house, in the house surrounded by the desert of his childhood. Adam lay on the bench, waiting, shading his eyes against the glare. As he had so often waited as a boy, on that bench, he waited for Father Thomas.

Father Thomas, a neighborhood fixture for forty years, said mass every day at the Church of the Sacred Heart, two blocks away. Most of the neighbors were devout Catholics, and Father Thomas was constantly in and out of the homes up and down the block. He baptized their children and confirmed them, counseled and married them, heard their confessions and, when he must, gave them the last sacrament and absolution. Every Monday and Thursday afternoon at the end of the school day, there he would be, ambling down the street on his rounds, stopping before every house. For as long as Adam could remember, Father Thomas was embedded in the cycle of life on their block. Regardless of the weather there he was in his black flowing robes, idly fingering a rosary as he walked. For more than thirty years, Father Thomas had stood at the foot of the steps or sat in an Adirondack chair on their porch. He never pushed his faith. Mindful of the power of grace, he tended to the spiritual needs of his parishioners and was no less attentive to neighbors, like the Grants, who did not share in his faith. For twelve blocks, nearly as far south as St. Ignatius Church, he ministered to every neighbor without exception. Often Father Thomas even ventured onto the soccer field at St. Ignatius where the boys played soccer most afternoons. He knew each Jesuit priest at the St. Ignatius parochial school. They, however, found it difficult to tolerate his presence, though they would never admit it. When they saw Father Thomas with the boys, their vigilant impulses took hold. Boys could be influenced by the likes of a Father Thomas, he a Franciscan. Without fail one or two of the Jesuits would briskly cross the field to engage him in idle conversation, their nostrums laced with ecclesiastic undertones and matters of the mystery of faith. The boys seldom had a clue to what the Jesuits said. They were young, and talk of souls and redemption did not in the least interest them. The boys, however, were perceptive enough to know that when a Jesuit came between them and Father Thomas, it was best to leave.

A quiet-spoken priest, Father Thomas deeply believed in the redemptive power of grace. At the edge of the soccer field he stood his ground with “fine and proper ecclesiasts,” his averted eyes occasionally conveying more than his contrite lips would admit. Jesuits, he once told Adam when he was sixteen, could dissect grace with precise, holy logic. Father Thomas, however, said that grace resided in each person without the need for codified logic. Grace shone in Eleanor, he said.

For thirty-four years Eleanor had lived as a fixed point of light on her block. She knew every neighbor, and they her. In the shade of her Mulberry tree at the edge of the porch, Father Thomas could be seen on a Monday or a Thursday. Like Eleanor, his tenure, too, was long and abiding. As the twins grew, he came to wish them happy day on each birthday. He ate cake and ice cream and drank ice-cold lemonade in the shade with them. He knew all who came to the birthday parties and fit right in. A thousand times he denied that his black cassock was too hot in summer.

He was there, too, when Uncle John came to stay. Monday was their day to sit and talk out on the porch or inside in cold weather. Adam enjoyed listening, often sitting on the porch floor between them. If he had not gone into the priesthood, Father Thomas admitted, he would have been a scientist, some kind of evolutionist at that. He saw no contradiction between the mystery of faith and the wonders of the natural world. His faith admitted Darwin. Eleanor often took time away from her gallery to come home and wait for Father Thomas to come ambling down the street. She enjoyed listening to Uncle John and Father Thomas debate the world and its eternal flux. Differences they argued over mattered less than the ends to which their dialogue strove. Eleanor encouraged her son's interest in the Monday afternoon impromptus. Adam needed the influence of good men and what better men were there?

Six months into the weekly debates between Father Thomas and Uncle John, at the advent of spring, time deserted him. Uncle John became too weak and wracked with pain to continue. Still, he was not satisfied with Father Thomas' conjuring up Zeno's paradox. "I'll leave it to your God, Father, to settle the argument."

The following Sunday, Uncle John asked for Father Thomas. With the family gathered about him, he asked the good Father to bless him. The request caught Eleanor by surprise, but her eyes said yes. Father Thomas bent over Uncle John and whispered his benediction. Uncle John gripped Eleanor's hand and quietly, smiling, surrendered up his life.

During that last painful week, Eleanor forgot how witty her brother could be. Father Thomas reminded her. The problem posed by Zeno had stayed with him through his years of training for the priesthood in Chicago and even after taking his vows. He'd waited so many years to find someone with whom to argue it through, anyone not a priest.

"You see," he said, with Adam and Cynthia listening, "Zeno posited that it is not possible to cross a room by halves. A half forever remains one more measure of distance. No distance is ever crossed by half steps. So, where is the end?" Uncle John, he said, believed that if the time remaining to him was reduced to ten to the minus power of twenty-four, what remained for him was an eternity. The scale of it mattered not. Kepler called God the divine calculus. Still, Newton was not so rash as to impose a mechanistic, linear design upon nature and life. Poor Zeno had but "half measures" to reach the undiscovered country, always a last measure yet to cross. And so, John chose Newton.

The time also came when Father Thomas sat with Eleanor. She had slept most of the night and into the day. The doctor was concerned. She had not wakened since before eight o'clock the evening before. He did not think it a coma, though. He said that she was gathering in her final strength. When she woke, he told Adam and Cynthia, they must be prepared for what might appear to be a rallying. She might appear alert and energized. But it would not last. She would shine bright, as does a light bulb just before its filament fails. Cynthia, bitterly, said through tears, "What do doctors know of eternity?"

That evening as the air cooled, the sun having surrendered the day, Adam called Father Thomas. The nightly Stations of the Cross were but half complete, but Father Thomas came immediately. Entering the room, Eleanor stirred and smiled at seeing him. She became awake and alert. Adam and Cynthia sat by her bed, talking of the little things that made up her days around the house. Neighbors had been coming by at regular intervals to ask about her. Many left behind something they had made to eat. Father Thomas squeezed Eleanor's hand and made the sign of the cross. Her moment of brilliance did not last. He kissed the purple strip of sacred cloth and hung it about his neck. As he bent down to apply extreme unction,

Eleanor winked and whispered, "Just this once, Father." Eleanor Grant smiled and closed her eyes, the lines in her face softened. She whispered, "I see another half-measure to cross."

At the graveside Father Thomas blessed her casket and the open ground that had been prepared. He stood with Cynthia and Adam as the bearers lowered the coffin. "I have been a priest for more than sixty years. In that time, not more than a handful of faithful have I known who filled their lives with such grace and dignity. Your mother was such a rare person. If there is a God, she is surely with Him now."

Although he had been retired nine years, Father Thomas was still allowed by his diocese to live on at the rectory. He still kept to his Monday and Thursday walks, greeting those whom he had baptized, confessed, married, and ministered to in sickness and grief. Between three and four in the afternoon, there he would be, making his way down the street. The children now were different, but the questions were the same. Adam had heard how the old priest never failed to stop in front of the Grant house. A young couple now lived in the house, Presbyterians. Father Thomas always stood long enough to say a Hail Mary before moving on. When asked, he'd say, "That's where Eleanor Grant lived. We all so miss her." He would add, even if not asked, that Eleanor Grant had been called before her time.

<++++++++>

Alexander's left foot was planted at the edge of the chasm as he stared down at the canyon floor hundreds of feet below. He had not wanted to come. He hated the desert. With an incessant wind pressing stubbornly at his back, he bent forward at the waist. His knees buckled. With a thousand feet of sheared rock wall below, he struggled to keep his balance. The sword-like monolith rising from the canyon floor and half way across to the other rim looked to be about eight hundred feet high. He wondered, could a good athlete make it? Might one at a good run, with a pole in hand, possibly make it to the top of that white-capped spire? In his youth he might have imagined such a feat, a triumph to awe the world. The dry heat on his parched skin, the biting sand in his watery eyes, and the numbness in his knees all conspired to confuse him. What was he doing here?

Why had he come? He did not believe in any of it, not now. This fool's errand had already cost him one son. Adam, his only living son, was now in danger. No good could come of this, only betrayal and shame. Why had he not refused? Duty demanded that he be elsewhere, if not to grieve for Herman, at least to console Carol and comfort Marianne. The confusion at the Cockroft house had given him no time to speak of what must be done. Marianne demanded that he take Herman's sons in hand. It was all a blur. Now, here he was in the desert, at the edge of oblivion. One step and it could all end—no more betrayals, no more shame.

"Hey! Which of you sorry bastards is up to taking a leap across this hole in the ground? If you make it, I'll include you in my will." Alexander reached out to the radiating heat of the canyon. Molten air, he imagined it. Below, he saw no sign of human presence. At the edge of the streambed a deer stepped boldly out of the shadows into the light, a magnificent six-point stag. The stag raised his head, nostrils flaring and teeth showing. An involuntary spasm rippled up Alexander's spine. That buck was staring at him, yes, at him! "What might you tell me? Get gone! You do not belong. Get away!" Alexander stiffened his legs and leaned forward to return the beast's stare. But he saw nothing. Could it have been a mirage? He rubbed his eyes and looked again. Nothing!

Had he ever asked himself when he ceased to love his eldest son? Without conscious effort, he tried to recall anyone, even Marianne, ever asking him if he did, or had, or could? Alexander could not think of a time when Herman, the boy or the man, had asked him. Now Herman was dead. "Yes! Spit it out! Spit it out. I loved him. In my own way, my own way, I wanted to love him."

A dark truth rested with those who had lived with Herman. His death had changed nothing, except the end of his pain and frustrations. Herman had lived life in one inexorable drift from insecurity to disappointment, from loneliness to alcohol. Alexander hated his son's weaknesses. He had made excuses for Herman, stubbornly insisting that, in spite of everything, he was a talented administrator. His mania for order and procedure attenuated his flaws. But men like William Henry Schwann saw advantage in them and used Herman for their own ends. Herman believed that he was not a bad person, not good, but not bad. He did admit to himself that he was too weak to resist the temptations of material comfort or the flatteries.

Had Carol ever loved Herman? She had once thought that he had good prospects as a provider and was of a notable family. Herman, for his part, expected little emotional investment from her as her suitor or as her husband. In time Carol's demeaning characterizations of Herman emerged. Alexander remembered all of them. He had never liked her. Could Herman have done better in choosing a wife? Herman's sons, what was there to say? They but spent, idled, and wasted so long as Herman provided.

Alexander stepped away from the abyss. "Am I now to be their provider?" He did not care who heard him, not now, and certainly not here. "Not so much as a kroon or mark, do you hear?"

A massive weather front was moving in. Great phalanxes of moisture-laden clouds were lining up to unleash sheet lightning, sudden flash floods, and havoc on power lines and roads. One thin gap in the cloud mass at the western limit of sky could deceive all but the seasoned desert dweller with a false and dangerous promise of relief.

From where Alexander stood, the half-familiar landscape stirred up a faint echo of the momentous shock wave on one long ago dawn. As it was then, 45 years ago, his companions were committed to a secret business at hand. "And then what, what now?" Only now there would be no blinding light, no second sun, no second coming. Alexander licked at his sour, salt-stained lips. His tongue felt like sandpaper. He could smell his own acrid perspiration. His sputum was thick and frothy, hardly enough to spit out. He had forgotten why he was here, why he had come. Had he agreed to come? Could he have refused? Was he too weak to refuse? Or, too afraid? Was he that feckless? If Herman had lived, it would be he who came. What good was it for either of them to be here? Poor, poor Herman, he could not have refused. But Herman was free now, free of his unfulfilled desires, frustrated ambition, absolved of concern for his own soul. Alexander envied his son's newfound freedom. For once, he envied Herman.

"Alex, Goddamn it, what the hell are you doing? Get back from that rim! Get back in the car!" Pretending not to hear, Alexander stood still. Yes, it was possible to ignore Schwann! It was a new, delicious sensation. He would claim that he simply had not heard. Why blame him for hearing loss due to age? Schwann, to deal with being ignored, turned to the man standing fifty feet from Alexander. "Goddamn it, man, you got us lost!"

Alexander heard Mueller's low, suppressed grunt perfectly. Had he also heard Schwann grinding his teeth and clenching his fists? Without turning Alexander said, his words spilling over the lip of the chasm, "You got us lost a long time ago. You, me, Mueller, we're along for the ride to nowhere."

Mueller heard that, but he pretended not to hear. He never questioned orders. And yet, if Schwann wanted Alexander retrieved, let him be the one to do it. What did Mueller care if Alexander Terman went over the side? That's one less old fart to deal with, he told himself. Yes, Schwann would make him pay. He understood that. Alexander was yet of some use, whether he liked it or not. With measured deliberateness, Mueller silently came abreast of Alexander. Blowing steady and strong, the wind had picked up again.

Alexander listened to the incessant, snake-like hiss of loosed grains of sand scraping Mueller's shoes. Where would that sand end up? Where would he end up? By nightfall, one more layer of time would come to rest at the top of time. What story might that thin layer of sand tell? Would it record his coming, his going? Alexander turned back from the ledge. If the day was to end badly, he was determined to face it on his own two feet.

Since landing at the rudimentary airport south of Chinle, Schwann and party had lost their way. Nothing was working according to plan. Alexander had balked at coming, but could not refuse. He had succeeded only in forcing a small delay. Herman's last act, an irony in itself, caused the delay. Schwann was bitterly inconvenienced. Then, a weather hold at the San Francisco airport kept Schwann's plane at the General Aviation hanger for another three hours. The pilot's apprehensions also frustrated Schwann. Only once airborne did Schwann tell the pilot where they were headed. The pilot questioned whether the plane could set down on the airstrip outside Chinle. He said that they should keep to the flight plan for Albuquerque. Schwann threatened, accusing him of cowardice. The pilot set course for Chinle. On the way, Schwann swore at him almost non-stop. Over Chinle, the pilot circled three times before he chanced the landing. On the ground, Schwann discovered that the telephone lines were down. The commandeered car was unreliable. Getting lost was an indignity for Schwann.

Walking slowly back to the car, Mueller took hold of Alexander's arm. His grip was tight, intent on causing pain. Alexander hated Mueller but was too exhausted, too drained of will, to resist.

"You really are a sorry bastard, Herr Mueller." Mueller outwardly ignored the taunt. He hid his vicious glare behind steel-rim dark glasses. Alexander repeated his taunt, "You're a sorry, mean bastard."

"Just do as you're told, old man."

Mueller's meaning and purpose centered on his prospects for inflicting pain. He exercised his Teutonic talents on command. He lacked emotional content to recognize what anyone other than Schwann thought of him. At the moment his impulse to be violent strained to act. It had been pent up too long. Adam Grant had become something of an obsession. Alexander would have to do to salve his suppressed urges, if only for the present. How much simpler things would have been, if only he had been given free reign earlier. But the "Little Prussian" could not, dared not, act on his own volition. Yet, his moment of direct action against Adam Grant would come. He knew his master's intent. Then he would grab, brutalize, and extract what words only served to frustrate, thwart, and deny.

Schwann stood beside the car, spitting at the ground. The wind caught up his sputum to stain his pant leg and shoe. He turned around and spit again. This time his spit landed on the car's fender, "psit-psit." A horned lizard scurried out from beneath the front tire, fleeing and bobbing his scaly head. Schwann cursed. He was sweating and could not clear the sand from his mouth. He shouted into the wind, "This goddamn piss-hole." No one took notice. He had not reckoned the necessity of his being forced to come to such a vile place. Adam Grant, Alexander's son, had forced him to come to this piss-hole.

"Get back in the car, Alex. We've wasted too much time in this goddamn..." Mueller, holding Alexander firmly in his grip, stood mute. Had he heard?

"Damn you, Mueller, move!" Mueller glared at his master through his dark glasses and pushed Alexander into the back seat of the car. Alexander moaned at being jostled which drew a tight, menacing grin from Mueller.

Their predicament could have been foreseen. That is, foreseen by anyone familiar with local road conditions. Somewhere south of Chinle, the pavement had given out. Four miles farther on, the driver had lost the track of the dirt drift that sufficed for a road. The airport mechanic had called it the Sawmill Turnpike. "Easy enough," he had said.

Slumped down hard against the back seat, Alexander had cared not that they were lost. It amused him. A wrong turn, two, or was it three? Admitting that he was lost, the driver, Mueller's man, had slammed on the brakes five yards from the canyon's rim. The horrid screech of worn out brakes jarred everyone's nerves, except for Alexander. He was already beyond the far edge of caring. Getting out of the car to see, Mueller swore at the driver. Instinctively he fixed the blame on the driver before Schwann assessed their situation and directed his spleen at him. Aroused, Alexander stared out his window. "What a shame! You missed it by three feet."

Schwann had demanded to see the map. The driver got out to spread it out on the front fender, holding it down with both hands against a stiff gust of wind. "Here, here is where we are. Look!" Schwann jabbed his finger at a point on the map. "This is Bat Canyon. Damn it, Mueller, get things straight for once in your life. No more mistakes, do you understand? Not one more mistake, or else!"

Mueller had ignored the threat and bent over the map. He studied the smudge made by Schwann's finger. He looked about in every direction, as if by looking he could find their bearings. He saw where

Bat Canyon was on the map. He saw the turnout area to the north marked in red, a place called Spider Rock. His posture, sullen and tense, could not disguise his distaste for the mission. They had been driving aimlessly on a dirt trace marked as road. In every direction, the landscape was dominated by piñón and juniper. In front of the car was Bat Canyon. That is, if it was Bat Canyon. Did that mean Monument Canyon was to the east? But if that were the case, where had they missed the turn? Rimrock, the airport mechanic had said, was beyond Spider Rock, beyond Monument Canyon, and then east-by-south toward Fort Defiance. What had he said about getting lost? "Don't take that road to Three Turkey ruin. If you do, you are lost for sure." There was only one fork, he said, the left fork. They had passed by three left forks, if that was what they were.

"I don't like this one bit, Henry. We should not have come."

"Alex, shut up! You are becoming unreliable. I would not want that, Alex. You do understand that, don't you?" Alexander did not respond. His watery eyes were fixed on a distant point across the canyon's rim. "Until I have what I must have, don't let me think you a liability. You must talk sense into him. He will regret it if he does not listen. Both of you will regret it."

"He already does, Henry."

"What the hell does that mean?" Schwann's tone was at once confrontational and sarcastic.

"I was just thinking."

"Don't think, Alex. Thinking only confuses you." Schwann folded the map and got into the back seat next to Alexander. The two institute security guards, one the hapless driver, crowded into the front passenger's seat. Mueller took the wheel, cursing the driver for getting them lost. He ground the gears into reverse. Mueller hated manual transmissions, but was a capable driver. Turning the wheel hard and forcing the transmission into third gear, he derived a pleasure bordering on viciousness.

Earlier, on the paved road out of Chinle, Mueller had told the driver to downshift and swerve the car to deliberately hit a snake writhing its way along the road's shoulder. Jarred into alertness,

Alexander had complained that it was so unnecessary. The driver, Helmut, had grinned, "I got the butt end of that one, sir."

Alexander, too exhausted to care, retreated into himself, ignoring the erratic drift that Mueller stubbornly steered. To him, a desert was a dead thing suited for nothing more than the testing of lethal weapons. For that alone the desert served men. The time for such weighty matters, however, was long past. Such tinkering with nature was all but forgotten. Or, was it? His son, Adam, was out there in the desert. Wasn't he tinkering with nature, with human nature? Alexander wanted to believe that Adam's effort had come to something. Schwann believed it completely, else why come? Now, five men were lost on this flat, forbidding expanse of arid earth. Alexander wanted nothing to do with any of it. The idea of living longer, what did that mean to Schwann or to the "Little Prussian"?

Slumped over in the car seat, Alexander grimly acknowledged to himself that he had glimpsed something of the price paid to alter the way of things. Nothing good came from such ambitions. Yes, physics had changed everything, had bent, battered, and burned out the souls of men. He had played his part. Beyond Trinity what truth was there in any of it? He was a burned out soul, his dreams hollowed out at the edge of night in the desert, in the company of men he hated. Now, Schwann dared to show him what future awaited his only living son. As he dozed, with his head pressed against the tattered upholstery of a Navajo mechanic's "loaner" car, Alexander no longer cared what happened to him. He prayed for oblivion.

Schwann had bitterly complained of the heat from the moment he exited the plane at Chinle. If Alexander could have marshaled the strength, he would have chided Schwann. What did he know of heat? He had never faced the heat of radioactive debris clouds and shockwaves following a detonation. The desolation and emptiness Alexander now dreamed of made him recoil from the thought of having to be here again in the desert. His own dried sweat stuck his face to the car's stained armrest. Why was he here? Delirium gripped Alexander. His mind slipped back in time, far back.

The staff car with Alexander and his fellow physicists had bounced and bobbed and rattled along the rutted roads on the trip to

Omega Building. Their makeshift device made to test critical mass, ruefully nicknamed "the guillotine," had functioned with remarkable success. How much was required for chain reaction? Oppenheimer insisted they had to know the exact quantity. He insisted that they had to know if there was enough plutonium for two bombs, not one. Only then could the test at Jornada del Muerto be made. A young man appeared in the mist of Alexander's dream. "You got to drop that slug of pure urchin right through the center. The boat will work. You'll see!" And it did. The plutonium slug slid through the center and the counter measured the effect. A slide rule calculation confirmed what until that moment was but theory. The amount needed for critical mass was now known.

When Alexander's great moment came, that July night, it was cold, wet, and full of tension. No stars were seen. The desert's grip held everyone's attention. Alexander and three companions had driven down from Los Alamos to Obscuro in silence. They wondered if there, beyond Obscuro, their theories would be proved correct. In the predawn gloom they stood in wait, hunters in a blind. One asked, "How big do you think it will be?" Another shrugged, "Who knows? Ask Teller, he's taking bets and passing out suntan lotion." Beyond the bunker and the trenches, "The Beast" slept. What if it turned out to be a still-birthed event? They had toiled, doubted, and waited so long. "We'll see it best here, on Compania hill," Teller had boomed. "In seconds we are going to know a lot more, you'll see."

Alexander squeezed his eyes shut and sank his head deep into his shoulder. A sudden glare and an indescribable silence enveloped him. Then, a queer, greenish-hued dawn enveloped Alexander. He saw a fantastic, boiling plasma rising into the stratosphere, The Greene Lyon. "No! God no! No!"

"Alex, for Christ's sake, get hold of yourself!" Schwann was violently shaking his shoulder.

The car had pitched and slid sidewise, tossing Alexander against the back of the front seat. He smelled stale sweat and tasted blood in his mouth. Blood dribbled down his nose and onto his shirt. He strained to focus his eyes, to dispel the unimaginably intense light that had invaded his brain. Muscular spasms rippled through his arms and legs. "I…I was dreaming that…"

Schwann grabbed at him. "Having a goddamn nightmare, were you, Alex? Get a hold of yourself." His tone was threatening, laced with disgust. "Mueller says you are no longer reliable. Perhaps I should let Mueller have his way with you."

Alexander stiffened and returned Mueller's fixed glare framed in the rear-view mirror. He knew. Mueller wanted to deal with him in his own way.

"Is this hell, yet?"

"Don't go fey on me, Alex." Schwann stared out the window with his dry, wind-scratched eyes. So far, the desert had definitely had the best of him. Schwann did not belong. His pupils had narrowed to yellow-hued slits, reptilian. He was intent on having what Adam Grant denied him. He would not have a desert or any man stand in his way.

Mueller ground the gears into second to take the next rise. At the crest, Alexander sat up to breathe through the open window. He watched Mueller strain to make out what was ahead. Four houses appeared, each two or three rooms in size and widely separated by a sheep coral and open space, only to disappear behind low growing trees and brush. Four or five abandoned cars and a truck, desert corpses, sat rusting away behind the last house. Penned up in a brush ramada beside the road, sheep stared back at them. Alexander saw a house made of rough-hewn logs, mud, lumber, and a single re-used window and door. A thin plume of smoke escaped from its peak and drifted eastward and away.

A half hour later they had seen little sign of human habitation. At four o'clock, they approached a turn-in to the left. They were still lost. Hours had been wasted. Mueller stopped the car at the rude sign nailed to a pine post bound up with rusted barbed wire. Schwann read it aloud, "Tumecho." Schwann ordered Mueller to drive to the houses. Gears ground into first as Mueller spit out the window.

A woman with a porcelain dishpan in her lap sat on a wooden bench near the front door of the first house. Mueller stopped the car fifteen feet from the old woman. She did not raise her head, took no notice of them. The hiss of escaping steam from the car's radiator was high-pitched and steady. Mueller cursed. "That goddamn Indian pulled a fast one. He knew we would break down!"

What choice did the mechanic at Chinle airport have? Mueller had waved money in his face and commandeered the car. Picking up the bills thrown at his feet, the man could tell that Mueller was not one to fool with. He had tried to warn them about the radiator leak. They were not going to get far without making stops to refill the radiator. The gas gauge registered a full tank, but had not worked for years. No, George Curly figured, this bunch was not going to leave the Res, not in his car. With the five twenties in his hand, he handed the man in the light beige suit a Canyon de Chelly National Monument map. It marked some roads on the rim as unpaved. To Mueller's question about Rimrock, he gave the standard, vague response any white man deserved. "Not far. You can't miss it."

Now, with steam rising steadily from the hood, Schwann cursed at Mueller for not watching the radiator more closely. "Mueller, that savage told you what would happen!"

"Don't tell me what…"

"That's enough, Anton! Just get on with it." Schwann wiped his brow with a soiled wet silk handkerchief. "Time, we're wasting time. Find out where we are. Get water for that radiator."

Alexander, stiff and weak, struggled to get out of the car. "Don't drift off, Alex."

"No chance of that, Henry. Where would I go?" Alexander smiled, wondering if Schwann had picked up on his tone of voice. It no longer mattered. Alexander had forgotten why he was compelled to come. He did not want to know. The old woman sitting beside her door made no move to get up. Was she aware of her visitors? He imagined that the old woman knew George Curly's "reconditioned run around." She could have told him that George Curly hauled three sheep from Hastin Klah's outfit that morning in it. As for her visitors, they were coyotes, and up to no good. Men in suits never are. It was best to wait and to watch them.

Schwann hastily examined the map. There was no "Tumecho" marked on the map. And if it had been, what would Tumecho be?

Fifty feet to the right of the hogan, in two manufactured homes, lived Widow Tumecho's two married daughters and their husbands. Her brother, Hosk-Ke, was inside the hogan. From the edge of the clearing, at a safe distance within earshot, children watched. Sheep in the brush ramada huddled together at the far side of the enclosure under a lone tree that afforded shade. Of a make-do appearance, the compound was clean and orderly. Two pickup trucks on concrete blocks, long cannibalized for parts, were planted beyond the sheep ramada. Both had been scraped clean of paint by blown sands. Chickens now used them for shelter and nesting for their eggs.

Alexander stared at the hogan and the old woman with the dishpan in her lap. She slowly stood up and walked inside. Did he hear a door latch slide into place, or just imagine it? Something had distracted Mueller when she slipped away. Pivoting awkwardly on his heels, he looked in every direction for the old woman. Schwann, too, was visibly unnerved. He waved to Mueller to check the houses. Mueller knocked on every door. No response. He stood beside the empty chair by the door of the hogan. In frustration, he pounded on the door. Schwann paced nervously in front of the car.

Alexander walked, stumbled, and aimlessly drifted about. He was cold in spite of the heat. He wanted to lie down. He set himself down in the chair beside the hogan and leaned his back against its wall. Wiping his eyes, he squinted at the children crouched behind bushes. They watched the white men.

An outhouse, its door on rusted hinges, faced east, and a clothesline separated it from the two houses. He thought it odd to see the outhouse face due east. He watched the sheep, how they stared intently at the spectacle of Mueller pounding on doors. Forty yards south was a crude earthen dam and a patch of garden and cornfield. Frayed, dried corn stocks bent and swayed in the wind.

Nausea welled up in Alexander's stomach and chest. He tried to stand. He made for the privy. His entire being was focused on the outhouse's construction to ward off the pangs surging through his intestines. Made of barn boards and corrugated roofing, it tilted slightly on its foundation. The door hung ajar. He wanted to empty his bowels, urinate, and throw up all at once. Spasms coursed through his back muscles, legs, and arms. He wanted to fall down. A few steps from the outhouse, he heard Mueller. "Goddamned savages! No plumbing!"

Desperate to control his bowels, Alexander yelled at Mueller: "Don't step on that snake!" Mueller reflexively jumped to one side. Alexander bent over laughing. One could have been there. Fighting off the constriction in his chest, Alexander stopped short of the outhouse to catch his breath. He counted, "One, two, three steps more to go, just…"

"Heat got you Alex?" Schwann stood by the car, arms folded across his chest, rocking on his heels. Pain never failed to amuse Schwann, even pain that he had not inflicted.

"Shut up, Henry"

"Anton, get a bucket, anything. There's water in that dam over there." Mueller did not respond. No one but Schwann ever called him by his first name, not to his face. Nor did he like hearing Schwann use it. "Get something, Anton, anything. You can do that, can't you?"

The sarcasm stiffened Mueller's back. He stood very still, facing Schwann. He had big feet, size 14-E, made larger by the shoes' thick, black soles and white cotton socks. An angry gust of wind stirred the dull brown soil at Mueller's feet, dusting his scuffed shoes and dirty socks. The flap of his jacket blew back, exposing his thick, black belt cinched tight against his rock hard, round belly. The in-seam of his pants rubbed up against his scrotum, a constant irritation relieved only by his scratching. He was a titan with deep-set, brooding eyes and a face that belonged in a Kaiser's helmet. But for all his size, in the presence of Schwann, he seemed small, a diminished being. Herman Cockroft had taken perverse pleasure in calling him "the Little Prussian with an itch." Herman also had chided him as one having never been seen with a woman. Nearly bald, with only a wisp of close-cropped hair about his temples and the back of his nape, Mueller personified the sexless, brutal eunuch. As he faced Schwann, he gave concrete form to the enslaved will of a displaced Prussian Janissary.

Bent over and gasping for air, Alexander watched a mute Mueller stand his ground. He had seen such men, men who hated commands, yet always obeyed with perfect abject obeisance. He had seen Mueller's kind strutting their way about the streets of Tartu, keepers of an alien iron rule. Mueller blinked and cocked his head to one side. He scraped the ground with his left foot and stared back at Schwann. The eastbound wind hissed its sand-laden purr. The open ground before Widow Tumecho's hogan had, if only for an instant in time, become a proving ground of enslaved wills.

Bent over in pain within feet of the outhouse, Alexander stared at Mueller, then at Schwann. With effort, he straightened. He entered the privy and sat down on the one-holed bench. He was no longer nauseated. He grinned through the pain intensifying in his chest. He was determined to watch the standoff even through a pile of vomit. He'd seen Mueller act like that often enough to Herman. But, for him to stand up to Schwann, that was new, unthinkable. Could it be the heat? Could being lost have brought it on? They had lost their bearings toward one another. What of the bodyguards, Helmut and Guenther? What use were they? Were they nothing but dead weight?

Alexander looked down and cupped his head in his hands, distracted by the ants at his feet. He leaned forward, half out the privy's door. On its rusted hinges, the door swung faintly with each gust of wind. At his left foot the ants probed and retreated, determinably seeking an invisible path leading them toward an unseen objective. Alexander let the ants be. It was Mueller with a rusted gallon can in hand that interested him. Mueller stood at the lip of the earthen dam, hesitating. Then he was gone, over and down the side of the dam. Alexander tried to breathe, tried to compose his thoughts. What was he doing here?

"Alex, damn it, where are you?" Schwann's head pivoted from side-to-side, like a lizard. He licked the air with his long, meaty tongue. "If I did not need you..."

"Yes. If you didn't need me, I would not be... If you did not need..." A raging fever flared up and clouded his brain. Lack of sleep and dehydration had sucked dry his reserves. The core of his being, reduced to nonentity, was now but an exhausted appendage to

Schwann's tragic, comedic drama. He wanted to lie down, to close his eyes, to sleep, to forget. A distant, angry voice spewed out demands—meaningless, useless demands. He no longer cared to listen. "Why am I here?"

An agitated wind brushed against the privy door. The heat of the day died away as a late sun turned deep red low in the west. At the edge of the brush ramada, a confused jackrabbit froze in place. To the south beyond the compound, a monotonous creaking noise synchronized with each shift of wind. Wood scraping against wood, it became an empty, mournful portent of desolation that seized Alexander's attention. He watched Mueller slog back to the car carrying the water can, spilling half its content on the ground, on his pant legs, on his shoes. Those shoes, black enormous shoes caked with thick, rust-red mud were what Alexander saw. Mueller had slipped on the mud at the water's edge. Mud an inch thick peeled off his heels with every step. He cursed, kicked, and scraped at the ground in frustration. His shoes would never again shine. Alexander smiled at the irony—he sitting on a one-holed privy in the middle of nowhere, Mueller staring down at his ruined shoes, Schwann trying to read a map.

As he filled the radiator, the sound of a motor distracted Mueller. He cursed the water can, spilling muddy water on his pants. He looked like an old man who had pissed on himself. The sound was intermittent but coming closer, from the west along what passed for a road. A column of red dust marked the vehicle's advance. At fifty yards a faded blue pickup appeared. Spattered in dried mud and dust, the windshield obscured its occupants. Both headlights were missing and the front grill was bent and rusted, a testament to its use in pushing vehicles out of ditches. Three bodies could be vaguely seen in the front seat. In the pickup bed six people sat clinging to its sides. Schwann motioned to Helmut and Guenther to stand with him by the car. For the second time that day, Schwann betrayed an uncharacteristic emotion—vulnerability. The pickup came to a stop. The occupants stared at Schwann impassively. To them he was not master of the moment.

Guenther, who was closest to Schwann, unbuttoned his jacket. The butt of his holstered pistol was visible, its safety strap unbuttoned. Gripping his belt with his left hand, Schwann made a clenched fist with his right. Dressed in his spotless Savile Row suit, pale beige alligator shoes slit along the insteps, a white collared pressed silk shirt, and dark blue tie, Mr. William Henry Schwann shielded his face with his light brown felt hat—the epitome of urbanity, a tycoon. But in this remote desert reach, his eyes lurking behind dark metallic sunglasses, he was somehow diminished. In Widow Tumecho's front yard he was a caricature of something alien. He was a trespasser. The Navajos waited for Schwann and his companions to consider their position and leave, to retreat.

Alexander, in delirium, conjured a movie with Indians on war ponies circling a wagon train of settlers. "Yes, you're not so big now. Go on, big man; let's see you order them around." A grim, weak smile broke out on Alexander's parched, cracked lips. His mind swam with violent images.

Two men and a woman, the woman holding a baby, were in pickup's cab. In the open bed sat six men and women, along with wood apple boxes filled with pots, food, wrapped packages, and blankets. Only the scraping hiss of the intermittent wind gusts interrupted the enforced silence. The Navajos showed no sign of getting out of the pickup. A minute passed in silence. Finally, a male voice, quiet, deep, and unhurried was heard. His words were undecipherable to the strangers.

The sound of a door latch being opened and the creak of seat springs signaled that the driver was getting out of the pickup. About thirty years old, the young man was tall and muscular. He wore a red Pendleton shirt, cuffs folded back on each arm, and a turquoise and silver bracelet on his right wrist. He wore faded jeans. As he raised his left hand, his silver and inlaid turquoise ring caught the light. He stepped forward, a formidable presence framed by the rays of a dying sun. He wore a three-strand turquoise and abalone shell necklace with a large silver sandcast *Naja*. The *Naja* resembled folded protecting hands, a turquoise stone set into its axis. A faded, dark blue cowboy hat shaded his eyes. The hat was streaked with dried sweat and red dust, a crown for a man used to hard work. The brim sported a leather band with small silver conchas inlaid with greenish-gold turquoise. For all the weathered and worn appearance of the man's face and hands, he exhibited a vital presence, pure form and substance.

He stepped smoothly, deliberately, over the open ground in light brown, hand-tooled cowboy boots. The stiff leather creaked of newness. He knocked at the door to the hogan. Had he not seen Widow Tumecho's unbidden visitors? He gave no hint of it. Patience, a thin commodity to Schwann, failed him. He determined to be recognized. Pivoting on his heels, the dust at his feet roiling up, he addressed the Navajo who now had his back to him.

"You there!"

But the man, standing at the now opened door, appeared oblivious to Schwann. Schwann cleared his throat and stamped his left foot on the ground.

"Do you speak English? You there, Indian, do you…" Still the young man did not turn.

From the pickup the others stared at Schwann and at Mueller. They watched, impassive and stolid. Strangers whose intent was not known could be assumed to be ill omened. The young man was now talking at the door of the hogan.

A minute passed, perhaps two. The calm, unhurried Navajo voices mingled with the sharp, plaintive yips of a mongrel puppy held by a woman in the pickup's bed. It squirmed and yipped until a firm hand settled it back onto the floor. With the sun now low behind the hogan, an old woman stepped into the fading light. She looked toward the pickup, waving her right hand, "*Yá'át'ééh.*"

Alexander heard and closed his eyes. He tried to fix in memory the image of the man standing at that door. He was so beautiful, more so than any man he had ever imagined existed. The sureness of his step had captured Alexander's imagination. The young man's arms swung so smoothly at his sides, rhythmic, effortless—grace personified. His hands were jeweled talons. His necklace swung in unison with each step, catching the light. The whole being of the man was that of a great hawk with speckled breast feathers and proud mane. Aloft on that flat expanse of ground, he was the master of light and air, a perfected being.

Struggling to his feet, Alexander leaned forward for a better view. The Navajo was absorbed in conversation with the old woman who had earlier mysteriously evaporated with her dishpan. Schwann still stood by the car, looking tense and confused. For the first time, Alexander saw a mute and diminished William Henry Schwann. In this place his presence served only to amplify the form and substance of another man.

The sun slipped away, and with it the heat retreated, leaving graying shadows to gather about Widow Tumecho's compound. Four confused and frustrated white men stood in this place beyond the known or knowable world of William Henry Schwann. Each one harbored unspoken frustration and regret. Alexander, however, did not regret. Here, he had seen such a beautiful man. He had witnessed the diminishment of his hated familiar in his too finely tailored suit. With his suit hanging loose on his withering frame, Schwann was no match for such a man. A prolonged spasm of involuntary twitching worked its way across Schwann's face. His lips twisted. His head jerked sidewise to shake off the spasms. The veins of his neck pulsed violently, the exhausted channels of anemic, senescent blood. What next? Alexander cared not. He had glimpsed the eclipse of his age-old associate, now nemesis.

The older man who had sat in the pickup now stood beside the young Navajo. How had he gotten there? Without sound or a hint of movement, he had crossed the open space to stand at the door with his companion. The wind smothered their indecipherable words as they spoke. A stray dust devil skirted the rounded sides of the hogan. Like billowing sails on ships of the desert, the men's shirts caught up the agitated air. Their arms, great bowsprits, rose and swept the air before them. Such men were beings true to the wind, true to the course they set. They belonged.

With unhurried steps, the two Navajo men crossed the open ground to face the white men. Steady and sure as two China clipper ships with wind at their backs they came. Schwann and his minders leaned back and away at their approach. Trapped by uncertainty and the dimming light of a departed sun, Schwann stood transfixed, unable to marshal his defenses. Straight and tall as a mast, the older Navajo led. The men's leather boots creaked softly as they plowed the disturbed sand at their feet. Their hard goods about their necks whispered on the wind, as would well-tempered fittings secured to sturdy masts under full sail. Alexander recognized these men, these masters of the moment.

Coming to a halt at five feet, they eyed Schwann and his men squarely and completely. Then, they turned and walked to the car. They paid no special scrutiny of Schwann, scarcely noticing him. Mueller, however, was another matter. Their estimation was plain: Of the five trespassers, Mueller was the one to keep in view. Unbidden strangers always were trouble, and these five were up to no good. White men in suits driving over dirt tracks of Monument Canyon and Coyote Wash could only bring trouble. It was best to keep clear of them. Their purpose would show itself in time.

Occupied with pouring muddy water from a rusted tin can into the radiator, Mueller had left the matter of speaking to the Navajos to Schwann. But it was Mueller whom the Navajos watched most. At George Curley's car, they faced Mueller and stood waiting for the inevitable barrage of questions. Such white men were not about to introduce themselves or make acquaintance. Only the big man in an ill-fitted suit was engaged in an act with a purpose. Cars, like horses, demanded care.

With no words forthcoming to break the ice, the tall Navajo raised his right hand slowly and deliberately and looked directly into Mueller's eyes. He did not speak. He waited for this big, rough-looking white man to speak. But Mueller stood stone still, looking intently at the Navajo's wristwatch, one with a silver and turquoise band. On his firm, slender frame the man's jeans were close fitting, faded and worn smooth about the knees and pockets from long exposure to sun and hard work. He took out a pack of Camel cigarettes bulging from his shirt pocket. The older man took a pull-tie bag from his shirt pocket and proceeded to roll a cigarette. Obviously, he preferred to hand-roll his own.

The wind was dying, in retreat at the advance of twilight. In his element, the elder Navajo man was patient, calm, one who belonged. Alexander again admired the form and substance of such a man, a being not diminished by the likes of Schwann. The elder Navajo's nose was long, a proud nose that cleaved the air not by force but by its very being. Alexander rubbed his eyes to take in the whole of the man. He saw a man of capacities, one others looked to for guidance and action. His peppered hair was tied back Navajo style with a bright red bandana. And there was Schwann—decrepit, debilitated, and debased. For the first time, Alexander believed that at last he understood Schwann's true measure.

Alexander was deep in the moment, as immobilized as a fossil encased in Baltic amber. And yet, transfixed by the drama before him, his mind drew in the image of his only living son who had chosen to live in this desert, a place such as this. At last, finally, he glimpsed the bond between such men as these Navajos and Adam. His son chose to live apart from Alexander's world, apart from men with thinning blood and stale seed. The desert was no place for the likes of Schwann or Mueller. This desert belonged to men of open purpose and simple, practical virtues.

"Mister, you come to see Little Mother Tumecho?" Mueller stared hard at the Navajo, his bloodshot, pale eyes blinking to ward off the blowing sand. Half empty, the can he held had a leak. It dripped down onto his shoes.

"She rests now. You must go away." Hearing the Navajo speak English, Schwann stirred and walked briskly to Mueller's side. The elder Navajo said with finality, "You must go." He did not tense or show sign of noticing Schwann.

Schwann's hands shook. He clenched them to gain control. Palsied spasms ran up both arms and into his neck and jaw muscles. "Now look here, you!" At his side, Mueller was on the edge of rage, had been all day. Since the hasty pre-dawn departure from the Oakland airport, he'd been constrained, too tightly wound not to lose control. Reflexively, his hand cleared the flap of his jacket, the pistol showing.

"You are lost. If you do not belong, it is easy to get lost." The elder Navajo smiled and stretched his neck to look in all four directions, perceptively, calmly. He fixed his eyes on the white men standing in his sister's front yard and the lone figure leaning unsteadily against the side of the outhouse.

"What do you want?" He knew how to speak to strangers.

Mueller withdrew his hand and let his jacket fall back into place. "We are lost. Show us the road to Rimrock. You do know Rimrock, don't you?" As an insult, Mueller snapped his neck to one side, showing his tense swollen muscles. Sweat dripped from his chin. "Yes. You understand me."

"This Widow Tumecho's place. Maybe you want to buy a rug?"

"Look, we don't want anything from you. Just tell us the way to Rimrock."

The younger man, his arms wrapped tightly about his chest, walked to the car behind Mueller. Mueller unfolded the map on the hood. The Navajo looked. "Um, this map's not so good. Tourist maps are no good."

Mueller pointed his finger unsteadily at the map. The Navajo continued to smile and glance at the map, not touching it. "This is not a good map. You want Highway 7 maybe, see Spider Rock?"

"We want to go to Rimrock. Which road is that? Can you mark it on this map?"

"We got many, many rocks." The young man backed away from the car and map. "Park people give you that map? They don't drive out this way much."

Schwann was now beside Mueller and pointing at the map, waiting to extract some sign of the direction. With no answer, Schwann's expression became that of a startled child. The Navajos in the pickup bed, without being noticed, had surrounded them. Four more had emerged from the houses. The children who had been watching from behind the bushes of the sheep ramada now ran about the open ground laughing, though their eyes never left sight of the men. The air smelled of musk and sheep dung. At a distance, Alexander sniffed the air, taking in its elusive, delicious, earthy scents. The smells were somehow familiar to him, sweet, earthy, and very old.

He had caught scent of wet sheep's wool and sage. He hungered for his mother's cooking. He sniffed at the air, thinking of his mother's lamb soup with cabbage.

Two women now stood near the outhouse watching Alexander. They stood quietly, their bright blue blouses and shining velveteen skirts caught up in the intermittent breeze. Broad hipped and high cheek-boned and their skin deeply bronzed, they eyed Alexander impassively. A third woman, young and thin, crossed Alexander's field of vision. Her deep-blue velveteen dress billowed out as she walked. Her silver and turquoise necklace and earrings swayed with each step, making Alexander dizzy. He listened to the soft tinkling about her neck, a synchronized murmur of sound embedded in color and light. He felt a lightness of spirit that had eluded him for sixty years. The dying wind shifted and cooled by degrees. Alexander's insides turned. His lungs burned. His chest smoldered. Delirious, he stood, stumbled, and fell to one knee. An old woman's hand reached out to steady him.

Schwann swung around looking for Alexander. He did not know that Alexander had deserted him. Alexander gripped at his chest and bent over to vomit. "No! No! Not now! Not here!," he thought. He struggled to stand, raised one arm above his head, as if to shield his eyes. He spun unsteadily in a circle, reaching for something above his head, something that was not there, a monstrous creation he knew too well.

"Anton, get hold of Alex! Get him into the car!"

Mueller tossed the tin can away and went to grab hold of Alexander. He caught Alexander as he again fell to his knees. Mueller pulled him to his feet and dragged him to the car like a sack of coal. Schwann opened the car door, and Mueller roughly put Alexander in the back seat.

"Heat prostration, the damn fool has had it," Schwann growled.

"Dead weight," Mueller cursed, his eyes narrowing to menacing slits.

"Shut up, Anton."

With Alexander reduced to an inert object of pity, a burden, Schwann seethed with pent up rage. They were lost. His intent had been frustrated. Night was coming. "Indians" were mocking him.

The handsome young Navajo tipped his hat. "Too old to stand is not good."

He looked to his elder. "Luke Many Goats says you must go now. You now got water for George Curly's radiator. Go back to Chinle." The elder pointed to the north and turned away.

There was nothing more to be said. Mueller got in and started the car. The others got in. He turned the wheel and drove back on the dirt track that led in a westerly direction, grinding the gears and giving no sign of trying to avoid ruts. Alexander, unconscious, leaned hard against Schwann. He tumbled headfirst, forcing Schwann to cradle him like a child. Cooled by air streaming in the window, Alexander roused himself. He opened his eyes. "Ah, we have arrived. Sweet Jesus!"

What had Alexander seen just beyond his reach, as he sat in the one-hole privy? A tantalizing chimera, a thing bound up in blinding brilliance, white-hot and churning? He was again lost in time, standing in a bone-chilling, tense dawn. He, the son of Earnst and Friida Jogeva, was at last a proud man. This brilliant little urchin from the dusty streets of Tartu longed for the chance to make one's self new, to have a new beginning. Again, time slipped its groove. He was now far from Tartu, a place beyond the stream of great things. A sharp pang gripped his chest. Again, time slipped its groove. A blinding, penetrating heat pierced the deepest recesses of his optic nerves. His parents stood beside their humble door waving. "Time to come home," they said.

It felt good, the cool air streaming through the open window. It tempered the fire that raged within him. He ached from standing at the edge of the canyon rim staring into the abyss. He felt the grains of sand driving past his feet. The abyss of sheared rock wall below his feet hovered in shadow. He imagined that the desert wind moved with purpose. It had pulsed hard against his back. He had braced against it, struggled against it. His impulse had been to take that one step, that last step. In the dying of the light, a house appeared.

Alexander was hungry and very tired, but home was in sight. Mother would have fresh black bread and hot Nami-Nami soup waiting. He reached out with his right hand. The wind, cooled by a fresh sea breeze, was at his back. It propelled him through the threshold of the opened door.

Steering through the deepening gloom, Mueller held stubbornly to a northerly course. At last, the Canyon de Chelly Visitor Center appeared, and then the outskirts of Chinle. He stopped the car in front of Rose Bia's Cafe. Schwann commanded him to ask about a hotel. For the moment, Schwann had surrendered. It was out of character for him. Rimrock could not be found in the dark, not over rutted traces of dirt road. For the night Rimrock would have to remain beyond his reach, somewhere safe out there, away and beyond Indian Highway 7.

Entering the cafe, Mueller stared at the men sitting at the counter. They ignored him. It was Chapter Night. The cafe would empty out soon, as the men went to their meeting to talk of rain, of grazing conditions, when to move stock into *Tseyi*, and of the strangers parked outside Rose Bia's place.

Schwann waited in the car, determined not to have to deal with more "Indians." A red Ford Wrangler rolled up behind George Curly's car. The crackling sound of a two-way radio made Schwann sit up. He saw a tall, well-built Navajo with a holstered sidearm get out and approach the car.

"Good evening, gentleman. Nice evening for a country drive." Schwann stuck his arm out the window and gave the man a dismissive wave. In the front seat, the two security men sat staring straight ahead. They pretended not to notice the badge.

Clyde Yazzie made a second attempt to engage Schwann, his eyes on Mueller inside the Cafe. "You gentlemen are planning on returning George Curly's car sometime this evening, is that right?" Schwann gave the policeman a second long, disdainful look.

"George, the mechanic over at the airport, called me. According to him, you promised to return his car by 4 p.m. Have I got that right?"

"We got held up," Guenther said without turning his head.

"Looks like the radiator ran out of water, what with that steam rising from the hood."

"We figured that out, Officer," Schwann replied with sarcasm.

"Call me Clyde. We like to know people by their first names out here." Officer Yazzie stepped back to get a better look at the car's occupants. "What with this not being the tourist season, we don't get too many folks in town after dark. You plan on staying maybe at the Thunderbird Lodge?"

"We're on our way to see someone."

"I see. Who are you planning on visiting? Maybe I know them."

Schwann took his eyes away from Officer Yazzie. The two security men remained rigidly still in the front seat, their eyes trained on the visor mirror. They watched Schwann, awaiting his command.

Clyde Yazzie kept his broad, steady smile as he focused his eyes on each man. A cautious man, Clyde paid closest attention to the two men in the front seat. He did not like talking to men who wore dark glasses, not with the sun having set. He also watched the big man who was in the cafe speaking to Rose. He stood at the rear passenger side window and looked at the man who appeared to be asleep in the back seat. Taking a good second look, he shined his flashlight on Alexander's face. Clyde stiffened and stepped back. "What's the matter with him?"

Schwann growled, "Nothing, he has a touch of sunstroke."

Clyde took his hat off and wiped the sweat from his brow. "You never know what sun can do to a man out in it too long, do you?"

Officer Yazzie turned and went to his vehicle. Picking up his radio mike, he spoke quietly in Navajo. "Mary, this is Clyde Yazzie, over." The radio crackled. "I'm in front of Rose Bia's Cafe, Mary. We got five men in George Curly's car, five *bilagáana*, well, four anyway, and one *ch'į̨́idii*."

The radio crackled and spit, a confused woman's voice was heard. "Better send me some backup. Notify the State Police. We're gonna have to sort out what these men are up to, over."

Schwann had not understood a word, but he grasped the essence of what the Navajo cop had said. He reached over to feel Alexander's skin. It was cold, stone cold. Preoccupied, it had completely escaped his notice that he was sitting next to a dead man. Alexander's mouth was partly open, his lips twisted to one side. His eyes, wide and vacant, stared straight ahead. How many miles back had Alexander slumped back against the seat? Schwann had ignored Alexander's saying that he was in the company of men he hated. Alexander Terman, son of Friida and Earnst Jogeva, had deserted them without notice. Nor would he, or could he, acknowledge that at last Alexander was free. Guenther leaned over the front seat to look. Schwann started to speak but for once words failed him. Dejected, he slumped back in his seat.

Officer Yazzie went into the cafe and spoke to Mueller. He spoke of *ch'į̨įdii.* Rose, nervous and animated, dropped her coffee pot on the floor. "*ch'į̨įdii?*" A dozen Navajos and a stray family of tourists gathered on the sidewalk, a good distance from the car. A man, brushing the side of his jacket as if shooing flies, caught the mood. In silence, the crowd dispersed.

"Poor George Curly, he's gonna need a sing for his car, maybe have to junk it," one man said. At a distance of forty feet, men stood at the curbside. What was Clyde going to do?

Mueller had by now returned to stand beside Schwann. Officer Yazzie reached out his right hand for the car keys Mueller's held. With his left hand on his gun holster, Officer Yazzie spoke to Schwann and to Mueller. "Until the State Police get here, you men better sit back and relax. You have some story to tell. It is best you get it straight."

Returning to his vehicle, Clyde took his pistol out and pointed it at the ground. For the moment, with onlookers watching, the advantage was his. He did not doubt that the men were armed. They looked like trouble. He had had his eye out for them since talking with George Curly. He had also questioned the pilot, who readily admitted that he didn't like having to fly them. This was not a usual flight, he had said. Three of the men were armed, he said, making no effort to conceal the fact. All that he wanted was to get back to Oakland. Whatever Schwann and party were up to, he insisted, it had nothing to do with him.

Clyde reassured the pilot, "You just file a proper flight plan. I'll round up your cargo." The pilot agreed. He'd refuel and submit a flight plan.

When Mueller had emerged from the Cafe, he was unaware of the development. He'd been occupied with the woman in the cafe. Reluctantly, she had allowed him to use the phone to call the airport and locate the pilot. No one had answered. What if he had known that Schwann was sitting next to a corpse, in the dark, on First Street in Chinle? What could he have done? For once, Schwann had no recourse, but to submit. Mueller was in no position to fend off his nemesis of the moment.

A long ten minutes passed before a black and white patrol car rolled up. "Clyde, what's the situation? The dispatcher said something about a dead man and four suspects."

"I'm glad you got here quickly."

"I happened to be up the road talking with your dispatcher. What's the situation?"

For the next two minutes, Officer Yazzie filled in Sergeant Wallace and Officer Smits from the State Police barracks in Ganado. He was succinct and stuck to bare facts. Even so, it took telling to construct the essentials.

"Seems these fellows landed before noon. They came in on a Learjet, one of those corporate jobbies. They gave George Curley a hundred bucks, said they needed his car for a few hours. George is no fool. It wasn't like he needed the hundred bucks to let out that old car of his. But, he was not about to say no to that crowd."

Yazzie pointed at the car. "They're packing guns. Anyway, he called me, said his car, as it's got this slow radiator leak, can't go far. He did not want to be responsible if anything happened to those characters. They sort of ignored his warning about the radiator, you see."

"I got word they were out beyond Monument Canyon, over by the Widow Tumecho's outfit. Her son-in-law called to say they had been there and were acting real funny. I figured they had but one place to end up after sundown, if they're not complete fools, that is. So, I hauled down Highway 7."

"I spotted them over by the turn-off to the Thunderbird Lodge. In town they parked just where you see the car now. So, I rolled up behind. I could see they were nervous and did not want to talk. I wasn't getting much out of that one the back seat. He spoke as if he was in charge. After a bit, I see that this other guy in the back seat is dead. He's dead as a doornail. That other gentleman was sitting there as if nothing special had happened. That other guy, the big one, was in the Cafe making a call. What I wonder is what they planned to do with the dead man."

"Well, Clyde, we'll see about that. For now, we have enough to hold on to them."

Clyde looked to the crowd that had reformed at a distance. By now everyone in town knew about the dead man parked on their street. "The folks around here are going to be pretty jumpy tonight. They don't like having a dead body parked out front of Rose's place."

"You mean chindi, don't you, all that ghost and corpse powder stuff and all?"

"That's right. I'll call for an ambulance. They'll come and get the body."

"We'll transport these men down to Ganado and sort all this out."

"Thanks."

"It's too bad about George Curly."

"Yeah, he won't ever get in that car again. I'll call for towing."

15

Born for Water

For five years Bayeta had found ways to avoid the matter of neighbors' feelings about Adam's laboratory. Of course Adam knew of the rumors and suspicions. At first the men in Rose Bia's Cafe quietly tolerated him. Some nodded, then looked away. On the street a woman's hand might rise to brush away an imaginary stray strand of hair as she averted her eyes. It was just so. But with time he became more a fixture of the environment than an object of gossip. Women now smiled shyly at him. Men tipped their hats without slowing their gait. A few, Johnny Kabito for one, would stop him on the street to say hello and ask about Bayeta. She was kin to some. However, Rimrock itself was not mentioned. That would have fed their anxiety over something they did not understand—what the laboratory was about.

Today, however, the laboratory was nothing more than a windowless building attached by a covered walkway to the house—no more gas venting, no air conditioning hum, no equipment running. Chanter of the Sun's House had called Adam *Tse-nis-na-sa*, knowing that he had freed his army of shrews. To the singer, it was a good thing that the animals had at last found their proper place. For Adam, the irony was that for the first time his shrews were free to be manic predators living brief, intense lives. There was no Navajo word for a shrew, not a specific one. Mr. Chee called them *Gah din'é Táchii 'nii*, *Táchii 'nii* signifying "Red-Running Into-The-Water-Clan." A weaver at Cameron, a *Táchii 'nii*, once pointed out to Bayeta the red sand and silt in the river, saying that *Gah Diné* meant the rabbit people. Now, Adam's "rabbit people" were free to mate, pursue scorpions, and live as they were meant. He missed them.

It relieved Bayeta knowing that the lab, for the time being, was idled. But it did smell. No matter what the singer said, she doubted that burning sage incense would mask the odor of formalin. Her people knew that smell, equated it with death. Funeral parlors reeked of it. "That's where," Johnny Kabito once told Adam, "the *ch'į́įdii* can get you." Adam promised Bayeta that he would purge the lab to get rid of the smell.

Sedated, Alberto would sleep into the evening. Mary promised to keep an eye on him while Bayeta wove. Martin had also returned, tired from raising the roof beams and installing plywood panels on Maria Klah's house addition. He offered to give Adam a hand with the purging procedures. Adam insisted that it was his "rite of disposition," something he would do on his own. Martin laughed, relieved to be excused. With a pat on his shoulder and a stern look, Adam signaled to Martin that they would not speak more of Martin's lapse. What was done was the past. What mattered now was to go forward.

It pained Adam greatly to think about Martin's betrayal. He could not begin to fathom what threat or coercion had made Martin do it. Except that Martin, more than once, had tried to express his fears that Adam was tinkering with something better left to nature alone, or to the gods, if one believed in higher powers. Could he have been threatened? If that was so, with what? He had nothing that could be taken away from him. As a single male, he had no family of his own to worry about. Money? Martin had never shown the slightest interest in money. Adam could not fathom the reason. He knew but one thing—a confrontation now would only make things worse. What was done was done, was beyond stepping back. Only the path forward mattered. It was for Martin to find his way out of the hole in his conscience. It was up to Bayeta, who was kin, to help him. Adam could but be patient and let things resolve themselves.

With a fresh lab coat on Adam walked around the laboratory making certain everything that needed to be covered or stored away was done. The electrical equipment was unplugged. Gas outlets were shut off and sealed with identifying tape. The walk-in freezer was empty. The two isolation chambers were covered and the glove boxes sealed. Martin had even erased the wall chalkboards and cleaned them. It looked as it did five years ago—waiting to come alive. Nothing suggested that anything extraordinary had taken place there. The silence gave Adam an odd feeling. He rechecked the pressure gauges mounted on the wall. Martin had disconnected the lines to the helium and hydrogen tanks and tagged them. The oxygen gauge read 1900 PSI, still operational. Three nitrogen tanks were still connected. Adam made a quick calculation and was satisfied that they contained enough gas to purge the laboratory. An hour was enough time to saturate the space. Once the interior was filled with nitrogen, he would open the doors and turn on the exhaust fans. Even the air ducts would be purged in the process.

Adam took a last look around and turned the nitrogen gas valves to full open. The lines hissed with compressed, super-cooled gas. Adam sat down at his workbench, sinking into a delayed melancholy. He had spent years examining life at the molecular level pouring over procedures, regimens, chemical assays, post-mortems, a mass of experimental data, and test summaries. He had extended the lives of shrews, his tiny confederates. His probing had picked away at cell functions, enzyme interactions, cell replication, and repair mechanisms. All done to answer one question: What is required to retard some measure of the advance of senescence and atrophy? His method was "basement science."

"You are a 'tinker, a tinker toying with nature's secrets,' " Vaughn had opined that evening at The Manse. Of all the people to say such a thing, Adam thought. At the time, he had dismissed the remark out of hand. But now what? "That silly puffer is an ass," Adam shouted as he sat at his workbench. "I can show them all a thing or two."

Adam eyed the wall clock, how slow the second hand moved. Had he opened the nitrogen tank valves? He rubbed his eyes and again stared at the clock. Why was he here? What needed to be done?

He thought of all his shrews scurrying over the desert's floor at last in search of their own destinies. He tried to stand, but lost his balance and sat back down. He felt his pulse. Fast, he thought. He was thirsty. He reached out, but the workbench was not there. He slumped down to his knees and groped for a bench leg, anything to hold on to. How did he get on the floor? The cool concrete felt good against his cheek. "I must be getting a cold." He stretched out. The built-up tensions of the last week drained away. He shut his eyes against the glare. He smelled garlic. Phosphene chimeras danced before him—purple, shimmering, floating spots drifting in a black pool of vitreous humor.

<++++++++++>

The high-pitched hiss told him what he feared. Straining against his desperate impulse to breathe, Martin rushed into the lab. Finding Adam sprawled on the floor, he grabbed his wrists. With his lungs on fire, he staggered toward the exit, dragging Adam. He dared not exhale or scream for help. That would only force him to breathe. His head pounded with a wrenching headache. Struggling with Adam's limp body, he glimpsed Adam's lips, which were a sickeningly purplish-blue. What he saw was oxygen deprivation, severe in the extreme. Martin stumbled ten feet short of the door. He grabbed on tighter and lurched toward the door's handle. Adrenalin surged through every artery and his lungs, driving him to the edge of panic. He bit down hard, drawing blood from his lip to fight off the pain tearing at his chest. At the razor's edge of consciousness, Martin felt his body failing him.

At last Martin crossed the invisible wave front of escaping nitrogen. Gasping for air, he pulled Adam beyond the door and slammed it shut with his foot. The day's late sun blinded him. He slumped to his knees. His throat gasped for air. Half through the second door, he cried out. Exhausted, in pain, head pounding, Martin slumped against Adam's body and lost consciousness.

How much time passed before Martin breathed and felt his pulse? He would never know. With his eyes still shut tight, he counted. Yes, his heart rate was slowing. He had a monster headache and wanted to vomit. For the second time, he passed out. How much time passed before Bayeta found the two of them collapsed at the lab's outer door? Martin roused on hearing her cries and pointed. "Find his pulse. Help him to breathe."

Mary, having heard Bayeta's scream, appeared. Bending over Adam, Bayeta shouted out, "Mary, get water and a wet towel. Find my father." She looked to Martin. "Martin, what…"

"God, I don't know! The lab is full of gas. Adam was on the floor."

Bayeta pinched Adam's nose with her fingers, put her lips to his mouth, and breathed into him. Counting out intervals in fours, she forced her breath into his lungs. Agonizingly slow, Adam's skin color began to turn from a ghastly reddish-blue to feverish-pink. He began to breathe on his own. He choked. Still unconscious, he dribbled phlegm out of his mouth and nose. Bayeta kissed him and brushed her hair from his eyes. She sat back, her tears wetting the concrete. "Martin, what happened in there?"

"Nitrogen narcosis," Martin said.

"Get the oxygen bottle outside Alberto's room."

Mary had returned with the wet towel. Unnerved, Bayeta smiled up at Mary. Her father came. Without a word, he picked up Adam and carried him into the house. Bayeta leaned on Mary and slowly rose to her feet. Together, they followed, drying their eyes and reassuring each other.

<++++++++++>

Half an hour later in the kitchen and still feeling the effects of his mind-splitting headache, Adam made light of the affair. Yes, he had been stupid. He related the euphoric sensation of drifting, floating in a pool of warm water. It was deep and a queer luminescence had gathered about him. It was like a happy drunk on a bender, he said. One perfect point of blinding light had held his attention. He had reached out, but the light retreated. It hovered, faded to deep indigo. He had never seen anything quite so beautiful.

The next thing he remembered was his headache and Bea kissing him. He smelled her hair. No, he tasted it. He could not move, but that didn't matter. She was holding him.

"I realize now, Bea, that a hallucinatory synesthesia had taken hold of me. It was so extraordinary. Wow!"

"Adam, you almost died. Do you know that? How could you be so…"

"Careless," he interrupted. "It is best that I own up to it."

She hugged him tightly. "I'll get you something for your headache, and then you must rest."

"It was a kind of rapture, Bea."

"Oh, Adam, how can you be so damn analytical?" Her tears would not stop flowing.

"A microscope will never reveal what I saw." He talked as if he had discovered some great secret. Had narcosis made him think that he had found a way to float down to the very edge of a cell's membrane? "I saw structures of organic molecules that are entirely unknown." He insisted that such detail had never before appeared on an X-ray diffraction plate. "We really see only shadows, you see, ghosts. We don't see the thing itself. But, I saw it plain. Yes, it was wonderful."

Martin stood at the door listening to Adam's confused ramble.

"Adam, what happened?"

"I made a stupid mistake, that's all."

"You never make mistakes, not like that. What really happened?"

"Oh, I don't know. Alberto was on my mind: What more should I have done for him. Then I thought, what if 70 years is not the average length of a life? What if it was only twenty or so years? What kind of a world would it be? Would we adapt to a fast, furious life like shrews? A child might grow to an adult in eight years. Parenting would begin before age ten. Then, the problem to face is what to do with those who live longer, say beyond twenty-two. Can we imagine people dying in pain and suffering from advanced age at 22?"

"You are not making sense."

"I'm not sure of anything right now. Maybe we already have a long enough time on this earth, time to work, play, have sex, travel, and raise a family—a full life. We live, make our mark on life, and give way to the next generation. What if only the privileged reap the benefits of life extension? Most people, ordinary people, would be denied it. In San Francisco, I began to ask just that." Adam continued to talk, still agitated by his headache. Martin listened, but was tired from the ordeal. He waved to stop Adam talking.

"I must go lie down. You must rest, too."

Two hours later, while Mary and Ninaba kept the hot quesadillas coming, Crystal poured the sangria. Both men were ravenous and ate with abandon. A large pot of thick chili with beef topped with diced red onions was next. George Slim did the honors of serving. Martin and Adam looked relaxed and rested from their ordeal.

"It is good to eat hot chili and drink cold sangria," said George Slim. Bayeta nodded and pretended that she had something in her eye. She sighed, a sigh of relief. Adam smiled at Martin.

"Bea tells me you've been to see Maria Klah, Martin."

"She is a good woman. When it is time, I would like you to stand with me."

"Martin, it will be an honor." They embraced across the table. Whatever had stood between them was over. They were again at ease with one another. Bayeta busied herself at the sink, bending over it intently. Her worry lines melted away. Harmony and balance had again come to her home.

Adam could not contain himself. "You know how much I enjoy reading Loren Eisley." They all nodded, knowing what was about to come. "Anyway, in San Francisco, I planned to put in this bit from *The Immense Journey*, but could not find the exact quote. So, I scrapped it at the last minute. I wish I had found the quote in time."

"Would it have made a difference?"

"Probably not, except to me. He believed that we are just past the threshold of being beasts, a little too curious for our own good. If we are wise, he suggested, we must stay as those humble creatures far back in our lineage, content to pour little gifts into the grave. No one asked me to research longevity. I decided. Did I ask myself if I should? Not once. Facing opposition, I dismissed it as the hobgoblins of little minds. I told myself that I was doing it for those like Alberto. Not true. I had begun to think about it before Alberto came into our lives. When he did come to us, I decided to continue, if only for him. His parents were exhausted from caring and gave him up. Alberto could have been a ready vessel. But he is not a guinea pig, nor one of my shrews. Was I tempted? An experimental procedure was just possible. I was tempted."

"Adam, you have given him extra years without subjecting him to anything."

"Will Alberto feel that I did all that I could?"

"Only Alberto can say."

"I want to believe that he knows that we did all we could. In the lab, he identified with each shrew. He counted their days. He had to wonder why the same result was not open to him." There was no need to remind Adam that he had had no choice. Alberto was not a shrew. Fatigue crept back on Martin and Adam before either realized it. Martin excused himself and went to bed. Bayeta put her arms around Adam as he fell asleep in front of the living room fire.

<++++++++++>

At sunset Bayeta woke Adam. They walked out to the patio and stood scanning the horizon for the first star. "Bea, he will be taken, if not tonight, tomorrow, if not tomorrow, the day after." His words had a sorrowful finality of defeat, of grief to come. With his eyes fixed on the eastern horizon, he waited for her to say something.

"I look at him when he is not aware of my presence. I watch how he responds to the smallest thing. He's like the child I have always wanted, a boy with such innocent eyes. He talks to himself, often with the word "when" in his sentences. Since Flagstaff he does not speak of when."

Adam nodded. "I must let go of seeing life by objective measures. Alberto has brought me up short. Fantasy and dream have sustained him." He turned to Bayeta. "I need to tell you what to expect."

"Please, Adam, not now. I don't want it said, not out loud, not yet. Please."

Bayeta's last reserves were now breeched. With his strong enfolding arms about her, she hugged him tight. "Adam, I have something to tell you." Mary interrupted before she could say what was on her mind. Someone was on the phone, something to do with Adam's father.

<++++++++++>

Static on the line made it hard to make out what was said. It was the Navajo policeman, Clyde Yazzie. In his unhurried manner he related the situation, as he knew it. Adam listened.

"Why, do you think those *bilagáana* came to Chinle?" Had Adam expected them? "Three of the men were armed. Poor old George Curly, he took the money for his car only because they had guns. When they drove off, the pilot was left behind. He was supposed to refuel and wait and was told not to file a flight plan. That was when George Curly called me. I went out and questioned the pilot before noon. He said all he knew was that a place called Rimrock was mentioned. Do they have business with you, Dr. Grant?"

It was not unusual for a Navajo to take time to come to the point. That Adam would expect. But, Officer Yazzie was asking a lot of questions. Adam had never heard a Navajo ask so many questions. Still, he was a policeman.

"Clyde, you are asking questions that I have no answer for, I'm sorry."

Clyde appreciated the humor. "Anyway, I would have liked to have been there to see the Tumechos playing with them. When I caught up with them in front of Rose's, that's when I saw that they had a dead man in the car. The thing is, folks aren't used to pistol-packing white men parked on the street at dinner time, not with a dead man in the back seat."

There was a long pause before Officer Yazzie again spoke. "This Schwann fellow said the man is your father. I am sorry to have to tell you this, Doctor Grant. I would have called sooner but…"

Adam interrupted, not quite understanding the gist of what the officer was saying. "Clyde, you had your hands full."

"I hate to have to tell you all this. It was 6:40 p.m. when I rolled up behind them. I got out to take a close look at them. I told that fellow Schwann that George Curly expected his car back. He wasn't one for talking. Then I tried to speak to the other gentleman sitting in the back seat. That's when I saw that he was not breathing."

"You mean that was my father in the car, sitting there dead?"

"He looked peaceful enough. Still, I never figured on a thing like that. From the way the others acted, I guess they had no idea they were driving around with…well you know. That's pretty much it."

Officer Yazzie waited for Adam to respond. When Adam did not, he said, "There will have to be an autopsy. The State Police are transporting the body to Ganado."

"Then, I need go to Ganado."

"Yes. You will need to make a positive identification."

"It's a bit complicated here at the moment. It will take me time to get there, Clyde."

Adam had more questions, many more. But this was not the time. If it was indeed his father, dead, being driven in an ambulance to Ganado, why? What had made his father come in the company of Schwann? He felt a sense of loss and sadness. Now nothing could be done to repair the long estrangement between them. In California he had felt a change, a connection with his father. Had he only imagined that his father had reached out to him? Adam had not expected it. Now, Alexander Terman was being driven in an ambulance to Ganado, a place he would never have imagined being taken to under any circumstance.

"Don't worry about those men."

"They have not come to see the sights, Clyde. You do know that."

"The State Police might not keep them for long. This Schwann guy called his attorney."

"From what little I know of him, I imagine he'll try pulling strings."

"Tell you what I can do. The State Police are pretty straight. I'll call and make sure they run the gun permit checks. That will take hours, half-a-day minimum. Who rides around with a dead man in the car? Maybe they can't hold Schwann, but the others they can. I figure it will at least be Thursday morning before the Staties are done processing them."

"They can't go far without a car."

"Good point. I can see to it that the State Police drive them back to their plane at Chinle when done with them. That could buy some time."

"Then, it's settled. I will start out for Ganado. That should take two hours."

"I will meet up with you there at Whispering Pines Funeral Home."

Having heard part of the conversation, Bayeta had waited by the fire in the living room for Adam. He then called Cynthia. She took it hard. She and their father were close. Though he was emotionally limited, she had made allowances. With his personal history could he have helped being emotionally crippled? She kept saying through her tears that it was a cruel fate that he died alone in the desert, died with no one holding his hand. Adam said that Schwann was with him.

"Adam, he really hated that man, you know."

Adam did not argue with his sister, not over this. "When can you come?"

"I'll start out as soon as I can pack a few things."

"It will be a long drive."

"I'll be there as soon as I can make it."

"Before you leave, will you call someone there in Los Alamos for me?" She said that she would call Donald Ryder for him. He rang off and took a deep breath before making the call to Marianne.

Marianne's answering machine took his message. He could not bring himself to leave details on a machine. He liked Marianne. Explanations would have to come later. Adam took another deep breath. Whatever he had thought about Herman, he knew that he had to inform Carol. On hearing Adam's voice, however, Carol began a tirade verging on abuse. Why had he not come? Even poor Herman deserved respect in death. Through her tears and recriminations, Carol blurted out that the Berkeley police were certain that Herman did not shoot himself. Was Adam involved, she asked? Why had he up and disappeared? The police wanted to talk to him. "You are involved in this Goddamn mess."

Adam could hardly contain his anger. "Carol, are you implying that it is not suicide?"

"As if you didn't know! They found size 14 footprints in the rose bed outside the library window. What size are your shoes? Tell me that! Tell me that! Herman was not a happy man, but he would never have put a bullet to his brain. He was too weak to do that. Never!"

"Carol, what are you saying?"

"What size shoes do you wear, Adam? Tell me that!"

"Carol, something has happened here in Arizona."

"Just tell me where you were. I don't give a damn about Arizona. Tell me!"

Bayeta waited, listening to Adam trying to tell Carol about Alexander. But Adam could not make her listen. She was venting. He put the phone down with a look of surprise. "She hung up."

"You're not serious. What did she say?"

Adam looked stunned. "The Berkeley police now have evidence that Herman did not commit suicide. Carol asked me my shoe size. They found evidence of someone standing outside the library window."

"What have shoes to do with anything?"

"Everything. The police want to ask me more questions."

"If it is not suicide, what will happen now? Did you tell Carol about Alexander?"

"She was too hysterical for me to get a word in." Bayeta told Adam to call her back. "I won't go through that again. I'll try again to call Marianne. She actually loved him. Tomorrow, after I've made arrangements at the funeral home, I'll ask Cynthia to call Carol. She will listen to Cynthia."

"Who did you ask Cynthia to call just now?"

"Donald Ryder. He's living in Los Alamos for the moment."

Bayeta asked him why he would call Ryder.

"Oh, I don't know. He is no longer working for the San Diego Tribune, but he is still a reporter. There is a story to tell; it needs to get out. Whatever Schwann thinks he can do to me, the more publicity the better."

"Don't leave me here, not alone to deal with everything."

"I'll be back by late morning. Nothing will happen before then. I promise."

<++++++++++++>

Adam arrived at The Whispering Pines funeral home at 10 o'clock. He was relieved to see Officer Clyde Yazzie parked on the street. It took only moments to formally identify Alexander's body. Adam signed the release for the postmortem autopsy and viewed the body of his father one last time. He could not think what to do next. Seeing Alexander's tie hanging outside his jacket, Adam straightened it and tucked it neatly inside his jacket, as he had worn it in life. Mr. Sterling, the funeral director, said he would fax a confirmation of identity to the State Police.

"You have plans for burial? We are at your disposal to assist in any way and take care of formalities. Our staff can prepare your loved one for viewing. He is at peace now, in God's hands." Officer Yazzie was standing discreetly outside the door. At the mention of burial, he shifted his stance and looked away.

"There is a plot in Gallup that is available. The service should be held there."

"We have a fine place of repose here, sir. I can show you, if you like."

"No. Gallup will be his final resting place. I bought it for another purpose. It will do."

"Whispering Pines will see to your every wish, sir." Mr. Sterling bowed. "Pardon me, Dr. Grant, was Mr. Terman from these parts? Are his roots here?"

"No, he was born in Estonia a long time ago. During the war, he came to this area. San Francisco was where he resided. It will not miss him, though. Here is as good a place as any."

Mr. Sterling gave that perfected slow and formal bow that marks a man of his profession. The gesture gave Adam a momentary shudder. In life, no one had ever bowed that way as a sign of respect for Alexander Terman. His world was made of men who fawned over one's superiors, but never with so gracious a bow. What could his last thoughts have been as he sat next to THE William Henry Schwann? What irony to be in the back seat of George Curly's loaner car in front of Rose Bia's Cafe. In death, he had obstructed Schwann's purpose, but would never know it.

Officer Yazzie asked Adam what he planned to do.

"Alexander is with his god. I doubt that it matters much to him now where his bones rest."

"Gallup is better than Ganado, I think. Yes, it is best."

"You mean that Ganado is on the reservation. You don't want people worrying over his spirit wandering about. In Chinle they saw his body in George Curly's car. Clyde, you have a way of making plain what's on your mind without actually saying it."

"It's my Navajo nose, Dr. Grant. Mischief was what they were up to. If it had not been for the customers in Rose's place watching, I would not have got out of my truck. The way they rolled into town at sunset. I followed them from White House Trail into town. When that big one, Mueller, got out and went into the Cafe, I caught a glimpse of his weapon, a nasty looking thing. So, I parked behind George Curly's car and called it in. I almost didn't get out. If I had not, they might have driven off and headed out your way. You'd have had to deal with four bad characters and a *ch'į́įdii* on your own."

"You'd have come along, Clyde."

"Go over to the State Police barracks. Give Joe Hansen, the duty sergeant, the information he needs. And, while you are at it, get a good look at those men."

"I already know what Mueller looks like."

"I'll call ahead and tell Hansen to expect you. He's one who always sees that the paperwork is done right. They're not going anywhere until it is done. Takes time. Then, too, there's the matter of the weapons. We don't allow concealed weapons on the Res. Those aren't deer rifles, and this is not the season. It's not a matter how many permits they might have. If they're not FBI, they can't carry. Hansen will run a check for Arizona permits. We don't recognize California gun permits."

"I see. And, all that takes time."

"Count on it. Hansen didn't like the look of those characters either."

"Are you driving back to Crystal?"

“My family is over at Sonsela Butte for the blessing. Later, I can drop by Rimrock for coffee.”

“Come for a late breakfast, and there will be fresh biscuits.”

“*Yá’át’ééh*.”

<++++++++++>

On the outskirts of Ganado, south on Highway 63, Adam found the State Police substation. It was one building with an attached trailer that had barred windows. He spoke to the dispatcher at the front desk. He was to wait. Sergeant Hansen was questioning one of the men brought down from Chinle. He’d be finished soon, the dispatcher said. He could help himself to coffee if he wanted. Adam poured hot coffee into a Styrofoam cup and sat down across from the dispatcher. He heard loud voices from one of the rooms down the hall. He assumed it was Sergeant Hansen questioning Schwann or someone in his party.

“Busy night, officer?”

The dispatcher grinned and said, “They don’t get busier.” Adam wondered what Officer Yazzie had told Sergeant Hansen.

“He wants a hold put on the four men from Chinle. Hansen can fill you in. He plays it by the book. That’s what’s got that old guy in Room 4 so riled up. He thinks he’s some kind of big shot. Says he’ll have Hansen’s badge. He should not have said that. As I said, he plays it by the book. Nothing makes Joe madder than some clown demanding special treatment.”

“I’m glad to hear it.”

“You are Dr. Grant, right? Clyde says you’re OK. Joe will see to it that those goons are held until the judge holds session. He’s a stickler when it comes to strangers packing heat. They can’t be ordinary poachers or anything like that. They might not get out of here ‘til Monday. The judge, you see, he never holds court on weekends.”

The dispatcher had a big grin on his face. In the time it had taken Adam to drive from the funeral home to the barracks, Clyde Yazzie had indeed acted quickly. With coffee in hand, Adam walked down the hall to stretch his legs. Outside Room 4, he could see four men through the door's small view window. He recognized Mueller. Adam studied the features of each man. They all had sullen, twisted faces. Mueller was bigger than he remembered. But he'd only seen him before at a distance. He looked big enough for size 14 shoes. The other two, sitting beside Schwann, were not as large. They were muscular, with thick arms and thick necks. They were built for what they were.

As the door to Room 4 opened, Adam stood back. "Dr. Grant?" A pleasant looking man in uniform extended his hand. "Clyde said you'd be coming by. I appreciate that. Please accept my condolences for your loss."

"Thank you Officer Hansen. I am sorry that any of this has happened."

"Don't be. You had nothing to do with it, Dr. Grant. Matter of fact, we haven't had enough excitement around here lately. This sort of thing breaks the monotony."

"My father was eighty-seven. I assume it was natural causes. When I last saw him…"

"When was that, Doctor?"

"It was late last week in San Francisco. He did not look well, acted a bit off. One minute his wit was sharp and on point. The next, he seemed distracted, almost...well, I don't know, lost in thought?"

Hansen nodded and made a note on his clipboard. He stiffened and focused his attention on the moment. "An hour ago, I assumed that this was all just an unfortunate event. People do die in unexpected ways. You said your father was eighty-seven, right? What with the heat, declining health, and age, it could have been natural. We'll know more tomorrow."

"I understand. Is there anything else I can tell you? I mean…"

"Dr. Grant, Clyde tells me that you are making arrangements with the funeral home. That's all I need for now, that and your release form for the autopsy."

Adam remembered something. He was not certain, but then he did not believe in coincidences. "There is one thing. You might check to see if that Mr. Mueller wears size 14 shoes."

Sergeant Hanson smiled. "He's big enough. Is that important?"

Adam took a card from his wallet. "Call this Lieutenant Kestos, Berkeley Police Department. He may see a connection to the death of Herman Cockroft. Alexander Terman was also his father."

"You interest me, Dr. Grant. You could have walked out of here without telling me that. We've already been in touch with Kestos. When we queried the Berkeley police to confirm Mueller's driver's license and home address, they replied with a hold request. How did you know about Mueller?"

"An inquest is to be held into the death of Herman Cockroft, the late director of The Evergreen Institute, Mueller's employer. He was found dead Monday. Outside his library window, that's where his body was found, there are imprints in a flowerbed of size 14 shoes. Mueller has big feet. Maybe there's nothing to it, but I don't believe in coincidences."

"Doctor, this is for certain turning out to be an interesting night. It can't hurt our reputation if we help the Berkeley police in their case. And, like you, I don't believe in coincidences either."

"I'll say goodnight, then."

Hansen hesitated. "You know what? I have some questions of my own." Adam looked confused.

"Oh, I mean for that Mr. Schwann. They're a pretty tight group. I don't like it when people clam up. Add that to this Mueller business. Could be a lot going on here. That Schwann acts like a big shot. He's in charge. Says he's some multinational something or other. His lawyer is on his way. I'll probably get a call from my higher ups in Phoenix ordering that we cut him loose. He was not carrying a weapon, you see. The one in charge never does. But I have every right to hold the other three until a judge sees them on a possible weapons charge. It just doesn't make sense, does it?"

"What doesn't make sense?"

"Look at it like a policeman. We get this call. There's a beat up old car parked on the street in Chinle with five men in it. One is dead. One says he's worth billions. He wants my badge. The three others fit the profile of goons. What's it about, men like that driving around the desert in that old car with a rusted out radiator and three of them packing enough firepower to start a small war? Clyde says that they were on the back roads over by Monument Canyon and Bat Canyon for most of the day scaring the be-Jesus out of the locals. What's with the Lear jet on the tarmac waiting to fly them out?"

"Sounds pretty fantastic, doesn't it?"

"You bet." The sergeant gave a knowing look. "I figure you're the one they came for."

"You do have quite an imagination, Sergeant Hansen."

"We don't get big shot types coming our way." He gave Adam an appraising look. "I was on extra detail when you built that place, Rimrock, right? Five years back, wasn't it? One doesn't forget a project like that, all that scientific stuff being hauled over those miserable ruts of road. One never forgets a thing like that, not around here you don't. Word was some scientist was going to live out there and experiment, some such thing. That was you, right?"

"Sergeant, at the time even I was surprised."

"See what I mean? Now, here we have this Mr. Schwann cooling his heels in my interrogation room. Wants his lawyer. He wants my badge. Maybe I'll have to let him go. I can't charge him for being too stupid to know when his seatmate has checked out. He won't say, but I figure he and his party were headed for your place for sure, and they weren't coming to pay a social call."

Adam smiled. "That does present something of a mystery, wouldn't you say?"

"That it does."

"So, you can't hold him."

"I'd like to know what he's up to. His sort roaming around, no good comes from it."

"I have never actually met him, you know. Recently, I learned that he, or his company, was behind some funding for some of my research. Had I known, I would not have taken the funding. Now it appears that he thinks he has rights to my work."

"You say you've never actually met him. Would you like to now?"

"It is time that I met William Henry Schwann. Would you mind? You could watch through that one-way glass of yours. He might tell me why he was sitting with my dead father in the car."

The Sergeant was not sure it was a good idea. It could compromise any investigation going forward.

Adam persisted, "Sergeant Hansen, what can it hurt? Later, you could deny that you heard a thing."

Sergeant Hansen agreed. Adam watched as two officers removed the other men. Mueller looked especially nervous at being separated from his master.

As he entered Room 4, Adam sized up Schwann. He was old, obese, and looked mean. He was tapping the desk with the index finger of his left hand. Seeing Adam at the door, he glared. "You have been a thorn in my side, Dr. Grant."

"That's of your own making."

"Alex did say that you have a way of getting quickly to the heart of the matter."

"Do you?"

A tense silence followed. Schwann stopped tapping on the table. Adam looked down at Schwann, just a man, an old man not in command of the moment. Schwann rose from his chair and planted both of his hands firmly on the table.

"I'll be direct, Dr. Grant. I didn't get where I am by waiting on others to make things happen. I anticipate. I pay for what I want, for what is rightly mine. For five years every cent that The Evergreen Institute put into you came from me. I expect a return on my investment."

"Herman never so much as hinted that."

"Herman was stupid. He should have told you we owned you from the beginning."

"You are owed nothing from me."

"I have rights to your research and I want it. I will have it."

"Why do you want it so much? You already have billions, what will more money get you?"

"You think I want it because it is worth billions?"

"I'm not so naïve as to think you are doing this just for profit."

"An astute observation, Dr. Grant. Maybe we can do business." Schwann paced behind the desk, alert and intensely focused. "What do you know about power, Doctor, I mean real power? Power is the only true measure. With power I can break any man. I can and I will break even you. I have more power than you can possibly imagine." Adam dismissed Schwann's rant with a wave of his hand.

"There are millions who will pay dearly for more time. They will surrender their will and their souls for more years. Do not delude yourself that profit is what motivates me. What matters is control, Dr. Grant, power."

Adam abruptly changed the subject. "How well did you know my father?"

"Forty years. He was once a damn good physicist, knew how to turn ideas into profit. A born tinker, that's what he was. I paid him well and used his knowledge to advantage."

"And along the way you destroyed his son."

"Herman was weak, damaged goods. He was adequate until he took to drink."

Adam turned to leave.

"I'm not done with you, Dr. Grant!" Schwann grabbed for Adam's shoulder. Adam brushed Schwann's arm away.

"You brought my father along to use as leverage. Now he is dead." Schwann started to speak but Adam cut him off. "And here's a hot piece of news for you, Mr. Schwann, the Berkeley police believe that Herman's death is a homicide."

Schwann reeled back on his heels and looked taken unawares.

"Did you intend for Mueller to go that far? Now he is a liability. Your enforcer, the 'little Prussian,' has become a liability, a threat. Mueller was the only weapon you had left. He won't be able to help himself or you."

Schwann backed away. He was not in control. Desperate to regain some measure of control, Schwann blurted out, "Herman's death was unfortunate. What kind of a man are you, anyway? Your own brother dies and you up and leave?" Schwann sneered, glaring at Adam. The look in his eyes, however, was one of panic, loss, and rage.

"To you he was no more than a shill. You even counted on his death to keep me in California where you could use less subtle pressures on me."

Wiping his forehead and speaking rapidly, gasping, Schwann trailed after Adam who was at the door. "Don't be stupid, Grant. It's not too late. We can still do business! I'll give them Mueller. He's the one. I never told him to use force, never. He is unstable. I see that now. Yes, I'll tell them that he's out of control, out of control. Me? I had no idea. It's too bad about Mueller. He served me for thirty-five years. I brought him over from Germany, you know. I will be sorry to lose him."

"Go home, Mr. Schwann." Schwann retreated and slumped into the chair by the table.

Sergeant Hansen walked Adam to his car. "Thanks, Dr. Grant, I got it all on tape. My superiors may quibble over the expectancy of privacy, that he never waved his right against self-incrimination, that sort of crap. You're not a police officer, so what was said is not privileged. He never asked and I never said it was safe to talk in there. Besides, he had already talked to his attorney by phone. I'm sure that he was told not to say a word. It's not my fault that he couldn't keep his big mouth shut."

"Can you hold him?"

"The Berkeley cops may be able to work it up to accessory before or after the fact." Sergeant Hansen grinned. "I'll call Kestos and send him a copy of the tape. His lawyer is due. We'll probably have to cut him loose and let the police in California handle him."

"If you need me, I'll be at Rimrock."

<+++++++++++>

Adam arrived home after 5:00 a.m. Unable to sleep until Adam returned, Bayeta was at her loom.

"You actually met this Mr. Schwann?"

He put his arms about her. The loom, lit by a floor lamp was within Adam's reach. He looked intently at the open warp and admired the emerging design.

"I had a dream today in the lab. Like this weave, our life has more to come before it is complete. But, I can imagine the whole. There is no need to change the pattern, not now."

“Adam, I’m glad you think that. But, we can’t see how each new thread will lie down until it is before us. There is more to a weave or to life than simply waiting for it to work itself out.”

“Have I missed something?”

Bayeta smiled contentedly as Adam carried her to bed. A heavy, cold rain was on the roof.

At sleep’s door, Adam’s head touched the pillow and his consciousness imploded. Bayeta stretched out to watch over him. How perfectly the shadows of bare warp strings had framed his form in the studio. The whole of him was secure within her web. For all of his obsessive searching, he was anchored to her. She saw the way he looked at the weave in progress. He had dared so much, yet no evil had touched him. An overturned tractor had taken Hastin Gani, a man who had never reached beyond his grasp, one satisfied with a well-plowed cornfield, sheep, and his dream to raise a healthy herd of Holsteins. A bullet had taken Herman, a flawed man who wanted nothing more than to belong, to be a man of importance. Alberto was to be taken for no good reason, to be taken because of an error in the coding of his life’s thread. She prayed, fearing that some monstrous thing still stalked the desert for a fresh victim.

At her touch, he smiled. She whispered, “Adam, you are going to be a father.” But he had lapsed into deep sleep, beyond hearing. “Adam, I am going to be a mother.” She laid her head on his chest. “In the morning, I will tell you again. Then you will know how much we are woven together.”

<++++++++++>

North to south along an invisible line at the 111th meridian, rain clouds stretched for eight hundred miles. At the eastern limit of the Hopi Reservation, the system had stalled, waiting for the winds. Sheet lightning split and fractured the sky to the Utah border. The Navajo Radio Service announcer read out a flood advisory in effect from ten in the morning for Canyon de Chelly and the Chuska Range drainage.

It was nine o’clock when Bayeta answered the kitchen phone. Adam, awake, was sitting with Alberto. Alberto had no appetite but wanted to taste the fresh fruit Mary had sugared down for him. He sucked on the juice and smiled. He gave Mary a wink, as she wiped juice from his chin. "Twice the taste and half the calories," he said, insisting that he was much better than yesterday.

Bayeta came in. "A Sergeant Hansen is on the phone." Adam went to take the call.

"This is Adam Grant."

"Good morning, Dr. Grant. I'm calling to inform you of a development this morning." Adam sat down. "We had to release Mr. Schwann about an hour after you left."

"You said that might happen."

"He hired a taxi to drive him back to Chinle. I'm told that he got his pilot out of bed at the Thunderbird Lodge and insisted that he be flown out." Adam listened but said nothing. "From what we gather, Schwann made the pilot refuel the plane without checking with George Curly or anyone at the airport. A note was left in the fuel truck cab. It said to bill Schwann and Company. Seems they are not too careful about leaving fuel trucks locked out there."

"So, they will have to hope for payment for the gas," Adam interjected.

"The thing is, Schwann will never pay for it. What with it being dark and all, seems like they filled that Learjet with the wrong fuel. The mechanic who came on duty at eight says the octane mix in that truck is not for jets." Adam was now standing, suddenly alert. "We are not sure, sir. But the way we figure it, the plane got airborne and headed west. Most likely, it flew by Flagstaff sometime after seven this morning. Our Flagstaff office reports an aircraft of the same general description being spotted trying to gain altitude on the east flank of the San Francisco Peaks. The storm was dumping a lot of rain about that time to the west. There must have been a lot of turbulence. With unsettled air and poor visibility, those peaks can be dangerous. The civilian air patrol is due to go up within the hour, as soon as the visibility improves, to take a look."

Adam asked if he thought the plane went down. Hansen said, "The pilot radioed the Flagstaff tower asking for a fix on his position. They lost contact with the plane before they could do so. I thought you should know."

"Thank you. What about the other three?"

"We still have them. They will appear before the judge first thing tomorrow morning. They'll make bail and, my guess is, disappear."

"Thanks for letting me know."

"I've also called Officer Yazzie. That Mueller is a piece of work. We can't figure if he's just mad or plain crazy. Whatever is going on with him, he's one to watch out for."

"Will you call me when you have something definite?"

"Count on it. The news wires will pick this up just as fast, though. This Schwann character, if he is splattered across a mountainside, will be big news. Our barracks commander has already heard from the Governor's office."

It surprised Adam to hear that William Henry Schwann had disappeared. The man had tried to project an image of being invincible, what with money and power at his disposal. If so, why would such a man personally involve himself by coming to Arizona? He had men like Mueller at his disposal. Was it that he did not trust his own men to carry out his orders? Herman had failed him. Alexander had turned. Mueller only complicated matters. What of Vaughn or Valentine, or others? Adam could not suppress the rich irony of it. He was back at Rimrock, safe. He had been fooled, cajoled, pressured, and followed without success. Could it all have come down to his pursuer being lost on the San Francisco Peaks due to pilot error? Bayeta came into the kitchen as Adam hung up the phone.

"Adam, please wait to tell others, except for my parents." Adam was confused. "Of course, Mary and John should know. But, let's not talk about it to others, not yet."

He thought that he understood her caution, her impulse not to unnecessarily worry others. Ominous winds brought black rain. Black rain was more than an elemental force sweeping in from a distant ocean. Her neighbors would say that black rain had pulled the plane down from the sky. No pilot would be so ignorant as to use the wrong fuel. The NTSB might conclude just that, but many Navajos would understand the real cause. Schwann had come in the guise of a skin walker. He had made a threatening appearance and was to be avoided. The man had sat with a corpse in the back seat of George Curly's car, sat there as if nothing out of the ordinary had happened. Only a skin walker would do such a thing.

Their innocent miscommunication ended with Bayeta smiling at their secret, the one she had told him in bed. Adam smiled, knowing that his wife was right to advise him not to speak of the potential danger from Mueller and the other men.

Cynthia arrived before noon. Donald Ryder was with her, having volunteered to do the driving. After consoling Cynthia, Adam told her of his intention to have Alexander's body taken to Gallup for burial. She agreed that he would not have wanted to be buried in Albuquerque. As for taking the body back to the Bay Area, even she saw the wisdom of not allowing anyone there to make a spectacle of his funeral. He had, she confided, told her how he had come to loathe his life in California. He had never cared for Carol. His grandsons were wastrels. That left only Marianne. She, of course, would want to come for the burial.

It was settled then. With the plan laid out, Adam took Ryder into the library. Ryder asked if he could file a story, the real one, warts and all. He wanted the focus on Schwann and his manipulations. Adam agreed. Ryder would have his exclusive at last, and be back in play as a reporter. And, what then? Well, it was trout season. Unless he was quick about it, the big ones would be fished out within a week.

One or two details still did not jell with Ryder, however. Why would Schwann, powerful as he was, make such a trip in the first place? And, how was he to spin Alexander's role? Adam shrugged his shoulders.

"Just say that he was an innocent passenger caught up in something he had no knowledge of. He had simply come along to visit with family. Say that he became sick late that day. His passing in Chinle was an unfortunate, unintended outcome. End of story."

Ryder agreed. It was barely plausible. But stranger things do happen. "What about the scene in front of the cafe?"

"It was getting dark. Not being used to desert heat, they did not recognize that he had expired. Alexander was still sitting up, I am told, with his eyes open when Officer Yazzie first saw him. He said that Alexander looked to be smiling."

Ryder could see the irony of it. There slumped Alexander, in the company of Schwann and his henchmen. If he knew that he was dying, why not do it in a way certain to complicate things?

After Ryder left, saying that he could be reached at the Thunderbird Lodge, Mary told Adam that Alberto was awake. Adam felt guilty for not attending to Alberto's needs sooner and went to him.

"Adam, I want to sit outside. I want to feel the wind."

"The rain could resume at any minute."

"You promised." Adam considered the matter in silence. What difference would a few drops make?

Bayeta heard their plan. "What are you thinking of doing?"

Adam turned and told her it was what Alberto wanted. Stepping back into the hallway, he added, "It could be his last day, Bea. He wants me to take him up the hill, up beyond the garden. Martin has put up a brush Ramada, there."

"Adam, why?"

"Alberto knows his own mind. He does not want to die in his room. He believes in *ch'į́įdii.* He believes and does not want his spirit to linger in the house."

"How can he believe that, he's a...?"

"Catholic? Does the Catholic doctrine of spirit differ so much?"

"You can't subject him to that weather out there, not in the open."

"Bea, all I know—what I feel—is that he has found a way to let go, let go on his terms. I will sit with him and read to him. He wants to experience all that he can."

Adam carried Alberto up the hill and laid him on the pile of soft cushions that Martin had prepared. The ramada provided a dry shelter against easterly winds. A small patio table was set beside Alberto's pallet. On it was a copy of *The Decameron* and a fresh vase of cut desert lilies. Adam took a deck chair and settled in next to the boy. He talked to Alberto of many things, the good times. Each time Adam paused, he listened to Alberto's breathing. Alberto's eyes were closed but he was listening. The ring that Bayeta had bought for him in Albuquerque was in his hand. The wind sang softly as it filtered through the ramada. Rain spattered tentatively on the roof. A jackrabbit scurrying for cover ran across the opening facing east.

Adam put his reading aside and watched over Alberto. Along a solid front of black, upwelling cloud mass, sheet lightning scraped and seared the far rim of Canyon de Chelly's western side. Sharp, crackling thunderclaps pierced the space between sky and earth. The vegetal promise of rain hovered over the red earth. There followed a long moment, a hesitancy and stillness in the air, before the first drops of black rain began to fall. Adam adjusted Alberto's covers and noticed the smile on his thin lips.

Bayeta climbed the hill. With effort she suppressed the look of anxious care on her face and knelt to take Alberto's hand, to feel his forehead and adjust his blankets. She did not speak. Words would only draw tears.

At three o'clock, Widow Tumecho arrived. Her eighty-eight years had slowed her steps to an ambling slow waltz, yet on she came, erect and determined. She made the climb to Alberto's "nest", as that was what he told Bayeta it was. The Widow bent over and whispered in his ear. He closed his eyes and smiled.

Turning to Adam, she cupped her hand, "He calls me his Juliet. I am his best girlfriend."

Their friendship of five years had spawned a wry humor that only they two shared. The Widow had often spent afternoons huddled with him in conspiratorial banter. Alberto made up fantastic stories drawn from his reading. Ovid's *Metamorphoses* was a favorite source, full of changelings and lust- struck women. She could relate a Navajo story to match each fantasy. It amused both to interrupt the other, carrying the stories forward, ever weaving two traditions together. Their crazy quilted stories, always with a heroic plot, ended well. Juliet and Romeo forever young.

Alberto nodded off. Widow Tumecho and Bayeta withdrew to the house. There, they stood by the door watching the approach of the black boiling mass of clouds. Taking Bayeta's right hand in hers, the Widow said, "Rain comes to make new corn, fresh grass. Maybe people get wet. What it matter?" She was very old and knew the power of rain. Thunder boomed overhead. Sheet lightning stretched from Ganado in the south to Mexican Water and beyond to the north. Bayeta led Widow Tumecho indoors.

Adam, now alone with Alberto, adjusted his blankets and sat back to warm his own hands. But he could do little to warm them. It did not matter. He watched over Alberto, whose body convulsed with pain between shortened intervals of calm. The morphine drip only masked the pain. A sudden, desperate gasp told Adam that even the drug had failed Alberto. Alberto gripped the blanket and opened his eyes. His dilated pupils absorbed the blinding light from a burst of sheet lightning. He tried to raise his head toward the light, as if to meet it head on. Adam felt Alberto's hand surrender its grip. Alberto's face, ravaged by years of muscular decline and debility, softly melted into a relaxed, angelic pose. The wind came up, bearing hard against the ramada. Adam wiped the stray drops of rain from Alberto's cheek. In the time it took the lightning to touch earth and the rain to meet the ground, Alberto had left his pain behind. Adam drew the blanket over Alberto's head and took up Alberto's well-worn missal. He knew the extreme unction text almost by heart. "In the name of the Father…"

The rain inexplicably retreated. At the end of the reading, Adam made the sign of the cross. He was not Catholic, but he knew what should be said. Martin, who had retreated to the house, came to stand with Adam. He, too, knew the words. "For I saw a new heaven and a new earth…"

As Martin spoke, Bayeta, with Widow Tumecho at her side, came up the hill. Mary and Cynthia followed. "And God wipes away all tears, and death shall be no more, not sorrow, not crying, there will be no more pain, for all that is passed away."

When the doctor from Ganado arrived, he wrote on the death certificate that the time of death was 4:47 p.m. The notation read, "Cause of death cardiac arrest due to myocardial infarction." Another notation was added as to Alberto's underlying condition, progeria.

At the house, Bayeta and Mary washed Alberto's body and placed him on his bed. Adam had retreated to the library. He said he needed to straighten up some papers. He could not bring himself to admit that he needed to be alone with his thoughts. The record he had kept on Alberto's disease was on the desk, but he could not touch it. It began in part by stating that Alberto was a one in eight million baby. In his first three years of his life, there was no hint that his life's thread was flawed. For three years he walked and was learning to talk like any normal, healthy toddler. He was a bright child, so active and ready to take in the measure of the world about him. However, a shortened measure of fate was embedded deep within him. Once begun, the unraveling and falling away could not be arrested. By the time he was five, it was apparent to anyone who saw him that something had gone wrong. To the doctors, he was a clinical curiosity. Genetic testing provided the awful truth with a precise diagnosis. He was not expected to survive to age fifteen. Ninety percent of progeria victims die short of age twenty. And so the record went.

At Rimrock Alberto had watched over the experimental animals with desperate interest. It excited him and gave him hope. That so small a being as a shrew, its life's limit measured out at two billion heartbeats, could defy the defined limit was magical. Did it matter to him that the animal's confinement was artificial? Living wild and free, two years was what time allotted it. For the shrew, a longer life promised added frantic nights to crush insects between its jaws, more owls to evade as it crossed exposed moonlit expanses, and desperate hours at the edge of starvation. The fate of a natural shrew was delimited. Alberto also understood that there was no such thing as a progeria shrew. He never asked Adam why then did he seek to extend shrew lives and not Alberto's.

When the boy of seventeen first came to live at Rimrock, Adam had told him, "My wife tells me that I am like Born-for-Water. Such people are born to explore, seek. My search is to find answers." He did not, not then, speak of life extension.

Adam found his wife sitting at her loom, her hands resting in her lap. She was not weaving and would not until she had exhausted her grieving. "When?"

"Did you say something, Adam?"

"When did you know?"

"I was sure a few days ago. I'm in my second month."

Adam rested his hands gently on her shoulders. She turned and drew herself up into his arms.

"This is a good place to bring up our children."

"Please, one at a time, Adam."

"Twins run in my family, Bea."

They held on to each other for a long time. They listened to the rain and watched the lightning move on toward the east. They would have a good cry. Then, they could do what had to be done.

16

Into the Light

Beyond the half-opened sliding glass door, a soft patter of rain roused Adam from a deep sleep. He rolled over to reach out for Bayeta, but she was not there. Dawn's first light was spreading across the patio and into the bedroom. The aroma of fresh brewed coffee prodded his senses toward full wakefulness. There was a muffled, intermittent rustling of a small animal hidden in rabbit bush near the door. That the necessities of the day should begin so gently, he was grateful for. Friday would be a hard day to cope.

Finding his slippers, Adam walked down the hall to Bayeta's studio. Ninaba was sitting to the side of her daughter's loom, her hands at rest in her lap. With the last words of whispered prayer, her hand rose to gently brush the open warp of the unfinished weave. She prayed in the language of the loom. She did not turn her head upon hearing Adam enter. A lamp on the floor beside the loom cast its soft, warm glow to frame the uncompleted web. Her hand returned to her lap. He saw clearly that Ninaba was well satisfied with what her eyes saw and her heart felt.

Adam retreated to the kitchen to pour two fresh cups of coffee and returned to the studio. Ninaba had not moved. He set a cup down on the floor to her right. Her eyes were alert and focused. She reached out and took up the cup to warm her hands. Adam sat down on the floor behind her right shoulder. It was not easy for him to talk with Ninaba. She genuinely liked him and approved of the marriage in spite of how, at the time, some of the people and her kin felt. She, too, had to resist the pull of a lifetime of proscribed behavior. Yet, a mother-in-law must accept and respect a daughter's choice.

"My daughter makes me proud. This web is like no other. She walks in beauty."

"It is not yet complete."

"Silly boy, to you that is just so. Do eyes have to know the whole before one can see?" Adam looked intently at the weave and at Ninaba's expression. "Grandmother of my grandmother, one who made such a web as this, she also made it for her man. He suffered much in that bad place, Bosque Redondo. It was a time of sadness and hunger. The Blue Coats made him plow up dirt to make corn. The corn did not grow. His spirit was made into a small thing. She made it for him to put on his shoulders when he walked away from that place. Then, he was again a proud man, free." She reached out to stroke the weave. "It was just so."

The advance of day shook off the heavy cloak of darkness, exposing the skeins of dyed wool hanging on the drying racks. How brilliant the wool shone as it soaked up a new sun's gifts, Ninaba said.

Ninaba believed the color red alone existed in the First World. The light of the world had yet to be brought down by Coyote from the Sun's house. Ninaba greeted each dawn of her long life waiting for the shroud of night to retreat and for light to advance to freshen the forms of her world, as if for the first time. She understood how light is born, how it grows, and how it retreats to sleep beyond the western edge of earth. For her, it is ever becoming. One thread at a time gathers up within the web the color of its nature and comes into the world. It takes time to bless the world with all the colors, each dawn to dusk. Newtonian optics was no match for such a delicate understanding of the way of things. Could Newton have sensed the subtlety of Navajo optics, had he but known? Before the first sun and first moon brought light into the sky, one color only existed. Coyote's labor was necessary and good. How could the weaver capture and hold the colors of life without Coyote's gift?

Adam returned to the kitchen to review his list of calls to make. Ninaba followed, holding the note Bayeta had left for him. "Back by nine," it said. "Call John about Father Thomas, and tell Cynthia when to expect us."

Things were in hand, almost. John would drive Father Thomas to Gallup. Cynthia called a minute later from the El Rancho hotel. John and Father Thomas were to meet her there for breakfast. Donald Ryder would also be at the hotel. Jonathan and Martha Hardesty were due to arrive at the Albuquerque Airport at ten o'clock, meet up with Marianne there, and the three of them then drive to the funeral. Would they arrive in Gallup before 1:00 p.m.? Jonathan, ever the cautious driver, would keep to 65 miles per hour, not New Mexico's speed limit of 75. Adam told Cynthia not to expect them until after one. Did the delay matter? To Cynthia, the efficient one, it did. As children, it was Adam who allowed the when and how of things to fall into place, never forcing them. Cynthia was just the opposite. Tardiness to her was a sign of poor planning.

At first light Bayeta had driven out to the field of lilies and then on to Spider Rock. As a young child, she half-believed in grandmother's story that Spider Woman took bad children away in the night and ate them. This was just so, grandmother had told her. Did she not see the top of The House of Spider Woman, how it was strewn with the bleached bones? They were there for all to see. To a young girl's eyes, it seemed so. Eventually, her mother took her on her own and explained that it was a "just so" tale, and not to be taken seriously. Bayeta looked very closely, uncertain what to believe.

"They do look a lot like bones, Mother." Ninaba had answered, "Not all things are as they seem."

That spring when George Slim had put up her first loom, Mother told her again not to worry over such things. Was it not so that Spider Woman gave to the *Diné* knowledge of spinning and weaving? Was it not Spider Woman who gave The Twins two feathers? One feather protected them from harm. The other feather was for "the threads of life." Grandmother, too, was quite certain of what she said. For Crystal, Spider Woman would guide her hands all the days of her life.

As she made her first web, Grandmother whispered: “This is like no other. Straight and firm you make each row.”

From the shadows down among the cottonwoods, a Meadowlark’s flute song rose up. Rich and full, it spoke of spring. Bayeta faced the new sun and listened to the lark, Spider Woman’s companion on her journey to the Sun’s house far in the west. The lark’s song reached out to her across the canyon floor, up the wall of time, and into the present. Back on the road to Chinle, she heard the sound of a car’s approach. The car carrying a family of tourists made the last turn and came to a stop. Anxious to see what guidebooks called a natural sandstone formation, they got out to look. They would wonder at the geology, consult a statistic in their guidebook, take a picture, and depart for the next attraction. Bayeta turned to leave. She had started out to pick desert lilies for Alberto. They were in bloom early this year. Tears fell silently at her feet.

<++++++++++>

Nestled on a low hill overlooking the Rio Puerco, the graveyard was not impressive. Most of the graves, long occupied, were but sporadically tended to. Did it matter to those at rest? The open ground of the newly dug graves was surrounded by a profound silence and stillness. About seven acres in extent, the cemetery numbered less than four hundred graves. To the south the eroded flank of Remnant Butte clung to the horizon. The Zuni Buttes hovered in the haze beyond. A line of cottonwoods and ponderosa pines marked the limits of the graveyard from the surrounding desert. A light breeze stirred their leaves and branches. The quickening in the wind, the harbinger of long, hot days to come, was palpable.

Discretely, the funeral director performed his functions. The two caskets were borne to the gravesites draped with purple cloth, each bearing a single rose, a lavender hued Rose of Sharon. Folding chairs had been set out in a semicircle, the refreshment canopy set up behind the seating area. To keep the dust down, the funeral attendants had moistened the ground and sprinkled it with lavender water. The caterer’s open-air canopy and seating area provided shade, cold apple cider and cranberry juice, and trays of Lorna Dunne and Fig Newton cookies. Pavane, by Gabriel Faure, Alberto’s favorite, played softly from an unseen sound system. Cynthia had seen to it that every detail was just so. Father, too, deserved to be buried with dignity. Alberto, beside him, would have appreciated not being alone. Father Thomas was to officiate without the customary dirges and mournful musings of loss. Father Thomas and John were due at any time. Those already present stood in the shade of the open-air tent. Bayeta was arranging two baskets of desert lilies. Adam stood to one side talking with Luke Many Goats. The Widow Tumecho and her two daughters were at the serving table, glasses of iced apple cider and cookies in hand. They eyed the open graves warily. Martin had come with Big Eagle's Claw. There was a kin relationship between Maria Klah and this man. Bayeta would find time to speak to him and learn how it is that she should know him. Some who came had never met one or the other to be laid to rest. That fact did not alter the sadness of the occasion.

Though denied a full measure of life, the "aged boy-man" had endured so much. As a sign of respect, Big Eagle's Claw wore a sand-cast silver *Naja* with a double strand necklace of silver melon balls and squash blossoms. Bayeta immediately recognized it as an old piece, one handed down one to another for one hundred and fifty years. Gray Whiskers, himself, had made the *Naja* when interned at Bosque Redondo. Gray Whiskers' powers to make beauty had long been legend. There were many hard goods worn to honor Alberto, each catching and holding the beauty in the light. The sign of respect was also for Bayeta. In the days to come, Bayeta would tell each wearer of hard goods that they were welcome to bring them to the sing and place them in the ceremonial hogan where Martin was to be sung over. It would please them to know that Crystal Bayeta, daughter of George Slim and Ninaba, had not forgotten the ways of her people.

As she watched Big Eagle's Claw hand Adam his *Naja*, Adam smiled and handled the necklace with great care, admiring the silver and rubbing the turquoise stone set in the *Naja*. Luke Many Goats grinned and nodded approvingly. Big Eagle's Claw made a sweeping motion with his right hand from his chest to the *Naja*. Bayeta understood. Adam had just been given the very one made by Gray Whiskers. There was none finer or more recognized on the reservation. So much beauty had been lost to museums and collectors to be trapped behind glass. In the early afternoon sun, Adam adjusted Gray Whiskers' gift about his neck. One does not refuse a gift. Adam looked and saw that Bayeta was watching. "I will wear this until you take me to The Window. On that day, I also will make you a gift."

Luke Many Goats and Tall Boy nodded approvingly. Big Eagle's Claw had made a friend. Together, he said, they would ride into *Tseyi* and spend time together. Bayeta smiled. She saw that Adam and Big Eagle's Claw were now friends. Maria Klah's kin were more than neighbors. They were united to Rimrock by friendship between men, not women alone.

John Sanderson arrived with Father Thomas. Adam gave Father Thomas a cool glass of apple juice. Two minutes later, Jonathan and Martha Hardesty parked their car and walked up the small knoll to the gravesite. Marianne was with them. Adam saw Ryder park his car and wave. All was now in readiness.

Father Thomas motioned for everyone to assemble and led Adam, Bayeta, Cynthia, Martin, and Marianne to their places. With a crisp breeze blowing, the fresh dug earth infused the air about them. Father Thomas gathered in his thoughts and marked his Bible with cloth strips. Led by Widow Tumecho and Ninaba, a cry went up from the women. Father Thomas folded his hands to pray. Sunlight bathed the edges of the casket's purple coverlets.

"Thou preparest a table before me in the presence of mine enemies. Thou anointest my head with oil. My cup runneth over…"

When he concluded the service for the dead for Alberto Muñoz, a child of the Church, the Good Father turned to his left to address the casket of Alexander Terman.

"A man not of the faith," he said, "yet, Alexander did have faith, faith in God." Father Thomas saw no need to parse the difference between a loving God and an angry God. None of that mattered, not now. He spoke of a young man gone before his time and an old man whose life had run full course.

"Man born of woman, living for a short time, is filled with many miseries. He cometh forth like a flower, and is destroyed, and fleeth as a shadow, and never continueth in the same state." In the space of the reading, the sun's transit moved on, and shadows spread over the opened ground. The grave attendants took their places, and the earth received the mortal remains of Alberto Muñoz and Alexander Jogeva Terman.

"Let us pray," Father Thomas said. He had spent his life listening to his neighbors, Catholic and unbeliever alike. He knew how to comfort all. He read from the rite for the burial of children.

"Praise Him, O ye sun and moon: praise ye Him, All His hosts." The women wept with the reading of Psalm 148. Father Thomas raised his aspergillum to sprinkle holy water on Alberto's casket. "Thou hast received me because of mine innocence." He turned to Alexander's casket. "Look in the tenderness of Thy mercy upon the soul of a father, and forgive his sins…"

At the sight of the aspergillum, Ninaba and Widow Tumecho moaned, more a sad hum than a moan. Made of silver, they saw it for what it was. A Navajo healer would use a wand made of feathers and dyed yarn. The difference mattered little to them. Whether of silver or bright bird feathers, a wand held the power of the Gods through song and prayer. Father Thomas ended the prayer for the dead and turned to Bayeta. She dried her tears as she opened Alberto's worn copy of Longfellow.

> "As a fond mother, when day is o'er,
> So Nature deals with us, and takes away
> Our playthings one by one, and by the hand
> Leads us to rest so gently, that we go
> Scarce knowing if we wish to go or stay
> Being too full of sleep to understand
> How far the unknown transcends the what we know."

Bayeta bent over Alberto's grave and let fall the desert lilies she held in her right hand.

Adam stepped to her side and cleared his throat. "Our father," he said as he turned to Cynthia, "was a man from a world now all but forgotten. He fled the home of his birth only to find himself a prisoner trapped inside a magic mountain. On the most important day of his long life, the same day Cynthia and I were born, he once said a friend gave him a book, *The Magic Mountain.* His friend, another physicist, told him it contained a cautionary tale. Thomas Mann wrote about people who lived apart from the ordinary events of the rest of the world. Hans Castorp, the protagonist, found that he was unable to leave that high place on the mountain. Ultimately, he does flee, freeing himself and coming down from the mountain. Yes, in the end, he came down, he came back into the world."

Adam paused to find his marked passage. He looked at the Navajos waiting intently, whose people had their own story of exile and wandering, of family and land left behind, the tale of "The Visionary" of The Nightway. Soon, at Rimrock, he would again be reminded of it. There, "The Visionary" would again come among them. Today, however, was a day to cry and be sad for Alberto and for the stranger who had died sitting in George Curley's car outside Rose Bia's cafe.

Adam continued, "Alexander Terman is at rest, having at last freed himself of that which made him a prisoner. Yes, he came down from his magic mountain. God give him rest."

Inserting Alexander's name, Adam read, "Farewell, honest Alexander. Farewell. Your tale is told. It was long and hermetic." Adam paused to focus his eyes. "Moments there were, when out of death, and the rebellion of the flesh, there came to thee, as thou tookest stock of thyself, a dream of love. Out of this universal feast of death, out of this extremity of fever, kindling the rain-washed evening sky to a fiery glow, may it be that Love one day shall mount?"

Adam read without irony. Alexander had been lured to "that wretched place in the desert," had enlisted in a "universal feast of death." He had lived long enough to realize that the atomic age had not banished war. It had only made future annihilation all the more tenable, a legacy of the fears and hates spawned by his dead Europe. Alexander had made his last journey in the company of Schwann. But, he had come not to injure, but to help his only remaining son.

Father Thomas leaned heavily on Adam's arm as he gave the final benediction. Then, he whispered in Adam's ear: "Your mother, God rest her soul, would be happy and proud of you."

"If only that were true, Father."

"Adam, I was not speaking of your talent, great as it is. It is Crystal Bayeta who makes you a whole person. Eleanor is at peace knowing that you wed a weaver. A woman who weaves sees the pattern and texture of all things. A weaver measures each person's worth by the strength and durability of the fibers of their being. It was Eleanor who taught me to see each person in such a light."

"Father, please come to visit us at Rimrock."

"I'd be delighted. But my time is short. The Good Lord is becoming impatient. He has been whispering to me. He needs me to help him deal with his pestering Jesuits."

"Do they still give you the green eye?"

"Just like when you and the other neighborhood boys played soccer on their field. The boys still play there, and I still talk with them. I tell each one not to settle for half measures. Such talk infuriates the good friars. They see me, and out they come. If they had it their way, no one would dare to sin. So, I keep telling them, if not for sin, what need is there of redemption? But they are pragmatists, always ready to settle for half. Odd, is it not, to be a teaching order that fears error?"

"Crystal and I will come to Albuquerque. Then, we will bring you to Rimrock."

"And we can talk more about what wonders are in store."

"Father, we are expecting our first child, about November 1st."

John and Mary, standing near Bayeta, overheard. They embraced her. Embarrassed, she gave Adam her sternest look. She would have kept silent until her belly showed. She wanted to avoid seeming boastful. Adam, however, was filled with this news. If only Alberto had known. If only Alexander could have lived long enough.

Jonathan and Martha turned to Widow Tumecho and her granddaughters. They, too, had heard and crowded about Bayeta to congratulate her. Widow Tumecho caught Adam's eye and winked.

Adam embraced his friend. "Jonathan, I am so grateful that you and Martha came."

"To bury Alexander and Alberto on the same day is a hard thing," Jonathon said.

"You knew Alexander better than most, Jonathan. I think he found some measure of grace, don't you? In a taxi last week, we made a kind of peace between us. Those words that I spoke had something to do with that. I think he came here to warn me, to be at my side when I needed him most."

"Schwann and his ambitions have come to nothing."

"Let us hope so." Adam looked relieved. "You must be tired from the flight and that drive from Albuquerque. Would you like it if Martin drove your car to follow us?"

"Yes, that sounds fine."

Cynthia said her goodbyes and offered to take Marianne to the Albuquerque airport. Marianne squeezed Cynthia's hand and said that she wanted to speak to Adam on a personal matter. Without asking, Cynthia walked toward the parking lot and waited at the bottom of the knoll.

Adam was standing with Jonathan and Martha by the graves. Jonathan searched his jacket pocket for a moment.

"By the way, something in yesterday's San Francisco Chronicle struck my eye. It was just a one-column news item, short and impersonal. I don't know why it stood out, but it did."

He unfolded the clipping and read an excerpt, "Police said the woman was an itinerant bag lady. She was known to frequent the Palace of Fine Arts grounds. Identified as Katy Elkins, seventy-two years of age, she was pronounced dead at the scene. Her death is being investigated as a homicide."

His hand trembled as he wiped back a tear. Adam took the clipping Hardesty held out to him. Jonathan asked, "Is she the same person you talked about at dinner the other night?"

"I am certain that she was. She expected to die of pneumonia in winter, not like this."

"I called a friend who works for the paper. They are running a follow-up piece today. Three boys, teenagers, were drunk and came on her in the park. They chased her from one spot to another for almost half an hour. A dozen people saw all or part of the scene. No one tried to stop it. No one called the police. They beat her to death with beer bottles and then just staggered off."

"Senseless, isn't it?"

"They are in custody. A neighbor identified one of them. He lives two blocks from the Palace, the son of a prominent lawyer. They all come from good families."

"Jonathan, will you call someone for me, your friend on the paper, perhaps?"

"Of course I will."

"I'll talk with Cynthia first, but I think she'll not object. With Alexander buried here, there is the matter of an unused crypt at Forest Hills. I have the deed with the executor papers he sent me last year. My attorney will claim her body. She was afraid of being buried in a common, unmarked grave."

Silence had come over the other mourners. By twos, threes, and fours they spoke their condolences to Bayeta, Adam, and Marianne and drifted slowly toward the parking lot.

Adam saw that Marianne, alone, was waiting to say her goodbyes.

"Things seldom turn out the way we dream, do they?" Marianne said.

Adam sensed what was on her mind. "I know you are anxious to get back to San Francisco. You are concerned about your grandchildren. When I can, I will…"

Marianne gently pressed his arm. "I know you have a lot on your mind, Adam. You must sort things out here. Time has a way of getting ahead of us, and it is impossible to satisfy everything that comes one's way. For the present, I will try to take the boys in hand. Later perhaps, when things settle down, I may call you and ask for your help. I know you will do whatever you can. But, for now, see to your own. Alexander, God rest his soul, left us all with a bit of a mess to clean up."

Adam hugged Marianne. "I appreciate your understanding, Marianne. Thank you."

<++++++++++>

For Adam and Bayeta, the return home was something of a blur, lost in their memories and sense of loss. Neither said much. What was there to say?

Mary moved into Alberto's room. Jonathan and Martha were settled into the third bedroom. Martin had ready moved into the spare room at Maria Klah's house. His room was taken over by George Slim and Ninaba. Of course they could have had Alberto's room, but that would not have suited them. His spirit was still strongly felt, though no one could speak of the loss. Renewal must replace loss.

Two hours later, rich aromas of pungent lamb stew, braised venison with rosemary, and hot fry bread floated on the air. Bayeta had used sage, wild onion, Indian pepper, and a pinch of chili in the stew. The roasted venison was to be served with tart chokecherry chutney. Fresh salad greens, asparagus, and baked acorn squash were already set out on the table.

Adam stood to give the toast. "Lately, I have struggled to understand the meaning of my work. Now, I leave it to others to manage for good. Alberto's life was brief, but wonder shone in him. Alexander's life was marked by war and insecurity. At the end he found peace. This I believe. For us, life moves on. Let us raise our glasses to Alberto and Alexander." The toast was drunk in silence. Adam continued.

"What comes now? Crystal has summoned a singer, Chanter of the Sun's House. For nine days and nights a ceremony will take place to heal and restore the balance. I am told that it is The Nightway, that for hundreds of years it has served to maintain and restore the balance of this world. As Crystal so often reminds me, we are all blessed to walk in beauty." He did not complete the prayer's words, as it was too close to their loss to admit.

<++++++++++>

On Sunday, with dawn stretching its arms out across the patio, Chanter of the Sun's House and his assistants stood before the temporary hogan. Bayeta brought out two thermos bottles of coffee and a large platter of Ninaba's fresh fry bread. George Slim was at her side. All sat down at the patio table. Of those things to which she could not speak, her father would speak. All was in readiness, Mr. Chee said, and thanked Bayeta for having him to dinner.

"It is unusual," he said, "for The Nightway to be performed this late in the year. It is best to sing it when bears and snakes hibernate.

It is just so. Chanter of the Sun's House says that the mountains are greening. The month of shedding antlers is ending. The time of delicate leaves is coming. Even so, Chanter of the Sun's House has come with his *jish*."

Mary, who had quietly joined them and stood behind Bayeta, asked if that is how it is decided. Mr. Chee understood that she was an anthropologist.

"It is good that you wish to know," he said, "No one has seen snakes emerge from their holes. The Nightway must be complete before then. Yes, everything is late this year. The People are unhappy because they cannot go down into *Tseyi*. The sing will make everyone not so sad. When the sing is finished, the snakes will come out. Then, we go down to *Tseyi*."

Chanter of the Sun's House had deftly calibrated what was winter and what was spring. The right conditions mattered most for the welfare of The People. The *bilagáana* calendar did not dictate the timing of the seasons, not here. Mr. Chee added that it is dangerous to conduct a sing out of season. "This winter's time will hold on long enough, just long enough."

Chanter of the Sun's House turned to Bayeta. "Daughter of George Slim, soon you will be a little mother. That is good. Come and go as you wish. The child in your womb will hear the words of the gods and be blessed. We must drink more coffee. Then, we will begin."

"Martin," she said, "has gathered cane reed and juniper boughs to make *kétahn*."

The singer smiled. "Mr. Chee also makes prayer sticks. He is soon to be *hataali*. With Little Nose and Tommy Hosh-ki to help, all will be made ready."

With their coffee cups emptied, Chanter of the Sun's House and his assistants left to begin the first purification rite. Martin appeared with an armful of reeds and juniper boughs. There were many *kétahn* to make, eight to begin with. These would be the first to be made on this day. They were called *Tsay-Ge-Gih*, prayers of *Tseyi*. The Nightway was given to The People at *Tsay-Ge-Gih*, inside *Kinneh-*

Na-Kai, White House Ruin. It was to be just so, for the power of *Tsay-Ge-Geh* held constant, unchanging for hundreds of years.

Adam watched from the bedroom door as four dancers appeared at the hogan with Martin. He held a *kétahn* and prayed with the medicine man. A place to sweat had been prepared. Adam went back to the kitchen when the sweat bath began. It was best not to watch when Talking God and Calling God brought the patient out from the sweat bath. The prayers and songs would be repeated four times. Talking God and Calling God would purify Martin. He was to be made holy, brought back into harmony.

Martin was sung over many times on the first day. With the help of the Gods, he was purified and given medicine. He did all that was expected of him and gained strength and protection from evil. He sat on the drypainting prepared for him, and the gods sang over him. He was sprinkled with pollen and brushed with eagle feathers. Martin sat on the drypainting *Jay-Who-Tay-Ho-Zhon-Zhi*, four mountains of sand. More songs were sung. Many *kétahn* were made. With each new drypainting, Martin was placed upon it and the gods came. After sundown, Monster Slayer, and his twin brother, Born for Water, appeared. Chanter of the Sun's House sprinkled pollen on Martin. With his eagle wing feather, he stroked the patient's body, removing the pollen. With the light in full retreat, the masked god impersonators came for Martin.

At full dark, all who came to witness the first day of the healing were satisfied with the result. With ceremony concluded, Jonathan walked out into the evening with Adam. They talked to Tall Boy and Big Eagle's Claw about racing horses. Tall Boy asked if Adam was going to race. "I have but two legs. How fast are the horses?" It felt good to laugh again.

Many were camped a short distance from the house and the up slope to the west. Once the *Hataali* had blessed and burned incense in Adam's lab, some accepted its convenience as shelter. Adam had turned on two of the computers and loaded them with Alberto's favorite video games. This pleased the children. Trays of cookies and a washtub full of iced sodas were brought in. The lab became a giant community hall with chairs, bedrolls, hot plates for brewing coffee, and family dogs.

Bayeta would see to it that a water truck hauled in fresh water every day. Johnny Kabito volunteered to bring two loads of dry firewood, more, if needed.

Returning to the house, Jonathan asked Adam if he had given more thought to the proposal for forming a longevity advisory panel. The San Francisco experience, he said, made it clear that Adam had to be involved. The pharmaceuticals and health care industry needed oversight. Unintended consequences had to be addressed. Physicists had their Union of Concerned Scientists. It was important that biologists take the lead in framing the debates over recombinant DNA, cloning, stem cell therapy, genetic profiles, and the prospect of extending the life span.

"You stirred things up by not recognizing the need beforehand," Jonathan said.

Adam was sympathetic, but noncommittal. He abruptly changed the subject. "I stood there for two hours watching things from Bea's studio. The patio door was open and I could hear the chanting."

"You didn't go into the hogan?"

"It was not my place to do so. I listened. Much of it is repetition and reiteration, exacting and demanding. It takes great presence of mind to hold to the discipline of iteration, reiteration, and recapitulation, as it is with committees. I know that I am not suited for such a challenge."

Nothing more was said. Adam's insight contained a hidden text, Jonathan guessed. He had kept to his disciplined regimen of experimentation, to his search for answers. Solving a problem, not anticipating the consequences was his aim. For him, it was for others to examine and evaluate his research. Would they put it to good use with the checks and balances? No answers came to Adam. For the first time in years, Adam went to bed with no routine to face. It felt strange, a kind of newfound freedom.

<+++++++++>

At dawn on the second day, Adam again watched the *Hataali* direct the making of prayer sticks. Prayer sticks called *Tsay-Ge-*

Gih, meaning Canyon de Chelly, were made. Many *kétahn* were required for the morning's sing. Chanter of the Sun's House instructed the dancers to go and place their *kétahn* on distant, high bluffs. The wind carried the prayers to the gods' ears. When they returned, Martin was sweated and sung over. Song and prayer filled every hour until dusk. Fresh sandpaintings were made, sat upon, and destroyed. Each time, the pigments and sand were gathered up and returned to their places of origin. At sunset Talking God and Female *Yé'ii* appeared. Then The-God-Who-Cries-Dodi and a second Female *Yé'ii* appeared. A final ceremony for the day was conducted with Martin sitting on a buffalo robe. His body was sprinkled with pollen. Talking God appeared at the door to the hogan. A treatment with square sticks, *Bah-Lil*, was rubbed on his body. Three more gods appeared. With the sun setting, the sing ended for the day.

The third day began much as the preceding days. Martin was sweated and prayed over. All was made holy. Prayer sticks were made. The trickster Coyote appeared, and prayer sticks were made for him. Prayer sticks were made for The Wind. The gods watched, and a strong wind swept down from the Defiance Plateau to the south. At sunset, a final ceremony of the day, *Ith-Ye-Ith-Tahl*, was conducted. A small piñón tree was laid before the hogan door. Talking God and Female *Yé'ii* appeared. An eagle's feather was tied to the top of the tree. Martin wore the mask of the god. The Female *Yé'ii* took the mask from Martin and attached it to the tree. The rite ended. All was holy.

On the fourth day god impersonators appeared with food trays. Bayeta put her weaving aside that afternoon to take part in the preparations. She did as Changing Woman would, grinding corn and making fry bread. At the long tables set out for the evening's feast, a young boy and girl, Maria Klah's children, took their places at the head. All the children were excited, eating popcorn and running about in play. This night was for being sociable and having a good time.

Bayeta took part when it was proper todo so. And, she wove. Occupied so, she emptied her mind of pain and loss. Adam listened to the prayers and the occasional sound of a rattle coming from the hogan. He began to sense when to expect the gods to appear.

By the fifth day, he waited with anticipation for their coming. The ritual cycle was repeated again and again with pragmatic, calculated emphasis to insure the power of each action. The dreamlike quality of ritual had affected Adam. He listened to the songs and watched for the god impersonators. It was like that long ago night when he waited with Uncle John for shrews to come upon the circle of scorpions. Again, Adam waited and watched. The dance of life and death, old as time, appeared for him.

Listening to the hourly mixture of Navajo sprinkled with snatches of English, Adam walked with Jonathan into the throng gathered at the tables. He overheard the word *Tse-nis-na-sa* many times. Chee had done his work well. Adam had never liked being called *Tse-'atse-sa'*, as it reminded him of Widow Tumecho's loss. Bayeta, too, was pleased. His reputation as a wizard was beginning to fade. And, Adam vowed not to be seen again standing alone at the rim. All who came to the sing could see that the lab offered only shelter from wind and a place for children to play video games. Its alien noises and venting gases no longer rose up over Rimrock day or night.

Each day, more Navajo arrived and crowded into the hogan. Maria Klah's children, Mary and Billy, were paid special attention. When the newly made masks were taken into the hogan, Martin blessed each one and handed them back to the Chanter. Now, he was a holy one.

Adam had kept to the house most of the fifth day, watching from the privacy of the studio. Mr. Chee came and sat with Adam at the far end of the patio. Some time passed before he spoke. "Black God is coming. He comes with Talking God and First Man and First Woman. The People will sing. There will be talk of grasshoppers and locust. They will talk of disease, those first brought by the white man. Everyone will be told to keep the masks holy. If the masks are holy, the crops will be good. Bad things will not again come to The People."

"And if the masks are not kept holy, bad things will happen."

Chee looked toward the hogan. "That is so. Evil comes to The People on the summer winds. It is why it is good that The Nightway is completed before summer."

<++++++++++>

On the sixth day, at dawn, Big Eagle's Claw waited at the kitchen door. He came to drink coffee, he said. Sitting at the table, he was in no hurry. After two cups and fry bread he spoke.

"Chee has made one big *kétahn*, one with six names: Talking God, Calling God, Fringed Mouth God, Humpback God, Male *Yé'ii*, and Female *Yé'ii*. Martin will hold it. Prayers will be sung over him." Big Eagle's Claw drank his third cup in silence. Adam and Crystal Bayeta waited for him to find his words. "This big *kétahn* must be taken to a high place." Bayeta nodded that she understood. Big Eagle's Claw brightened.

"Little Mother knows what must be done. I will take it to a bluff in the *Chus-Kai*. Pollen Boy and Pollen Girl live near that place. But I have no rainbow to ride. I need help to take the *kétahn*."

Bayeta looked to Adam. "Speaking of rainbows, it is fishing season. Wheatfields in the Chuskas has big rainbow to be caught."

"I'll go and get my pole," he said, giving her a sly look.

John Sanderson, who had arrived late last night, joined them at the breakfast table. Big Eagle's Claw shook hands with John, and asked him if he, too, fished. John nodded that he did. "It'll be good to ride in your big car," Big Eagle's claw said.

Adam and John walked out with Big Eagle's Claw and watched him go into the hogan. The kétahn was in his hand. A moment later, the low, rhythmic, hypnotic sound of the chant was heard from the hogan. Then, silence.

Big Eagle's Claw, the kétahn in hand, returned to the house and was delighted to see that Adam had brought out a third pole. The three sat down in the kitchen to plan out the fishing expedition. They were hungry for the taste of fresh fish.

High above Teddy Chee Spring, close to the Arizona-New Mexico Border, Big Eagle's Claw climbed up to a high place, eight thousand feet above sea level, where a stiff wind blew. He planted the kétahn, said a prayer, and returned to where Adam and John waited for him. On the way back to Indian Highway 12 and on to Wheatfields Lake, nothing was said. Each man was occupied with the thought of catching the big one.

Before sunset they returned to Rimrock. Between the three of them, they had caught ten fine trout. Since it was early in the season, there were many trout. Big Eagle's Claw laughed at remembering how he thought it wasteful, watching his companions throw the small ones back. To his mind, catch and release was impractical if they wanted to eat fish that night. But, he admitted, the fishing proved good. He, too, had released two small ones.

Tall Boy was waiting at the house when they returned. If Big Eagle's Claw went now, right away, he could watch the unmasking of the gods in the hogan. Yes, Tall Boy said, dancing was to go on all night until dawn. Many unmarried women had come to dance. Tall Boy was anxious to meet them, see if one liked him. Tomorrow, the young women would see him race his new pony.

Adam and John said they would fry up the fish. On the drive home they had argued over how best to prepare the fish. Big Eagle's Claw settled the matter: "Roll them in cornmeal and sage. Fry them in a hot skillet with bacon fat."

After dinner, Jonathan asked Adam to join him in a walk. They wandered about watching food being cooked. It was a night for dancing, sitting around the fires, and being sociable. Rimrock had never looked more alive. On the first night of the sing, Adam had wondered if people would become restless over nine days and nights of ceremony and leave for home early. Now, seeing so many families and young couples crowded about the campfires and the tables heaped with food, he knew that everyone was having a good time. Mary, who was watching the comings and goings at all hours, was also having a wonderful time. She did not take notes openly, though Adam and John knew how desperately she wanted to put to pen what she was witnessing. She kept her writing pad on the kitchen shelf with the cookbooks and recorded briefly what she had experienced whenever she came into the house. Every detail excited her.

Bayeta divided her time between weaving, spending time with Martha and Mary, and taking part in ceremony. This was the first time Rimrock had been completely embedded with her people. The sing was for Martin's sake, but she had been anxious over what The People would think of Rimrock. Rumors about the lab had floated about the reservation for years. She feared that some might choose to err on the side of caution and stay away. But come they did. All came to share in the power of the sing. Curiosity also played a part. Some had come to see up close this man Crystal Bayeta had married. It was known that Ninaba and George Slim approved of the marriage. And so he must, in spite of the rumors, be a good man. If he were not, the gods would not have come to Rimrock.

The dancing continued until dawn. A great fire burned all night, its flames higher than a man's head. Everyone was having a good time. Adam went to bed, exhausted but content. He slept until after eleven and would have slept longer but for the sounds coming from the hogan. The eighth day ceremonies would go on into the night and last until dawn of the ninth day.

John Sanderson returned to Albuquerque. Mary stayed on, thunderstruck. Hour by hour, everything excited her. With effort, she kept silent and in the background. Whenever she returned to the house, she smelled of smoke. Her clothes were dusted with pollen. Her notes took up more than two notepads. This was an experience of a lifetime. She regretted that John had to return to his duties as department chair.

Martha was content to be with Bayeta, to watch her weave and to help Ninaba with the cooking. Her maternal feelings, long suppressed, had reappeared. Jonathan and Adam took daily walks about the compound and the nearby mesas. Jonathan openly spoke about his uncertain health. He still had "fire-in-the-belly," he insisted, for one more campaign. He was determined to promote a longevity forum. He used the lab computer, when he could bribe the children to give up playing video games for an hour, to consult each recipient of Adam's research. To a person they were impressed, disturbed, and committed to doing something. None wanted to see a breakthrough of such magnitude loosed on the world without a proper airing of its potential impacts on the social and economic landscape. An oversight body was needed, they insisted. Safeguards were needed to avoid unintended consequences. Not one wanted to see it in the hands of "Big Pharma." Thanks to Don Ryder's exclusive reporting, which was grabbed up by newspapers from New York to Los Angeles, William Henry Schwann's death had brought to light his attempts to subvert Adam through The Evergreen Institute. Many had been suspicious of the institute for some time. The new co-directors, Drs. Hessen and Valentine, were labeled "invidious puffers". Hardesty insisted that nothing good could come from an institute in bed with the pharmaceuticals.

By his leaving San Francisco so suddenly, Adam had drawn William Henry Schwann out of the shadows and exposed his dealings. The question of the potential for good or for unintended problems from Adam's discovery remained. What would a world do with billions human beings living well beyond seventy or eighty years? Could social, economic, and political institutions cope? Food, housing, and medical care were only the tip of the iceberg. Could governments contend with the demands of a superannuated constituency? Could familial relations adjust to the attitudes and competing needs of four generations at once? What of the struggles between the haves and have-nots? Every resource imaginable would be fought over. The definition of the good life would forever be altered. One of Jonathan Hardesty's informants ruefully quipped that the movie, Blade Runner, in which humans had been driven underground, might become the reality. Would people be expected to check into death chambers when they reached a certain age? Would the prime directive be to apportion resources only to the fit and young? Unthinkable! Inevitable!

At sundown the great drypainting for the Fringed Mouth God was made. Chanter of the Sun's House, Mr. Chee, and Big Eagle's Claw shared in its creation. Bayeta was at her loom when the singer came to tell her that it would be good for Adam to be present. Her friend, Mary Sanderson, having shown great respect, was welcome as well. Bayeta listened to Chanter of the Sun's House. She did not hear the word *bilagáana.* She was pleased that Adam was welcome. The People, having come to know him, now accepted him. Some spoke of him with a new name, one of respect. She liked the new name, *hooshdódii*, whip-poor-will. It fit. He did whistle to himself when he was content. It was almost song-like. In these last few days, after a long period of silence, she had again heard him whistling to himself.

At sunset, Adam walked with Bayeta to the hogan. Many people washed their hair with yucca suds and were sung over. It was her wish, too. Outside the hogan, Adam stood with Mary while Mr. Chee washed Bayeta's hair. Her hair washed, they entered the hogan. The god impersonator in the black mask, Grandfather of the Monsters, stood with the singer. A Female *Yé'ii* stood next to the singer. Bayeta and Mary sat with the girls and women on the south side of the hogan. Adam joined the men and boys lined up along the north side of the fire.

The god impersonators removed their masks in turn. Bayeta sprinkled cornmeal on the black mask. The god impersonator placed the mask over Bayeta's head and a cry went up. The singer spoke to each child and adult. As he spoke to Bayeta, he looked in Adam's direction. "Always remember the Holy People. Never talk about what you have seen tonight." He turned to Adam and Mary and repeated his words in English. Both nodded assent.

The initiation rite continued. Adam felt dizzy standing still for so long in the firelight, watching, waiting, his mind becoming overwhelmed with what he was witnessing. He knew not to leave before the rite was complete. He did not want to leave. He felt something, a bond with those present. Bayeta's eyes were fixed on the fire's flames through the eyes of the mask, through the eyes of the god. She sat in the midst of her people. The singer bent over to sprinkle her with pollen. Adam felt an involuntary spasm ripple up his arms. He had no recollection of being so blessed; all the same his bare arms and forehead were smudged with grains of pollen.

The rite ended. The initiates filed out of the hogan, Adam among them. He now walked with The People, with the Milky Way stretching across the pitch-black vault of an early spring night. Martin stood outside the hogan. The assistants appeared with fresh ground pigments. A new drypainting was to be made. Martin would sit upon it and be sung over. Afterwards, the dancing would last until dawn. The People, secure within the four mountains, would continue as before.

Dark, threatening clouds had moved in across the sky on the third and fourth days, but no rain. For eight days and nights, no rain fell. At dawn on the ninth day, Bayeta watched dark masses of cloud stream in from the west. The air was humid, smelled of rain. From her studio, she listened to the call of Talking God, as he approached the hogan for the last time. The assistants followed with fresh pigments and sand to make *Uh-Tah-Gi*, Heaven. Tall Boy and Big Eagle's Claw stood by to add more pine boughs to the dressing places. Talking God and Calling God led the procession. All the gods appeared and danced in front of the hogan.

With her weave all but complete, the last task was a challenge. The space between the weft line and dowel was less than one inch. Bayeta had already removed the shed rod and had put aside even her smallest batten. Now the heddle stick had to be removed. It took all her strength to tamp the weft yarn down with her comb. The needle she used to thread yarn with was hard to draw through the last of the exposed warp. At feeling her own tension, she stopped just short of completion. She reached out for a curved sacking needle, resolved to complete the weave before nightfall.

She saw Martin standing on the buffalo robe laid out before the hogan. Male God and Humpback God guarded the dance ground and made everyone keep quiet. To ward off evil, Monster Slayer, Born For Water, Shooting Goddess, and Water Sprinkler sang and waved their hands. The gods now blessed Adam. Tall Boy and Big Eagle's Claw stood with him. Soon, she would lie down to rest, knowing that all was good. She had not slept more than two hours at a time for days. The sing would end, and Martin would begin a new life as a man with a wife and family responsibilities.

By late afternoon black clouds threatened the western limit of *Tseyi*, a roiling mass heavy with the promise of rain. Dry lightning came to earth. And yet, no rain fell on Rimrock. Bayeta feared the rain would begin by nightfall. She rose from her nap and put on a fresh skirt, a blouse, and her finest jewelry. Joining the throng gathered outside the hogan, she saw Mr. Chee approaching her. "The crooked snakes come down to earth. Hear the noise they make."

"Will the sing end before it rains?"

"Only the gods know."

"You have come to tell me something, yes?"

"My jish, tonight Chanter of the Sun's House will bless it."

Together, they entered the studio. For the first time, Mr. Chee saw the weaving. Bayeta made no sign that she heard him gasp for air. He stood at the loom. His eyes were afire and fixed on the weaving. Bayeta stroked her weaving comb with her right hand, as if to smooth out its grain. Infused with a lanolin patina, it glistened in the light. "This comb is very old. It is made of ironwood. My grandmother, Ruby Yazzie, born of *Kinyaa'áanii*, gave it to me. I was very young. Grandfather, born to *Tó dich'il íí nii*, made it. I used this to make my first web."

Mr. Chee held out both hands, but his eyes still riveted to the weaving. He took hold of the comb as if it were a newborn child. "It is good to know how such a web as this came to be."

"This comb made the weaving that you see. Its work is done."

Mr. Chee touched the weaving, as if to assure his eyes that it was indeed real, then turned and walked out of the studio through the open glass door and into the twilight.

The gods danced. The Red *Yé'ii* danced. Calling God's dancers followed. Talking God led the *Yé-Be-Chai*, the Holy People. At the edge of a great fire, the gods danced and The People sang. Sheet lightning scoured the sky south to north, and still the rain held off.

Before dawn, Bayeta returned to her studio. With her curved sacking needle, she worked for an hour. Her fingers ached. The light was not good. None of that mattered. What mattered was that her work be completed before full day. At the edge of day, thunder continued its roar. Bands of lightning stretched out against the sky south to north. Still no rain fell. Lightning lit up the studio as she took up her knife to cut the weave from the loom. Bayeta used a flint knife, its edge sharper than a metal blade. She cut clean and quickly. As she cut the binding strings that held the weaving to the top dowel, she prayed.

"It is *nizhóní*, beautiful.
This covers it all,
All is beautiful behind me,
All is beautiful below me
All is beautiful above me,
All is beautiful all around me."

The singing outside of the hogan became one with the thunder. At the last moment, the moment before full day, Bayeta cut the last string. The weave was now free of the loom. She folded it carefully and went to stand and watch her people gather for a final blessing. They stood around a dying fire to soak in its warmth. Adam stood warming his hands with Widow Tumecho beside him. Chanter of the Sun's House was sitting on a bench with Mr. Hardesty. Both men were smiling. A silence descended on the gathering when Bayeta walked into the circle. She came to stand behind her husband. In the steel-crisp air of a new day's first moments, with a dying fire's glow upon him, Adam looked tired, a little cold. He stood very still, warming his hands and facing east, waiting for a new sun. All who stood about the fire were tired. The long night was at an end. They had stood in wait for her. She, too, looked to the east. The first blush of a red sun's light slipped over the Chuska Range to divide the land from the sky. Dawn departed from the circle of life for another day.

The dark clouds overhead thundered and roiled up. The fire's red coals hissed with the first, tentative drops of rain. Bayeta unfolded her weave. About Adam's shoulders, she hung the new *honalchodi*. It settled perfectly about his shoulders. Before the soft amber light of the dying fire and a new red sun, the *honalchodi,* woven of alternating horizontal bands of red bayeta, deep indigo, and un-dyed white wool, flowed in beauty. It danced upon his frame. Adam turned to embrace his wife. A cry went up from around the fire pit. "*Hózhǫ! Hózhǫ!*"

<++++++++++>

Another long, hard winter had ended. Late rains flowed down from the Chuska Range into Wheatfield Creek, Whiskey Creek, and Tsaile Creek. Their hidden waters would nourish the canyon floor over the long days of summer. The People would return to the depths of the canyon as they had for generations, down to the place of emergence to nourish their souls. The growing corn would reach deep down to quench its thirst. With the drying out of the surface sands, the sun's heat would again become embedded in the red rock walls and radiate warmth long after each sunset. The bone chill of winter would be forgotten.

Two days after the ceremony ended, Adam went to the rim for the last time. He bent down to feel the heat within the weathering rock. Rain had come and gone. He scanned the void to the far rim and down to the ribbon of green clinging to the canyon floor and talus slope. By midsummer the heat would become intense, the winter's snows and frozen landscape forgotten. A hard time would come again. It was just so, the cycle of life.

In the shadows of a cottonwood tree at the stream's edge, the six-point buck stood stone still, reluctant to surrender ground. He saw man standing at the rim. Adam backed away wanting the deer to tolerate him, to allow that he too belonged. He hoped that much. He had come to know the importance of avoiding impulsive action without knowledge of its consequences. The massive sandstone record of *Tseyi* spoke of this, spoke in its familiar, silent language of the effects of time, water, and pressure. Live in the present, he told himself. Summer is coming—white-hot days and cool nights warmed by the radiated heat bound up within *Tseyi's* massive walls—the time of plenty.

Driving into Chinle, Adam found the mood at Rose Bia's Cafe cheerful and expectant. A young man at the counter announced that it was time he moved his horses down into *Tseyi* where the grass was now thick and green. Another man said he was going down in two days to plow his field and plant corn, beans, squash, and tobacco. As if a bugle had sounded, the men drank down their coffee and hurried out the door. Someone, the waitress told Adam, had seen Auntie Yazzie with her wagon, two horses, and many sheep. Before he headed out the door, Johnny Kabito seconded the sighting. He was on his way to lead tourists to Newspaper Rock, Sleeping Duck Ruin, and White House Ruin.

"They want to see everything," Johnny said laughing. Today he could take them only as far as White House Ruin. By then they would be hungry and want to eat. "It is just as well. This spring was a tough one, worst in forty years. It will be two weeks before I can take them past White House Ruin."

For weeks, the men had nursed their coffees and listened to Johnny's prognostications. Today, however, they had preparations to make for the migration. Johnny could waste his time in Rose Bia's Cafe drinking coffee. He was waiting for the late rising tourists who breakfasted at the Thunderbird Lodge. In fifty years of leading tourists into *Tseyi*, Johnny had picked up their habit of starting out late. He had picked up so many bad habits. Still, he was part of *Tseyi*. He possessed common sense about the limits and dangers of sand, water, and time. He would drive visitors into *Tseyi* at ten and be back a little after one in the afternoon. That was the "program" that most of the tourists wanted.

Big Eagle's Claw entered the cafe as Johnny Kabito was leaving. He and Adam were to ride into *Tseyi* together. Big Eagle's Claw had saddled a big Appaloosa for Adam, one he had ridden before. It was Tall Boy's horse. He knew the horse to be sure-footed and patient, and not easily spooked by vehicles. Today Big Eagle's Claw would show Adam "his" *Tseyi*. They would ride into a sacred place alive with sounds and sights of Navajo returning after a long winter. Beyond White House Ruin, there would be only the two of them.

At White House Ruin Big Eagle's Claw walked the horses to water. Adam wandered into the ruin of the once five-story complex of white plaster and stone. Cottonwoods cloaked the crumbling walls in shadow. The ruined rooms opened to the sky. A tree ring date of 1050 had confirmed that the ruins were a thousand years old, abandoned even before the coming of the Navajo. It was older than the Great Pueblo Period of Chaco Canyon to the east. Above the ledge upon which the main ruins nested, the sandstone walls were streaked and stained dark red from millions of years of spring runoff. Navajos had no need of carbon dating and tree rings to tell them this was ancient ground. It was as old as The Nightway. Chanter of the Sun's House had spoken of White House Ruin. "*Kinneh-Na-Kai*", he had said, "is there for all to see, the place where the first Nightway was sung." Chanter of the Sun's House believed that a male god and a female god lived at *Kinneh-Na-Kai*. So long as The People lived in *Tseyi*, the world would remain, of that he was certain. Each generation would be born, live, and die surrounded by the four sacred mountains with *Tyeyi* the place of emergence for the fourth world.

Farther into the canyon beyond White House Ruin, Sliding Rock Ruin came into view. One hundred and fifty feet long and approached only by eroded hand-and-toe-holds, it invited closer inspection. But Big Eagle's Claw had something else in mind. There would be another time for Adam to satisfy his curiosity.

Half an hour later, Big Eagle's Claw reined in his horse. Above them was a massive vault of stone, The Window. Wind, ice, and time had done their work. With the horses tethered in shade among cottonwoods lining the seasonal wash, they climbed up to the sandstone ledge. Gaining the smoothed and rounded sandstone platform directly beneath the arch of stone, Adam and Big Eagle's Claw sat down and looked out over the canyon floor below. Adam listened to the wind whisper in his ear. He took Gray Whiskers' Naja from around his neck and held it out. Big Eagle's Claw smiled and accepted it. "Warm days have come. This blue bird has returned. It is a good thing to live long and to listen for his song."

<++++++++++>

Adam returned home before sunset. Mary had left with Jonathan and Martha at seven, before he drove to Chinle. Adam agreed to come to Albuquerque in May to talk with John about a half-time appointment. "Be a teacher, Adam. You have discovered something of great value. Now it is time to tend to the needs of students." Of course John was right. Through teaching Adam would find the balance of what it meant to be a scientist living in the world and not apart from it. In time, perhaps, he would find a new line of research, something "reasonable" to explore. Bayeta saw advantage, especially for her child, of living half the year in a city. Rimrock had become a lonelier place without Alberto. In time the pain and its grief would pass. Yes, half each year would be good.

Martin, newly restored, now lived with Maria, Tall Boy, and the Klah family. George Slim and Ninaba were at home in Crystal. George Slim was anxious to get his corn in and had missed his own bed. On the last night of the sing, two hundred people were present. They had come to see the gods dance. By dawn, with the gods departed, The People began to say their goodbyes. Crystal Bayeta had watched from her studio as the hogan was dissembled. Within half-an-hour, only a smoldering fire pit remained.

Adam found his wife waiting for him out on the patio. Together, they faced the setting sun. Their eyes drew in the deep red glow of sunset. She reached out and smoothed out her weave snugly about his shoulders. It was the same gesture she had made on the last dawn of the ceremony.

"This *honalchodi,* my husband, is the web of Crystal Bayeta. In old age you will walk on the trail of beauty." He was at last truly home, enfolded within a world created and protected by Crystal Bayeta. She would soon be a mother. She whispered, "In beauty you walk on the trail of old age."

Adam reached out and drew Bayeta into his blanket. He pressed her body into his. Tonight, Rimrock was for them alone. He whispered softly, "In beauty, on the trail of old-age we walk together."

Made in the USA
Middletown, DE
19 August 2021